THE EVER AFTER HOUR

A GAME OF LOST SOULS

BOOK THREE

LISA SILVERTHORNE

AWARD-WINNING BESTSELLING AUTHOR

LISA SILVERTHORNE

THE EVER AFTER HOUR

A GAME OF LOST SOULS

Devilish Debts

Forbidden Soulmates

Another Reality TV Season!

Angel of death Talia Smith and hot Hollywood hunk, Jack Casey face a new and darker challenge when Talia is stripped of her wings and halo and falls from Heaven.

Into Jack's arms.

Lucifer is hellbent on dragging Talia to Hell.

Forced to run, Talia and Jack battle demons, hellhounds, and the true darkness of Jack's past to escape Hell's clutches.

Guarded by a rogue faction of the death angel guard, Talia and Jack seek refuge on the set of their reality TV show's third season. Losing the game this time means eternal damnation.

With time running out and Lucifer's forces gaining strength, Talia and Jack risk losing each other for eternity.

The Ever After Hour is the third book in *A Game of Lost Souls*. Dark, irreverent, and always romantic, this is an action-packed 13-book fantasy romance with the fate of Heaven and Earth at stake.

Two lovers caught in the middle of a mythic battle between good and evil that begins with a simple wager with the King of Hell.

THE EVER AFTER HOUR

Copyright © 2021 by Lisa Silverthorne

Published by ElusiveBlueFiction.com

Elusive Blue Fiction Logo designed by Samantha Romage

Cover Design and Book Layout by Lost Souls Studio

Cover Imagery by Benny Productions, Brusheezy, Creative Fabrica, Creative Market, Chesire Studios, Deposit Photos, Dreamtime, Obsidian Dawn, Pixabay

ISBN-13: 978-1-7365530-5-3 (Hard Cover)

ISBN-10: 17365530-5-4

ISBN-13: 978-1-955197–32-8 (Trade Paperback)

ISBN-10: 1955197-32-6

ACKNOWLEDGMENTS

A big thank you, again, to VERA for all your help and support in getting this series out into the world. Always the bright light in the darkness. Couldn't have gotten through this craziness without it. And you. Thank you.

A huge thanks to SUSAN for your magical and brilliant word alchemy. You made blurbing and marketing tasks fun and sometimes mind-blowing. Thank you for your clarity and wordsmithing.

Novels by Lisa Silverthorne

Standalones:
ISABEL'S TEARS
LANDFALL
PACIFIC BLUE TATTOO

A Game of Lost Souls series:
THE CINDERELLA HOUR
THE PRINCE CHARMING HOUR
THE EVER AFTER HOUR
THE FALLEN HEARTS SEASON
THE RISING SPIRITS SEASON
THE ETERNAL SOULS SEASON
THE ROYAL WEDDING HOUR
THE HEAVENLY HONEYMOON HOUR
THE DIVINE NEWLYWEDS SHOW
THE CELESTIAL COUPLES SHOW
THE ENOCHIAN APOCALYPSE SHOW

Curse and Crown series:
THORN & BLADE

The Spiral series:

BETWEEN

REPRISE

AVENGE

The Resurrectionist Papers

GRAVE RECKONING

Short Story Collections

THE SOUND OF ANGELS

THE MAGIC OF ORDINARY THINGS

TIMELESS

Science Fiction Writing as L.S. Silverthorne

Standalones:

REDISCOVERY

Experiencing True Purple series:

RECOMBINANT, Book 1

HELIX, Book 2

SPLICE, Book 3

1

Azrael, Archangel of Death stared out the portals of High House with trepidation. His turn at the tribunal like his charge, Muriel had faced weeks ago. It was his responsibility and he would face it—no matter the outcome.

His charcoal wings twitched, reddish gold halo faded as he awaited the seraph's arrival. A moment he had dreaded since he had accepted Lucifer's first wager.

He brushed a thick lock of silver-black hair away from his face, dark grey eyes soft as he passed the portal overlooking High House's glistening spires and the tall trees towering above the distant walls of the Garden, where God's experiments first began. Traces of gardenia scent hung in the cool, fresh air.

Soon, he had to face the Maker and confess his transgressions. Before Lucifer did. He had broken the protocols and used a forbidden power.

It was his story to tell, not Lucifer's.

But first the seraph. Seraphina, one of the highest-ranking angels in the Heavens, had summoned him to High House. To discuss these wagers. And this feud with Archangel of Death, Samael, and his guard.

If she condemned Azrael, he would be reeducated—a fate no loyal angel deserved.

A reset of his memory and a reminder of his protocols. Wiping away connections, memories, and associations—anything that threatened his obedience. His keeping the protocols.

Like seraphim and archangels, angels of death were critical to the ethereal and physical worlds. Reeducation had been a desperate safety measure after Lucifer's war and fall from the Heavens.

The seraphim had to know another civil war was brewing. Lucifer had much more in mind when he proposed these wagers to Azrael. Regardless, war was coming. And some things within the realm of angels were worth fighting for, too.

One of them was Talia.

He might be the first archangel since Lucifer's fall to earn reeducation and its devastating effects. He'd delayed the completion of Muriel's reeducation, begun after Talia won Lucifer's first wager. Azrael sighed. When he had looped and rewound time to save Talia from a human death after her incredible sacrifice. To save another human's soul.

The *whup, whup* of wings behind him shook him out of his thoughts, his mouth going dry.

A Watcher angel with flowing wheaten hair and fluttering white robes floated beside him in the vaulted entryway of High House. Her wings were a soft ivory, wing tips whispering against the currents that flowed through the spires and the nave. Like most gathering places in the Heavens, there were no doors or windows, only portals and openings. Angels used air currents like humans drove on highways. Obstructions like doors and paned windows interrupted those air streams.

Air was life here.

Angels breathed differently from humans. Air flowed through their bodies, not requiring them to breathe it in or out. This continuous current gave them buoyancy and drift. They could pull air in and out with breaths, to raise and lower their bodies in flight. Or have the satisfaction of taking a calming, deep breath. But most angels simply let the air flow through them.

Beyond the two white double doors at the other end of the nave was the cavernous Cloud Chamber of Judgment. Where seraphim presided over other angels. Where he

had been summoned to explain the wagers.

And what happened to Talia.

Azrael turned away from the opening, straightening his tall, lanky form and closed his eyes. Shuddering at the memory of those dark moments on the steps of Eolowen, the grand hall. And in anticipation of facing the seraphim.

Facing Seraphina. He stiffened. The seraph presiding over—he sighed—the Incident.

He shuddered. Seraphim.

Six-winged, fiery-eyed angels with burning halos and terrible powers summoned lesser angels to the platform (or pyre as Azrael called it) that overlooked open sky. Seraphim detested walls and being contained. They floated in the Heavens around the platform, silent, wings in constant motion, circling like vultures, communicating questions without a word.

Here, he would speak his truth, telling them the events as they transpired. The story as it unfolded.

There would be no trial, no testimony, no pronouncement of guilt. No demands, cross-examinations, or witnesses. There were only the protocols and what was in an angel's heart.

His story.

After appearing at High House on their summons, Azrael would return to Eolowen while the three seraphim residing at High House ruminated for a time about the interchange. And decided what to do.

When they came to a decision, it just happened. There was no warning, no ceremony, no arguing. It just happened.

Peace and order maintained.

Had they evolved beyond interacting with the lower tiers of angels? Beyond speech and compassion—even for angels? Or was their power so absolute that a thought made it all come to pass? Almost like the Maker?

He was about to find out.

The Watcher motioned him forward. He flicked his wings and let out a breath, rising into the nave's air currents. Toward those double doors. Regardless of what happened, there would be atonement for his actions. And everything he'd done to save one of his best angels of death.

Talia had rare gifts for an angel, powers that she'd just begun to discover. Gifts desperately needed by the guard. And he'd given her the gift of preemption. Envy within the guard had already caused division, but this gift had caused outrage in some lesser angels. And the special treatment had led to Archangel of Death, Samael's death angels to even hold a strike.

If they knew that Talia had been given a soul to learn compassion for humans, there could be war. A deep bend of the protocols, but it had saved her from a terrible fall into Lucifer's realm.

The white doors opened. Into the quietest part of the Heavens.

Endless, serene blue skies, picturesque white clouds scuttled along the strong, sweet air currents and streams of glistening sunlight. An angel could float forever in this infinite peace. Where seraphim spent most of their time communing with the thrones and the results of His Creations. Not the living creatures, but the systems that turned galaxies and planets. The order of things. How it all interacted.

And sometimes, they hovered and listened to the lower hierarchies of the Watchers and movers and soldiers responsible for maintaining order.

Or presided over egregious acts of rebellion. Like his latest act of collusion.

This time, with God's own Scribe. Seraphina was anxious to experience his side of the events that had led to Talia falling from the Heavens toward the lowest of Hellfires.

And his deliberate breaking of protocol that led to The Incident.

The Watcher stared at him as the great doors opened into the tranquil blue skies and cloudscapes that stretched toward an infinite horizon. Where the fiery wrath of seraphim floated in front of the shimmering white stone platform in the tallest spire of High House.

Azrael soared through the open space and landed on the platform that had a curved stone banister and sunlit lectern that he leaned against. Facing the blinding glow of the seraphim floating around the platform, beat of six sets of wings like a pervasive heartbeat through the solitude of infinite sky.

The words slammed into his head, fast and furious, the seraphim bombarding him all at once.

Explain these wagers and why you entered into them with the Fallen One.

Why did you give an angel of death a human soul of her own?

Why did you allow one of the guard to be taken by Lucifer for losing an unfair wager?

The heat of their presence burned as they circled, enveloped him, temperature rising along the platform.

He called it the pyre for good reason.

Wing feathers curled, tips turning black. His face burned, cheeks stinging. His halo began to thrum, reddish gold light spinning faster. Sweat prickled across his forehead, charcoal grey robes becoming sticky as they clung to his skin. The air smelled of ozone and lightning, the intensity sweltering until he felt the air currents shift.

Seraphim surged past him on both sides, soaring onto updrafts that lifted them above his head and the platform. The air cooled, allowing him to collect his thoughts, but the heat quickly returned, the guttering of white flame lifting his gaze from the podium.

Seraphina burned in Holy white fire in front of him, eyes white flame, wings ablaze like solar flares as she hovered near him. Enough to blister his skin if she moved any closer. But close enough for him to understand the threat.

Of instant oblivion if he did not cooperate.

The seraphim did not tolerate insurrection of any kind. And he had volumes of his own insurrection to share. Retribution would be swift and permanent if they found him accountable for the Incident. It hurt him deeply to talk about it.

Tell us the story of this incident.

Seraphina's command filled his head, drowning out the other two seraphim. Her Holy flame burned white, identifying her as the most powerful angel of the three. Any one of them could burn him to cinders with a thought, but her question was the first one he had to answer.

"The incident," he began, feeling sick, "happened when Talia lost Lucifer's wager." He bowed his head, the words so painful to say much less hear, but his existence depended on his story. On his heart. For Talia, he would hold nothing back. "Forcing me to strip her of her wings and halo and cast her from the Heavens."

The image of her terrified gaze, pleading with him to save her after she'd given everything to the first and second wagers. Until Lucifer cheated and then demanded that Jack Casey be the second soul she must take—the human that Talia loved more than her own existence.

Azrael winced at the memory of Talia's wings burning away as she fell through the clouds. Falling toward Hell and eternal banishment from the Heavens.

Lucifer had counted on her refusing to end Jack's life or watch him die. So, again, she'd sacrificed herself to save Jack.

How were you forced? Seraphina demanded, an edge to that question when it popped into his head.

"I agreed to the consequences," he said with a hiss. "An agreement I had no right to make on Talia's behalf. An agreement I made to prevent Lucifer from telling the Maker about my transgression from the first wager."

Explain! The word pounded against his forehead. Seraphina was already losing patience.

"In order to protect Talia from turning against her human charges, I agreed to Lucifer's first wager, intending for Talia to save two souls while learning what it meant to be human. By being human."

He stared down at the podium, wondering how he'd made such a mess of everything when all he'd intended was to protect his guard. Protect his human charges and uphold the mission of every angel of death in the Heavens. Crossing over humans with kindness and compassion.

"Talia ended the first wager by sacrificing her human soul for another human being," he continued. "Showing me that she had found her compassion and had learned to love God's Chosen at last."

But there was a problem. Seraphina's statement.

Her six wings beat the air with a steady rhythm, the heat just close enough to remind him it could incinerate him if it got any closer.

"Yes, there was a problem," said Azrael. "Talia fell in love with the man whose soul she saved. Jack Casey. To a point where it completely changed her. It broke her, something I should have anticipated. But I failed in that task, too. I couldn't bear her pain in the moment that she lost Jack, when she sacrificed her human soul for him."

Continue.

"So, I used my archangel powers," he said, squeezing his eyes closed. It sounded so premeditated and treasonous when he said it aloud. "I looped that moment in time. The moment her human life ended. When she put her body in front of Jack and the fatal gunshot hit her instead. I rewound that moment and sent Muriel as an angel of death to prevent Talia's premature death."

Then Muriel did not act alone?

A question! It wasn't an out-and-out pronouncement of his guilt. Was there hope of saving Muriel from reeducation?

He nodded. "On my order, Muriel deflected the bullet, only grazing Talia's shoulder. But the moment I returned Talia to Heaven, took away her human existence, and returned her to her duties, the problems that I created started."

Explain. Seraphina again. Hovering. Staring. Evaluating.

He hoped that she would hear him out completely before incinerating him.

"Talia was falling apart after being separated from Jack Casey. I had given her what her heart craved above everything else. And then ripped it away from her, leaving her empty and aching for something she could never have. It was cruel."

He waited for the response. For the next question.

The seraphim shifted. Circling above him.

Discussing, he realized, his wings beginning to tremble. He hadn't even gotten to Talia's fall yet. But they had to understand what he'd done to Talia before he could continue his story.

In a blink of the eye, Seraphina hovered a short, burning distance from the podium again, her eyes white fire.

Continue.

He pulled in a shuddering breath. "I had given her a human soul and it still existed within her. Causing her pain, but it kept her connected with the human that she loved so completely and selflessly. And it was my fault, not hers. Then Lucifer returned, threatening to expose my insurrection to the Maker, my rewinding time to save Talia's human soul. If I didn't agree to a new wager. And yes, I was selfish. I tried to keep my actions from our Maker, but not to keep them hidden. It is my story to tell, not Lucifer's."

Why did you save Talia's human soul? Seraphina asked.

"I hated what I'd done to her," he confessed. "I took away the one thing she ached for—love. And I also harmed Jack Casey in the process. He loved her completely. More than his own life. He proved that by battling Lucifer's human champion to his last breath to stay with her. Jordan Bellamy. The first soul that Talia had to cross over for the second wager."

What were the stakes of this second wager? One of the other seraphim, but Seraphina kept her position of discomfort in front of him.

"Lucifer threatened to kill or take Jack Casey's soul if I didn't agree to the wager. Sending Jack to Hell would have destroyed Talia and Jack hadn't earned damnation. All of it was payback for my protocol-breaking rewind of time. But then, Lucifer made Jack's soul the second soul that Talia had to take in the wager. Somehow, he got someone to change Jack's Book of Life and Death. Entries were forged, events changed. A premature death rewritten onto the pages after Talia had saved him."

Talia refused to take Jack's soul.

It was a statement by Seraphina, staring at him through that white-hot Holy fire, wings alight with the deadliest power in the universe. Except God's.

"Yes, causing her to lose the wager. Causing…the Incident."

You took her wings and halo and made her fall into Lucifer's clutches.

Azrael squirmed at Seraphina's statement. But she already saw what was in his heart. He couldn't hide it.

"Not exactly."

The heat increased, a searing light buffeting his skin. Like a magnifying glass against the sun. The edges of his soot grey wings sizzled. Charring.

Explain this, not exactly.

He held up a hand, blocking the heat building against his face and neck. "I freely admit my guilt," he began. "I started investigating the source of this forgery, beginning with Pravuil, God's Scribe."

Has the forger been identified? Another seraph's question.

"Not yet. Pravuil is still investigating the changes made to Jack's Book. But while working with Pravuil, I discovered a loophole to the consequences of Lucifer's wager."

Explain. The heat of Seraphina's presence increased as she moved closer.

Azrael began to sweat again.

"Since Talia still had a soul at the time of the wager, I knew that stripping her of her wings and halo would have a different outcome. Angels stripped of halos and wings would fall from the Heavens and land in Hellfires. Like Lucifer and his followers. But Talia's fall was… shorter."

Explain!

Emotion from a seraph? Was it anger? Was he about to be disintegrated in a burst of Holy fire?

He exhaled and tried to keep his hands steady. "Talia fell to Earth because she still had a human soul," he said.

Where is your angel of death now, Azrael?

Seraphina's question was sharp and jarring. A demand. The heat increased, snapping against his skin. Crackling across his halo that had begun to wobble.

"As I said, she fell to Earth." He pulled in a breath. "And…someone caught her."

Caught her?

He felt shock and surprise in that response. Seraphina's eyes blazed with intensity. The white fire singed his eyebrows and the ends of his hair. He closed his eyes against the heat.

"Yes. Caught her. In his arms."

2

JACK CASEY STOOD ON THE POSTAGE-STAMP-SIZED PATIO OF HIS FIRST-floor shithole L.A. apartment, wondering what he'd done to make Talia walk away from him tonight after the finale. After saving his life from that falling stage light. Like she'd been done with him and he was on his own now.

He took a long pull from the cold can of Coors Light in his hand, feeling lost, his heart aching. It felt good to wear faded Levi's and a jean shirt instead of that grey show uniform, but he longed to see the luminous grey of Talia Smith's eyes again. And that look in her eyes reserved only for him. That glow that told him she still loved him.

He bowed his head, staring at his old checkerboard Vans slip-ons and the almost-healed gashes across both palms, the events of the last few weeks flooding back. But his brain rushed back to tonight at the Microsoft Theater and it almost felt like a dream.

He'd asked her to marry him.

In front of a huge audience and on live television. The fact that she hadn't given him an answer spoke volumes and he was struggling to process it all. Then the stage light fell and everything turned into chaos.

It was just after midnight, a chill in the December air, skunk smell of weed hanging in the air as multicolored Christmas lights blinked on the rotting wood wall separating him from the five screaming neighbor kids and their monster-sized dog that barked all night. While their mom sat on the patio and drank cans of Natural Ice, half of them ending up over the fence and onto his ~~square foot of broken concrete~~ patio. Along with the monster-sized dog dumps in the sliver of grass that they never cleaned up. Thank God the neighborhood weed smell covered the pervasive stink of sunbaked dogshit.

Sirens wailed nearby above the whup, whup of police helicopters slicing through the night. Constant rush of cars along the interstate.

Pop, pop, pop of gunshots. Squeal of tires. Kids next door screeching. Another lovely weekend in his crappy L.A. studio foxhole.

There hadn't even been a closing party for the show. The fallen light had disrupted everything.

He stared at the Christmas lights around the apartment complex, feeling empty. Two weeks until Christmas. Alone again. Broke again —after giving his last dime to Lenny to clear his coke debt. Until he got his last paycheck. He smiled. And his quarter share of one million dollars.

At least with the money, he could move out of this shithole and hang up his combat helmet. While he went out for casting calls, something he hadn't done in years. But without Talia, it all felt empty. This wasn't the life he'd expected after *The Prince Charming Hour finale*.

Losing her again was breaking him into little pieces.

And he had no way to contact her. No cell number. No address. No vague clue where she lived. Not even a Twitter handle. She'd disappeared right after the stage light fell and he hadn't even gotten the chance to talk to her. To finish the conversation that he'd started onstage. After winning her heart and finally, the match.

Why hadn't his life changed? Why wasn't Talia here with him? He couldn't even send her a text. He sighed and finished off his beer, setting the can beside the back door as more gunshots rang out.

Monday, he'd go to the studio and find someone to connect him with Talia. He wouldn't quit until he found her. He needed to hear her voice. Stare into those intense grey eyes. Feel her in his arms again. He needed to know that she still loved him. That her reaction on *The Prince Charming Hour* finale had been real and that she hadn't changed her mind about him.

Beer cans crashed against the concrete next door followed by the sound of a door closing, muffling the shouting kids and barking dog.

And then he was all alone in the midnight darkness with the police sirens and more gunshots.

Something fluttered overhead in the dark. A strange rustling sound. Like a loaded clothesline in a strong wind.

He glanced up.

A dark shape spiraled through the indigo Los Angeles sky, city lights washing out the stars.

Jack stepped off the concrete, into the thin strip of cold grass beyond it. Hoping he didn't step in anything as he watched the oscillating object.

He swallowed a breath. Had something fallen out of a helicopter?

It was small. Moving fast.

As it slipped closer, he saw the flutter of cloth, a pearly dove grey in the twinkle of city lights. Smoke trailed up in coils from whatever it was. Flash of tangled raven blackness and something wintry pale. Beginning to slow its descent.

His stomach dropped.

It wasn't a something…it was a someone!

He threw out his arms as someone whumped into them. Knocking him to the ground.

Untangling the folds of soot-covered, dusty fabric, he pulled back the smoking layers and his heart bounced into his throat.

"Talia!" he shouted.

He cradled her against him, her clothes smoldering and burnt.

"Oh, my, God! Talia! What happened? Where'd you come from? How'd you get here?"

Gathering her tighter into his arms, he carried her to the back door and kicked it open with his foot. Once inside, he kicked the door closed, carrying her over to the Murphy bed against the far wall.

That he'd already pulled down from the wall and turned down the covers.

Gently, he laid her on the bed, brushing ash off her beautiful face and out of her raven black hair. He pressed his ear to her chest. Desperate to hear a heartbeat.

Everything was so muffled. A chill rolled over him. He couldn't hear anything!

Frantic, he slid his fingers against her neck, feeling for a pulse. But nothing registered.

"Talia!" he shouted. "Talia, it's me! Jack! Oh, please don't be dead!"

He fumbled his phone out of his jeans' pocket and it slipped out of his hand. Cursing, he grabbed it off the faded blue comforter and tried to dial 9-1-1, but his hands shook so hard he kept taking screenshots instead of bringing up the SOS slider.

Until a groan echoed through the tiny studio apartment.

He rushed back to her side, a hand against her face. She had a long, thin burn across her forehead and two blackened patches smoking on the back of her dress.

She groaned again.

He stroked her hair and face, desperate to see those beautiful, intense grey eyes looking back at him.

"Talia! You're okay, you're okay," he said in a tight voice. "Everything's going to be all right now. You're safe."

She shrieked and tried to sit up, but fell back against the bed.

"Ssssh, easy," he said softly, laying his hand against her cheek. "You're okay."

Her eyes snapped open and she peered around the room, eyes wide like a deer in headlights.

Gently, he ran his hands through her hair, brushing it off her face and cheeks as he moved in front of her.

"Talia, it's me, Jack, I—"

"Jack!" She lurched forward and threw her arms around him, trembling and crying.

He crawled onto the bed and slid his arms around her, holding her against his chest, gently rocking her. Letting her cry.

"I don't know where you came from or what's going on," he said, holding her as tight as he could, "but I can't believe you're here. In my arms."

She clung to him, shaking. He'd never seen her this way before.

"I'm here," he whispered, laying his face against her hair. "It's all going to be okay."

It seemed like forever until her sobs quieted and her tight grip on him loosened, but he would have held her for a lifetime.

At last, she turned her face toward him, her tear-filled eyes so wide and afraid as she stared at him.

"Where am I?" she asked finally.

He smiled, brushing hair out of her eyes. "My place."

"Your place?" she cried.

He nodded, a hand against her cheek. "Glad you dropped by," he said with a chuckle. "I was planning to send out a search party to find you after the show ended."

She looked confused, like she hadn't heard him or didn't understand.

"What's wrong?" he asked. "You have no idea how happy I am to see you, but how did you just—fall out of the sky?"

The fear burned in her eyes again and she jerked her hands up toward her shoulders, trying to grab hold of something.

"What is it? Did you lose something?"

"My wings!" she cried, fumbling for something along her back.

"Don't worry, your halo's still intact," he said with smirk.

"It is?" Her hands shot above her head, against her forehead. "No! It's gone!"

Puzzled, he sank back on the bed. That had been a joke. What exactly was going on here?

"Talia," he said, squinting. He didn't even know how to start this conversation. "I'm a little confused. I'd just been out on my patio, wondering how to find you when you just dropped out of the sky into my arms. How exactly did that happen?"

Was he dreaming? Had he fallen and hit his head on one of the dogshit bricks in his neighbor's yard? Stroked out after one beer?

She bowed her head. "There's so much going on, Jack," she said finally. "I don't even know where to start."

He stretched out on the bed and propped his hand underneath his head. "Page one is a good place to start."

"Page one?" she said, staring at him.

"You know, like a book. At the beginning."

"Oh, a book. I know what those are."

He chuckled. She seemed more like the Talia he'd first met on *The Cinderella Hour* with her sexy sense of wonder that he'd found so enchanting. Along with her arsonist's sense of humor that had quickly burned most people to the ground, including him.

She bit her lip and glanced around at the yellow walls and the old pine hardwoods. At the creaky Murphy bed and the burled maple dresser, the one Dad made for him. Across to the old green couch with the crooked white clock hanging above it and the old, dented Harvest Gold appliances in the kitchen that stood between the Murphy bed and the living room.

"This is your place?" she replied, a funny look on her face.

"In all its glory," he said, grinning, as he patted the comforter. "And this is my bed."

She nodded, not picking up his hint.

He slid closer, bed creaking, and ran his hands down her bare arms. Down to her hands that he entwined with his fingers.

"I've dreamed of getting you into my bed," he said in a soft voice and leaned toward her.

His lips parted, pressing against hers in a long but gentle kiss.

Until the end of the bed thumped up and dumped him into the floor. Head first. His face smacked against the pine floor. He struggled up on his knees as Talia's laughter rang in his ears.

He threw himself against the end of the bed and wrestled it back against the floor. Damned Murphy bed.

She was still laughing as he laid his face against the comforter and looked up at her.

"Davy Pierson, I'm not," he said with a chuckle.

"Davy Pierson?" she said, her brow wrinkling with that sexy little shadow she got on her forehead when she didn't know what he was talking about.

"My smooth, bad boy heartbreaker character on SanFran Confidential. Got the girl in every episode." He glanced at his hands. "Unlike Jack Casey, who's as smooth as a broken computer mouse."

Again, that hot little shadow appeared on her forehead. "What's a computer mouse?" she asked.

"Yeah, I know, old technology," he said with a shrug. "Like my acting career." She looked really confused, not what he'd intended. "You know what a computer mouse is," he said.

She just shook her head again.

"You probably use a laptop with a trackpad these days."

"Trackpad?"

"Glide pad?" he said and moved his index finger in the air. "Move the cursor with your finger? Like on a tablet or a Kindle."

He had to sell his laptop and tablet or he'd have shown them to her. His Kindle was in his Explorer, but she was still shaking her head. Something felt really off here. He didn't understand her confusion. How did someone her age not know anything about technology?

And she still hadn't explained how she'd just fallen out of the sky.

"Talia," he said, an edge in his voice. "Tell me what's going on? Can we go back to the beginning again? Where you tell me how you fell out of the sky?"

She covered her face with her hands. She was trembling. "I don't even know how to start. And you aren't going to believe any of it." At last, she slid her hands away, revealing fresh tears. "And I'm terrified that you'll hate me when you know everything."

He laughed and with slow movements, he sat down on the bed, making sure it wasn't going to bounce up and toss him in the floor again. He slid his hand into hers and gripped it tight.

"There's nothing you could ever tell me that would make me hate you."

She sniffled. "Promise?"

He held up his right hand. "I promise."

Talia sat up straight and took a deep breath. "Jack, do you believe in Heaven?"

He groaned. "You're not one of those door-to-door religion people, are you? I hate those dudes!"

She gasped, her eyes widening, mouth falling open.

"Talia, I'm kidding," he said with a chuckle.

"But it's worse than that, Jack," she said, doom in her voice. "So much worse than that."

He laughed and pressed her hand to his mouth, kissing her fingers. "Impossible."

"Try me," she said, her gaze frozen on his face.

"Well, unless you're like the Angel of Death, I think we can work through this, Talia."

Loud, shaking sobs shook her entire body as she collapsed on the bed, face pressed against the comforter.

"Okay, I suck at comedy," he said, laying a hand against her hair, stroking, trying to calm her down. "I'll stick to the dramatic parts from now on."

The patio door creaked. He jerked his head around. Flash of darkness fluttered. Something hard smacked against his head and he crumpled.

3

"Jack!"

Talia stared up at the charcoal robes and spread of dove grey wings, the familiar face looking back at her. Long, rich, sable hair. Round, grey eyes. Without that horrid gold glimmer. Except for the white-gold halo spinning above her head.

"Muriel? Oh, Muriel, you're free!" She struggled off the bed and threw her arms around Muriel. "I'm so glad you're okay."

"You, too," said Muriel, looking relieved. "We've been looking everywhere for you. Should have looked here first." She glanced down at Jack slumped on the floor and smiled. "He's cute. You keeping him?"

Talia frowned. "He's not a pet."

"He can sleep on my bed any day."

"Muriel!"

"Sorry," she said with a shrug. "Haven't been out of High House long and we've been looking for you for hours."

"We?" Talia said, raising an eyebrow.

Muriel nodded toward the back door. "Anahera and me. And some of the guard. She's checking to make sure we weren't followed. And putting up wards."

Talia winced as she bent down to Jack and laid her hand against his face. "You hit him really hard."

"I didn't mean to," she said with a moan. "He shouldn't have been able to see me. It took me by surprise."

Her eyes widened. "Wait, he saw you?"

She nodded. "Even heard the door open. How's that possible?"

"I don't know," said Talia, the fear returning. "We need to know if it's just Jack or if all humans can see you now."

"I'll blast past some of the tourist traps," said Muriel with a shrug. "See if they see me. If they do, I'll just say, welcome to Hollywood and keep going." Muriel glanced at Jack again. "Does he know what happened to you?"

"Not yet," said Talia. "But Muriel, he caught me when I fell out the sky."

"What? Are you kidding?"

She shook her head. "No, I couldn't believe it when I looked up and saw his beautiful smile and those sizzling light green eyes staring back at me." She reached out and gripped Muriel's sleeve. "Muriel, why didn't I keep falling? Into Hell?"

Muriel glanced over her shoulder at Jack's patio door and then back at Talia, looking scared.

"We're not really sure." She shrugged, wings twitching. "Azrael might have had something to do with it, but he's been summoned to High House. They just opened the door and set me free. Then Anahera came to me and led me off. Only when we touched down on Earth did she tell me what happened to you. And that Azrael had tasked her to search for you. Here, on Earth."

Seeing Muriel's halo and wings made Talia ache for hers, knowing they were forever lost to her now. Her back ached from where her wings were burned away, her head feeling off-center without her halo. Yet, she'd never felt so relieved in her life to land on Earth. She smiled. In Jack's arms.

She was beginning to feel lightheaded, the ache between her shoulders turning sharp.

"We were expecting to charge through the Gates of Hell to find you, Talia," said Muriel. "We brought half the guard with us, ready to at least bring you out of those Hellfires. And then we tracked you here." She glanced down at Jack's inert form on the floor. "Wow, he's much hotter up close, Talia," she said. "You sure you're keeping him?"

"Muriel!" she cried.

"Because if you weren't—"

"I'm keeping him!" she snapped. "I mean, he and I are…"

She didn't know how to answer that question. In the final moments of *The Prince Charming Hour*, just before their crowns matched, Jack had proposed to her. Gave her a ring and—

Oh, no! The ring!

She jerked her left hand into the air, excited when she saw the silver ring still on her ring finger. It had been loose and she'd pressed her fingers together to keep it on her hand when he took her in his arms and kissed her on stage. And then the stage light fell. She threw both of them backwards—into the throne—to prevent Jack from dying.

And then everything happened so fast. The summons back to Eolowen. Lucifer gloating. And Azrael making such a production out of taking her wings in front of the entire guard. *Why? Why had he done that? To humiliate her further?*

And then that horrible fall through the Heavens, careening toward the burning glow of Hellfires in Lucifer's domain.

She'd blacked out a moment and then felt arms around her. Expecting to look into Lucifer's leering blue eyes. She cried when instead, she saw Jack's beautiful oval face and his smoldering, light green eyes smiling back at her.

She didn't how or why she was back here on Earth. Much less back with Jack. She had been despondent when she returned to Eolowen, knowing she'd lost him forever. And here she was in his apartment. How?

With a sharp snap of her left hand, she held it out to Muriel and pointed at the ring.

"Jack proposed to me, Muriel," she said in a quiet voice.

"What? Seriously?" She took hold of Talia's hand and turned it over, examining the silver band. "And I missed that? I'm gonna throttle Azrael for making me miss the most romantic moment in angel history ever. Congratulations! But how is that going to work? Jack, do you take this angel of death to be your lawfully wedded wife? 'Til uh, death do you part…oh, wait."

Talia rolled her eyes. "Very funny, Muriel."

"I was actually being serious. How does an angel of death marry a human?" She nodded at Jack still on the floor. "And how'd he take it when he found out his fiancée carries a scythe and smites humans for a living?"

"I don't carry a scythe! Often." She glared at Muriel and crossed her arms, but the pain was horrific. She yelped and let her arms uncross slowly.

Muriel laid a hand against her chin. "Although, he must have taken it pretty well when he found out that his ex-girlfriend sold her soul to Lucifer and was trying to kill him to keep her boyfriend's show from tanking. Sorry, saw it on angelcam during one of my reeducation sessions."

"Lower your voice," Talia snapped. "He doesn't know she's really trying to kill him. Or even that she sold her soul to Lucifer. He doesn't know a thing about the angel situation either—much less any demons. And he doesn't know I'm an angel of death yet." She sighed. "Was. And he's asked me a bunch of times how I just fell out of the sky. I was trying to tell him when you clubbed him in the head."

Muriel plopped down on the edge of the bed and leaned back, halo tilting. "Well, you're going to have to tell him everything, Talia."

"Why?" she asked.

"Because when Lucifer figures out you're not coming for holiday, he's going to come looking for you. To claim his door prize. Jack's place is the first place he'll look. That's why Anahera and I are here. To stay and protect you from Lucifer's wrath." She nodded over at Jack. "And guard your blond Hollywood hottie. Lucifer is still expecting to collect his soul, too because of the lost wager. And because Jack's ex is still trying to end him in Lucifer's name for cash. He have a brother?"

Talia dropped down on the floor beside Jack and laid her hand against his soft blond hair, running her fingers through it. Looking to see if there was a knot or a gash on his scalp.

"He's really out," she said, worried that he hadn't come to yet.

"He just thinks I'm a knockout," Muriel said with a smirk. "Hey, I'll take it."

"Well, you're not taking him," she said, smiling at him. "I love him. And I'm going to marry him."

"Talia," said Muriel, sitting up. "Not to smite your dreams, but you need to tell him everything first. Because he can see us. And there will be demons showing up to drag you to Hell. And take his soul. Lucifer himself might even show up, so Jack's going to see more wings than the local bar at happy hour."

She bowed her head. "I know. I've been trying to tell him for some time."

Muriel motioned toward her. "And he won't stop asking about your fall from the sky. Or those wounds on your back and forehead."

The patio door creaked open and Anahera slipped inside, her form shadowed, wings glassy, short red hair tousled, the white light from her halo illuminating the floor. Her grey eyes were wide as she crept into the apartment. Then she saw Jack on the floor by the bed and rushed over, dropping down on one knee. She laid two fingers against his neck.

"His heart still beats," said Anahera, glancing up at Talia. "What happened?"

"He can see us, Anahera," said Muriel, leaning on her elbows. "It startled me, so I knocked him out." Then she offered a sheepish grin, looking anxious. "I didn't mean to hit him so hard. I wasn't expecting him to react to me."

Anahera's mouth dropped open. "How can he see me? He's human."

"I don't know, but he can," said Muriel.

"Help me put him on the bed," Talia said to Anahera who nodded.

Talia bent down and slid her arms underneath his armpits. Anahera took hold of his feet.

Very gently, they lifted him out of the floor and laid him on the bed. He was still out cold. Making her worry even more.

Anahera reached out and gripped Talia's burned sleeve. "Talia, I'm so sorry about what happened. I wanted no part of this, but Muriel convinced me and part of the guard to come down to Earth and fight for you. We're here to help. To protect you and Jack."

At last, Muriel sat up, a dark look on her face. "We need to find a way to hide you and Jack from Lucifer long term, until I can discuss this with Azrael. If he comes back from High House. He said not to worry, that he had a few maneuvers that Lucifer didn't know about."

"Like shortening a fall into Hell," Anahera said with a grin.

Muriel gave her a knowing smile. "Yes, like shortening a fall into Hell. Azrael had everything to do with you landing on Earth." She chuckled. "With Jack catching you, too. That's pretty romantic which is surprising if it was orchestrated by Azrael. Didn't know he had it in him."

Anahera checked Jack's breathing and then looked over at Muriel. "We won't be able to hide our halos or wings from him now." Her gaze fell onto Talia. "How are you going to explain this to him?"

Talia sighed and sank down beside Jack on the bed. She was so tired.

"I wish I knew," Talia replied. "I can't just say, hey, Jack, I'm an angel of death. I just lost a wager with Lucifer, so I fell from the Heavens and these are my angel friends protecting me. Shall I order pizza?"

Muriel stood up from the bed, staring over at Jack. "Better think of something, Talia," she said. "Because he's waking up."

Jack groaned and moved his head.

Her stomach sank into her feet. How would she explain this without totally freaking Jack out? Or losing him forever?

4

JACK GROANED, HAZY IMAGE OF HIS SHITHOLE STUDIO FOXHOLE COMING back into focus, creak of the Murphy bed confirming his fears. He felt sick, his heart hurting.

It'd all been a dream.

He'd only dreamed seeing Talia. It was all just a damned illusion and she was still out of his life.

The Murphy bed creaked again. His vision was still fuzzy, but his hearing was just fine. He hadn't moved. So why did the bed creak?

A hand touched his brow, fingers sliding through his hair in soothing strokes, easing the sharp pounding against his temples.

"Talia?" he mumbled.

She leaned over him, smiling and he couldn't halt his grin.

"Oh, God, I didn't dream you!" he said, his voice breaking as he pulled her against his chest and wrapped his arms around her, holding on with everything he had. "You're real. Please tell me you're really here."

"I'm really here, Jack," she said as his mouth found hers in a desperate kiss.

Then someone cleared their throat. He froze glancing right and left.

"Please tell me that's not Lenny with a tire iron," he said in a quiet voice.

"Worse, Jack," said a female voice.

He struggled to sit up from the bed and saw a dark-haired woman standing at the foot of his bed. Arms crossed. With large grey eyes almost as bright as Talia's. He couldn't keep his mouth from falling open when he saw the dove grey wings unfurled at her back and the white-gold circle of light rotating above her head.

Beside her stood a taller woman with short red hair and darker grey eyes. And similar dove grey wings a little longer, the pattern of feathers a little different, more angled. The circle above her head spun a bit slower with more gold light.

"Friends of yours, Talia?" he asked. "Victoria's Secret models? Please, God?"

"Who's Victoria?" Talia replied. "And why does she have secret models?"

Jack couldn't rein in his smirk. "Because they look like that." He swallowed a breath and leaned up on his elbows. "I hope I'm not dreaming this either."

"He's adorable," said Muriel, sitting down on the edge of the bed.

The bed didn't move or try to close.

"You sure you're keeping him?" Muriel asked and uncrossed her arms. "'Cause he's adorable."

Jack smiled, but Talia gave him an annoyed look. "Muriel!" Talia snapped, anger flashing in her grey eyes, so much brighter than her two friends.

She held up her left hand and the woman called Muriel rolled her eyes. What was that about?

"So, are you, two actors?" Jack asked. "Headed for a Christmas performance somewhere?"

The taller woman shrugged and gave Muriel a funny look. "Performance?"

"Uh, yes," said Muriel, glancing over at Talia. "We're performing in a theatre production of—"

"Of Angels Heard on High," Talia replied.

High all right. Maybe too much skunk weed had filtered over to his patio? He'd have to send his neighbor a fruit basket.

Muriel hesitated and then nodded. "Yes, it's downtown. A small local production."

Something didn't feel right here. And those halos were way too high tech for a local theatre company.

"Oh, like a Civic theatre show?" Jack asked, glancing at the two women and then at Talia.

"Yes," Muriel replied, her gaze still on Talia. "Civic theatre."

"At the Dolby?" Jack asked.

"Yes, the Dolby," the other woman replied.

Jack gave them a hard look. "Dolby seats almost four thousand people."

Muriel sighed. "You're up, Talia."

"Jack, I—"

Jack scrambled off the bed and stared at them, feeling a strange sense of dread.

Something was really off here, but he had no idea what. Those wings looked so realistic. Like high-end stage or screen production costumes or expensive props. Especially how they moved. And he couldn't even respond about the halos. Battery power couldn't produce that kind of glow or brightness. And no LED light he'd ever seen had that kind of ethereal glow.

But the thing that disturbed him most were their eyes. They all had the same type of grey eyes that Talia had, not as bright or alluring, but similar. It made him apprehensive. What the hell was going on here?

"Look, I don't know what's going on here, but you two aren't actors and if those wings and halos are props, they're the most expensive ones I've ever seen. And way beyond a local theatre company's budget. Like performing at the Dolby."

He turned his gaze back on Talia, eyes narrowing. "Who are you? And why did you fall out of the sky, Talia?"

Talia got up from the bed and he took a long step backward. Toward the back door. Was that even Talia? Was this a massive prank?

Or something Rachel put together? To push him back to the flake again? Or push him off a cliff?

"Are you even Talia?" he asked.

Her eyes turned watery and she bit her lip. "Jack, please," she said. "You kissed me. You held me in your arms. It's me...I swear it."

"Talia, you need to explain it to him," said Muriel.

"Explain what to me?"

Cold fear rose in his chest, spreading to his fingertips, his mouth going dry.

"It's a long, complicated story, Jack," said Talia, moving toward him.

He backed away. "Why did you fall from the sky, Talia?" he demanded, his voice rising. "I've asked you half a dozen times and this isn't making any sense. Either I've just stroked out or you're not real."

"I am real, Jack," she said, holding out her left hand. "I'm wearing your ring, remember? You proposed to me with it earlier. During the finale of The Prince Charming Hour."

"And you didn't answer me."

Tears threaded down her face and it made his chest ache. "I couldn't then, but I love you, Jack."

Those words tore through his heart and burned into his stomach.

"Do you hear me, Jack Casey? I love you."

He laid his hand against his heart and then held it out to her, palm up.

Grinning through her tears, she closed her hand and pressed against her heart.

It *was* her. He ached all over now, not even caring about the truth. All he wanted was her beside him. Forever.

"Talia," he said in a small, tight voice. "I love you, too. Now until forever."

Talia threw herself into his arms and he just held her. And then she began to sink.

"Talia?" he cried, fear blooming cold through his chest. "Talia!"

Her eyelids fluttered, but she kept sinking.

He gathered her in his arms and carried her to the bed. He laid her down and slid his arms free. His shirt sleeves came away bloody.

"Oh, my, God! Talia!" He took her hand in his, frantic. "What's the matter? What's happening?"

Muriel was beside him, hands against his arms. "Let me, Jack," she said in a quiet voice, her unblinking gaze reassuring. "She's why Anahera and I are here."

"Who are you two?" he asked, feeling frustrated.

The halo above her head brightened, wings unfurling.

"Angels, Jack," she replied and nodded at Talia. "From Heaven. Like Talia."

He couldn't speak, the words stuck halfway up his throat. Angels? As in Biblical, card-carrying, winged, halo-spinning, harp-playing, cloud-surfing angels?

"Like with highways and Roma Downey?"

Muriel laughed. "Much better than that, Jack," she replied, her light mood fading. "Talia's been hurt—her wings are gone—and we're here to help. She's also in danger—and so are you. We're here to keep you both safe, but see, humans can't see us unless we let them. So, we're still trying to figure how you can see us. But right now, Talia needs our help."

He sat down on the bed beside Talia and laid his hand against her hair, stroking. "Well, I'm not leaving her side. I'll take care of her. Whatever she needs."

Muriel nodded, moving to the other side of the bed. "Right now, we need to stop this bleeding."

Jack turned Talia on her side as Muriel laid her hands against the torn and burned cloth at her back.

"I'll get something clean for her to wear," said Jack, jumping up from the bed.

He rushed over to the dresser and pulled out the first baggy T-shirt he came to: his Van Halen *1984* T-shirt. He groaned when he saw the angel.

"Really?" he muttered, grabbing another T-shirt.

Rush. *Clockwork Angels*. He pulled the next shirt in the stack. Aerosmith. *Get Your Wings*. "Seriously?" he snapped with a sigh.

He grabbed the next one in the stack. Neil Young. *Sleeps with Angels*.

"Okay, stop it already!" he said with a growl.

Muriel turned around, watching him. When she saw the three T-shirts in his hand, she burst out laughing.

"Angel fetish, Jack?" she asked.

His face turned red. "Music," he replied. "Music fetish."

Without looking, he pulled the next T-shirt out, his gaze on Muriel as he handed it to her.

She smirked at him as she unfolded it. Nirvana. *In Utero*. He groaned. The one with a winged woman on the album cover.

"Aw, come on!" he shouted.

Muriel burst out laughing. "You're a keeper, Jack."

He opened the next drawer and pulled out a pair of blue jersey cotton pajama bottoms. He handed them off to Muriel and turned toward the bathroom.

"I'll get the first aid kit," he said.

"No need for that, Jack," she said and handed the clothes to Anahera as the taller angel started gently sliding Talia's arms out of the burned and torn silky fabric that had once been a dress.

Or something. Jack didn't know anymore. Was she really an angel? Maybe that stage light had actually crowned him and he was still lying on the stage floor of the Microsoft Theater, hallucinating after it split his skull open?

He turned around, facing the wall, hands in his pockets while Muriel and Anahera dressed Talia in one of his T-shirts and pajama bottoms.

"And a gentleman, too?" Muriel quipped behind him. "She got the whole package with you, Jack."

He shook his head, staring into the dresser mirror at his thin face, messed up blond hair, tired green eyes, and unshaven jaw. He looked like a recovering addict. Accurate.

"She got the twenty percent off, damaged goods box," he remarked, smoothing his hair. "The washed-up actor with a flake problem model. Without the instructions and a few screws missing."

"You can turn around now, Jack," said Anahera.

He turned around.

Talia lay on her side, dressed in his Van Halen T-shirt and blue pajama bottoms. Muriel had her hand pressed against Talia's back, white light vibrating against her shoulders. Some sort of healing light?

His heart smashed against his rib cage at seeing her hurt. He stepped around to the other side of the bed and sat down, laying his hand against her hair. Stroking. Wanting to comfort her. Wanting to fix this. He felt helpless and he still didn't understand what was going on.

Muriel chuckled. "You still believe that, don't you, Jack?"

He sat up. "Because I see him every time I look in the mirror." He sighed. "Or open my wallet—that echoes."

An issue of *Variety* appeared in his hands. He jumped, pages rustling.

"Front page, Jack. Hot off the press, er, the website. This is Monday's issue. Your phone's gonna blow up on Monday."

The headlines gleamed up at him. *Smash Hit Prince Charming Hour Finale Watched by over Forty Million Households.*

He laughed. "Nice try, Muriel."

"You'll find out when every contact you ever made in Hollywood is breaking down your door come Monday morning," said Muriel with a shrug. "This show has convinced lots of studio execs that you're leading man material, Jack. You're about to get flooded with film and TV offers."

He shook his head, unable to process that. "How could you have Monday's issue of Variety or know what's about to happen?"

She tapped her temple with her index finger. "Jack! Angel. Remember? We exist outside your time stream, so we can wade into it anywhere. At any time."

He held his breath, unable to process that, but he remembered what had happened after *The Cinderella Hour*. But those were offers to reappear on *The Prince Charming Hour*. Not movies and television.

Was Muriel just jerking him around or was he about to get his acting career back?

"I'm really going to get to act again?" he said in a quiet voice.

"In whatever project you want, Jack," said Muriel, that white light moving across Talia's head now, across her brow where that long, thin burn had blistered.

He couldn't even process that statement. Whatever he wanted? Like a return to *SanFran Confidential*? Or a big budget action film? A superheroes movie! Writing his own ticket. What every actor dreamed of.

His gaze traveled to Talia who looked so frail and pallid. The fear returned, cold and sharp in his belly. She was badly hurt. She needed rest and attention. He didn't care who called him on Monday. He was sticking right here in this crappy little apartment, at her side, taking care of her. Hollywood could wait. Besides, if Talia was in danger, he wouldn't let her out of his sight.

"It's just a job," he said, leaning over her again, stroking her hair. "I'm not leaving her for some stupid script pitch."

"Not even for a billion-dollar franchise?" Muriel asked.

He frowned. "What franchise?"

"A new property for a huge blockbuster fantasy series. The one everyone's talking about."

His eyes bugged out, mouth falling open. "That series?"

She nodded. "They lost their minds when they saw that duel you fought, Jack." She pantomimed a swoon. "And when you told Talia goodbye."

"I told Talia goodbye because I thought I was going to die in that fight." He rubbed his forehead. "But I don't care about any of that right now," he said, feeling confused and uncomfortable. "I'm staying right here. With her."

Muriel gave him a funny look. "But this is your dream, isn't it? Your chance to be back on top again."

"She's my dream, Muriel. And she saved my life twice," he said, sliding his arm around her. "It's time I return the favor. If they really want me, they can wait. When she and I can talk about living on location somewhere. She'd have to agree to that—because I'm not letting her out of my sight again."

Muriel was grinning at him. "Like I said. She got the whole package, Jack."

Jack laid his hand against Talia's face, careful not to touch the white light from Muriel's fingertips. The heat startled him.

Perspiration beaded across Talia's cheeks and clung to her neck. She was running a fever.

"She's getting worse," said Jack, gripping her hand in his.

"It's Separation Fever," said Anahera, looking worried.

Okay, now, he was scared shitless if the angels were scared. "What's that?"

"When an angel falls from Heaven, the sudden separation sometimes causes illness," said Anahera. "Fever."

Fury burned in Muriel's grey eyes. "So does having your wings burned off your back and your halo taken."

"What? Can't you guys just carry her back to—wherever she's supposed to be? So she can heal?" He shook his head. "I'm so out of my element here."

Muriel walked around the bed and sat down in front of him. She laid her warm hand on his shoulder.

"Jack, I don't think you understand exactly what's happened here."

He gave her a sharp nod. "I have no freakin' clue. I'm lost, Muriel."

"Understandable," she said and glanced over at Talia who groaned. "See, Talia was just cast out of Heaven. She had her wings and halo stripped from her."

"For how long?" he asked.

"Forever, Jack."

His eyes burned, turning glassy. Talia was the nicest human being —angel? Whatever she was. He loved her with his whole heart, but right now, he had no idea who or what she was. How could she be cast out of Heaven?

"Why?" he demanded, eyes blazing. "What could she have possibly done to deserve that?"

"Absolutely nothing," said Anahera, shaking her head.

White fire burned in Muriel's eyes, blocking out her grey irises.

Scaring the living shit out of Jack. *Game face, dude. Act your way through this.* He held his breath.

"Jack, Talia's boss, the Archangel of Death lost a wager with Lucifer."

"Wait. What?" He couldn't process that sentence. His brain just wouldn't let it enter and kill the remaining brain cells he had left.

The white fire dissipated. Grey, more human eyes returning.

"I'm sorry this is all hitting you at once, Jack," said Muriel, squeezing his shoulder. "There was a wager."

He stared at her a moment. "With Satan. Prince of Darkness. Keeper of Hellfires. King of Mean."

"Yes. With Lucifer."

This wasn't happening. He was being punked. Where the hell was Kutcher right now? And his camera?

He laughed. "And the Archangel of Death."

She nodded.

Okay, then. He'd officially lost his freakin' mind. Had someone dropped a roofie in his beer? Or a tab of acid? Had he done some 'shrooms and not remembered it?

"And just what was this wager?"

"Talia had to take two souls in seven weeks while on The Prince Charming Hour."

The slow burn began in his chest, rising into his brain, stoking his anger.

"So, that whole show was just a bet? For Talia?" he demanded.

"So was the first one," said Anahera.

Muriel whirled around and shushed her.

His anger was white hot now. Had he just been a bet to her this whole time? A wager? Toy with the human's heart and take souls? Get big laughs on Angel TV? Weren't angels supposed to be guardians or something?

He crossed his arms. "So, I was just a bet to her? Get the human to fall in love with an angel and then break his heart? And then kill him for his soul. That's hilarious! You dudes should have your own show.

A Game of Lost Souls. Damn—and I've been playing it for two seasons."

He stomped up from the bed, his head spinning.

"Jack, no!" Muriel shouted at him. "It isn't like that."

He kept his back to them, his eyes stinging. God, he felt used. Humiliated. Did Talia ever really love him or was he just a bet to her?

It hurt bad, his whole chest on fire.

He grabbed hold of the door handle to the patio door. Remembering the stage light that fell. And a cold chill washed over him, the painful reality sinking in…that light had been meant for him.

She was supposed to kill him and take his soul, but he moved at the last minute. Had she been winding him up this whole time only to kill him at the end of season two? He winced, the pain sharp in his gut.

He'd just been a bet to her. An outcome to keep her wings. Nothing more. The rage made him shake all over. He'd been played by all of them.

Even Talia.

"Guess I just moved at the last moment," he snapped. "And didn't die like I was supposed to. Messed up the devil's little wager."

Anahera was in front of him in a blink, her hands gripping his wrists.

He jumped, startled.

"You didn't die like you were supposed to because Talia grabbed you and fell backward. Out of the stage light's path."

"Guess she felt guilty at the last moment," he said, the edge in his voice razor sharp. "Like someone looking back at the puppy they just left on the side of the road. Before they drove away."

Anahera's eyes filled with glistening tears and she bowed her head. "Oh, Jack, no. She was devastated when Lucifer told her that yours was the second soul she had to take. And she refused to do it. Knowing it would cost her everything. Especially you."

He glared at her. "Me? She was supposed to kill me, remember?"

Blink. Muriel was beside her.

"Damn! Don't do that!" He shouted.

"Jack. Do you know why Talia agreed to the second wager?"

"Another shot at killing me? Slowly?"

"To return to you here on Earth. Her first wager was to save you. You were on the fast train to overdose city, Jack, and that was your fate. Written in your Book of Life and Death. She was supposed to change that. And then she fell in love with you."

But it was still a bet. And it stung. Bad.

Muriel's eyes softened. "I know this has to hurt, Jack," she said, "but after she won the first wager, she was returned to her angel form. And she couldn't be with you anymore."

Anahera nodded at him, studying his face, his eyes. Like she was looking into his soul and it made him uncomfortable. But he couldn't look away.

"That second wager was the only way she could return to you," said Anahera. "But when she accepted it, she had no idea that Lucifer would name you as the second soul. When she refused to let you die, she saved you again. Sacrificing herself. Her entire existence as an angel. And an eternity in Hell with Lucifer. Because she loved you that much."

A cold wind brushed across his heart and his breath caught in his throat, eyes tearing up. Damned for eternity. He bit his lip, looking away. That was a lance through his chest. His breath caught, knees buckling. He grabbed hold of the wall, his hand over his mouth.

"That's right, Jack," said Anahera in a sad voice. "She gave up her existence to save you."

"And I'm not worth that," he muttered, his voice breaking. "How could I doubt her like that? When she means everything to me."

Muriel slid her arm around his shoulders. "It's a lot to process, I know. And finding out you started out as a Heavenly bet in her life has to be as tough as learning that she's an angel of death."

He swayed, his brain on overload, threatening to detonate. Holy shit…Talia *was* an angel of death.

"What the hell does that mean?" he said, rubbing his forehead. "That the woman I love is a black-winged, scythe-carrying, black-hood-wearing, death angel killing machine?"

Muriel nodded. "That's about right. But she only carries a scythe in extreme circumstances."

Wait a minute…the woman he was going to marry was a black-winged, scythe-carrying, black-hood-wearing, death angel killing machine? Sweet! Guess that explained her arsonist's wit. She'd be indispensable in contract negotiations. Maybe he could even fire Phil, his agent?

Who needed to give up fifteen percent when his fiancée was an angel of death? She could put the fear of God into any contract negotiation. Striking bad clauses would be cake with that scythe!

"Okay, then," he said with a nod. "Angel of death. Right. I think I can get used to that."

Muriel gave Anahera a shocked look and then turned her surprised expression back to him. "So, you're fine with that?"

He nodded again. "Nobody will mess with me if my girlfriend's an angel of death. I'm kind of liking this. One word from me and she'd Schwarzenegger their asses all over the pavement. With or without a scythe."

Muriel burst out laughing, shaking her head. "Jack, you're one weird human. I can see why Talia gave up everything for you."

"And I need to show her that it wasn't a total waste," he said and glanced at the door handle.

He started to let go, but it turned in his hand.

And the door began to glow red.

"Uh, friends of yours?" he asked, stepping backward.

"Red's not my color," said Muriel, pushing Jack behind her as Anahera stepped in front of him.

The door thumped hard and then blew open, backward onto the patio.

"But it's certainly mine," said the cheerful British voice from the patio.

"Ah, shit," Jack muttered. "And I bet he's not a census taker either."

"Only for Hell," said a tall, thin man with sun-blond hair and pale blue eyes like Robin's eggs.

He looked like a GQ model as he stepped into the apartment in a black tailcoat, black pants, white shirt, and red bow tie. He smiled, but the glint in his eyes was empty of compassion and empathy.

And it chilled Jack to the bone.

"And you've got a change of address coming, Jack Casey. And so does my dear, Talia. I do appreciate both you arriving at the same location. Saving me the trouble of hunting you both down."

Jack gritted his teeth, glaring at this strange dude invading his shithole apartment. It wasn't much, but it was his shithole apartment. He backed toward the bed, standing in front of Talia.

Muriel and Anahera shuffled backward, wings stretched wide, blocking whoever this dude was from his path.

"Two little angels of death trying fruitlessly to protect their little human pet. How very cute. Now, pat him on the head, tell him he's a good boy, and then hand him over. He's mine now." He motioned at Jack. "After all, I won him fair and square."

"Won me?" Jack snapped. "Who the hell are you?"

His dangerous smile stretched into a grin and he bowed. "Very perceptive, Jack. I am Lucifer. I'll be your flight attendant on this all-expense paid trip to Hell. I hope you like hot weather and don't forget to pack your swim trunks. The Lake of Fire is beautiful this time of year."

Holy shit. This was the Devil?

He'd never believed in any of that Heaven and Hell stuff. He'd always thought the Devil stories were written to scare kids and control adults. And because some dudes up in the clouds made a bet with him in it, he was now Satan's chew toy in Hell for all eternity?

He gritted his teeth. Hell no. He wasn't putting up with this shit.

"You can just go back to Hell, devil dude. I'm not gonna be your chew toy because you made some bet. I never signed a damned thing. Keyword being damned. Forget it." He glanced at Talia. "And she's staying right here."

Lucifer stared at him a moment and his grin unwavering. "I do like this one—lots of spirit. Breaking you will be so much fun, Jack. Especially while my dear, Talia watches. It will provide minutes of entertainment."

Jack pointed at him. "You think I'm scared of you? I'm not. There's nothing you can do to me that I haven't already gone through.'

"Jack, don't," Anahera whispered.

Lucifer's smile didn't waver. "You think you've been through Hell here? This is Disneyland compared to what I can inflict upon you. I am the originator of torture, Jack. I taught Genghis Khan. Vlad the Impaler. Hitler. How do you think your pathetic empathy and compassion—your heart—will stack up against those devoid of all humanity?"

Jack stood his ground. He didn't care what Lucifer did to him. For Talia, he'd take it to protect her.

"Do your worst," he snapped, hands on his hips. "I'm not letting you take her."

A deep laugh rumbled through Lucifer as he tossed his head back. "Believe me, I always do my worst. It's what I do best. Oh, we're going to have so much fun torturing you, Jack." He leaned against the wall, looking smug. Jack wanted to punch his face. "And when it's your soul, Jack, it means you can't die and escape. Think about that for a moment while I just give you a little demonstration."

Something moved in the room. A blur. A shadow. He saw it out of the corner of his eye.

He glanced around the room. Everything was so deadly still that it made his hair stand on end.

Muriel and Anahera crouched low, wings extended, halos thrumming in the silence as they watched the room.

Something growled. Jack's skin began to crawl. A deep, throaty caterwaul like a mountain lion or a panther.

"Jack, stay close," said Anahera, glancing around the room.

A flash of red. Rush of air. Glint of fangs.

He whirled right. Then left.

Something brushed past him with a hiss. Something dark and sinewy. Lean and muscular.

His mouth went dry. Something that could tear him apart.

Muriel was turning, hand raised, moving in almost slow motion as the shadow sprang.

The shadowy panther shape leaped at him, knocking him to the floor. And it began to change, fluid smoky body stretching into female curves. Spine shortened, legs lengthening until a shadowy woman sat on his chest. She leaned toward him, lips pursed into a kiss, red eyes burning.

He slammed his left hand upward. Grabbing her by the throat.

It screeched, fangs bared, trying to sink them into his flesh.

He heard Lucifer's guttural laugh as he drew back his right fist and hit the demon as hard as he could.

And then Muriel and Anahera were on it, slamming it with white-hot Holy fire. Until it vanished in a trail of smoke.

As Jack got to his feet, Lucifer's GQ look had degraded. Horns were beginning to protrude from his forehead, a pointed, leathery tail twitching against his tailcoat. His feet moved stiffly, heavily now, like he had two left feet. Jack's skin began to crawl again. Or hooves.

"Now, how did you know that assassin demon was there?" Lucifer demanded, waving an arm at Jack.

"Like it was a big secret or something," Jack snapped. "I saw it."

"Jack, you saw it?" Anahera asked as she backed up against Jack, Muriel on his other side, posture stiff, gaze flitting through the room.

Outside, the flutter of wings filled the silence.

"Good thing I did. Sorry, I get cranky when something tries to tear my throat out."

"The guard!" Muriel cried.

Lucifer looked pissed. He pointed a finger at Jack. "I don't know how you're cheating, little human, but I will be back to fix whatever little trick you're playing." He smiled at Muriel. "I'm allergic to feathers."

"Thought you taught Vlad and Khan and Hitler," Jack taunted. "What's a matter? Scared of a few angels? Party's just starting."

Lucifer's blue eyes turned blood red, his gaze murderous.

"I can't wait to flay the skin from your body, Jack and bleed your soul into ribbons."

"What's stopping you?" Jack replied.

"Just waiting for Talia to join the party, Jack. To watch you roast on my spit."

In a puff of smoke, he was gone as a dozen grey-winged angels flew through the open back door and into his crappy little apartment.

Muriel grabbed him by the shoulders and shook him. "Jack, are you insane!"

"Yeah, but what's that got to do with anything."

"Taunting Lucifer is a very, very bad idea," she shouted. "And how'd you really know that assassin demon was there?"

"Like I said, I saw it."

Muriel let him go and began to pace the room as the other angels took up places throughout the room. Damn. He only had eight beers left.

"Sorry I don't have enough beer for everyone," he announced.

"How could he see that demon?" Anahera asked Muriel in a soft whisper, but Jack heard it.

"I don't understand what's going on here, Anahera," said Muriel, talking fast and sharp. "I need to talk to Azrael."

"What did Lucifer mean when he said I was cheating?" Jack asked.

Muriel sighed and rubbed a hand over her face. "Because you saw his assassin demon at the same time we did."

"So?" Jack said with a shrug.

"So?" Muriel turned toward him, hands on her hips. "Jack, humans can't see ethereal beings, light or shadow, unless they want to be seen. If all of you saw what was on the other side, you'd lose your minds."

Jack sank down on the edge of the bed beside Talia. "Kind of like right now."

She knelt beside him. "We don't know how or why you're able to see these things, Jack, but we're trying to figure it out. We've never dealt with this before. And apparently, Lucifer hadn't either. That's why he left. But he'll be back."

Anahera was on his other side now, looking over him at Muriel, fear in her grey eyes. "He and Talia can't stay here," she said. "Lucifer blew past every ward I set."

Muriel got to her feet, wings unfurling as she began to pace. "All right, we need someplace isolated that we can defend. Not in the middle of a big human city with people all around. But where?"

Jack felt his pocket vibrating. He slid his phone out of his jeans pocket. Thirty-two missed calls. Fifty-six text messages.

"What the hell?" he said, staring at his phone.

"Guess they aren't waiting until Monday, Jack," said Muriel. "Variety must have published early."

His gaze shot to Muriel. "Who?"

"Hollywood."

The landline rang, scaring the hell out of him. First message on his answering machine.

"Oh, my, God, Jack! Have you seen the ratings for tonight's finale?"

Jack grinned when he recognized that voice. Armand Gianni.

"You won't believe the calls I've gotten tonight, asking me to read scripts. One of those calls was from Herb. Pitching a new show to me and Izzy. Something called The Ever After Hour. I texted you, but I know you use this number to screen your calls. When you hear this, call me. Herb said he can't get hold of you and asked me to try."

The machine beeped. He stared at it in surprise when he saw 104 messages on the machine. He'd cleared that machine when he got home. Why hadn't the phone rung until now?

He turned around, staring at Muriel.

"Sorry, I muted the phone and the machine when I saw the stats for your show. Didn't want to hear that thing going off every second."

The phone rang again. He groaned. "Like now?"

She nodded.

"I can fix that," he snapped and walked over to the phone. Unplugging it from the wall. "Problem solved."

"What about all those offers?"

He shrugged. "The last thing I need right now is a bunch of job offers that I don't care about." He moved back to the bed and sat down beside Talia, stroking her hair.

"You got a brother, Jack?" Muriel asked.

He shook his head. "Just four sisters, why?"

She smiled. "Just curious."

He flicked through the growing number of text messages until he saw the one from Herb Rutherford.

Doing a new show for the spring season. Called The Ever After Hour. A couple's show, to see if our new matches can stay together.

Armand Gianni and Mark Banks are both interested. Jack, we'd love to have you and Talia back for a third season.

Your performance on the finale broke records, Jack. And broke audience hearts. They want you and Talia back on their televisions.

Call me tomorrow. Name your price. Just call me.

Jack couldn't halt his grin. Name your price? He'd never seen those words directed at him before. He held the phone out as he leaned down to Talia's ear.

"Talia, they want us on a new show. Called The Ever After Hour. If nothing else, it'd be a few weeks isolated at a luxury estate. You've gotta get well, so we can talk about this. And some other things." He sighed. "Like that ring on your finger. Got some plans to make. Unless Lucifer turns me into wall art or something."

"Jack!" Muriel cried. "That's brilliant!"

Jack turned his head back toward the grey-winged angel, her gold halo spinning faster as she grinned at him, dropping down beside him.

"What? Lucifer turning me into wall art?"

She laughed. "No, an isolated estate! With enough of the guard, we can ward and protect the perimeter while Talia recovers. That way, we can control the environment and protect the two of you until we can talk to God's Scribe and Azrael about what to do next. After he's been released from the seraphim."

He frowned. "The what?"

"Highest order of angels. Deadly powerful."

"So, you want Talia and I to appear on The Ever After Hour as a couple? So, you and the other angels can protect us?"

"Exactly! It's isolated, but there are cameras everywhere. Even if Lucifer moved against you, he'd have to be careful with hundreds of angels underfoot. This is perfect. We just need to get Talia well." Some of her enthusiasm faded. "And to agree."

Holy shit, he couldn't believe it. Was he about to do a third season of reality TV? When he had all these amazing offers coming in? He was starting to understand what Hell might be like. Still, if it kept Talia safe, he'd appear at a circus and let clowns hit him with cream pies. And he hated clowns.

"Well, you don't have to convince me, Muriel," he said, gripping Talia's hand in his. "Keeping her safe is all I care about. I'm in."

"Excellent!" Muriel floated up from the floor, her wings fluttering. "We can do this, Jack. Keep her safe until Azrael tells us how to keep her out of Lucifer's hands."

He was going back for season three. But this time, he'd have Talia at his side. Working with him. And if it kept her safe, he'd do a hundred more seasons. He shook his head. Jack Casey, reality TV star. Not what he'd wanted as an actor, but as a dude hopelessly in love with apparently, an angel of death, it fit.

Another game of lost souls. He just hoped that by the end, he didn't lose his and Talia's both.

5

Azrael stood atop the podium, sweating as the seraphim circled him.

The flurry of activity startled him. They moved in frenetic arcs, two then all three. Banking against the clouds, rising on the updrafts, and then dropping into a free-fall. And back again.

He had no idea what was happening and it made him uncomfortable. He didn't know whether their actions were propelled by anger or some sense of discussion regarding his story so far. Or were they simply building up enough Holy fire to burn him out of existence at any moment?

And in a blur of movement, all three of the seraphim hovered in front of the podium, just far enough away that they didn't set his robes on fire. Or his wings.

Who caught the angel of death?

The question entered his head like a bass drum.

"Her human charge. Jack Casey."

Why?

Such a simple question, asked by children and adults alike. And it calmed him that Seraphina would ask for his motivation. She and the other seraphim already read what was in his heart. Already knew his reasons for doing what he did, but it puzzled him that she would even ask him why? Was she wanting him to confess his reasons?

But he only had one answer for that question. It was the reason behind everything he'd done since he'd tried to save Talia from Lucifer's clutches by agreeing to that very first wager.

"Love." He stared unblinking at the mighty seraph hovering near the platform. "Jack Casey loves Talia more than his own life. He will protect her as she heals. And I sent members from the guard to protect them both."

How can one human and lesser angels stop Lucifer?

Seraphina's next question was impatient. The seraphim beat their wings, circling again, swooping together as a single unit as they rose through layers of clouds and halted. Hovering at a distance. Conversing. Considering. He sighed.

Questioning again.

He understood why. At first glance, it seemed like a waste of resources. And impossible for a fallen angel and a human to combat the King of Hell. Lucifer was as powerful as a seraph, but weakened without his halo and wings. And what he lacked in raw angelic power, he made up for with hordes of demons and his fallen angel comrades.

"I have discovered that Talia possesses some rare powers not seen in the guard for centuries. They are just beginning to awaken and they need time to mature. And some of her other abilities are beginning to appear in her human charge. This is a startling development and it has never happened before. We don't understand how or why it is occurring. For these reasons, both need our protection. Especially after my deception with Lucifer."

Continue.

"I understand the impossibility of this situation, Holy Hosts," he replied. "But only in normal circumstances. And the current situation within the death angels guard is anything but normal. The same goes for the archive and God's Scribe."

In an instant, all three seraphim floated around him. Above him. Beside him.

Explain.

"Books of Life and Death have been altered. Forged. Penned by someone other than Pravuil, God's Scribe."

Impossible!

A seraph exploded into a ball of fiery wrath, shooting across the endless sky, cutting across the serene blue in jagged white streaks of fire that set the clouds alight.

"And someone here in the Heavens is trying to kill God's Scribe in order to change the Books at will."

Where is your proof?

Azrael lifted his hand into the air and a Book from the archive appeared in his hand. A Book of Life and Death. He turned the spine toward the seraphim.

"Pravuil and I discovered this Book hidden on the shelves and shadowed to keep angels of death from seeing it. As you can see, on the spine, the name of the Book's owner is written. As all Books of Life and Death are created. On the spine of this Book, there is a name. Pravuil's. Written in the old language. First, only humans have Books. Second, only God's Scribe can create a Book. Someone used something very old and very dark to craft a Book for God's Scribe. And write his ending with the Holy essence. In an attempt to kill him. And take control of the Heavenly archive."

He had never heard a seraph shriek until this moment.

Seraphina's piercing note, shrill and furious, resonated through the room, shaking the walls, and cracking the podium.

The shock wave filtered out across High House, shaking its spires, and rattling the Heavens all the way to Eolowen.

He did his best to stay composed, hoping they would still read what was in his heart as they considered the rest of what he had to say. He hated conveying this ugliness, but it had to be uncovered and handled. He was an old soldier and he would fight the good fight, but he would also identify who he thought was responsible. And protect the foundations of the Maker's realm and all that He'd built.

Including the human charges that God loved so much.

Remaining at the podium, Azrael watched the seraphim tangle together in a frantic communion, floating between jagged, smoking, fiery swaths of clouds. He knew Lucifer was behind this plot, but in order to gain access to the Heavens—and the Books—he had help. He'd turned someone. And not just a lesser angel. Someone with rank. And access.

"Holy Hosts," he called out. "You need to know that Lucifer is behind these acts, but he had help. Lucifer needed assistance to attack the archive. Not a Watcher or angel of death. Someone with rank and access. Someone that could orchestrate a rebellion, one that hasn't been seen since Lucifer's fall. A rebellion that whispers at the edge of the Heavens. One that slithers around the Garden and one that tiptoes into the archive with the intent to commit murder. One with the means and opportunity to start a war."

In the blink of an eye, the seraphim hovered around the platform. The heat of their presence was sweltering, roiling across him in waves. He squinted, doing his best to weather the force and the flame.

"I believe in my heart that one among us has joined Lucifer's cause. Intent to start a Holy war."

Name this conspirator!

Seraphina's voice thundered through his head.

He remained silent a moment, letting them read what was in his heart. And then he took a deep breath, the traitor's name on his lips as he faced the seraphim.

6

GUARDED BY A DOZEN ANGELS OF DEATH, JACK STAYED UP ALL NIGHT with Talia. He sat on the creaky old Murphy bed and held her in his lap, pressing cold compresses against her face and neck, bandaging the two bloody wounds between her shoulder blades, and applying burn ointment to the blisters across her forehead.

Three more times, Muriel laid hands on Talia's back and that white-gold light enveloped her body, spilling onto Jack.

Her sleep was heavy, fevered dreams making her call out and moan, but he held her through it all, whispering in her ear that he was there and she was safe. He wrapped her in a green and blue quilt when she began to shake and threw it off her when she began to sweat.

He leaned against two pillows against the wall, the clock by the bed glaring 6:07 at him in big red letters. In another hour, the sun would rise. He was so tired, but he wouldn't sleep until she was resting comfortably. And this fever dropped.

Even now, his brain reeled from the events of the last six hours. It was overwhelming and he still couldn't process it all. He went from aching for Talia on his patio, feeling utterly lost, to her just falling out of the sky and into his arms. Wearing his ring and telling him she loved him.

He didn't care how. And just when he thought everything was going to be okay because he had her back, it all went sideways. The freakin' clown car pulled up and a hundred clowns got out. And he hated clowns. Suddenly, there were angels of death in his face—hell, in his living room—telling him the love of his life had only been interested in him on a bet. That she was also a scythe-carrying, black-winged angel of death.

And then the whole realm of crazy town came to visit. Assassin demons. Lucifer. A whole guard of angels of death. And him apparently seeing things he shouldn't be able to see. While the assassin demon tried to rip out his throat and string his intestines across the room like Christmas decorations.

He didn't even want to get started on that.

And now, suddenly, he was the hottest ticket in Hollywood and everybody was blowing up his phone—even Armand Gianni—and his answering machine with offers he couldn't even dream about until tonight. Even when he was bad boy heartthrob, Davy Pierson on *SanFran Confidential*.

He was only twenty-six. He still had time for those roles. Right now, he needed to protect the love of his life. Talia had never acted like she needed his help with anything. But from the beginning, their attraction had been instant and she had fascinated him with her beauty, her wit, and her sense of wonder. He fought through two seasons of reality TV challenges to show her that he needed her. And that he loved her.

Even after he'd proposed to her on the finale of *The Prince Charming Hour*, he still thought he'd lost her. Until he saw his ring still on her finger tonight. He smiled. When she told him that she loved him. Had all of that only happened last night?

Anahera smiled at him as she sat down on the edge of the bed and checked Talia's wounds.

"You're taking really good care of her, Jack," she said.

"Thanks," he replied with a tired smile. "So, what happens to her when these wounds heal? Is she still an angel? Of death?"

Anahera sighed, her wings flattening against her back. "We don't really know. This has never happened before."

"An angel falling from Heaven?" he asked.

She shook her head. "Talia did nothing to earn that fall, Jack. And most of the guard is deeply troubled by it. Angels that rebel and war against the Heavens are stripped of their wings and halos and cast out. Talia did none of that. She just lost a wager that she didn't even make."

She knotted her fingers together. This situation had even unnerved the angels. It had sure freaked him the hell out. Must be bad up there. It sounded terrible to kick out one of their own when she'd done nothing to earn it. It made him hurt all over for Talia.

"None of us understands how she could be cast out like every rebellious angel and then land on Earth instead of Hell." She smiled. "In your arms."

"Craziest thing I've ever seen," said Jack. "Not used to people just falling out of the sky. Much less the woman I love." He laid his hand to Talia's head and ran his fingers through her long, black hair, cradling her.

"So much is happening that we don't understand," Anahera continued. "Archangel Azrael making a huge production of Talia's fall in front Lucifer. Your sudden ability to see angels and demons. By the way, Muriel walked all through the neighborhood to see if any other humans could see her."

He sat up straighter, eyes wide. "This neighborhood? She's liable to be mugged and carjacked—even without a car."

Anahera laughed. "Muriel would have smited anyone that tried, but no one even saw her, Jack. She tried everything, but no other humans except you can see us. It's all very confusing."

"I believe it," he replied. "I know I'm confused about everything right now."

"Until we're able to confer with Archangel Azrael, who leads this guard of death angels, we will hold fast to our mission. To protect you and Talia. For now, Muriel thinks that television show filming location you mentioned is our best fortification against Lucifer. The one that's isolated. It won't be impenetrable, but it will be defensible."

Jack nodded. He had to agree. An isolated location with all the cameras might be their best chance. And maybe it would help her heal, too? He worried about how all of this had affected her. She'd been through a terrible trauma. It must have been devastating. He understood a little of what that was like, after being cast out of everything he ever cared about. He'd been ready to give up. *The Cinderella Hour* was a lifeline and kept him from drowning—for a little while.

Until he thought he'd lost Talia and overdosed on coke. If Talia hadn't been there, that night would have been his last. A one-line epitaph in *Variety* and on the evening news. A last, single addendum to his Wikipedia article. No, Talia saved him. His soul and then his life. Maybe she shouldn't have? He bit his lip. All of her pain had been his fault.

He still had to work out his pain over the wagers, but he couldn't argue with the fact that this poor kid had her wings burned off, her halo torn away, and then she was literally thrown out of Heaven. Falling who knew how far, expecting to land in Hell. For eternity. But landing on Earth instead. In his arms. He couldn't even fathom the trauma that would come from that. And he couldn't help but feel responsible. Maybe she should have just let him go that very first time on *The Cinderella Hour*?

Regardless, she wouldn't go through it alone. He'd be at her side. No matter what.

He just wanted her to open her eyes and let him love her. Help her heal.

"When she's conscious again," he began, still stroking her hair, "and feeling a little better, I'll tell her about The Ever After Hour."

"But Jack," Anahera cried, glancing from Talia to him. "We can't keep you or Talia safe here. We have to take you both somewhere we can protect you. She has to go where it's safe."

Jack nodded. "I know. I get it. But she still needs to agree to it. Because of these wagers, I don't know if she'll ever want to see another season of this show again. After what she's been through, I don't want to force her into anything. You and Muriel may need to help me convince her to go where she can be protected."

"Agreed. We'll do our best."

"I'll contact the director as soon as Talia agrees. I just hope she agrees. But this time, it'll be different. She and I will be a team. That might change her mind." He smiled. "Also, she was friends with Morgan Boyer and Mark Banks. And she and Izzy were pretty tight by the end of season two. That might help. She'd be surrounded by friends. And me."

Anahera squinted at him, looking puzzled. "Why did you leave yourself out of that group, Jack?"

He couldn't hold back his sigh of disappointment. The wagers still hurt. He was struggling to get past that. His head got it that she'd made two huge sacrifices for him, but both were because of the wagers. His heart needed to know that she really loved him—without a bet in play. Especially now that she was earthbound and had lost her abilities as an angel of death. In a strange way, they were on equal footing. She was living a human life now.

Would she still love him? Now that she was trapped here? When she realized that her fall and all her pain had been his fault?

"I just don't know where I fit into her world right now," he said in a quiet voice. "When she realizes she's stuck living like a human being, she may not even want me anymore. Now that she has no wager to satisfy."

"Oh, Jack—she loves you so much. You'll see."

"Hope you're right."

She patted him on the shoulder. "Especially when I tell her how you held her in your arms all night and nursed her back to health."

"But Muriel did all the heavy lifting in the healing department. I just used a little human first aid."

She smiled at him. "And all the love you could give. That can heal faster than any other power I know."

He leaned down and gripped Talia's hand in his as he pressed another cold compress against her flushed face. Hoping that her fever would break soon. Right now, she needed a lot of rest after the horrors she'd been through. Before he had to move her someplace safe. He sighed. From the Prince of Darkness and his squad of assassin demons and who the hell knew what else? Literally. He hoped that *The Ever After Hour* was prepared to handle a shitload of angels of death and demons. This show would never be the same after this clash of Biblical proportions went down.

7

Talia felt like she'd slept for days. Angels didn't sleep, so this was way beyond anything she'd ever experienced (even for the brief time she was human) and it was so strange. Surreal. Especially with the fevered heat that made her ache and sweat and dream. She'd never experienced an illness before. Not even when she was sent to Earth in human form for Lucifer's first wager.

Lucifer.

She shuddered, the darkness writhing around her. The memory of his first attack through Devin Van Fossen came back to her in the fire and stillness. And all the times he'd stepped into other people to taunt or seduce her. But he'd never been able to control Jack that way.

It would crush her heart if she ever saw Lucifer's gaze staring back at her through Jack's beautiful, light green eyes.

Where was she? How much time had passed?

Time. It was such a strange concept now that she'd been cast out of Heaven. Time was a river that she could enter from any bank and every bend. She could wade through it or submerge herself, stick a toe or a finger in it. Brush across its surface with her wing tips. It was a destination not the rhythm that she moved to like her human charges. And now, it controlled her.

She wasn't human, but she was powerless and in their world now.

What would become of her? Would she eventually fall from the Earth and into Hell? Or would Lucifer find her and drag her there? Why hadn't Azrael fought for her? Why had he even allowed such a wager, knowing this could happen?

And what would happen to Jack? Lucifer promised to reinstate Jack's original premature death back into his Book of Life and Death, like he had control over the archive and God's Scribe.

Shouldn't that have alarmed Azrael?

And still, Azrael let it all happen. It made her furious every time she remembered standing in front of the guard. Her colleagues. Angels of death like her. Witnessing her halo being snuffed out and wings burned away.

Why had Azrael made such a production of stripping her of her wings and halo? Humiliating her in front of the guard—and Lucifer like that.

Had Jack really caught her when she fell to Earth? Or had that just been a hallucination? Her wanting desperately to return to him.

It was all so fuzzy. She had a vague memory of Muriel and Anahera—and Jack's apartment. She chuckled. And poor Jack so confused by their presence as they pretended to be actors in a Christmas play. Her heart swelled, remembering Jack's arms around her. Kissing her. Until the bed tilted and knocked him into the floor.

No, it was real. It was all real! Jack *had* been beside her.

Even when she felt the world rising. The last thing she remembered was his arms around her, fear burning in those sexy, light green eyes as everything went dark.

She struggled against the pervasive dark, wanting to climb out of this deep, black hole, back into the light. From a great distance, she felt arms around her, someone holding her.

Jack.

All she wanted to do was open her eyes and look into his face and tell him how much she loved him. How sorry she was about how those wagers made him feel and how hard she'd fallen for him that first season on *The Cinderella Hour*. And that she'd do everything in her power to stay with him. Now that she'd lost her halo and wings.

Talia hurt all over. The pain in her back was a constant ache, the ghost memory of her wings flexing, the shadowy feel of muscles twitching and feathers shifting. The comforting feel of wings unfurling like sails behind her, the force of the wind when she caught an updraft. The freedom of soaring above the clouds with the wind flowing across her body, running through her hair, through the tips of her wings.

But the steadying, gentle presence holding her was calming. It anchored her, gave her the strength to fight back against the hurt and the pain. And this sweltering fever burning through her body. She'd never been ill before. Angels didn't get sick like humans. Not like this. It was something she'd never experienced and it frightened her.

Again, at a deeper level, she understood what her human charges endured now. Many passed from the Earth after a lengthy illness just like this one. And so much worse. Things that ravaged their minds and bodies. It made her so sad to think that their last moments had been spent in such confusion, pain, and distance. Unable to say a last word to those they loved.

Like when she'd disappeared from the stage last night, unable to even touch him one last time. Kiss his lips. Tell him how much she loved him. How much he meant to her.

But the heat was dissipating now. The pain not so intense. The sensations were penetrating this horrible, dark fog. And slowly, she began to feel the heat and weight of arms around her. Felt the heaviness of a quilt around her. The heat of his skin against hers, the faint, comforting scent of cedar that clung to his clothes.

She heard the soft creak of the bed. Felt its shakes as he shifted. Felt the gentle rise and fall of his chest against her back.

At last, she felt her voice break free from the silence, a groan cracking the barrier until she heard her own voice again. Raspy and weak, but she moaned.

The sound sent a jolt through him as the bed shook. Then creaked. "Talia?"

The urgent rumble of his voice, warm and buttery. Like hot caramel. Warm velvet. And every note wrapped around her heart and cradled her, urging her up and out of this horrid heat and darkness.

"Jack?" she whispered, struggling against the force and the dark to open her eyes.

It took the combined force of all her will to push her heavy eyelids open.

And then she was staring up at his beautiful oval face, looking thin, his sizzling, light green eyes so tired, a shadow along his jaw where he hadn't shaved. Soft blond hair disheveled, looking like he'd just woken up. She loved seeing him wake up in the morning. Like the night she'd held him in her arms while he slept. She wanted so many more of those nights, those memories. She wanted all of him. For the rest of her existence.

She reached up to his face and with shaking fingers, she ran them along the smooth curve of his cheek, along his jaw, and down his neck to his chest, wanting to wrap her body around his and kiss him until she fell asleep in his arms. She wanted to mess up his hair and tangle her fingers in the soft blond strands as she smashed her lips against his hot mouth and showed him just how much she loved him.

"Talia, how do you feel?" he asked in a sleepy voice, his eyelids heavy.

He was asleep on his feet. Had he been up with her all night? Holding her in his arms? Taking care of her like she'd once taken care of him?

He was so sexy and she loved that he was a little bit vulnerable and unsure. She loved that he needed a little encouragement. And his aching honesty that sometimes brought her to tears. He was everything she'd ever wanted and this time, she'd have him. This time, she'd stay with him. And be the woman he wanted and needed.

"It hurts," she said, her hand falling to her side.

"Your back?" he asked in such a sweet, concerned voice.

She nodded.

His hand slid under the soft shirt that had replaced her tattered angel's robes, gentle strokes rubbing her lower back and her shoulders. His hands were warm and soft against her skin, his loving touch washing over her in waves.

"Talia, I'm so sorry that this has happened to you." His voice ached, almost breaking before he got the whole sentence out. "I'm sorry that I caused all of this."

Her heart sank and she looked up at him, her hand against his face again. "You? You didn't cause any of this, Jack."

He bowed his head, hand still rubbing her back. "If you'd just let me go in The Cinderella Hour, you'd still be in Heaven with your halo and wings. And Lucifer wouldn't be hunting your right now. I'm so sorry."

Talia forced her other hand up to cup his face. "Don't, Jack—your death was premature. It wasn't what had been written in your Book. And I got the privilege of saving you. It wasn't for a bet. And it was a choice I'd make over and over again." She ran her fingers through his hair. "And that choice saved me, Jack. Saved my wings and my halo. But it didn't save me from falling."

He nodded. "I feel so guilty about that."

"From falling in love with you, silly," she said with a smile, pulling his face down to hers for a gentle kiss. "And the reason I fell from Heaven was for saving you, not letting you die." She leaned up and covered his mouth with soft little kisses. "And when I did fall, you were the only one who caught me."

At last, a smile lit his face and those watery, sleepy green eyes. He kissed her back this time, a tender, satisfying kiss that wrapped around her like the warm, cedary quilt from his bed.

She pressed another kiss against his lips and patted his cheek. "And you've been up all night taking care of me. You need some sleep." She patted the creaky Murphy bed. "Lay down beside me and get some sleep, please."

That troubled look hovered in his eyes again. He needed to say something.

"What's the matter?" she asked, unable to hold back the look of concern creasing her forehead and burning in her eyes.

"A lot has happened since you passed out," he said, still rubbing her back.

She felt her stomach twist and tumble. "Like what?"

He looked up, the corners of his mouth quirking into a smile. "I don't even know where to start." He let out a heavy breath. "Let's see, Lucifer stopped by for a few laughs—and to drag me and you off to Hell. After his assassin demon tried to rip out my throat."

"What? Jack, are you all right?"

He nodded. "And then half your squad of death angels showed up for the party, but nobody brought enough beer, so Lucifer and his designated driver shuffled off to rob a liquor store or something. After promising to attend my next bash here."

"The guard is here? My guard?"

Again, he nodded. "Let's see, what else," he said, glancing toward the back door. "Oh, yeah, apparently, I'm the only human on this planet that can see angels and demons."

Her eyes widened and she stared at him in shock. How could he see all of this as a human unless angels and demons allowed it? How did he have this strange gift all of a sudden? It made no sense.

"How is that possible?" she asked.

He just shrugged. "I've been in Hollywood for a while, so I've been trained to spot demons and angels of death. I've killed my career enough times that death angels just hang close to wait for it."

She frowned at him. "Not funny, Jack Casey."

She tried to keep her angry face on, but that smirk and the twinkle in his eyes quickly pushed it away. She could never stay mad at him, no matter how hard she tried.

"And in other news," he continued, "the finale of The Prince Charming Hour was apparently watched by over forty million people. And yours and my name got specifically mentioned as making that happen. So, now, my phone's been blowing up with offers for blockbuster action films to the lead role in the biggest fantasy series of the last two decades. That every A-Lister in Hollywood is trying to snag." He pulled in a deep breath. "And Herb's doing another season of

Cinderella Hour called The Ever After Hour, bringing back couples from the previous two seasons. To see if they'll stay together."

He gazed at her, a funny look on his face. She hadn't seen this look before. His eyes were a little sad, a little vulnerable, and a little hopeful. But expectant, like he was waiting for her to respond.

"So…what do you think?" he asked quietly.

She shook her head, giving him a confused look. "That's amazing, Jack," she said, his odd look intensifying. "Congratulations."

Then a cold burst of fear rolled through her. Was he telling her goodbye? Was he leaving her to go after one of those new offers? Was he going back to his old life? A life that didn't include her?

"Are you trying to tell me goodbye?" She felt her whole world crash around her feet.

He hung his head a moment, sighing. "No, of course not!"

Finally, he looked up and saw the first tears collecting in her eyes. The ones she couldn't hold back at that thought. And then his hand slid away from her back, stroking her hair and face.

"I'm not going anywhere without you," he said in soft, deliberate voice. "And you're not leaving my sight."

At this, she laughed, a grin rising on her lips. "You scared me."

"Sorry," he said, his gaze falling again.

And again, she couldn't read this complex expression on his face. It made her anxious. She'd always been able to read him so well, but this look puzzled her.

"See, Lucifer wants another play date, but this time, at his place." He twisted the edge of his blue and green quilt around his fingers. "I hate hot weather and having my skin flayed from my soul. And Muriel and Anahera said they can't keep us safe here in my shithole apartment if trench warfare breaks out with Lucifer's demons."

He was stalling. Hedging around a question he didn't want to ask. At last, she understood his look. He needed her to agree to something.

"You're not telling me everything, Jack," she said finally.

He shrugged. "Busted." He twisted the quilt tighter around his index finger. "Look, you and I need to go somewhere much safer than my place. And season three, The Ever After Hour is being filmed in a new, more isolated location this season and…"

Anger burned through her now. She glared at him, wanting to put her hands on her hips or cross them, but she couldn't.

"Jack Casey! After everything I've been through after two seasons of crazy and painful reality TV challenges, fighting for and nearly losing you twice! After losing my wings and halo and falling from the sky! And now, you want me to sign on for season three? No! Forget it!"

He looked contrite, staring at her with those sizzling, light green eyes. Melting her heart and singeing her cheeks with heat.

"It's been retooled for couples, Tal," he said in a timid voice. "Morgan and Banks are coming back. Gianni and Izzy. And they want you and me, too."

Her eyes narrowed and she let out an angry breath. "No way."

"But we'd be a team this time, Talia," he countered. "Working together instead of being apart."

Working together? Then she wouldn't have to watch other women all over him or other men trying to kill him. He had this cute little smile on his face, eyes so hooded and sleepy, his bed hair so sexy.

"And on location, at this isolated place, Muriel and your death angels' guard think that they can better protect us." He chewed on the inside of his cheek. "They think they can keep us much safer there than my shithole studio. So, whatta ya say?"

Then she wanted to laugh. That complex expression and cute, sexy look was about getting her to say yes to something. All the emotions rushing through his head at the time, giving him such innocent and boyish charm. Jack Casey never looked innocent. If anything, he looked like he did it and he was proud. And it wasn't manipulative like Lucifer. She loved watching the range of emotions build, rise, and then fade from his face. But she wouldn't tell him that honest and innocent expression had already won her over. That he'd had her with the words *we'd be a team*. And those smoldering green eyes.

"I'll think about it," she answered, staring at him with her unblinking gaze.

He glanced around the room. "Not too long, okay? Because uninvited assassin demons really make me cranky. Especially the ones trying to seduce me."

Talia bristled. Remembering the one she pulled out of Rachel Daniels after she'd tried to bully him during a challenge on *The Prince Charming Hour*. Na'amah. She'd been tall and voluptuous, working her dark spells on Jack for some time through Rachel.

She didn't want another one of those things coming after Jack. They were deadly—even if he could see it coming. He was in every bit as much danger as she was now. But the one thing that terrified her was that Lucifer knew Jack was her weakness. He'd try to use Jack against her. And that included harming him right in front of her. The memory of Lucifer pushing Jack closer and closer to an overdose on *The Cinderella Hour* still frightened her. And even worse, when he declared war on Jack during *The Prince Charming Hour*. Those memories burned like indigestion in her stomach.

Here, in his own place, Jack was no longer safe. And neither was she. She had to get someplace safe, but she also needed to get Jack out of here. Someplace where the guard could protect him like they were protecting her.

She glanced over at the back door to Jack's patio. Sunlight streamed through the window. It was morning. Again, she patted the bed beside her as she stretched out of his arms. Feeling already cold.

"Jack," she called, "you need to sleep."

He struggled to keep his eyes open.

Nodding, he held back a yawn and laid down on the bed beside her in his faded Levi's and jean shirt, sleeves bloodied from where he'd caught her. His Levi's were a little baggy, but she loved how they fit his lean body. He slid his arms around her, his face so deliciously close to hers again. He smelled warm and cedary, a touch of soap, and she snuggled into his chest as he closed his eyes. It only took a few moments for him to fall asleep. He must have fought it for hours to take care of her.

Then Muriel was leaning over him, hands on her hips.

"Glad to see you back with us, Talia," she said and Talia shushed her.

"Whisper," she said, a finger to her lips. "He just closed his eyes."

Muriel reached out with thumb and forefinger and cast gold light across his eyes.

"And he'll sleep really deep for a bit," she said. "While we talk about the bad situation we're in."

Talia nodded, watching the steady rise and fall of Jack's chest. Muriel made sure, with a little help, that Jack got some rest.

"Jack told me."

"Everything?" she demanded, hands on her hips. "Because bad doesn't begin to cover it."

"He told me about Lucifer being here and he told me about the assassin demon. And the guard arriving." She shook her head, imploring Muriel with a look. Had Jack left something out? Not told her everything?

She'd lost her sense to detect lies.

Muriel mulled all that around and shrugged. "Okay, he covered the big points. Did he tell you we need to get out of this place before they all return? To that new show's location?"

She felt the slow burn of anger begin. "So, he'd already agreed to do the show and didn't bother to ask me? Knowing how I might feel about it?"

Anahera was beside her now, soft-spoken and kind.

"No, Talia, we wanted to move you there last night, but he said you had to agree first. He didn't want you facing that unless you agreed to it."

She smiled. She'd jumped to that conclusion and misjudged him. She'd never done that before. What was the matter with her? Had removing her wings also removed her patience and her trust? Jack had earned her trust over and over.

"I should have known better," she said and glanced at his peaceful expression and boyish good looks. "Losing my wings has changed me in some strange ways. This one makes me uncomfortable. I've always trusted Jack. He takes care of people and he doesn't use them."

Anahera nodded at her. "My senses tell me the same thing."

"We done with the feelings yet?" Muriel snapped, wings bristling. "Because you're in grave danger, Talia. And Lucifer promised to flay Jack's soul right in front of you, after dragging you both to Hell. That makes me a little uncomfortable, especially since no one's heard anything from Azrael."

"What? Nothing?" Anahera's wings stretched and flattened against her back.

Muriel nodded, her halo tilting. "As far as anyone knows, he's still in the Cloud Chamber under their magnifying glass. Pravuil's frantic. He's got the rest of Azrael's guard around him. And another dozen Watchers that Azrael placed to sound any alarms."

"Pravuil?" Talia asked. "Why?"

Muriel laid a hand against her halo as it spun rapidly, the light brightening. "Watchers are reporting he's safe in his inner chambers. The guard says no one's tried anything."

"Tried anything?" Talia felt the fear rise in her again.

The look on Muriel's face told her everything even before she'd uttered a word. Pravuil, God's Scribe, was in great danger.

"Someone tried to destroy him, Talia, and take over the archive," Muriel replied, the anger sharpening her features.

"An immortal ethereal being? The Maker's Scribe? Is that even possible?"

Muriel looked sick as she glanced at the floor, her wing feathers rustling. She looked anxious. Afraid. She'd only seen Muriel afraid once. When she was fighting the beginning of the reeducation process that would erase her memories and thoughts, resetting her behavior.

"Yes, Talia," she said finally, staring at her with a frightened, unblinking gaze. "Someone created a Book of Life and Death for God's Scribe. They hid it in the archive. And ended it."

Talia sat up on the bed, the magnitude of that statement settling on her.

It felt like the first moment she'd fallen from the Heavens without her wings. A wild free-fall through the clouds, air rushing past and no wings to level her out. And the long, long plunge toward the Earth that felt like it would never end.

How had the Scribe's powers been accessed when God had only one? How had someone gained access to create a Book of Life and Death? For an immortal creature? Immortals didn't have books in the archives. Someone got control of one of the most powerful abilities in the Heavens to create that Book for God's Scribe. Books of Life and Death could be changed and given a beginning and ending.

And then someone used the highest order of death angel powers to write an ending. For God's Scribe. It was an unthinkable act.

"How?" Talia shouted. It was all she could get out.

"That's why I need to talk to Azrael," said Muriel, crossing her arms. "First there was a forger that changed Jack's Book. And now, someone's brought a Book into creation for an immortal being. If God's Scribe dies, then that will leave the archive unattended. And worse, it now means that with a scribe's powers, any immortal can now die."

Talia gasped, the realization terrifying. "Even the Maker. And Muriel, the forgery in Jack's Book hadn't been the goal. It was a test."

Muriel whirled around, staring at her with wide eyes. "A test?"

She nodded. "A test. Of the stolen power."

"What kind of test?" Anahera asked, her nervous gaze flicking from Talia to Muriel.

Talia finally understood it all. "If someone could grab a scribe's power and use it on any Book and have it work, then creating a Book would be the next test."

Muriel was nodding, the color draining from her face. "And from there, any immortal could be written out of existence."

"With one stroke of a Scribe's pen."

Anahera snapped to her full height, wings unfurling. "That's why Azrael was so worried," she replied as she paced between the bed and the dresser. "That's why he let everything play out like it did. Why he let you fail the wager, Talia. Why he took your wings."

Talia squinted at her. How did that explain why he'd humiliated her in front of Lucifer?

Anahera was grinning now, glancing at her and Muriel, searching for their understanding.

"Not following you, Anahera," Muriel said with a frown.

"He was very concerned about the forgery to Jack's Book and some rare powers awakening in you, Talia," Anahera continued. "But he didn't step in and stop Talia from losing the wager. Because he needed Lucifer to think he was winning. That's why he made the huge production of taking your wings, Talia. Lucifer needed to see you fall."

"What rare powers?" Talia asked. She had no powers now, but she didn't know what Azrael meant by that.

Talia gave Muriel a confused look and Muriel just shrugged. "I don't know what she's talking about, Talia. I was still in High House when this all went down."

Anahera was still grinning. "Don't you both see? Talia didn't really fall from Heaven."

"I did to!" Talia snapped. "I remember every moment, Anahera."

Anahera waved her hands at her, wings rustling, halo spinning faster.

"If you'd truly fallen, you'd be in Hell right now," said Anahera.

"She's got a point there, Talia," said Muriel, a hand to her chin. "Even Jack questioned how you landed on Earth."

"Azrael used the soul you accidentally received to fake your fall, Talia. So, Lucifer would try to claim his prizes, giving Azrael time to uncover his accomplice and stop them from killing God's Scribe."

Was he using her and Jack as bait now? Now that she was powerless to protect herself much less Jack. Then she felt something uncomfortable pulling at her back. The bandages that Jack had applied must have stuck together.

"Muriel, help me adjust these bandages, please," she said, reaching over her shoulder. But she couldn't reach the bandages.

"Sure thing, Talia," said Muriel.

She moved around Anahera and lifted up the T-shirt. She let out a shriek and stumbled backward, wings extended to keep her from falling.

"Holy pearly gates and harps!"

"What's the matter?" Talia asked.

Muriel just opened her mouth and pointed.

"What is it?" Talia demanded. "You're scaring me."

"Your back," Muriel said with a gasp.

"It really aches," said Talia. "The pain's been so sharp."

Muriel was nodding, her gaze still fixed on Talia's back. "I can see why," she said. "Because they're growing back!"

"That's impossible!" Talia shouted, trying to reach around feel between her shoulder blades.

Anahera rushed around Muriel and lifted up the T-shirt. She thrust her hand over her mouth, her dark grey eyes wide.

"There are two new wing buds, Talia," she said in a hushed, reverent voice. "Pushing up through the skin. That's why they're hurting."

Muriel was shaking her head. "Angels can't regrow their wings."

Anahera was smiling now, pointing at Talia as she let go of the T-shirt, letting it fall against her back. Catching on what felt like adhesive in two places between her shoulder blades.

"Well, this one can," said Anahera. She moved over to the mirrored dresser and tilted the mirror. "Turn your body and look, Talia."

Talia turned away and then looked over her shoulder into the mirror. She grinned, her eyes misting. Right between her shoulder blades, two dove grey wing buds the size of walnuts had broken through the skin and were beginning a chrysalis-like process of becoming silky new wings. That's why Jack had blood on his sleeves. The tiny buds had just broken through the skin when he caught her.

Her wings were growing back. They weren't gone forever. Maybe that's why she'd had those vivid images of ghost wings? And maybe even the fever?

"One of those rare powers Azrael mentioned?" Muriel asked, still staring at Talia's back.

"Maybe this was Azrael's test?" Anahera replied. "The fall to Earth. If her rare powers were awakening, maybe he needed to see if she'd regrow her wings? Instead of him returning them to her."

Muriel was grinning now. "Because he needs a rare power to

combat the forces attacking the archive and God's Scribe. And casting her out under the guise of the lost wager, puts her on Earth to evolve from the ashes of her descent. My Heavens—it's a Phoenix shift!"

"A Phoenix shift? What's that?" Talia asked.

"A fabled event when an angel's power is destroyed, it comes back twice as strong. Or when latent powers emerge after a trial by fire." Muriel shrugged. "When I was being reeducated, I had nothing else to do but meditate and read."

Anahera reached out and gripped Talia's wrists. "Azrael made the big production of burning away your wings, Talia, because it had to be a trial by fire. To release your rare powers. Only through this Phoenix shift can we stop whatever's happening in the Heavens."

"That crafty ol' archangel had this up his robe sleeves the whole time," said Muriel. "All this time, he was honing his secret weapon through Lucifer's wagers until Lucifer made his move. Talia was Azrael's wager."

Anahera glanced at Jack, sleeping soundly beside her. "Still one question left unanswered," she said and pointed at Jack.

"Yeah," said Muriel with a sigh. "Doesn't explain why Jack can suddenly see angels and demons. I'll save that question for Azrael."

Talia reached over and ran her fingers through his hair. Maybe her powers were returning along with her wings? And with them, she could protect her and Jack from Lucifer and his demons.

The rattling of the back door onto the patio startled her.

She gave Muriel a fearful glance as both angels of death turned. Muriel chirped a high-note and the guard assembled around her in a blink. A wall of angels between whatever clawed at that door and her and Jack.

"Roundel formation!" Muriel ordered.

The guard circled around the bed, wings extended until they'd formed a closed ring of gold light around her and Jack.

"Prepare to repel on my mark," said Muriel, arm raised, halo burning with fire.

Whump! Something heavy landed against the door. It bowed with shadowy energy.

Something strained against that earthly door. That would give with the next hit.

Talia wrapped her arms around Jack and pulled him close, wishing Muriel hadn't put him out like that. He wouldn't wake up until she released him.

"Hold positions," Muriel said, her voice steady. "Wait for it."

Whump! Door bowed again. Something whined outside the door. Shadows rushing through the sunlight. Massing around the door.

That was about to give.

"Ready defenses," she ordered.

All around her, golden shields of light materialized around the circle and on Muriel and Anahera's arms as they stood in front of the circle.

Whump! Door splintered, exploded into the apartment as demons flooded through the opening.

Talia gasped.

And Cerberus. Three-headed hound guardian of Hell. With his two-headed brother, Orthrus.

"Mark!" Muriel shouted.

8

IN A BLUR, A CADRE OF SHADOWY ASSASSINS IN SHADOW PANTHER FORMS sprang at the guard. Caterwauling. Fangs bared. The raspy, guttural growls chilled Talia as she knelt on the bed, gripping Jack's wilted, enchanted form.

Thunk! Shields collided with teeth and jowls.

Claws raked the hardwoods. Shadows leaping.

Fire sizzled, burning through shadows.

Creatures shrieked. Screeching as they fell.

The dozen angels of death crouched, shields aloft.

"Keep those shields up!" Muriel ordered as she engaged Cerberus, the three-headed hound turning toward her, three jaws snapping. "Repel these beasts all the way back to Hell!"

But the assassin demons just kept coming. More and more shadow panthers.

"Tighten formation!" Muriel shouted, straining against Cerberus' rapid-fire attacks. "Anahera, cap the well!"

"Can't!" she called out, dodging Orthrus' two heads, both with huge, razor-sharp fangs.

"Death angels!" Muriel commanded. "Wings on high! Shields to the sun!"

The death angels guard shifted, wings fluttering into vertical positions as the golden shields of light tilted up over their heads.

Shadows fell around the circle in droves and still, they kept coming.

And then Muriel fell when dozens of assassin demons rushed her.

Anahera leaped toward her, throwing a ball of Holy fire into the spinning snarl of darkness.

Assassin demons scattered.

"Where's the hound?" Muriel shouted, her voice strained.

"What?" Anahera cried.

"Cerberus! Quick! Find it!"

"Oh, no—and Orthrus."

Talia felt a cold wind against her heart as a silence descended, everything falling still.

And like a landmine, assassin demons exploded through the room until it turned dark, the light from the guard's shields barely cutting through the blackness.

And in a blur, Cerberus leaped over the guard, Orthrus beside him.

"No!" Muriel shouted. "Protect the center! Hurry!"

And with a blink, Orthrus was on Talia's chest, yawning jaws snapping at her face and neck.

And Cerberus was on Jack, its three sets of teeth grabbing hold of him. Dragging him out of the circle.

Orthrus had her pinned down. She couldn't move. And she had no powers to dislodge it.

"Jack! JACK!"

The drag thumps echoed through the room above the squalling of assassin demons that were overwhelming Muriel and the guard.

"Muriel!" she screamed. "Cerberus has Jack!"

Then Anahera was beside her, knocking Orthrus to the floor with her shield. It whimpered and rolled, two heads foaming as its red eyes filled with rage.

One of the death guard engaged it, shoving it out of the circle as Anahera leaped into the air, wings frantic as she sailed over top of the guard formation, over the lunging assassin demons, and toward the back door.

Talia shoved through the guard, but Muriel's shield went up in front of her, blocking her path.

Cerberus dragged Jack across the back door's threshold and he was still out cold.

"No! JACK!"

Like a bolt of lightning, Anahera landed on top of Cerberus, slamming her shield downward with both hands. Knocking the three-headed beast backward and out the door.

She grabbed hold of Jack and lifted him into her arms, wings beating as she shot forward, laying him down beside Talia on the floor. Behind Muriel. Who reached down and pressed her hand against Jack's forehead.

Releasing the sleep energy.

Groggy, his eyes slowly opened as Talia knelt beside him. He looked up at her with a silly, drugged smile.

"You're up," he said.

Three assassin demons leaped over them and into the circle.

"Guard!" Muriel shouted. "Form on our charges! Shields and wings to the sky!"

He frowned, looking confused. "You guys threw a party without me?"

"Party's just started," Muriel said with a laugh, smashing her shield into both of Orthrus' snouts. "And you're the guest of honor."

"I should go get more beer then," he said in a quiet voice and tried to get up, but Talia held him down.

He hadn't even noticed the massive force of assassin demons beating up the guard. Or the hellhound guardians that had just played fetch with him and dragged him outside.

"Jack, no! Stay put. Muriel, what'd you do to him?"

"A little too much angel's touch," she said. Then she shrugged. "So, sue me! I'm an angel of death not a guardian angel."

Shadow panthers screeched, lunging at the guard. They pounded the shadowy demons back with golden shields of light as Jack looked up at Talia, smiling.

"Or a box of wine," he said. "You like chardonnay best, don't you?"

She shook him. "Jack! Look! We're under attack. Stay down."

He waved her off and pointed toward the door. At Cerberus charging toward them. "That's just Bruce," he said. "He's the neighbor's monster dog. He doesn't even bite."

In a flash, Cerberus slipped through the line, one of its great jaws chomping down on Jack's left shoulder.

Yanking him backward. Leaving a thin trail of something very red.

"Go home, Bruce!" Jack shouted. "Home, boy! Bad dog!"

Talia leaped past Muriel, but Muriel slammed a shield in front of her, forcing her backward again.

Anahera was on Cerberus, shield hammering its three massive heads. One snout had Jack by the shoulder, all its teeth buried through the jean shirt and into his skin.

He winced, struggling. The pain had snapped him out of the angel fog.

"Holy shit! What is this thing?"

Anahera beat on it with everything she had, but Cerberus wouldn't let go.

That's when the assassin demons began to retreat. Her heart pounded into her throat. With their quarry. With Jack!

"Jack!" Talia shouted.

It dragged Jack across the back door's threshold as Muriel and the guard surged forward.

"Don't let it escape with Jack!" Muriel commanded, rushing forward.

Jack drove his right fist as hard as he could against Cerberus' snout.

It shrieked, letting go of its grip on his shoulder. He tumbled onto the concrete and scrambled to his feet. Diving through the threshold. Onto the hardwood with a thump as Orthrus lunged at him.

Muriel smashed her shield in front of Orthrus' two heads as Jack skittered backward on hands and feet. Shirt torn and bloody. Chest heaving. Light green eyes wild.

Together, the guard, along with Muriel and Anahera leading the charge, drove the hordes of assassin demons and hellhounds out of Jack's apartment. Into the sunlight. They scrambled away, disappearing in puffs of smoke.

And it was over.

Muriel staggered back into the apartment, Anahera at her side as the taller death angel backed inside, shield raised, eyes wide. In moments, the rest of the guard tumbled inside, shields burning. Anahera moved toward the remnants of the door and worked with the guard to reassemble it using their angel powers.

"Jack!" Talia was beside him now, a hand on his bruised face.

His shoulder still bled through the torn sleeve, deep punctures from fangs in his flesh.

He lifted his right hand, shaking and weak now, toward her face, cupping her cheek.

"You okay?" he asked, still pulling in breaths. "Those demons didn't get to you, did they?"

She shook her head. "No, I'm fine. But you're not."

"I'm fine," he said in an exhausted voice. "Those things were everywhere at once. So, now, we get to add hellhounds to the list of things trying to kill us." He glanced around at the floors, torn and overturned furniture, blood staining the pine floors. "Whelp, there goes my security deposit." He rolled his eyes. "Bet those hellhounds left dumps the size of trucks in the yard, too. Hope it was on the neighbor's side."

Talia laughed and smoothed blond hair out of his eyes.

Muriel motioned at him. "How can you tell he's back to normal?" she asked with a chuckle.

"The sarcasm returns," she replied. "And his jokes get better."

"They do?" Muriel said with a shrug then laughed. "Still, I'm going to be telling this story for a long time."

"About the assassin demons?" Talia asked.

Muriel broke into a fit of laughter. "No! Watching Jack Casey shout *bad dog* into all three faces of Cerberus, the Guardian of Hell's Gate! That was hilarious!"

Jack's face flushed and he glanced down at his hands. "He was a bad dog."

Muriel just laughed harder. "Heavens' Gate, I needed that. You have all the luck, Talia."

"Why?" she said, helping Jack to his feet.

"Because this one's priceless," she said. "Hold onto him before one of us snatches him from you."

Jack just shrugged and limped over to the bed, holding his left shoulder with his right hand. Talia walked beside him and sat down when he did.

"You shouldn't be up like that, Talia," he said, fixing her with a stare. He looked grumpy now. "That fever could spike again and you could pass out."

"And you could bleed out," she warned.

"I'm fine. Those wounds on your back are bad. You lost a lot of blood." He glanced around the apartment as the guard returned to their sentinel positions and made a sour face. "How long was I asleep?" he asked. "Looks like I missed all the fun."

She nodded. "Most of it," she said. "Like the part when Cerberus dragged you out the door. Anahera freed you, otherwise that hellhound might have dragged you back to Lucifer."

He sighed. "I put a fist in his snout that made all its eyes water and made him drop me."

"The second time."

"Second time?" He said, a frightened look in his eyes.

She nodded.

He glanced up from the bed and searched the room until he located Anahera. "Thanks for the save, Anahera."

She smiled at him. "My pleasure, Jack."

He laid his right hand on Talia's bare forearm. She felt his blood against her skin and it made her sad.

"You know we can't stay here now, right?" he asked, fixing her with his frightened stare. "Next round's going to make this one look like a day at the beach. We've gotta go someplace where we can defend it and this isn't it."

Talia sighed, bowing her head. She couldn't deny that logic. They'd almost lost everything just now. Jack was almost dragged off twice. Orthrus broke through the guard's defenses like they were nothing and sat on her chest. He could have ripped her throat out in a heartbeat. They had to fight Lucifer until Anahera could get to Azrael. And find out his battle plan for protecting God's Scribe and her returning powers. And Jack.

And she needed to know why Jack could see demons and angels.

She sighed. Looked like she and Jack were returning for another game of lost souls. Appearing as a couple on *The Ever After Hour*. At least it wasn't a wager. And with Jack at her side, she could overcome anything. Even a reality television show.

9

Jack paced the floor, stepping over the huge claw marks in the pine floors as the answering machine flashed full. So was his voicemail on his cell phone. He glanced at the death angels stationed around the tiny studio apartment. It was claustrophobic with him, fourteen death angels, and Talia. And not very romantic with fourteen pairs of eyes watching his every move. And then there were the assassin demons dropping in unannounced. And Lucifer. He redialed Armand Gianni, waiting for a response.

"Hello?"

"Gianni. It's Jack. How ya been?"

Gianni laughed. "You mean since yesterday?"

"Feels like a lifetime ago, doesn't it?" Jack said.

"It does. Until Herb Rutherford's phone call. You got his call, didn't you?"

"All eighteen of them."

"Wow, impressive, Jack. So, I take it you've gotten a few offers since Variety came out?"

Jack heard the laughter in his voice.

"Dude, I had to turn off my phones. Everything's full. I'll just tell them to call my agent."

"I heard you got a call from SanFran Confidential, too."

He'd listened to that message a few times already this afternoon. The one with Evan Bellows begging him to come back to the show. It made him feel funny. Part of him felt vindicated, but mostly he felt used. When he'd lost his place, couldn't afford to eat, and was withdrawing hard from an incredible cocaine addiction, no one even checked on him. They said he was the problem with the whole show. With the cast. Fired and forgot him. If it hadn't been for *The Cinderella Hour*—and Talia—he'd have overdosed.

No, he felt a certain loyalty to Herb Rutherford's show. They were using him, too, but that's how the game was played in Hollywood. And they'd treated him well on the show. Hadn't even threatened to fire him yet. But *SanFran Confidential* hadn't until season three, so there was still time.

"Jack?"

"Yeah," he said with a sigh. "I did. Still trying to process that one. They want me to come back as Davy Pierson. Huge salary increase. Top billing. Dumont's gonna freak when he finds that out."

"You're taking it?"

He'd never go back to that show. Too many bad memories. And he wasn't that naïve kid anymore. Or that coke addict.

"Nah, but it feels a little like karmic justice."

"You didn't deserve that, Jack."

He laughed. "I did. I deserved to be fired. But so did the rest of the cast. I was a twenty-year-old kid who'd never had that kind of success —or money. Had never done drugs like that. Rachel and Lare made sure I was a pro at it. I let it turn me into an arrogant dick. I don't want to be that dude ever again. So, no—never going back."

Gianni was quiet for a moment or two. "So, you coming back for Ever After Hour, Jack? Banks and I can't imagine the show without you." He laughed. "I've been at the studio signing contracts today, watching Herb tear what's left of his hair out."

"Why?" Jack asked.

"Because you haven't returned his calls. And since the entire country's fallen in love with you, Jack, he knows the show won't fly without you. He's terrified you've found your ego and think you're too big for his show now."

"Me? My ego left town years ago and hasn't moved back. I've been talking it over with Talia. She's supposed to give me an answer this afternoon."

"How are you, two doing after the finale?" Gianni asked. "I was worried when she disappeared on you. After you proposed to her."

"So was I," said Jack. "She's still wearing my ring, but she hasn't given me an answer to that question either. You and Izzy still talking?"

"We are," he said. "We just had lunch together. Well, Jack, I hope to see you on the new season. Let me know what you and Talia decide. And put Herb out of his misery soon. Before the guy has a heart attack."

"I will," he said. "Hopefully, Talia will give me an answer shortly. Then I'll call him and let him know. Take care of yourself, Gianni."

"You, too, Jack."

Jack cleared the call and gripped his left shoulder. It still ached from that hellhound sinking its teeth into his shoulder and dragging him out the door. He was still wearing the torn-up jean shirt and bloodied Levi's. He needed to take a shower and change. Blood had already soaked his left shoulder, the fabric torn and hanging.

Sweat clung to his upper lip and broke out across his forehead. He felt a chill from the draft at the back door. Anahera had reassembled the door, but it didn't sit quite flush on its hinges now, letting in a draft that made him cold.

He moved away from the torn green sofa and crossed over to the Murphy bed where Talia lay sleeping. He sat down beside her, leaning over to check her temperature with the back of his hand. Just a little warm. He hoped she was feeling better. His eyelids were heavy as he walked over to the dresser and pulled a light green hoodie and another pair of jeans out of the bottom drawer. He grabbed a pair of dark green boxer briefs out of the top drawer and went into the bathroom.

He jumped into the shower, the water hot. His shoulder throbbed, looking puffy and still leaking blood. The water hurt when it hit the angry red skin, so he kept his left shoulder turned out of the water stream. He struggled a little to lather up his hair and body, then rinsed off. He put some conditioner in his hair and shaved in the shower. After rinsing the conditioner, he turned off the shower and towel-dried his hair. He got blood all over the beige towel.

He dressed quickly, zipping the hoodie to his collarbone as he began to shiver.

Then he stepped out of the misty bathroom with damp hair. And heard Talia talking to Muriel and Anahera.

"We're not allowed to—you know that, Talia." Muriel.

"Why not? You practically drowned me in healing light."

"That was different."

"How?"

"You're not human."

"So, what's he supposed to do? Walk into a doctor's office and say, hey, I was bit by a hellhound?" She was silent for a moment. "I'm worried."

Jack frowned. They were talking about him.

"I don't know what happens when a human's bitten by a hellhound, Talia."

"It's not healing. And he's still bleeding." Talia sighed. "Muriel, it's been hours and he's still bleeding."

"Hellhound wounds heal slowly," said Anahera. "It probably just needs some time."

"Until he bleeds to death?"

He glanced down at his hoodie, left arm feeling weak as it hung at his side. Already, a red circle had spread across his left shoulder. Talia was right. It hadn't stopped bleeding. It wasn't gushing blood, but it was seeping blood. Enough to still soak his shoulder.

"Until who bleeds to death?" Jack asked, forcing a smile on his face, as he walked out of the bathroom, hands in the kangaroo pockets of his hoodie.

"Jack!" Talia cried, hurrying toward him. "Your shoulder's still bleeding." She turned around and glared at Muriel. "See, it's worse than I thought." She reached up to his face and stroked his cheek and forehead. "You feel warm, Jack."

He laughed. "Of course, I do. I just took a hot shower."

She shook her head, her hand blotting his face. "You're sweating."

"It was a really hot shower," he answered.

She turned back around, her wide grey eyes pleading as she stared at Muriel who just shrugged.

"It's against the protocols," Muriel replied.

"So are hellhounds attacking humans," Talia said, anger in her voice. "We are sworn to protect humans. We didn't protect Jack."

"We did our best," Muriel replied.

Jack waved her off. "I'm fine, Talia. How are you feeling? Fever down?"

"Don't you dare change the subject, Jack Casey," she shouted and stamped her foot.

Talia reached over to the zipper on his hoodie and unzipped it to his navel.

"I like this subject," he said with a smirk.

Gently, she peeled back the hoodie material from his left shoulder. It was stiff and damp now, sticking to his skin. He bit his lip and muffled a groan as she uncovered the rows of deep punctures where Cerberus had sunk an entire mouthful of fangs into the soft, fleshy part of his left shoulder. All the teeth puncture marks wept blood that dripped down his arm, staining the light green hoodie.

"Muriel, please—look at this. How can we keep him safe with this hideous wound festering?"

Muriel moved closer, her gaze encompassing now as she studied the wound carefully.

"Man, Cerberus really nailed you, Jack. Got one whole mouth around your shoulder." She made a sour face. "Wow, that is looking bad." She studied his eyes a moment. "How's the pain?"

He laughed. "Pretty exquisite."

"On a scale of one to ten?"

"Um, thirteen."

"Jack!" Talia cried, glaring at him. "Why didn't you say something?"

"Just gonna take some ibuprofen for it."

Muriel was shaking her head now as she looked the wound over carefully. "You're right, Talia. This is going to fester. We can't keep him safe with a wound this bad."

She turned toward Jack. "I'm going to apply a little angel healing, Jack."

"You sure?" he asked. "I don't want you to get in trouble because of me."

Muriel smiled. "You're sweet. Healing this is worth a little trouble."

She led him over to the Murphy bed and he sat down. Talia was at his hoodie zipper again, unzipping it and sliding it off his bare shoulders. Sending a burst of gooseflesh across his arms and chest. His lip was threaded with sweat, forehead beaded and face a mask of perspiration. Muriel laid the back of her hand against his forehead.

"He's running a fever. I'd better intervene before this gets serious, protocols or not."

"Thank you," said Talia as she turned back to him.

"Gonna feel a flutter through your shoulder, Jack. Then a sharp ache. I'm sorry. The pain might get rough for a little bit, but it'll stop."

Jack set himself, gritting his teeth as he nodded at Muriel. "Ready."

She laid her hand against the bloody punctures still seeping blood and her hand burned with heat and pressure. He winced and smashed his eyes closed, weathering the burning pain that rolled through every puncture and then throbbed like a toothache through the top of his shoulder. Into his neck.

His body stiffened as he rode out the wild wave of pain and fire until it began to cool. And recede. It took several minutes before he could breathe normally again.

"Better, Jack?" Muriel asked.

He shrugged. "I'll let you know after I regain consciousness."

"That good?" she asked with a chuckle.

He just nodded and sank back on the bed, his bare feet dangling off the bed. And then Talia was beside him, sliding a pillow under his head, draping the blue and green quilt across his bare chest.

"You need to sleep for a while," said Talia.

"I do?"

She nodded. "Sleep and when you wake up, you should probably call Herb Rutherford. And get us on the next season." She leaned down and gently kissed his lips. "I need to get you someplace far away from hellhounds and assassin demons."

He yawned. "And you think a reality TV show's gonna have less hellhounds and assassin demons?" he asked with a smirk. "This is Hollywood, Talia."

She laughed and kissed him again. "At least, on the show, I know how to deal with those demons and hellhounds."

"Except me," he said with a laugh.

"Oh, I especially know how to deal with you, Jack Casey." She grinned at him, eyes full of mischief.

Flirting. He was all aboard that train. He leaned up to her face, his lips almost brushing across hers.

"How?" he asked in a husky voice.

"I'll just show you," she warned and smashed her mouth against his.

It was a burst of fire that set him alight. God, he wanted her.

A sharp pain shot through his shoulder. He jumped, his face screwing up as the pain felt like a bullet, tearing through muscle and ligaments. He gasped, eyes smashing closed as he pulled back.

"Jack? Are you okay?"

It took him a few moments to recover. Finally, he nodded. "Sorry, pain was pretty intense for a moment. I'm okay now."

Her eyes were wide, filled with fear.

This huge bite was beginning to concern him, too. It just kept weeping blood and the pain got severe at times, ramping up to excruciating enough times that he wondered if it would ever heal. Anahera said they were slow to heal. Had Lucifer wanted to slow him down or was it all just his bad luck that Cerberus wanted a taste of him? Couldn't drag him off to Hell any other way than with his teeth?

"I'll show you another time," Talia said.

He frowned.

Her voice fell to a whisper. "When I can shove you onto the bed without a roomful of angels."

He grinned. "I'm so holding you to that."

"You'd better," she said and laid down beside him. "For now, get some rest."

He nodded. He'd call Herb tonight after he'd slept a little. With Talia in his arms.

IN A FEW HOURS, Jack awoke alone in his bed. The sun had already set and it was dark outside. The apartment had that dim, hazy, fevered appearance to it. Fever pounded through his temples and pain throbbed through his left shoulder. He sat up and threw the quilt off, glancing at his left shoulder that had been bandaged with thick, heavy gauze and tape. A dark red circle had stained it, leaving the bandage damp. He sat up, the pounding in his head making the lights look so dim.

The death angel guard still held vigil throughout the studio apartment. Talia sat beside Muriel and Anahera on the old couch, the crooked white clock showing seven o'clock.

He struggled to his feet and shoved his toes into his old beat-up Vans and with uneven steps, he moved toward the dresser. Grabbed hold of it when the room swayed and then waited out the shift. When it passed, he grabbed his light green hoodie off the dresser. Someone had washed out most of the blood. It just had a faint red stain on the left shoulder. He carefully slid his arms into it and zipped it up to his collarbone. Then he moved unsteadily toward the couch.

"Jack!" Talia cried, seeing how unsteady he was.

She jumped up and took hold of his right arm, leading him over to the couch, and sitting him down beside her. The back of her hand shot up to this forehead. She turned to look at Muriel.

"He's getting worse," Talia announced. "What do we do? I don't know how to treat a hellhound bite."

Anahera gasped and stared at him and then Talia, a strange look on her face.

"Anahera? What's the matter?" Talia asked.

Muriel squinted at her. "You heard back from the archive, didn't you?"

She nodded, her big grey eyes looking fearful.

"What'd they say about the hellhound bite?" Muriel asked.

Anahera bowed her head, staring down at her hands as she tangled her fingers together. "You're not going to like it."

He swallowed a breath. "Just say it," he replied.

She fixed Talia with her gaze and let out a quick breath. "The archive said that the hellhound marked Jack with that wound. To track him. So, Lucifer will always be able to find him." She pulled in a breath. "He'll also try to control Jack through it. It's like a connector or something."

Jack let out a hiss of breath. Guess there'd be no hiding from Lucifer.

"Oh, no!" Talia was on her feet now, her eyes a mixture of fear and fury. "How do we sever it?" she demanded. "There has to be a way to heal it and sever Lucifer's connection to him."

Anahera seemed to have been anticipating this question. She didn't blink when she turned to Talia. "Only death severs it."

Talia took hold of his arm and held onto him. "No," she said in a small voice. "This can't be happening."

"I've asked the scholars to research how to heal a hellhound's bite in humans," said Anahera. "Hopefully, they'll turn up something."

Jack sighed. Guess there was no escaping this devil bullshit. He'd just have to hope that these death angels found a way to heal the wound. Either way, he needed to get him and Talia out of this apartment and someplace that the death angels could defend. They'd make their stand at the isolated estate where *The Ever After Hour* was being filmed.

"I'll call Herb now," he said and turned to Muriel. "Get your people ready to move, Muriel. To this estate on the outskirts of the city. Maybe we can keep Lucifer busy until you hear from your boss?"

"That's our best hope right now, Jack," said Muriel who got to her feet. "All right, guard, prepare to move out as soon as we find out where this estate is located." She reached out and laid her hand on Talia's shoulder. "Are you okay with this, Talia?"

She nodded and glanced at Jack. "As long as he's safe, I am."

"We'll do our best."

Jack slid his phone out of his pocket as Talia made him sit down beside her. He chuckled. Four more voicemails and three texts from Herb. He hit redial on the last call.

"Jack?" Herb shouted in the phone. "I'm so glad to hear from you. I've been calling you for two days. Everything okay?"

"Sorry, things have been a little hectic here."

"I can imagine," said Herb. "Probably got all of Hollywood calling you right now."

"Yep, my answering machine and my voicemail box are blowing up. Had to turn off my phones to get some sleep."

Herb sighed heavily into the phone. "This show can't begin to compete with those offers. Is it true that your old show made you a massive offer, too, Jack?"

"They did."

"So, America's finally gonna get their bad boy Davy Pierson back?"

"Not unless they recast the role. I'm not going back to that environment, Herb. It almost destroyed me."

The phone went deathly quiet. "You're not?"

"Talia and I like this new incarnation of the show. And with Gianni and Banks returning, how can I ruin a television reunion? We're both in, Herb."

"Oh, my God! Are you serious, Jack?"

Jack couldn't hold in his smirk. Herb sounded so relieved and grateful.

"Sure am. Just tell us where to be on location and when. We're ready for another season."

"I can't believe it! Jack, please thank Talia for me and I can't wait to have you both on set again. This season is going to be the best one yet. Ever After Hour is officially a go, Jack! I'll text you the location information. You and Talia can sign contracts and get settled a few days before rehearsals and filming start."

"Looking forward to it, Herb. See you soon."

"Take care, kid. We'll see you in a couple of days."

"Have a good night, Herb," said Jack.

Herb laughed, his voice overflowing with relief. "I will now."

Jack cleared the connection and looked up at Talia. "Looks like The Ever After Hour is officially a go."

He just hoped that he and Talia survived the assassin demons, hellhounds, and Lucifer long enough to participate on the show. And just maybe they'd live through it all long enough for Talia's boss to find a way out of this mess?

10

SUNLIGHT DRENCHED DECEMBER'S EARLY MORNING COOLNESS, birdsong bright against the crisp, cloudless sky as Jack stepped outside his apartment, wearing faded Levi's and a navy blue hoodie over his dark grey Led Zeppelin t-shirt. Then he looked down and saw Icarus and his wings and sighed.

Again with the angels.

Distant sound of a helicopter dissipated in the crisp breeze as he rolled two blue suitcases out his front door, Talia beside him, her guard up as she glanced around them. Her grey eyes looked haunted in the sunlight, but no fever burned there. It had finally broken. She looked alert and a faint blush of color touched her winter-pale skin.

She was healing. And seeing her looking more like his Talia helped erase the memory of her collapsing and those bloody wounds on her back. Still, catching her in his arms on the patio would remain one of his favorite memories of her. It was the first moment he could remember that she'd needed him.

His heavily bandaged left shoulder burned, still seeping blood as the suitcases thumped along the broken concrete walkway toward his black Explorer parked in the space in front of his door. He felt dread heavy in his stomach, glancing around. Fearing more of those shadowy assassin demons would leap out at them at any moment. Or worse, a pack of triple-headed stray Hell dogs ready to rip his face off.

He sighed. Just another weekend in Los Angeles.

The lot was full. Most people were still sleeping. Steady hiss of cars rushing past from the nearby interstate, the air smelling like asphalt and exhaust fumes, a hint of red roses and eucalyptus from the tangle of bushes in front of the 70s style blonde brick apartment building. And skunky weed smell.

He glanced behind him at the open apartment door. Where a dozen angels of death stood silent and stoic in flowing charcoal grey robes, soot-colored wings spread, halos spinning with gold light. Their grey eyes were piercing. The sight of so many of them made him tense. And more than a little freaked out.

He was still trying to process the craziest twenty-four hours of his life.

His brain felt tired today, still struggling with one mind-exploding event after another. A rollercoaster ride that had left him exhausted and brain-fogged. Proposing to Talia. Talia falling out of the sky. A herd of death angels. A horde of demons. Hellhounds.

And if that wasn't enough, the woman he loved was an angel of death. Who'd loved him on a bet. Oh, one other small thing: Lucifer was real and trying to mount his head like artwork on his wall.

"Jack, are you okay?"

He glanced at Talia as she leaned against the Explorer, squinting at him. She could always read him like a book. Was that as angel of death Talia or wondrous, everything's new and amazing, human Talia? He didn't think he could take it if he saw those luminous grey eyes turn to white fire.

"Fine. Why?"

She reached out and rubbed his right shoulder. "You've been so quiet this morning," she said, those big grey eyes looking sad, concerned. "And everything's been happening so fast. Before I fell out of the sky into your arms, you'd probably never even thought about angels and demons."

She was right about that.

"I admit, I'm struggling with a lot of this," he said, chewing his lip. He ran his right hand through his hair as the wind blew it. "It was a landslide of things to get used to. Just need some time to deal with all of it."

"I know," she said, looking sad.

He laughed and reached out, caressing her face. "Here I thought I'd finally gotten you into my bed, alone in my apartment. Not realizing how close to dying I came with an angel of death in my bed."

"Jack!"

"I wonder how many times you wanted to smite me with your scythe since The Cinderella Hour."

She crossed her arms. "Does right now count?"

"Then fourteen of your closest death angel friends show up. Along with dozens of assassin demons. Hellhounds. And Lucifer. And nobody even thought to bring a bottle of wine."

"And that's the reason why humans can't see demons and angels," she said, her eyes turning glassy. "We don't understand how or why you're able to see them. I'm sorry, Jack. I never meant to cause you any trouble. If you want me to leave, I will."

His heart leaped into his throat as he pulled her into his arms, holding her tight against his chest, ignoring the sharp pain in his shoulder. "God, no, Talia! I thought I'd lost you again after the finale of The Prince Charming Hour. I'm never letting go of you again." He held her out at arms' length, sending pain down his left arm. He shoved it away as he gazed into those beautiful, stormy grey eyes. "Do you hear me, my beautiful and deadly angel of death?"

She smiled at him as the first tear fell. He wiped it away with his thumb.

"And you're okay with all of it?" she said, sniffling now.

He shrugged, a crooked smile on his face. "Let's just say, I'm struggling my way through all of this, Talia. Not sure I'm okay with it. But I love you, so I'll deal with it the best way I can."

A smile lit her face at last.

"You're not going to smite me now, are you?" he asked.

"Jack!"

She smacked his arm and he broke into a laugh as he pulled her back into his arms and kissed her.

"Nice save," said Muriel somewhere behind him.

He turned toward the apartment door. Muriel and Anahera floated along the walkway, wings whispering above the persistent surge of cars. They stayed close, grey eyes narrowed, gazes flitting around the parking lot.

With Talia's help, he lifted the suitcases into the back of the Explorer. His left shoulder was weak now and he worried it would handicap him during *The Ever After Hour's* challenges. He'd just keep that to himself right now.

Muriel and Anahera each held out a hand and two light blue suitcases appeared beside Jack's two blue suitcases in the Explorer.

"That should be everything you'll need, Talia," said Muriel, smiling. "That little task brought back some fun memories. Of you learning how to be human. And falling in love with Jack the first day you saw him. That, thank the Maker, I can still remember."

Talia's eyes got huge, her mouth falling open, cheeks reddening.

So, that first time they'd stared at each other across the stage in Studio 22, she'd fallen for him? He'd have felt that gaze from a mile away. It was intense, intoxicating, and it had nearly turned him into a melted puddle of heartache right there under the stage lights. He'd never felt such a sweltering rush of emotions in his entire life until he'd looked into her burning grey eyes.

And he'd been forever lost without her ever since.

Jack grinned, turning his gaze back to Talia. "So, you didn't hate me that whole season?"

"Just most of it," Talia said, looking stone-faced.

"Come on, admit it," he goaded, still grinning at her. "Your badass death angel self was totally over the moon for me! From the very first moment you saw me. Even after you found out my bad boy reputation was as solid as my acting career. And then you played me, acting like you weren't interested. When you were absolutely swooning for me! Damn. Played by the angel of death for two seasons."

"Jack Casey..." Those eyes burned with embarrassment, cheeks flushing red.

He leaned over and gently kissed her angry, pursed lips. "And you never knew," he began in a quiet voice, "that I'd lost my heart to you the very first moment you turned those sexy grey eyes on me. Melting me right there under the Studio 22 set lights."

Her cheeks flushed red. "Studio 22? But that was the first time you saw me."

He nodded. "Yes, it was."

Her surprised grin made that admission worth it. And so was the hot, anxious kiss she planted against his mouth.

He closed the Explorer's back door and opened the passenger side door for Talia.

"Ready?" he asked her.

She nodded and climbed in and he closed the door, hurrying around to his side. He opened the door, climbed in, snapped on his shoulder belt, and headed out of the parking lot as Muriel and Anahera appeared in the back seat. The shoulder belt pressed against his left shoulder, making it throb.

He frowned in the rearview mirror. "Hope your squad isn't planning to pile in with you. Otherwise, you're going to have a long ride back there."

"They've already gone ahead," said Muriel. "Ensuring that there aren't any surprises for you along the way. We're making sure the two of you get there safely."

"Good," he replied, his gaze back on the turn onto the street as he headed toward the 10, headed west toward the coast. "My insurance only covers the apocalypse, not demons and hellhounds."

Talia looked up at Muriel as she fastened her seatbelt. "Where's there?"

Jack grinned as he pulled his Ray-Bans out of his hoodie pocket and slid them on before he hit the onramp and merged into the dizzying rush of cars on the 10. He loved driving. It gave him a feeling of peace and freedom that only came from an open road, wind in his hair, and the smell of the ocean. And with Talia beside him, it almost felt like a date. It'd be their very first.

"Malibu. In about an hour. Along the coast."

"An hour?" Anahera cried, glancing at Muriel. "That's forever in human time."

Jack laughed. "The drive's half the fun."

Talia shrugged. "What's Malibu?"

He'd had a place there once a hundred million years ago. Living on the ocean was the one thing he missed most about his former life. He glanced over at her.

"We're going to the beach, Talia."

Her eyes got big. "The beach? I've never touched one of Earth's oceans before."

Something he'd get to show her, walking along the rocky coast, the surf a gentle rush against the soft sand, scent of salt spray washing away the smell of the city. And the golden hour giving everything that pure, ethereal glow that made the world feel a little fragile and a little magical. Especially with the woman he loved in his arms.

"Can't wait to walk along the beach and show you all the ocean's magic, Talia," he said, touching her face. "Closest thing to heaven here on Earth."

Talia smiled at him as she reached over and took his hand in hers, entwining his fingers a moment.

"I'd love to touch the ocean with you, Jack."

"Then it's a date," he said. "I want to show it to you before the show starts. It's being filmed at some estate in Malibu."

"Uh, Jack," said Muriel, apprehension in her voice.

"What's wrong?" he asked, changing lanes behind a black Ferrari to avoid a slow-moving van.

"This estate you mentioned."

"Yeah?" His stomach clenched. He didn't like the hesitation in her voice. "Don't tell me it belongs to Lucifer."

"Muriel, what's wrong?" Talia asked, turning around in the seat to stare at her.

"Well, not directly, Jack."

He let the heavy sigh slip between his teeth as he moved out of the fast lane to let another car get past his SUV.

"You were supposed to say, *why, no, Jack, that would be silly after a horde of demons and hellhounds battled a bunch of angels of death inside your apartment.* Right after the woman I love just fell out of the sky into my arms. And Lucifer came over to measure my head for his wall.'"

Muriel's jaw tightened as she glanced from Anahera to Talia. "Let's play two truths and a lie. I tell you three things and you tell me which one is a lie."

"Why not!" Jack cried with a grin. "'Cause this just gets better and better."

Muriel pulled in a breath. "Okay. I'm acting captain of the death angels guard while Azrael's away. Talia loves you with all her heart. And your ex-girlfriend and your ex-costar are letting the show film on their Malibu estate because they work for Lucifer and are still— trying to kill you."

"STILL?" Jack swerved, turning the wheel to quickly get back into his lane. His anger flared. "What does that mean?"

"Oh, the stage light," said Anahera in a quiet voice, a hand over her mouth as she stared at Talia.

"What do you mean, the stage light?" he shouted.

Talia glared at Muriel. "Jack and I never got the chance to have that conversation about Rachel and Lare."

"Holy Hell! Lare, too?"

That information washed over him like a rogue wave. And stabbed him in the chest like a red-hot poker. He thought Rachel was just talking trash, trying to hurt him when she said that the dude he'd considered his best friend hated him. She hadn't said that they'd wanted him dead.

Why? It didn't make any sense.

"Talia, you knew about this?" he shouted. "And you didn't tell me?"

She bowed her head. "There hadn't been time," she said and rubbed his right shoulder. "And I knew how deeply it was going to hurt you. It was too much hurt at the time. I didn't want her to see you hurt and vulnerable. I was afraid she'd break you with that information."

He winced, his chest aching, the hazy memories of Rachel leading him to slaughter came back with a vengeance.

He squinted, concentrating on the 10's heavy traffic as the memory of him pleading with Rachel to stop him from snorting all those lines filled his head. Rachel knew it was enough to kill him. She knew it and he knew it. And he'd begged her stop him. But she just urged him onward like a good little soldier.

"She already has," he said in small, tired voice.

He'd tried shoving those memories to the back of his head, but they came back to him at the worst moments. In the lonely hours before dawn when all the pain surfaced and those memories thrust themselves to the foreground. And the craving ate away at him. Until he saw Rachel's face. Laughing at him, cheerfully leading him to an overdose, knowing that those eight lines meant death to him. And she looked delighted by it.

And now, he'd be on her turf while the show was filming.

"What do you mean, Jack?" Talia asked.

His jaw tightened and he stared ahead at the freeway signs, eyes burning as the sun climbed higher in the sky, illuminating the highway. The smell of car exhaust and hot asphalt hung above the stale huff of the SUV's air conditioner.

"Jack?" Talia's voice bubbled with concern.

"I can't talk about this right now," he said.

"I'm sorry, Jack," said Muriel. "I just needed you to know what you were walking into before we got there."

He bit his lip and nodded.

"With no one in charge of the guard right now—and Azrael dealing with the seraphim—we've had to improvise. The guard has put together a series of connected wards that will create a Holy shield around the estate."

Jack ground his teeth together. Rachel and Lare's estate.

Then something came back to him from a conversation with Gianni. An article Gianni had shown him. Some architectural magazine from three years ago, showing Lare Dumont's house. With a picture of his partner, who lived at the estate.

He choked the steering wheel with his grip. Rachel Daniels. She'd been his partner at the time, living with him in his downtown penthouse condo—and his little beach house at Malibu. Shoving him so full of coke that he couldn't even feel his face anymore. Or anything for that matter. But her location schedule took her away from him several days a week for months. Now, he knew why.

Because she was out in Malibu at Lare's place. Laughing her ass off at his naïve, love-sick dependence on her and the coke.

They'd used him so effectively. Getting him hooked and then grooming him to take the fall to *protect* the rest of the cast. He'd been such an obedient little simp. Never susing that all of this had been a big setup. A plan that he'd unknowingly followed to the damned letter.

Talia's hand rubbed his right shoulder again, but he just felt cold inside, the memory of Rachel leading him to another overdose playing behind his eyes—over and over . The memory made him sick all over. Gave him the shakes. He'd tried to push those flashbacks down deep, but they just kept surfacing. And he couldn't get past them.

"Jack, talk to me," said Talia in a voice barely above a whisper. "You're scaring me."

His jaw tightened, eyes stinging. He couldn't. He just couldn't talk about it. Any of it. Not even that article. It hurt down so deep that talking about it just laid open those deep wounds. Laid them bare and invited the world to rub salt into them.

"Can't," he said in a tight voice and pressed his lips into a thin, quivering line as the 10 began its turn north. Into the California 1, the coastal highway.

He remembered moments along this rocky coast line, high out of his mind in the back seat of someone's Bentley as it carried him north. To a beach estate in Malibu. To be with Rachel for a weekend coke binge with the cast. And the days-long party that would leave him blacked out and missing time until he woke up beside Rachel in just his boxer briefs and a T-shirt. With no memory of undressing. Feeling violated and sick from all the coke.

But she'd just slide her arms around him, with him too baked to voice his no. He remembered shaking his head, trying to say no, to ask where his clothes went, but she just covered him with her naked body and fed him more coke. And he was gone again, barely aware of her presence as she rolled the T-shirt up and over his head.

Even when he passed on lines, she was at his elbow, teasing him with her touch, stoking and milking his cravings until he eventually caved. And he caved every time at her touch. Every. Single. Time.

And then more days missed. Lines forgotten. Appointments lost. And then she'd withhold coke from him. Making him ache for it. He chewed the inside of his mouth. Beg for it. Perform for it. Only then did she give him what he needed to stop the lonely emptiness and let him feel some semblance of enjoyment again.

To him, Rachel Daniels was a monster. And the memories in that house hurt from all directions at once. Could he even get through a day there? Much less seven weeks.

"Jack, please," said Talia, an ache in her voice.

He shook his head and kept driving. He'd fall apart if he talked about this. It was too jumbled and too raw. Especially her cruelty and how he'd just acquiesced to it. Allowed her to treat him like a toy. Or her purse poodle. Bad dog, Jack. No flake for you tonight. Now, lie still while I have my way with you.

He hit the steering wheel with his fist, fighting back the sting in his eyes. Dammit! He had to push this out of his head somehow, shove it back and blunt the pain before it all started to show through his game face.

Talia's hand was on his shoulder again, rubbing. Trying to calm and comfort him. But this one ran deep. It'd take a lot of salve—or flake—to numb this into a dark corner where he could ignore it again.

He reached over and patted her hand and then returned his hand to the wheel, still staring straight ahead as the 10 made the final curve north. Toward Malibu. He felt sick now. Wanting to keep driving north until he found a quiet little beach town where no one knew him.

But she kept her hand on his arm, fingers making soothing circles across his sleeve, the rhythm lulling him into a state of calm again.

11

TALIA WAS AFRAID FOR JACK, NOW THAT SHE KNEW THEY WERE HEADING into enemy territory, hunkered down beneath a chained ward shield to keep out demons. But what about the ones already in the house?

Rachel Daniels and Lare Dumont. They both wanted Jack dead.

And now that she knew they'd sold their souls to Lucifer, she and Jack were both in danger. Still, she knew it was better to face the enemies she knew than ones with no faces.

Like the hordes of assassin demons Lucifer had thrown at them last night.

She knew that the memory of Lucifer trying to force Jack into an overdose was playing over and over in his head. It would stay with him—and her—forever. Jack saw all those lines of coke laid out for him and knew it was enough to kill him. Knowing he couldn't stop himself, he'd begged Rachel to stop him. Talia felt the tears well in her eyes.

Jack Casey didn't beg, but that night, he'd pleaded with Rachel to stop him.

And Talia had been helpless, trapped behind a barrier that prevented her from stopping him. The entire time, Rachel just smiled and led him to the lines like his devoted lover. And he'd been powerless to stop himself from inhaling the drugs. Until he found one last sliver of fight left inside and blew the cocaine off the desk. Infuriating Rachel and Lucifer.

She knew that memory was eating away at Jack. And she couldn't do anything to help him. He wouldn't talk about it, much less in front of Muriel and Anahera. She'd try to talk to him again—if she could get him alone.

But she feared for him being in this estate. Rachel would do her best to hurt him further. And try to kill him. She knew that now, after Rachel paid someone to make that stage light fall on Jack. She hoped that she and fourteen angels of death would be enough to save them both from Lucifer. And his minions.

IN HALF AN HOUR, Jack turned off Highway 1. He followed a road that wound along the rocky coastline until he picked up a paved road that led away from the beach houses pressed together in a single line. They glided over a bluff with a panoramic view of the ocean.

For a moment, she couldn't breathe. Blown away by the incredible, dramatic beauty of the bluff with its rocky cliffs and outcrops and the sugary sand below with waves crashing along its length. At the top of that bluff stood a sparkling white villa that was all cubes and glass and light. It glittered with sunlight, the white walls reminding her a little of the grand hall of Eolowen and it made her tear up.

"Incredible," Talia said, barely finding her voice.

Jack sighed and chewed his lip, staring toward the distant ocean as the sun hung high in the sky, sparkling across the deep blue Pacific Ocean.

He pulled up in a long, wide driveway. It was also white and divided into squares by a black grid that matched the three garage doors. The entrance was all glass, a cascade of white lights hanging like starlight in the vaulted foyer where silver stairs wound up to the main level.

Jack looked stiff and angry as he unfastened his seatbelt and climbed out of the SUV. Talia hurried out on the other side and rushed around to take his hand.

His smile was weak, flat as he gazed into her eyes and then entwined his fingers hers. His hand felt hot, warmed from being in the sun. He walked a little heavier to his right, letting that left shoulder roll forward and his arm droop. It was bothering him.

Jennifer Collins rushed out the glass doors and ran across the driveway toward them. She wore a long-sleeved red blouse and black pants, clipboard and phone in her hands.

"Jack! Talia! Welcome to—"

"Summer's Revenge," Jack said bitterly.

She nodded, giving Talia a strange look, and then she gazed at Jack.

"Do you know this place, Jack?" she asked.

"Used to be a regular here a few years ago," he said in a quiet voice. "When Lare was just renting it."

"Of course! I should have known that." Jennifer seemed to sense that something was wrong with Jack, but she continued explaining about the facilities. "Talia, Jack probably knows this, but there are seven suites here, a game room, a pool, a sauna, a spacious living room, and some other amenities. You and Jack will be one of seven couples in the house along with the crew. And Devin, of course."

"Only seven couples?" Talia replied. She hadn't expected that, but it would make the interactions a little more intimate.

"That's right!" Jennifer said, smiling. "Each week, one couple will go home. You know most of the couples, but two we're calling *arranged marriages*, bringing former contestants together as a couple. It's going to be a lot of fun. But thank you both for being on the show. It probably wouldn't have gotten green-lighted without Herb promising that you two were onboard. He was losing his mind waiting for your call, Jack."

Jack nodded. "Had my hands full at the time and couldn't call him back until later."

"Here, let me show you to your suite and let you both get

unpacked." She stared at them a moment and grinned. "I'm so happy to see you two together."

Talia leaned into Jack and slid her arm around him, laying her face against his chest. He let go of her hand and put his right arm around her, squeezing.

"We're pretty happy about it, too, Jennifer," said Talia.

"Best moment of my life," said Jack and it made her tear up.

"Are you just in touch with each other or in the same place right now?" Jennifer asked.

"Same place," said Jack with a smirk. "In my crappy studio apartment, but we're looking for something better."

Hearing him say that made her want to spread her wings and soar. They were only tiny little buds right now, but they were growing back. She couldn't believe it! She'd never heard of this Phoenix shift that Muriel mentioned, but she needed her powers back. Now more than ever. She wouldn't tell Jack until she was certain.

"We plan to look for another place after the show," said Talia.

She didn't know what would happen after the show, but after everything she'd gone through, she refused to leave Jack's side. She'd earned her place there, even when her angel of death abilities returned.

TALIA AND JACK were placed in the Breckenridge suite. It was the farthest room south at the estate, the largest, and it faced the ocean. Talia was mesmerized by the incredible views. Jack set the suitcases inside the door with the help of a crew member that got all four inside the house and up to the suite. Then he disappeared with Jennifer, mumbling something about signing contracts. Leaving Talia alone with Anahera and Muriel.

The room had maple hardwood floors, white walls, white trim, and tall ceilings. It had no separating walls, just one open space that smelled like eucalyptus, sea spray, and jasmine. The south and west walls created a little alcove, like a bay window nook, with floor to ceiling windows. With a big bed.

It had a small kitchen just left of the door with sandy-colored countertops, a microwave, small sink, and a full-sized stainless-steel refrigerator. The little dining area in front had a round, glass table and four padded coral-colored chairs. A crystal chandelier hung over it, the crystals reflecting little rainbowed circles across the chairs.

"Look at this place!" Talia cried, walking through it, Anahera and Muriel floating behind her.

Beside the dining space was a large sitting area with two overstuffed turquoise chairs and a very soft turquoise couch. A marble coffee table had a trio of turquoise candles on gold pedestals, a clear glass bowl of sea glass in pastel colors, and a large gold starfish. A large flat screen television hung on the wall above a glass and white rock gas fireplace with little blue flames. Against the east wall was a desk with a padded coral office chair and white bookshelves.

The bed was huge and faced the wall of west windows. The mattress was nestled on a maple platform that was low to the ground. It had a padded white headboard, crisp white sheets, and a bright turquoise comforter. A white nightstand stood on either side of the bed with crystal lamps. On both sides of the bed were two, French-styled armoires. And a padded coral bench at the foot of the bed.

"This place is incredible!" said Anahera.

"Like this view," said Talia, standing at the window, watching the sun sparkle against the ocean, along the little sandy beach, and its rocky outcrops.

"And more than a little romantic," said Muriel. "Look at this bed."

The bed was equal parts romantic and terrifying. She and Jack would be staying together here. In this room. And there was only one bed.

"Muriel, what do I do?" she cried.

"About what?" Muriel asked.

She pointed at the bed. "There's only one bed."

Muriel grinned. "Lucky you."

"Muriel! You're not helping."

"There's a couch over there," said Anahera pointing at the living area.

"I can't make Jack sleep on a couch for seven weeks," Talia said, crossing her arms.

Muriel shrugged. "Then either you sleep on the couch or share the bed with him."

She was an angel of death. Angels didn't sleep. And she'd never shared a bed with anyone before.

Muriel rolled her eyes and took her by the shoulders. "Talia, you love him, don't you?"

She shook her head. "That's not the point. I've never been with a man like that before."

"Jack would never push you into anything. You know that!"

"No, of course not. That's not what I meant." She bowed her head, feeling frustrated. "I'm an angel…I don't even know the first thing about—"

"Ohhhh, right. That's a human thing." Muriel smiled. "Usually. There are cambions, children of demons and humans. Nephilims, children of angels and humans—"

"You're not making me feel better, Muriel."

"I just meant that it's a thing," said Muriel. "That angels have loved humans before. Physically. And nobody got smited, okay?"

Talia crossed her arms against her chest. She still had on Jack's Van Halen T-shirt and the baggy blue pants he'd given her. They had that touch of cedar and spice that was strong, warm, and intoxicating. Like Jack. But she had no idea about the mechanics of how humans made love. Kissing and touching Jack had come so naturally to her, but other things? He was used to women who knew what they were doing. Not some fumbling angel with no clue how humans worked.

"Talia," said Muriel, motioning toward the bed. "Jack Casey is a gentleman. When I was trying to heal the wounds from your lost wings, he turned his back so we could undress you and put you in his T-shirt and pants."

She loved the cedary scent of his clothes against her skin, knowing that he'd worn them. "I just don't want to disappoint him," she said, loving that he'd turned around like that.

"You won't," said Muriel, letting go of her arms. "He's fought long and hard to be with you. Don't forget that."

He had. Especially that sword duel against Jordan Bellamy that almost killed him.

"Muriel, I'm really worried about him," she said and sat down on the bed.

"I know," said Muriel with a sigh and dropped down on the bed beside her. "There's so much he doesn't know about Rachel Daniels. That's going to break his heart. And there's so much that woman did to him. Things he's just beginning to remember as he gets clear of the cocaine."

That thought terrified her. "He's also remembering when Lucifer tried to force him into an overdose."

"What?" Muriel cried, staring at her in shock.

"It's true, Muriel," said Anahera as she sat down on the coral bench at the foot of the bed. "I was there. Rachel Daniels did her best to get him to do eight lines of cocaine that she'd put down. While Lucifer looked on, laughing. Talia and I were trapped behind some barrier and couldn't get close to help him."

Talia was shaking now, the memory so visceral. "It was horrible, Muriel," she said, shuddering. "Jack couldn't control his craving. He was fighting so hard against it, but he couldn't overpower Lucifer pushing him to pick up that straw and snort it all down. All eight lines." She gritted her teeth, the rage hot against her cheeks. "And Muriel, Jack was begging Rachel to help him. To stop him from picking up that straw and putting it into the cocaine. She just told him to suck it up and get it over with." She felt tears against her cheeks. "He begged her to stop him, pleaded with her, telling her he couldn't stop himself. She just pushed him onward."

"My word, Talia," said Muriel, shaking her head. "I had no idea. Poor Jack."

"I know that's what was going through his head on the drive here.

He hasn't talked about that event, but I know it's eating him up inside."

"I assume you and Anahera got to him before he did all the coke?" Muriel asked.

Talia shook her head, eyes downcast. "Jack found the strength to blow the coke off the table. Which stopped the attack."

"Wow, impressive," said Muriel. "To fight through Lucifer's direct force like that and break free long enough to scatter the coke? That took some power, Talia. And some guts."

The door opened and Jack returned to the suite with a stack of papers in hand and some pens.

"Talia," he called. "Here's your show contract. Just need to sign everything that's marked and get it back to Jennifer by tonight."

He looked up and saw the three of them sitting on the edge of the bed and he made a face. She couldn't tell if it was a *what are you, three up to* face or a *why are you, three staring at me* face.

Talia rose from the bed and hurried over to take the papers as he glanced around the suite, taking in the layout and the furnishings.

"Thanks, Jack," she said and slid the papers out of his hand.

She leaned up and kissed him, making him smile.

"Miss me?" he asked with a smirk.

She nodded. "You should see our view of the ocean," she said, taking him by the hand and leading him over to the wall of windows.

He froze. Staring from the window to the bed, a haunted look in his eyes. He backed away, his face turning pale. She'd never seen him look so frightened before and it went right through her. Hurting deep. She didn't understand what was happening to him and she needed to know. She needed him to tell her.

"Jack? What's wrong?"

He shook his head, still backing away until he ran into one of the turquoise chairs and fell over it into the floor.

"Jack!"

She dropped down beside him, but he looked past her into the alcove, something very painful playing behind his eyes.

"What's the matter?"

"This is…where it—happened," he muttered in a faraway voice.

"Where what happened, Jack?" she cried, trying to get him to his feet, but he seemed lost in a bad memory.

"The night she…" He pulled in a breath, eyes smashed closed. "When she…"

What had Rachel Daniels done to him in this room? It made her shake with fury and she longed for her angel of death powers back. She'd smite that bitch right this very moment. What had she done to him?

She held his face in her hands, calling his name. "Jack! What did she do to you?"

His face scrunched and he struggled against something unseen. "She—" He sucked in another breath. Then another. And another. Shaking his head. Finally, he looked at Talia, biting the inside of his lip, and covered his face. "I was only twenty, Talia." His voice was thin and shaky. "I didn't want to—I mean I never said I'd…she didn't even ask if—"

With slow, deliberate movements, Talia put her arms around him, careful not to bump his left shoulder. He pressed his face against her shoulder, shaking.

"What'd she do to you, Jack?"

"There were so many drugs, Talia," he sputtered with a gasp for air. And sucked in another breath. "They kept me swimming in them. I barely knew my own name or what day it was."

"It wasn't your fault," she said, holding him close as she gave Muriel a desperate look.

"So much that I'd blackout for hours at a time. When I woke up, I'd be in the back of somebody's Bentley or on a couch somewhere. With no memory of how I got there. Or…" He pointed at the bed. "There," he said, his voice raspy now. "With my clothes gone and Rachel beside me…doing—things to me."

He dropped his face into his hands again and she pulled him close, just holding him. Horrified by his story. By the gaps in his memory that he struggled with. By the pain on his face at the snippets of images he couldn't put into a clear picture.

Rachel Daniels—and Jack's costar—had preyed on him. Rachel was a predator. She'd hunted a twenty-year-old kid who'd just hit it big with a starring role on the biggest show on television. And instead of nurturing this bright new talent, they'd fed on him, thrown him to the wolves, and watched as they tore him apart. And then they let him get fired, blaming him for all the debauchery on set when he'd never been the instigator. Only the victim.

She motioned at Muriel and together, they got Jack to his feet and over to the couch. Muriel frowned and pointed to his left shoulder. A red blotch was spreading across it.

"Hellhound bite's bleeding again," said Muriel as she pressed her fingers against the damp, blood-stained fabric of his navy blue hoodie. "I'm not supposed to, but I'll do what I can."

"Thanks," said Jack, eyes narrowing as Talia sat down beside him and laid her hands against his face.

"Jack, I'll go find Jennifer and ask to be moved out of this room."

He shook his head, looking at her with the saddest eyes and it went right through her. "It wasn't just this room," he said, an ache in his voice. "It's this whole house. I think I left half my memory here by the end." He shuddered. "And it's all starting to come back. Some of it's…horrible."

His voice was a raspy whisper and he was shaking. She just held him.

"You can't sleep in this room after all of that," she cried.

He looked at her. "I can if you're there beside me."

Her eyes widened.

"I don't think I can sleep in that bed alone. I promise I'll be a perfect gentleman," he said, sighing.

She grinned at him. "You'd better not," she said and kissed him.

That made him smile, the fear leaving his face.

But he was so incredibly tired. After staying up all night with her and then being awoken by all those attacking demons. And then the hellhound bite. He'd lost more blood than he cared to admit, weakening him. He needed to sleep.

"Here," she said, patting the sofa. "Why don't you stretch out on the couch with your head in my lap? I'll watch over you while you sleep."

His face brightened. "Still my guardian angel after three seasons, aren't you?"

"Now and always, Jack Casey," she said and nudged him. "Come on. Get some sleep and later, you can take me for a walk along the ocean."

"I'd love to, Talia," he said as he climbed onto the couch.

She put a pillow in her lap and he laid his head down. And in minutes, he was gone, sleeping soundly. She laid the back of her hand against his forehead and shook her head.

"Still got fever?" Muriel asked.

Talia nodded. She lifted up the edge of his hoodie and peered underneath it at the wound. The T-shirt beneath it was wet with blood again.

"This hellhound marker is really sapping his strength," she said.

Muriel nodded. "And it's causing him to remember things. Things that the cocaine blocked out before."

"What do you mean?" Talia asked.

Muriel turned away toward the window and stared out across the golden sunlight glittering across the deep blue ocean.

"Talia, that bite isn't just Cerberus taking a tasty nibble out of your Hollywood hottie. It was intended to mark him. To track him, of course, but it's also an attempt to mark his soul for Hell."

"Mark his soul for Hell?" Talia's mouth fell open. "No one can do that until he's been judged and there's no way he'd be thrown to Lucifer anyway. His Book of Life and Death was clear of anything like that."

Muriel sighed. "It was until that forger started rampaging through the archive. If Lucifer forged the ending of Jack's Book, he could have forged other parts of it. Like where Jack's to be sent. And when that happens, it starts to trigger a life review. You know how that works. We trigger one ourselves before we cross souls over."

She felt the anger burn through her. "And Lucifer's doing it just to torture Jack. To get to me."

"Exactly. With Jack here in this house, where all the cocaine use started, he's already awakening memories. The marker's accelerating it. The place where Jack fell in with a fast crowd that literally ran over him. These people belong to Lucifer. They've been setting up people for years to lose their souls."

Talia felt her anger bloom again. Even before she knew Jack, Rachel Daniels and Lare Dumont had sold their souls for success. And they became Lucifer's pimps, supplying him with souls.

"You're right," said Talia. "I can't forget that."

Muriel nodded, anger sparking in her grey eyes, turning them fiery. "These monsters were pros. They conditioned Jack. Groomed him. Made him into a raging drug addict, so he'd get fired and thrown into a downward spiral that would make him end his life. And fall into Lucifer's hands. But they did some pretty awful things to him, too. Things that the coke binges blocked out. Until now. The mark is making all of it surface. Lucifer wants him to suffer in front of you, Talia. You're right. He *is* using Jack to get to you."

Talia wanted to rage at Lucifer, to rip every golden hair out of his head and shove it down his throat.

"How can I help poor Jack?" she asked. "How can I protect him from round two of Lucifer's unbridled assaults?"

"It's you he wants," said Anahera. "Lucifer is trying to get to you through Jack because he knows that Jack is your weakness."

Muriel's expression was grim. "Anahera's right. None of us understands his obsession with you, Talia, but it's going to take all of us to keep Lucifer from taking you."

The thought of an eternity in Hell—with Lucifer—made her violently ill.

Muriel smiled. "And maybe Jack being able to see the demons is a blessing in disguise. It's hard to fight something you can't see."

Talia nodded as she ran her fingers through Jack's blond hair, hoping Muriel was right. Right now, they could use all the blessings they could get.

12

After a catered dinner in the beach house estate's large dining room, a vaulted space with exposed maple beams and glass filling the expanse with the setting sun and the Pacific Ocean, Jack had to face his demons as he sat across from Rachel Daniels and his former best friend, Laren Dumont.

They looked through him, like his chair was empty. It made Jack's anger flare, but he tamped it down tight. Getting fired from another show wasn't on his To Do list this month.

He reached out and slid his hand into Talia's. She sat on his right, smokin' hot in a short red skirt and his Van Halen T-shirt, black hair in ringlets down her back, those electric grey eyes burning through him like embers.

The oblong maple dining table had two dozen white leather chairs wedged around it, filled with familiar faces and some friends. The room smelled like teriyaki, pepper steak, and sweet and sour sauce after some Chinese takeaway, the bright rectangular chandelier drenching the table with white light and golden circles from the crystals.

Armand Gianni sat to his left, daytime soap star, good friend, and newly minted primetime television star after two seasons on the hottest show on TV right now. This one. Isabella Castilla sat to Gianni's left, her hand in his, that coppery bob with blue highlights shimmering under the lights. Gianni wore a long-sleeved light blue t-shirt and jeans, Izzy in a figure-hugging ivory sundress. Jack smirked. He'd never seen Gianni in anything that casual, but he was still Cary Grant in jeans and a T-shirt.

To Talia's right sat Mark Banks and Morgan Boyer. Banks wore a white sweatshirt and jeans, light brown hair still spiky. Morgan sat to Banks' right, her arm in his, wearing a flowered pink blouse and a short jean skirt, brown hair in a tight ponytail. Banks had been a good friend on *The Cinderella Hour*. Stopped him from sending Talia home that night, using his only veto after Morgan had lied and claimed Talia was playing him to get to Gianni. And that was after saving his life when he'd overdosed after finding Talia in Gianni's arms at the pool.

He owed Gianni and Banks a debt he could never repay.

He leaned over and kissed Talia, smiling as she blushed, those grey eyes only on him, like he was the only one in the room. She reached up and caressed his cheek then laid her head on his shoulder. He tilted his head against hers.

Jennifer Collins stood at one end of the table, clipboard in hand, Herb Rutherford seated behind her in chairs pulled in from the living room.

"Welcome, everyone, to the first reading for The Ever After Hour," said Jennifer, putting on a pair of red reading glasses. "In case anyone's forgotten, I'm Jennifer Collins, set coordinator for the production. Behind me is director, Herb Rutherford."

Herb leaned forward in his chair, wearing a grey jacket and black pants. "Welcome and thank you, everyone. We're thrilled to welcome you all back." His gaze went to Jack. "Especially you, Casey."

Rachel and Lare shot a glare at him, but he just smiled and thanked Herb.

"Every season needs a bad boy rule breaker like Casey," said Banks and everyone laughed, including Talia.

"Until he gets fired," said Rachel with a smug grin.

The room went quiet.

"If Casey gets fired, this show goes with him," Herb replied. "He's the reason this show's been number one for two seasons."

"That's what Evan said just before season three of SanFran Confidential started," said Lare, leveling his gaze at Jack.

Jack stared at him. Until another voice from his past rose through the room.

"Funny, Chung Liu said the same thing halfway through You and Me. When Casey stopped remembering his lines."

The room went deadly quiet.

Jack turned toward the other end of the table, his stomach dropping. Tyler Hughes sat there, dark hair spiky like Banks and beside him, Nicole Reardon, light brown hair loose around her shoulders. Her hazel eyes stared through him. He bristled.

His costars from *You and Me*, the one movie he'd done—that tanked. They were good friends of Rachel and Lare. Frequent visitors to Summer's Revenge. They'd kept the coke flowing on the set of *You and Me*, even bringing it to his trailer when he didn't join them. Making sure he walked away from that film just as messed up as he'd been on *SanFran Confidential*. Ensuring his fall afterward was complete and total.

But Devin Van Fossen's words came back to him from an interview on *The Prince Charming Hour*. Pointing him to the real truth about his reviews. He had to remember that when he was around these dicks.

He grinned. No revenge felt sweeter than succeeding despite these assholes.

"Need to run some lines, Jack?" Lare asked and Rachel broke into a fit of laughter.

Tyler snickered and Nicole just smiled, tossing her light brown hair over her shoulder.

He glared at them and then back at Lare. "Never again, Dumont," he replied.

"You mean, never again tonight. Right, Jack?" said Rachel, smiling at him.

He felt Talia's grip on his hand tighten as Banks reached out and patted him on the back. He gave Banks a nod of thanks.

"Stop it," Gianni snapped, voice raised. "Jack's clean. And you can't handle his success. Shelve your jealousy and be professionals."

"Armand's right," said Izzy, leaning her elbows on the table. "Keep it cordial or keep it to yourselves."

Jack glanced over at Gianni and Izzy, smiling. Gianni nodded at him. God, it felt good to show those monsters that he had friends at this table. When he turned back to Jennifer, she was smiling now.

"Now, I'd like to introduce you all to your competition and explain the new format and its challenges," said Jennifer.

She motioned to Izzy and Gianni. "Isabella Castilla, evening news anchor from San Francisco and Armand Gianni, star of the daytime drama, Crossing Paths. They met and matched on The Prince Charming Hour."

Her smile broadened when she got to Jack. "Talia Smith from…" Her voice trailed off a moment, glancing at Talia.

Jack glanced at Talia and smirked. "Alaska," he said.

"Thanks, Jack," said Jennifer, continuing. "From Alaska. And Jack Casey, star of You and Me and SanFran Confidential. Jack and Talia met on The Cinderella Hour and matched on The Prince Charming Hour. Propelling this little reality TV show into the number one ratings slot in the country. Over 40 million people watched Jack, in another unscripted moment, propose to Talia on live television."

He mouthed thanks to her and her smile broadened.

"And I see Talia is still wearing his ring," Jennifer replied. "Beside Talia is couple number three: Mark Banks who starred in the shows, Stop Already and The World According to Thomas. And Morgan Boyer, a hopeful actress from Carbondale, Illinois. They met and matched on season one of The Cinderella Hour."

Banks nudged Jack's shoulder with his fist. "Thanks to this guy, we did. Morgan only had eyes for Jack, but Jack taught me to fight for what I wanted." He leaned down and kissed her.

Morgan glanced at Jack and then Talia. "And Talia convinced me to give Mark a chance. Best move ever."

Jennifer began to introduce the next two couples as Jack's thoughts wandered.

Beside Banks sat one of the arranged marriages that Jennifer mentioned. Ryder Kurland, chief technical officer and distribution engineer from season two. A nice enough guy.

And Claire Olsen, a model from Alpharetta, Georgia from season one. She'd been fond of him. And he'd almost made one of the biggest mistakes of his life when he chose her as his match instead of Talia. He'd been angry and made a feeble attempt to salvage the game. So certain that she wanted Gianni, not him.

"And beside Claire and Ryder, we have season two finalist Eric Saunders, a financial planner and body builder who didn't match with a princess. And Riya Patel, an actress and model from Bhopal, India from season one who left us early."

Jack tried to remember the name or the face from two seasons ago, but couldn't. Riya was hot with long, shiny black hair, big, wide-set brown eyes, and full lips. And Eric didn't seem disappointed. He and Riya had been talking quietly with each other since they sat down, even throughout dinner.

"Next is Nicole Reardon, America's favorite Rom Com star. And Tyler Hughes—"

"Everybody knows Tyler Hughes," said Claire Olsen with a smile.

Everyone laughed. Except Jack.

Everyone knew Hughes, but nobody knew him well. If they did, they'd know he was a raging egomaniac that stole lines, stole scenes, and made sure he was the focus in every production. At that time, he hadn't been much better. Hurt and angry from being fired from his hit show and then dumped by a woman he loved, a woman killing him with coke, he'd railed against this dude's attempts to control everything. Including him. The set of *You and Me* became a battlefield. Hughes' ego against his and nobody won.

Hughes hated him because he'd gotten top billing, too stupid to understand that it'd been alphabetical. Hughes had been in the business almost a decade longer, but his star had been teetering on the edge of the A-List for a while. Jack's star hadn't completely shattered yet, the news that he'd been fired hadn't yet reached all the studios and casting directors. Like it or not, they'd been pretty equal box office draws at that time.

And now, Jack's star was rising fast again. Hughes hadn't had a hit for five years. That was a lifetime in the entertainment industry. And Nicole's had flatlined since she met Hughes six years ago. She was older than Jack, too. They all were.

"And our last couple is Rachel Daniels, star of Harbor Bay Medical and SanFran Confidential. She didn't match with anyone in season two. But she found her match in her former costar, Lare Dumont, star of SanFran Confidential, New Orleans PD, Hollywood Law, and over a dozen films."

Rachel tossed her auburn hair off her shoulders and leaned back in a see-through pink blouse with a cream-colored tank top underneath and blowsy linen pants. Her eyes were ringed in smoky eye shadow and liner, lips pale pink, freckles dotting her milky complexion. Beside her, Lare brooded, his chocolate brown hair almost touching his shoulders, beady but piercing dark eyes pinpointed on Jack. He was about Banks' age, his long face shadowed with stubble, perfect nose, and perfect chin combined to give him that heroic, alpha edge that so many women dreamed about.

That's why the casting director wanted a contrast when casting Drummond Turillo's partner on *SanFran Confidential*. They wanted a blond, baby-faced bad boy. Young. A rule breaker that did things his way, defied department rules, and clashed with Drum, the hero. Instead, they got a wide-eyed, baby-faced blond kid from Indiana with a huge heart that bled through his bad boy persona and rule-breaking behavior. To become the hero no one expected. Breaking hearts and forcing his way into the spotlight as the show quickly moved up in the ratings.

Everyone wanted more stories featuring Detective Davy Pierson. Wanted more Davy being the hero, more of this budding buddy cop shift that became the show's focus for almost three years. Until he got fired. People said the show was never the same after that, but it survived.

Maybe that was why Lare turned him onto the coke? And Rachel pretended to love him? To get him off the show? He hadn't meant to take anything away from Lare. He'd never intended to upstage him or take away his spotlight. He followed the scripts.

"…so please be respectful of all its spaces. This is Rachel and Lare's home and they have generously agreed to allow us to film season three here. And if you have any housekeeping or issues with your rooms, please come to me and I'll get with Rachel and Lare to resolve them."

Everyone nodded.

"And now, Herb's going to explain his vision for season three," said Jennifer, taking a seat in a white cloth chair off to the side as Herb stood up from his chair.

Herb leaned against the end of the table, smiling. He still had a bit of a paunch on his five-foot-ten frame. Balding, the fringe of dark hair around the lower half of his head shaved, Herb studied the cast a moment. His long, tanned face was creased around his mouth and eyes and across his forehead, eyebrows shaggy.

"Now, then, my vision for The Ever After Hour is obvious from the title," he said in his loud, booming voice that filled the space. "Which one of our couples will live happily ever after? With a million dollars?"

Talia sat up, turning toward Jack as she slid her hand out of his and around his arm. He leaned over and kissed her again and then turned back to Herb.

"There will be a series of challenges that I'm calling the Royal Courtship competition. There will be six challenges in all that will test each couple's commitment and trust. After every challenge, the lowest scoring couple gets sent home. You won't know your scores until the live dismissal show. Couples that are safe will be listed in no particular order either until we establish the bottom two couples. Then one of you will go home. Any questions?"

"How will couples be scored?" Morgan asked.

Herb gave her a knowing smile. "Depends on the challenge."

"So, we won't have any idea how we did on the challenges?" Nicole replied.

"No, you won't," said Herb, straightening as he stood. "That's where some of the trust comes from. You'll have to trust your partner through all the moments where you have no idea how you or they did on the challenges."

"Who will dismiss the couples?" Gianni asked.

"Devin Van Fossen is returning as the host. He'll be here tomorrow when we start blocking rehearsals and filming introductions and interactions."

Herb waited for more questions, but none came. Satisfied, he sat down and Jennifer returned to the table, clipboard in hand.

"All right, everyone. Free night tonight. Enjoy yourselves because starting tomorrow, things will get crazy." She started to walk away, but turned back.

"Oh, Mark and Morgan wanted me to announce that they're hosting a champagne welcome on the beach at sunset. It's a private beach, so there will be music and cold champagne. Dress casual and bring your dancing flip flops."

Everyone got up from the table, hurrying off. Morgan and Izzy scurried off with Talia. Leaving him alone. Until Banks and Gianni sidled up to him. Banks extended his hand and Jack shook it.

"Good to see you, dude," Jack said, smiling. "You and Morgan look good together. Things going well?"

"Jack! Things are great. Couldn't be happier. Morgan and I are smooth."

Gianni shook Jack's hand and then Banks' hand.

Jack pointed at him with his thumb. "No need to ask this dude how things are going. It shines on his face."

"Izzy's amazing," Gianni said, still grinning. "Gets better every day. She's in negotiations with one of the Los Angeles news channels. If all goes well, she'll be relocating to Los Angeles after the show."

"Congratulations, dude," said Jack. "Just invite me to the wedding."

"I will," he said with that smooth, silver screen Cary Grant delivery. "As one of my groomsmen."

He stared at Gianni a moment, not quite processing that comment. "Me?" he said finally. "You'd want me as one of your groomsmen?"

"Wow, Casey's ego's really tanked since The Cinderella Hour," Banks said with a chuckle.

"Nah," said Gianni with a laugh. "Just his acting."

Jack laughed.

Banks poked him. "So, how you been, Jack?"

He smiled, turning on his game face. "As long as I'm with Talia, I'm great."

"She looks happy, Jack," said Gianni, glancing over at her with Izzy and Morgan.

Jack chuckled, watching them talking a mile a minute and laughing together. Talia seemed happier in their company. She was probably already tired of his bad moods. And he just didn't have it in him to lay out the four years of misery he'd endured before *The Cinderella Hour*. And what had happened to him here. In this house.

She didn't need to know any of that anyway. She had her own issues right now. Not to mention the elephant in the room, er, the angels of death. And Lucifer. And everything else was way too crazy to believe.

It made his head hurt.

"You look tired, Jack," said Gianni, concern in those brown eyes.

Banks stepped closer. "Everything okay?"

He nodded, crossing his arms. "Yeah, just had some..."

He struggled for the appropriate word. *Let's see, assassin demons, hellhounds, and Lucifer showing up after a squad of death angels. And Talia dropping out of the sky.*

"Some maintenance and uh, neighbor issues at my place over the weekend. And the phone rang day and night until I just turned it off."

"Maintenance issues?" Gianni asked, face scrunching into a confused look.

"Neighbors?" Banks asked.

Of course, they wanted an explanation.

"Back patio door broke," he said.

Because apparently, Lucifer and an army of assassin demons broke it down.

"And neighbors got a little rowdy. Someone had a party, so uninvited guests showed up at my place by mistake."

A big mistake. Trying to drag Talia off. And him.

"Then my other neighbor's dog got loose in my apartment." Cerberus, the guardian of the Gates of Hell—and his bro, Orthrus. No big deal. Just tossed him around like a chew toy and tried to drag him off to Hell. "Uh, Bruce. Some Newfie-grizzly cross."

Gianni and Banks looked a little stunned.

"Where do you live, Jack?" Gianni asked.

"In South Park," he said, glancing away from their faces.

"What? No way!" Banks.

Finally, when he looked up, Gianni was staring at him, looking dumbfounded.

"Jack," he said in a quiet voice, eyes still wide. "I had no idea."

Jack just shrugged.

"That's why you signed aboard The Cinderella Hour." Gianni looked stunned.

He nodded. "It was that or move into my Explorer."

Gianni looked upset. "Jack, I had no idea that's where you lived."

Jack laughed. "And I still owed my dealer over thirty G's at that time."

Gianni gripped Jack's shoulders and he tried not to make a face when Gianni squeezed the hellhound bite.

"Jack, you practically live in a war zone. It's not safe."

"Yeah," he said with a grimace, trying to ease his left shoulder out Gianni's grip. "I can't have Talia in that environment. With the money from this season—and my quarter share of that million—I'm getting us out of there."

At last, Gianni smiled. "You're living together? That's fantastic news, Jack!"

"Wow, congrats, Jack!" Banks replied. "Best news I've heard in a while."

He grinned. "Best news I've had in a long while. Gotta make sure she's safe and happy." His voice choked up. "She means everything to me."

Banks chuckled. "Casey's got it bad. An incurable case of love."

Gianni nodded. "It's great to see the two of you together at last. She's absolutely crazy about you, Jack."

"And she'd go to the ends of the Earth for you," said Banks.

Jack sighed. "She already has, Banks. Twice. I hope I'm worth all her sacrifices."

"Jack…" said Gianni, hands sliding away from his shoulders.

The pain throbbed through his left shoulder, bandages already wet with blood again.

"I watched you get into a ring with hands so damaged you couldn't even grip a sword and fight a man almost twice your size for her. Knowing that he would probably kill you."

Banks' eyes grew wide and he glanced from Gianni to Jack. "When was that?"

"Did you watch The Prince Charming Hour, Mark?" Gianni asked, still fixing Jack with his gaze.

"I did." Then he let out a hiss of breath. "Wow, you mean to tell me that when Casey fought that guy in a duel for Talia's favor, it wasn't just a scripted event?"

Gianni shook his head in a slow, deliberate shake. "He slipped a couple of real swords on set. Used one that almost killed a competitor." He pointed at Jack. "Jack, here saw the glint and lunged under the ropes. And grabbed the blade. Otherwise, Zac Piersoll would have gone home in a body bag."

Banks was silent for a moment, wincing. "Seriously? You grabbed a sharp blade in motion?"

Jack nodded and ran his hand through his hair, remembering the pain. "I had on fencing gloves, but that blade cut deep."

Banks grabbed his right wrist and turned over his hand. The pink gash was still there, healing well, but still visible. It would be for a long time, leaving a scar. Jack turned over his left hand. Another healing gash.

"Damn, Casey!" Banks said with a gasp.

"With his hands slashed to bits, he and I fought our way through the finals. And a fight with Bellamy. And his real sword. Jack ran circles around him and we defeated his team for the win. But then Bellamy reminded the world that he'd challenged Jack to a duel if Jack won."

Banks was shaking his head, looking shocked.

"Thought I was going to die. I even told Talia goodbye. I figured I'd bleed out right there in front of the cameras."

"Damn, Jack," said Banks. "That's brutal."

"It was. Dude almost killed me."

Banks began to smile at him now. "Man, you deserve every accolade you got for that episode. I had no idea." He patted him on the back. "But you are the King of unscripted moments."

"Mark, you ready? We need to setup for the party." Morgan. From across the room.

"Gotta go. You guys are coming, aren't you?"

Gianni nodded.

"Wouldn't miss it," said Jack. "And if I did, Talia probably wouldn't speak to me if she missed time with Morgan and Izzy. Gonna be tough competing against good friends like this."

"No, it's better this way," said Gianni. "I already know who's got my back out there. And after The Prince Charming Hour, that's a very good thing."

"Armand," Izzy called to him. "I'm ready when you are."

"Agreed," said Banks. He leaned in close so only Jack and Gianni heard him. "And judging by the ugliness I saw tonight, I think Jack's gonna need us both."

Gianni nodded and it choked Jack up.

"Thank you, guys," he got out, his voice tight and broken. "Really means a lot to me."

Banks took a step back, his voice loud enough that the whole room heard him. "You got tons of the right kind of friends watching your back, Jack."

He chuckled and bumped Banks' shoulder with his fist. "Thanks, dude. Thanks, Gianni. You guys are the best."

He felt warm arms slide around his waist. "Jack? Do you want to go to the party?"

He turned. Staring into those luminous grey eyes made him lose his heart all over again.

"You're dying to walk along the beach, aren't you?"

She nodded. "With you."

He'd have walked barefoot through glass if she'd asked him to. "Can't wait to share some moonlight and beach with you," he said in a soft voice and kissed her.

She took hold of his hand. "Let's go then."

He laughed. "You heard the lady. See you guys shortly."

"Morgan got permission to change the bulbs on the lights leading down to the beach to purple," Mark replied. "So, follow the royal path to the beach, lords and ladies."

Jack bowed. "By your leave," he said and let Talia pull him toward the narrow hallway that zigzagged past two suites to the end of the hall.

To their suite. The six-paneled white door had a framed photo of the Breckenridge slopes and the word, Breckenridge in big gold letters. Jack unlocked the door and Talia pulled him inside.

She tugged him over to the couch and sat him down. He frowned when he saw the rolls of thick bandages, gauze, scissors, and the big tube of antibiotic ointment.

She grinned at him as she sat down on the coffee table in front of him and began unzipping his hoodie.

"This isn't how this moment was going to go in my head," he complained, wincing as she slipped the hoodie off his shoulders.

"Nobody noticed the blood on your hoodie," she said, picking up a roll of gauze. "But me. You need a little attention before the party."

He smirked at her as he leaned forward and slid his arms around her, pulling her close.

"Yes, I do," he said in a raspy whisper as he slowly pressed his mouth to hers.

Talia dropped the roll of gauze on the table, both arms sliding around him as she returned his kiss. Anxious, deep kisses, but she pulled back, her left hand bloody.

He cursed under his breath, letting her go as she reached for his T-shirt, rolling it up and over his head.

"No pouting," she said with a smile, one hand against his chest, stroking. "Your shoulder needs attention."

"So does the rest of me," he said as he felt her hand pull away.

And then she was cutting away the soaked bandage on his shoulder. It fell away as her mouth found his again. Another anxious kiss.

"All in good time," she said with a smirk.

"Tease," he said.

She laughed as she squeezed antibiotic ointment onto the huge, bloody bite, teeth marks on both sides of his shoulder. Then she laid a large, thick gauze pad across it. With the ointment clinging to the pad, she wound an elastic bandage around his bicep, under his arm, and over shoulder. Then around his back and across his chest, over the shoulder. And around his arm again. To keep it all in place. Then she used three clips to secure it.

"There," she said, rubbing his other shoulder. "That should help."

He made a face. Wincing.

"What's wrong?" she asked.

"Hurts," he said with a groan.

A look of concern washed across her face, intensified those grey eyes. "What can I do?"

"I think it still needs attention," he said.

She laid her hand against the clips. "I'll wrap it tighter."

"Allow me," he said, wrapping her in his arms, tight against his chest.

And kissed her. A slow, steamy kiss, his lips kissing her neck and nibbling her ear until she was gasping for breath.

Her cheeks flushed, hair bunched up around her neck, eyes wide. Mouth open.

She tried to say his name, but all that came out was a gasp of breath. Then she grabbed his face and smashed her mouth against his in a fiery kiss. His hands slid under that Van Halen T-shirt, cupping her breasts as she pressed him down against the couch, the weight of her body against his, her heart pounding like a drum kit.

He rolled her against the couch, pushing off that T-shirt in his way, fingers tangling in her hair as he sipped her hot mouth with deep, frantic kisses. He slid his hand across her soft, firm stomach in gentle strokes, across her hips. Up her thigh. Underneath that red skirt.

She gasped and grabbed hold of him with both hands, her face a mixture of shock and ecstasy.

The blur of wings startled him. He sat up as Anahera and then Muriel landed in the middle of the suite.

Sighing, he sank back against the couch cushion as Talia pushed the Van Halen T-shirt back down. She crossed her arms and glared at the two angels of death.

"You have the worst timing ever," she said.

Jack burst out laughing.

Muriel's face turned red and Anahera started laughing. "Okay, you've just embarrassed an angel of death. That took some work."

Talia's eyes narrowed. "No, it didn't," she said, glaring. "Just the worst timing ever did it. Timing is everything for an angel of death! Remember, Muriel? And our special abilities to see and touch the time stream give us extraordinary timing." She glared at her again. "Except *this* time."

Jack struggled not to snort he was laughing so hard.

Muriel sighed. "I'm never going to live this down."

"That's what eternity is for," said Talia.

Jack held his left shoulder, trying not to jar it from laughing so hard.

Talia's gaze snapped to him and the anger still burned in those grey eyes. Now aimed at him.

"And you," she said, "what ever happened to the Jack Casey nerves of ice?"

He struggled not to laugh. "Melted. Like a snowball in Hell the moment I saw movement. Sorry, but angels of death, assassin demons, and hellhounds are still on my *holy shit, what was that* list."

She was still glaring him, arms crossed.

"Don't blame me. You're the one that said I needed a little attention."

Her face turned as red as her skirt. And then the fire lit her grey eyes, the angry glare hitting him in the face. And so did the big coral pillow from the couch as she stomped away from him and slammed the bathroom door.

Okay, so maybe poking an already grumpy angel of death wasn't a good idea.

He looked up. Muriel and Anahera were laughing. "You are so dead, Jack," said Muriel with a snort.

"She's not going to smite me, is she?" he asked with a groan.

"Lucky for you she doesn't have her death angel powers right now," said Anahera.

He nodded. "Yeah, that look was locked and loaded, ready to kill. Guess I'm going to the party alone. And sleeping on the couch."

Muriel let out a snort. "If you're lucky."

"Unless you apologize," said Anahera, trying to help.

Jack shook his head, waving his right hand toward the bathroom door. "I think I'd rather take my chances with Cerberus," he said and rose from the couch.

Muriel was nodding. "Good plan."

He got up and opened one of his suitcases. He pulled out a black hoodie and a black T-shirt. He unfolded it. A Black Sabbath T-shirt. He stared at the shirt and rolled his eyes. Heaven and Hell. With angels smoking.

"Not funny anymore," he snapped and jerked it over his head.

He heard Muriel laugh again as he zipped up his hoodie and with a stiff shoulder, he opened the suite door and paused, not turning around. He hoped Talia would stop being pissed at him long enough to know that it wasn't his fault he could see her squad mates.

"Muriel," he called. "If Talia ever comes out of the bathroom, tell her I'm down at the party. Waiting to take that walk along the beach. If she'll still let me."

"I'll tell her, Jack," said Muriel as he closed the door.

13

Talia pressed a cold washcloth against her face as she sat in the spotless white marble bathroom. It had a huge glass shower with silver and turquoise tiles and a smooth river rock floor. And a dozen little shower heads. Beside it, a huge, deep tub shimmered white and two rectangular, white sinks with tall, silver spouts that hung above them. A huge, framed mirror stretched above both sinks, the gold frame interwoven with leaves and flowers. A small room with only a toilet was just inside the room on the left.

She couldn't halt the tears of frustration and embarrassment tumbling down her cheeks. His touch had sizzled along her skin, igniting her in ways she'd never even imagined. Sensations she never knew existed. She loved the feel of his bare skin against hers, ached to feel his body pressed against hers.

And then Muriel and Anahera barged in and ruined everything. The most private moment she'd ever known. Interrupted. Why hadn't Jack understood that?

She'd been too embarrassed to let it go. And then she'd yelled at him. He was the last person she'd wanted to yell at. She wanted to kick herself for that. He was probably fuming at her right now. How could she ever face him?

It was so quiet out there now. Had he fallen asleep or just walked out and left her in the bathroom? Were Anahera and Muriel still out there?

Finally, she couldn't stand the silence and crept out of the bathroom. The suite was dark except for the light from the west window and a lamp beside the couch.

The empty couch. Her heart dropped into her feet. He was gone.

She brushed the fold of Jack's Van Halen T-shirt down over her skirt and walked over to the window. The sun was hanging low over the ocean, stretching golden fingers across the cliffs and the waves, casting a shimmery glow along the beach.

"Talia?"

She turned around.

Sad-eyed, Muriel stood behind her.

Talia couldn't find any response. She shook her head, face scrunching up.

"Sorry for just showing up like that. High House made a bad impression on me. I didn't stop to think that you two are sharing this room. And that maybe I should knock first. Or look first. I am an angel of death."

"I overreacted, Muriel," she said, bowing her head. "I'm sorry. And I yelled at poor Jack over nothing. He was doing everything right and I just blamed him for everything." She sighed. "He probably hates me now."

Muriel took her by the shoulders. "He hates me now, not you."

Talia's gaze snapped up. "You? Why does he hate you?"

She snickered, a devious smile lighting her face. "I keep messing with his T-shirts."

Talia shook her head. "What does that mean?"

"Every time he pulls out a T-shirt, I just…well, rearrange them. So, he picks one with an angel on it. Or it says something about Heaven or Hell."

Talia burst out laughing. "Muriel…that's—hilarious."

"Yeah, it kind of is, isn't it?" Muriel said with a laugh. "Hey, angels of death have to have some fun, right?"

Talia's eyes turned sad again. "He's gone, isn't he?"

"He told me to tell you that he went down to the party. And he's ready to take you on that walk along the beach. If you'll let him."

She smiled. "Then he's not mad at me."

"Heavens no. He laughed. Made a joke. Changed shirts and told me to tell you where he was. After he yelled at me about the shirt."

Talia burst out laughing.

"Told you he was a keeper," Muriel said and nudged her toward the suitcases with her shoulder. "Now, go pick out a top that's going to explode his brain and wear it to the beach. Anahera and I are going to investigate the house and grounds and start chaining Holy shields together. Keep out as many demons as we can. Prepare the guard for the ones that slip through." She sighed. "And pray about the ones already here. Without someone to lead the guard, we've gotta come up with a strategy to go with our defenses."

Talia reached out and hugged Muriel "Thank you. I'm sorry I was so angry."

Muriel hugged her back. "Sorry for interrupting. Now, go knock his socks off."

———

IN THE TWO suitcases that Muriel and Anahera brought for her, she found a bunch of blouses. The one that caught her eye was a lightweight red blouse with what Muriel called cold shoulders. It had spaghetti straps, a V-neck, and deep cutout shoulders that flowed into loose chiffon sleeves that flared at the wrists. The back was cut low. She peeled off Jack's Van Halen T-shirt and shimmied into the blouse.

"Perfect!" Anahera cried.

Muriel squinted. "Almost," she said.

She reached out to the skirt and touched the waist band. The color red adjusted to match the blouse perfectly. She added a thin, gold chain belt that hung in rings around her hips.

"There." Muriel nodded toward the door. "Now, go drink some

champagne with Jack and watch him lose his mind." She motioned Anahera upward. "We'll just come back tomorrow morning. Late."

Talia laughed and grabbed her key off the coffee table. And rushed toward the door.

***

IT TOOK A FEW TURNS, but Talia found her way out of the house and toward a little sign that read, Beach. Just ahead of her, Claire Olsen clopped toward the path that led behind the garage, wearing flip flops, a blue sweater, and black shorts.

Talia rushed toward the path, keeping Claire in her sights as the path wound through rocks and wild flowers toward the beach below. Already, she heard the rush of waves and voices, laughter rising.

Purple lights lit the path all the way to the bottom. And the soft, sugary sand that flattened into a half moon of beach between towering basalt cliffs. A fire pit flickered below, the scent of charcoal and brine rising in the cool air. Clink of glasses. Pop of a cork.

She picked up the pace, her black flats clapping against the asphalt walkway. She glanced down at her feet. Correction, gold flats. Courtesy of Muriel's fashion sense.

When she reached the beach, she found a dozen folding chairs, a folding table, and large cooler arranged around a fire pit. Glass champagne flutes stood on the table in a rack, two bottles of cold champagne opened and out on the table beside a plate of strawberries and thin-sliced, white cheese squares.

Mark and Morgan filled glasses and passed them out. Izzy waved at her from one of the chairs, Armand Gianni beside her. Eric and Ryder sat in the circle, Claire and Riya talking softly in chairs beside them. Tyler and Nicole stood beside Rachel and Lare at the fire pit.

Where was Jack?

Morgan saw her and motioned her over. "Talia! Glad you're finally here," she said, grinning, as she handed her a glass of cold champagne.

"Where's Jack?" she asked.

Mark pointed past the fire pit. In the glow of the flames, she saw his silhouette at the edge of the water. Sleeves of his hoodie fluttered, hands in his pockets. Staring out at the water.

Mark squinted at Jack and then back at Talia.

"Everything okay?"

She nodded and took a drink of the champagne. For courage. "He promised me he'd take a walk along the beach with me. I've never seen the Pacific Ocean."

Mark frowned. "Thought you were from Alaska."

"The interior," she said. "And when I was four, we moved to Germany. And Norway after that. I've only been here in California a few months."

"Well, welcome home," said Mark, smiling. He handed her another glass of champagne. "Here, Jack'll need one, too."

"Thanks," she said and walked past the chairs, waving at Armand and Izzy as she headed across the sand toward Jack.

Walking in sand was hard and she struggled across until she touched the smoother, wet sand. But her shoes sank a little with every step. As she got closer, she caught a whiff of his cedary cologne and it set her alight at the memory of his body against hers, his lips against her mouth, hands against her breasts.

"Jack?"

He seemed a million miles away, watching the waves wash across the sand.

"Jack!" she called, louder, shouting above the wind and the waves.

At last, he turned, watching her with those sexy, light green eyes, his blond hair windblown like he'd just woken up, watching her with sleepy eyes and that playful smirk that made her want to smash her mouth against his.

"Sorry about—well, before," he said, hands still in his pockets. "I didn't mean to—"

She rushed up to him, her body against him and leaned up, kissing him hard on the mouth.

"It was my fault," she said in a quiet voice. "Don't you dare apologize."

That smirk bloomed into a smile as he leaned toward her,

returning her kiss. He pressed his mouth to her ear, whispering, "you're smokin' hot in that blouse by the way."

She grinned and kissed him again as she slid a glass of champagne into his hand. She took a sip of champagne and he kissed her lips again, sipping them in gentle kisses as the bubbles tickled her throat. He slammed his glass of champagne and kissed her again. Harder. Deeper. His arms slid around her, pulling her against him.

"I was afraid you were gonna stay mad at me," he whispered in her ear.

She kissed him again. "I could never stay mad at you. But this time, I was just mad at myself."

He shook his head, brow creasing. "Yourself? Why?"

"Because I was embarrassed."

He bowed his head. "Of me?"

She pressed his chin up and gripped it between her fingers. "Never, Jack Casey. Do you hear me? I've been proud of you from the first day I saw you staring at me across that studio stage."

He forced a smile. "Why would you be proud of me?"

"Because you've fought your way back from everything," she said and let go of his chin. "I was embarrassed because I was enjoying every touch and every sensation. And I wanted more. I wanted you to make love to me, Jack. Only you."

At last, he smiled.

She drank the last sip of champagne and wrapped her arms around his waist, careful not to bump his left shoulder.

"Ready for that walk?" he asked, laying his hand against her face, his fingers so warm and comforting against her cold cheeks.

"Thought you'd never ask."

SHE AND JACK walked up and down the small beach a few times and she picked up a couple of seashells and two pieces of pale green sea glass, reminding her of Jack's eyes. Arm in arm, they walked back to the party and got refills of champagne. She led him over to the folding chairs where everyone else sat. There were two empty chairs between Mark and Armand that she and Jack claimed.

"'Bout time you, lovebirds joined us," said Mark with a grin as he slid his arm around Morgan.

The fire pit crackled, scent of charcoal rising above the cold scent of sea spray and surge of waves along the beach.

"I promised her a long walk on the beach," said Jack, sipping his champagne. "A toast to Banks and Morgan for such a nice party."

He held his glass up and everyone lifted theirs into the air. Talia bristled. Except for Rachel and Lare. And Tyler and Nicole who kept their distance at the fire pit.

She was used to rude from Rachel Daniels. She hadn't expected her associates to behave any differently. Especially because it was Jack doing the toasting.

Morgan grabbed the cooler and pulled it over to the ring of chairs. Mark pulled out another bottle of champagne, popped the cork, and passed it around the circle. It was cold and crisp and every sip was like pouring summer in a glass and sipping it.

"I heard that we start the first challenge tomorrow," Eric replied, leaning into the group.

Ryder settled back in his chair and smiled at Claire who seemed a little taken by Ryder's blond good looks.

"Any idea what kind of challenge?" Ryder asked.

"Please don't let it be swords," Jack said with a groan.

Everybody laughed.

Armand patted him on the back. "I think Jack's earned the right to win an automatic exemption from any other sword challenges."

Almost everyone nodded.

"Yeah, Jack, that was a crazy story Armand told," said Mark.

Ryder pointed at Jack. "You wanna see crazy? Check out the footage of him grabbing that crazy Bellamy dude's sword as he plunged it toward Piersoll's face." He shuddered. "I can't even imagine how much that hurt. We all thought it was just the dull practice swords, but when blood started dripping from your shredded gloves, we all freaked out."

Jack bowed his head. "I couldn't let that bastard shish-kabob Piersoll right in front of me. I had to do something. Didn't have a clue how bad it was gonna hurt. Probably a good thing or I might have wimped out."

People winced and shook their heads.

"Casey, you're one crazy brave dude," said Eric.

Jack laughed. "Well, you're half right."

"I want to wish all of you the best of luck," said Eric, glancing down at his champagne glass. "I'm actually glad to see most of you return. You were standup guys, not backstabbing players like I expected. And you even tried to help when you could. That impressed me."

"Same, Saunders," said Ryder, lifting a glass. "A toast to people with integrity."

Everyone lifted their glasses.

"And I look forward to kicking every one of your asses, starting tomorrow," said Ryder.

The group laughed and drank their champagne, but Talia couldn't help glancing over at the fire pit where Rachel and Lare talked in quiet voices that didn't carry. And she wondered what they were already plotting to do to Jack. They had no integrity and would do anything and everything to harm him. She needed to tell him about his costars from *SanFran Confidential*. He still didn't know that Rachel was actively trying to kill him to save Laren Dumont's show and collect Jack's soul for Lucifer.

Jack didn't know the depths of their depravity yet. How they got money for their little projects or how they became stars. She had to make sure their operation stopped with Jack.

IT WAS after midnight when the party broke up. Jack and Armand helped Mark carry the cooler and table back to the estate while Ryder, Riya, and Eric brought up the chairs. Talia, Izzy, and Claire helped Morgan gather the glasses and empty bottles, taking them back to the house. Leaving Rachel and Lare with Tyler and Nicole, all of them still plotting around the fire pit. It made her queasy and she wished she could hear what they'd been saying all night.

And she wondered if they'd already managed to fix the game in their favor. Or worse. She worried the game had all been a big setup—by Lucifer—to get Jack back here and finish the job they started four years ago.

Were they truly Lucifer's minions or was this just Rachel Daniels and her partners plotting? Or was all of this an elaborate plan for Lucifer to get to her?

She still didn't understand why Lucifer was so fixated on her. It was more than just winning those wagers—that he had cheated his way through. No other angel would have honored his win.

Why had Azrael?

But now, she knew that Azrael had a reason to play into this whole debacle. He had planned to trap a forger and protect God's Scribe, but what was her role in all of this? And Jack's?

She needed to know. And she and Jack had to keep running from Lucifer until they found a way out of a one-way trip to Hell.

Jack was quiet when they returned to the room. When he closed the door behind him, he looked around the suite. Looking for Muriel and Anahera, she realized. She kept forgetting that he could see them now. She was used to angels just flitting past humans right and left without being seen or noticed. But it unnerved her every time Jack saw Muriel or the death angels from the guard enter a room. It was probably way more unnerving for him.

"Everything okay?" she asked as he walked over to the coffee table and laid the key on it.

"Fine," he said. "Why?"

"You're looking for angels, aren't you?" she asked, kicking off her gold flats beside the turquoise couch.

"Demons and hellhounds, too," he added. "Among other things."

"I can imagine," she said and moved over to him, rubbing his left forearm. "How's the shoulder?"

"Hurts," he said.

She reached over and unzipped his hoodie, opening it up. A dark patch of dampness seeped into the sleeve of his T-shirt at the shoulder, feeling a little stiff. Even through the heavy gauze pad she'd put there.

"It's still bleeding," she said, letting go of his hoodie.

He nodded, glancing past her. Around the room. He seemed a little distant and that worried her. Then she realized. He was dreading the night in this room. Remembering all those parties. His blackouts had been during nights in this house. He was probably afraid that just being here would awaken a flood of memories he wasn't ready to handle.

"Is it the night time here that's bothering you?" she asked. Might as well get it out there, to see if he'd talk about it.

His eyes widened. "What? How'd you know that?"

"Angel of death here," she said. "We have the ability to sense some things, Jack."

He shrugged. "If you already know, why ask me?"

"Because I don't know. I'm just sensing that you're bothered by the night and being in this room."

"You're partly right," he said with a sigh, rubbing his hand through his hair. "I'm afraid that being here will bring back the coke fiend I used to be. Or that Rachel will…"

He didn't know that she'd seen his whole fight against doing all that coke during *The Prince Charming Hour.* Would he talk about it?

"Will what?" she said in a soft voice and slid her arms around him, holding him close.

"Turn me back onto the flake again." His sigh was long and heavy this time. "And make me lose everything." His voice quivered. "Including you."

"She can't make you lose me, Jack," she said, laying her face against his back, that trace of cedar warming her all over.

He turned her toward him, staring into her eyes. "If they get me back onto the coke, you wouldn't turn your back on me?"

He needed to know that she wouldn't leave him in his moment of greatest failure. Like everyone else in his life.

"Of course not, Jack," she insisted. "I'd be here to help you get through it again." She shook him when he started to look away. "Listen to me! Being addicted is a lifelong battle. It isn't a switch you just turn on or off. And there may be times when you fall, Jack, but I'm not like everyone else. I'll be there to help you up, good or bad."

"Why would you do that?" he demanded, looking so angry and helpless.

Expecting her to give up on him like everyone else.

"Because I love you."

He tried to smile. Couldn't. "I love you, too, Talia."

She slid her arms around his neck. "You saw me at my very worst, Jack. My lowest point. When you found out my horrible secret." She bowed her head a moment. "I thought you'd just walk away at that point, but you stayed at my side. You held me all night in your arms, trying to heal me. You fought Lucifer for me. You fought demons and hellhounds for me. And you fought a crazy, possessed, sword-wielding guy that you were certain was going to kill you to stay with me."

At last, the corners of his mouth lifted.

"You've proven how much you love me and that you'll stay," she said, hands rubbing his neck, stroking his hair. "How could I do any less for the man that I love? In some of his worst moments?"

"Do I know this dude?"

She laughed and gently kissed him on the lips. And just held him.

14

THE NEXT MORNING, JACK WORK UP EARLY, THE WORLD STILL DARK, BUT Talia was already up and in the shower. He felt tired after bad dreams had interrupted his sleep.

Snippets of memories in this house.

Music a dull, persistent roar. Dizzy, blacking out.

Leering grins. Laughter.

Passed from one set of hands to another, walls twisting out of proportion, floors tilting.

Numb. Senses blunted. Riding wave after wave of euphoria. So far gone he couldn't speak.

Couldn't use his hands. Couldn't protest.

Struggling to purse his lips and shout no, but all that came out was air.

It wasn't a dream. It was a memory. And it made him shake all over.

He got up, barefoot, wearing only blue boxer briefs, and padded across the hardwood. Toward the white marble bathroom left of the bed.

Light from the bathroom filtered into the dark suite. Bright and ethereal. Reminding him of the first time he saw angels of death fight demons. Shower jets hissed in the quiet, falling like rain against the smooth stone floor.

Talia was in the shower. He smiled, wanting to join her.

He stepped into the steamy bathroom, mirror fogged, warm mist hanging in the air. The glass doors of the shower had all fogged up too, silhouetting Talia's shapely body as water rushed over every curve and every lean muscle.

"Talia," he called, moving toward the door.

He opened the shower door, grinning at her.

And she began to change. Hair turning flaming auburn, grey eyes too blue.

He backed away as horns budded out on her forehead and her feet became split hooves. Rachel leered back at him, a leathery pointed tail twitching through the water. As she began to laugh at him.

"Welcome home, Jack!" she called out to him. "We missed you! Welcome back to the party."

She blew white powder in his face and grabbed his arms. Pulling him into the shower as the bottom dropped. And he was falling.

He fell into darkness and brimstone, lit only by Hellfires burning bright and orange all around him. Until the cast of *SanFran Confidential* surrounded him. Shoving white powder in his face. Passing him around like their plaything, hands groping him.

He tried to shout Talia's name. Tried to shout no. Nothing came out but a scream.

And he was back in his bed. Shouting.

He forced himself up onto the side of the bed, shaking, sweating. It was still dark.

It had been a dream.

"Jack?"

Talia's sleepy voice whispered beside him. Like she was almost human.

His heart smashed against his rib cage. It made him so sad. Would she stay like this or would she eventually turn back into an angel of death like her friends? With terrible fire in her eyes? Able to stop his heart with a thought or cut him down with a scythe like the stupid cartoons of death? And those wings at her back, free to soar away from this desolate place at any moment. Leaving him earthbound for his short life as he aged and she didn't.

Why would a being like that want to be tied to a short, ordinary life with someone that could never learn to soar? At some point, she'd return to her world, leaving him behind. And there was nothing he could do to stop it. He loved her more than his own life, but right now, that felt like it would only last months.

With Lucifer, demons, and hellhounds after him, not to mention Rachel trying to get him back on the flake, he might only have weeks. At most. He felt like a condemned man.

"Jack?" she called to him again.

Hands slid around his waist, cool against his over-warmed skin as she laid her face against his back.

"What is it?" she asked in a soft, loving voice.

Her voice made him hurt all over. He just wanted to love her, to spend the rest of their lives together, but she was forever and he was just a spark in time. Just one sparkler burning itself out on some lonely beach in a sea of fireworks. Then she'd move onto the next soul. Forgetting he was ever here at all.

"Nightmare," he said in a gravelly voice, doing his damnedest to hold it all inside.

He couldn't tell her any of this. It would break her heart. And it would break his to give it a voice. Was there an ever after even possible for them? Or were these stray moments all they had? A few weeks at a time at best?

Could he even fight this? Fight forces he never knew existed until a few days ago.

Her grip tightened around him. "Do you want to talk about it?"

He shook his head and laid his right hand on hers, squeezing. "Then you couldn't sleep either."

She laughed, the sound like wind chimes in summer and it made him ache all over. He only wanted to stay with her, grow old with her, and love her through it all—fight anything and everything that tried to separate them.

But this? How could he fight immortal, paranormal creatures? And the Prince of Darkness, something he never thought existed? Evil was this dude's business and business was booming.

"Why don't you try to get some more sleep?" she said, her hand sliding up to his neck, stroking.

"Can't," he said, rising from the bed, her hands slipping away.

He felt like he was already losing her. Slowly. In inches and feet. Besides, if she ever saw him truly for what he was, saw him blitzed out of his mind on flake, her feelings would cool like a hot beer can in a subzero freezer.

And he already felt his resolve slipping. The memories in this house filtered their way into his brain, whispering, taunting. Playing on the deep, sweltering ache to do one more line. Burn with euphoria. Explode with that burst of energy that made him feel like he was king of the world. On top of his game. Invincible.

In this house, it was non-stop. Inescapable. And he feared it would slowly break him down. Into pieces.

She'd have no choice but to walk away when she realized she could never pick them all up again. Much less put them back together.

"I'm going for a run on the beach," he said. "I'll be back."

"Be careful, Jack," she said as he grabbed his blue running shorts off the dresser.

He pulled them on, and slid into his Vans. He zipped the room key in the front pocket and headed into the dark hallway.

15

TALIA, DRESSED IN A SHORT JEAN SKIRT, PINK TANK TOP, AND A WHITE half sweater, sat beside Jack at the first film shoot for *The Ever After Hour*. He wore jeans that were a little loose, an olive-green Henley, and tan loafers. The faraway, sad look in his eyes vanished the moment he sat down beside her at one end of a white leather couch in the sprawling living room that overlooked the ocean. He was now Jack Casey the actor in front of these people. Putting up the wall he'd kept there on every season of the reality TV show.

Protecting himself from any more hurt, she realized, wanting only to put herself between him and the horrible people that still wanted to hurt him. Including Lucifer.

Three couches stood in front of a huge white marble fireplace, end tables made of driftwood on both sides of each couch. In front of the fireplace, Rachel and Lare sat on a turquoise loveseat. A wall of windows let in swaths of light that pooled along the maple hardwood floors and a curved half-wall that separated dining room and kitchen from the rest of the space.

The room smelled like eucalyptus and the ocean with a touch of lemon, but the scent of frying bacon sizzled behind them.

Devin Van Fossen stood in the center of the room where a coffee table had been moved. He wore a dark blue, shiny suit jacket and khakis, a coral shirt underneath the jacket. His highlighted brown hair was stiff and unmoving as he flashed a toothy, over-white smile at everyone. He wore a wireless mic like all of them had been fitted with before entering the room, battery pack clipped to the back of pants and skirts.

Cameras were installed throughout the house and crew still tested some of them on ladders in the large open space. From the living area, Talia could see almost the entire house. Except for the upstairs bedrooms where Rachel and Lare slept. And another suite that Talia assumed housed Tyler Hughes and Nicole Reardon.

Fine with her that they were all in one place. Made it easier for the guard to watch them. And it kept them far away from Jack.

Behind them were shoulder-mounted cameras and three crew members handling them. Steve and Jennifer worked with Roy and Bill and a woman she'd never met handling those cameras. Herb sat in his director's chair, watching the first event unfold for the cameras.

Talia was nervous. This competition would be very different from the others, but being partnered with Jack made it all bearable. They had to win and keep winning until Muriel got to Azrael. Behind the chained ward shields setup by the guard, it was the closest thing to a castle fortress they had. Even with Rachel and Lare inside it—where they could be monitored.

Jennifer Collins walked up beside Devin Van Fossen, clipboard in her hand. She wore a green dress and black heels, dark hair in a ponytail, red glasses balanced on her delicate nose.

"Good morning, royal couples," said Devin, still grinning as he looked around the room. "So many familiar faces." He pointed at Mark Banks who sat on the couch to the right. "Mark Banks! Good to see you back. And still with Morgan."

"Good to be back, Devin," he said as Morgan smiled at the show's host.

"And Ryder Kurland back in an arranged marriage," said Devin, "and the fair princess, Claire from season one. I hope this match works out for you."

She smiled and said thank you, shoulder length brown hair dyed a bold red shade that accentuated her blue eyes.

Devin glanced across at the other couch where Eric and Riya sat beside Tyler and Nicole.

"Eric Saunders, back in an arranged marriage, too. Good to see you again."

"Good to see you, too, Devin," said Eric with a deep nod.

Devin turned toward the loveseat. "And Rachel Daniels, so good to see you here with your partner, the famous Laren Dumont. Lare, it's a pleasure to meet you. We are so fortunate to be filming here in your beautiful estate."

"Good to meet you, Devin," said Lare, his voice deep and penetrating, a charming smile on his long face. With his smoldering good looks, rich brown hair, and mahogany eyes, he looked like a television star.

But there was something dark in his eyes. Cruel and deceiving in a handsome, heroic way. He looked much older than Jack who still held onto his baby-faced looks even at twenty-six. He still looked barely twenty. Rachel was six years older than Jack who said she had aged from several procedures. To him, she looked forty with all the pulled and tucked skin, the sharp angles looking aged not chiseled.

The deals with Lucifer must not have included beauty, otherwise she'd have looked perfect. By human standards, she was still beautiful, but Talia couldn't see past her ugliness. And the memory of the things she'd done to Jack.

Rachel and Laren Dumont must hate that Jack still looked like that twenty-year-old kid they'd tried to ruin and end. They enjoyed ruining innocents. That was their hobby. And their business, even collecting valuables and antiques when their protégés offed themselves or self-destructed. To them, Jack was the one that got away. Was that why they were so hell-bent on destroying him? Now that she and Jack were together, she knew Lucifer had to be pushing them hard to deliver her to him through Jack.

"Armand and Izzy, one of our other success stories," said Devin, studying the couple who sat at the other end of the couch that she and Jack occupied.

"Yes, we are," said Izzy, smiling at Armand who leaned over and kissed her.

At last, Devin's gaze settled on her and Jack.

"And Jack Casey! Ratings juggernaut and fairytale hero of The Prince Charming Hour. With the beautiful princess, Talia. At last. Good to see you back with Talia at your side. It's been a pleasure watching both of you grow into this moment."

Jack glanced at her, smiling now, game face slipping. "She's my life," he said in such a quiet, aching voice that it made her eyes mist. "Now, that she's finally in my arms, I'm never letting go."

He leaned over and kissed her in a lingering kiss as he slid his stiff left arm around her. She pressed against him, hand against his chest, careful not to lean back against that shoulder.

"The show's viewers are going to love watching you and Talia work together on the challenges." Devin flashed them another smile and Talia felt no fakeness or agenda behind it. The show's host meant what he said. "I know I will. And I hope I don't have to watch you fight for your life again, Jack. I don't think this show will ever stop apologizing to you for Bellamy sneaking in real swords."

"Forget it," said Jack, smiling as he looked at Talia. "I lived and I got the girl, so happily ever after."

Talia turned Jack's face toward her and kissed him. "A match made in heaven," she said with a wink. His smile widened into a grin.

"Even after that left turn through Hell." He winked back at her.

"Well, we hope to take better care of our biggest star this time, Jack."

Talia glanced over at Rachel and Lare, watching the dark burn that ignited within them. Lare's eyes narrowed, his mouth twisting as Rachel openly glared at Jack. Talia was relieved that he wasn't looking at them. Didn't see the unbridled malice burning in their eyes, on their faces.

They hated Jack for his success.

Then she understood. Jealousy. They hated Jack for succeeding on his own. With nothing but hard work and persistence. Sure, he was immensely talented. And drop dead gorgeous. But hard work and persistence were much longer paths. To them, Jack's success was all luck, but they never saw his hard work throughout high school, performing nights at the theatre and working his way through college. And the staggering student loans.

When he moved to Los Angeles, he was already a seasoned stage actor with several commercials under his belt from working summers in the business. And he hit it big in early auditions, but for Jack, that long road of hard work and persistence continued after he got fired. Coming back from a near fatal fall and taking a chance on something crazy. Like this reality TV show. And her. He fought his way back, becoming the top ratings draw in the country for two seasons now.

And they hated him for that hard-earned success because they both had to sell their souls to achieve half of what he had. And he was younger, too.

She'd practically memorized Jack's Book of Life and Death. She knew all about him.

She didn't have a life to record and share with him. She was an angel of death who'd lived centuries, taking souls, and preempting premature deaths. She wondered if Jack even knew her at all. Not that he hadn't tried, but she didn't even know who she was now—after losing her identity and her wings.

"Just keep the sharp things in their cases and we'll be good," said Jack.

"Even the razor blades, Casey?" Lare asked, snickering.

Rachel laughed out loud, Tyler and Nicole chuckling.

A slow burn began in Jack, the smile gone. But she felt the pain behind that stone face. He was still very vulnerable to the drugs and fighting so hard against the pull. And they loved twisting that knife another turn—every chance they got.

"You mean the ones cutting all of you to pieces with your own jealousy?" Armand replied, glaring at the four of them.

Mark busted out laughing as Jack's mouth turned up at the

corners. He made eye contact with Armand and smiled at him, gratitude shining in his eyes.

Armand gave him a nod. She loved how Armand and Mark had rallied to Jack's side. She knew that he wasn't used to it. But the three of them had bonded through *The Cinderella Hour*. Armand became a close friend to Jack by the end of *The Prince Charming Hour*. And he'd emerged as Jack's staunchest defender against these jerks.

"Let's keep things civil, please," said Devin as he nodded at Armand.

Nodding his approval, Talia realized.

"Now, today we begin the first competition of the game," said Devin, gazing around the room. "The first competition will challenge your knowledge of each other as a couple and it has three parts. Called past, present, and future. For the past portion, each couple will draw six questions from the crown, questions about their partner. A point for every correct answer."

Jack glanced at her, fear in his eyes.

He was worried because he knew so little about her life. But he didn't realize there wasn't a lot to tell. Before she met him. Would they be able to get through these questions together?

"All of you answered these questions in the questionnaire we gave you along with your contracts. In the present part of the competition, our couples will play *Three Truths and a Lie* with their partner. One point each for spotting the lie. And in the future part, you'll be asked to identify your partner's statement about the future. One point for each correct answer. The couple with the most points will win the challenge. The couple with the lowest score will leave us on Friday."

Muriel told her to answer those questions with responses that Jack had heard before. Now, she understood why.

Several hands went up as Jack leaned down to her ear.

"I'm so screwed," he said. "How can I answer those questions?"

"Muriel warned me to answer those questions carefully," she whispered. "You'll do fine."

"Only if they ask me about Hell creatures and angels of death," he said in a sharp whisper.

"Jack," she said, feeling hurt.

Had she told him so little about her life that he felt like he didn't know her at all?

"Sorry, that wasn't directed at you," he said. "Every time I try to deepen our relationship, something unbelievable pops up in my face."

He was right. None of this had been fair to him. She touched his ring on her left hand, the silver band thin and shiny and a little scuffed up. She smiled. Like Jack.

"I know," she said, running fingers through his hair. "Forgive me?"

"Always," he said, pressing his forehead against hers, corners of his mouth rising into that hot little smirk as he kissed her.

"Any more questions?" Devin asked.

The room fell quiet.

"All right then," said Devin, clapping his hands together. "If you'll all follow Jennifer into the game room over there, we'll get started."

He pointed at the far end of the space that had a pool table, a row of stand-up arcade games, an air hockey table, and a dart board. Everything had been moved to the edges of the room with seven podiums in a half-moon around a table and another podium at the front.

"Cut and wrap." Herb called. "Shift scene."

Herb chatted with one of the script supervisors as they moved into the game room. Steve stepped out from behind the cameras, long hair tied back behind his neck, beard short and trimmed. He wore a coral T-shirt with *The Ever After Hour* logo on it in black, jeans, and white sneakers.

"All right, couples, this way. And don't forget, cameras are running all through the house except your suites. Twenty-four seven. He touched the earpiece in his left ear. "Cutting over to game room cameras one through four. Devin, from your mark, camera two then three."

Devin nodded and hurried ahead to the podium in front of the small table. With a large gold crown on top. As she and Jack drew closer, she saw that in the crown's center was a bowl with dozens of folded pieces of white paper. Jack swallowed hard when he saw the bowl. When they reached the brightly lit space, flashing with multicolored lights from the arcade games, she saw that each podium had the couple's names on it.

She was relieved that she and Jack were on the opposite side of Rachel and Lare. Armand and Izzy were beside them and that made Jack relax as he took his place behind the first podium. She caught a whiff of Jack's cedary cologne that hung above the scent of lemons and eucalyptus.

He leaned on the podium with his right arm, favoring it. She glanced at his left shoulder. Tiny dark pinpoints had seeped into the soft cotton fabric. Still seeping blood after three days. Even after Muriel had touched it with healing angel light.

Jennifer picked up the gold crown bowl from the table and faced the podiums as Devin got into position and finally turned his body toward camera two behind them.

"All right, my royal subjects, it's time to watch our couples show us how much they know about each other as they fight for their ever afters on…The Ever After Hour. The lovely Jennifer Collins will assist with this challenge. She'll go around to every couple and ask that they each draw one question and hold it, unopened until I request that they read the question about their partner. They will respond and the process will reverse, with the other partner reading and answering their question. And then we move onto the next couple." He turned to camera three. "All right, Jennifer, please pass out those questions and no peeking."

Jennifer walked up to Talia and Jack, extending the gold bowl toward her.

"Princesses first," she said with a smile without her glasses.

Talia turned away from the bowl and slid her fingers into the sea of folded papers. She took one and pulled it out of the bowl, hand closed around it. Jack stuck his hand into the bowl with a quick jab and snagged a paper that he gripped in his fist.

Next, Jennifer moved to Armand and Izzy. Then Mark and Morgan. Eric and Riya. Ryder and Claire. Then Tyler and Nicole. And finally, Rachel and Lare.

Devin paused, shifting toward camera one as Jennifer returned the bowl to the table and stepped out of camera range. Then he drew out the tension, watching them in silence until he finally flashed a smile for the camera and turned to Talia.

"Talia, read your question please."

She unfolded the paper and read it out loud. "What kind of car does Jack drive?"

"Now, for one point, Talia," said Devin, "tell us what Jack drives."

"It ain't an Alfa Romeo," Lare said with a laugh.

Jack glowered, right hand bunching into a fist.

"Cut," Herb called out. "Edit out that comment. Lare, no ad-libbing."

"Sorry, Herb," he said, still laughing. "Couldn't help myself."

"Try, Lare," Herb said, sounding annoyed.

"Okay, pick it up again," said Steve. "Rolling."

"Talia, tell us what Jack drives," Devin repeated.

Jack had his game face back on as she looked at him and smiled. "A black Ford Explorer."

"Correct! Jack, read your question."

He unfolded the paper in his fist, staring at it a moment. "Where is Talia from?" He looked at her and smirked. "Alaska."

"Correct. Two points for Jack and Talia."

Jack kissed her hard on the lips and she kissed him back. She kept track as the other couples answered their first-round questions. Armand and Izzy and Mark and Morgan got both questions right. Eric and Riya got one right and so did Ryder and Claire. Then Tyler and Nicole got both right along with Rachel and Lare who looked so smug that she wanted to smite him. She was so tired of them insulting Jack at every turn. She didn't understand that last insult, but she'd ask him later. If he'd even talk about it.

Jennifer brought the bowl around for round two and Jack gripped his folded question like it was a stinging insect, holding it tight in his fist. Then Devin was looking at her.

"Talia, read your second question please."

She unfolded it. "What was Jack's first job?"

"Coke addict," Lare called out with a snicker. Rachel broke into a fit of laughter as Jack's head snapped up, glaring at Lare.

"Trained by my costars—the experts," he replied, his stare deadly as both Mark and Armand broke out laughing.

"Cut! Roll it back, Roy. Dammit, Lare—enough."

"Rolling back again," said Steve. "And…go, Devin."

"Talia, what was Jack's first job?"

She thought back to his Book of Life and Death, grinning when she remembered that he'd been a lifeguard at the local YMCA in high school and through his first year of college.

"He was a lifeguard at the YMCA."

"Spot on, Talia!" Devin said, smiling at Jack. "Looks like Jack was a hero even back then. Jack, please read your question."

This comment brightened Jack's mood, but he didn't smile as he opened his fist and unfolded the piece of paper.

"What is Talia's favorite hobby?"

Then she saw the panic in his eyes.

Come on, Jack, she shouted in her head. *You know the answer to this question.* She loved flying above all else.

She could see the thoughts flashing across his eyes and he struggled for an answer.

"Jack, what's Talia's favorite hobby?" Devin asked.

He turned to her, staring into her eyes like he was trying to read the answer, but then that little smirk touched his mouth and the panic fled.

"Flying, Devin," he said, still gazing into her eyes.

"Correct, Jack! Good job."

She grinned at him and pressed a soft kiss against his lips which he returned with an anxious kiss, right arm pulling her close.

Izzy and Armand got both right and so did Mark and Morgan. Eric and Riya got one right. Ryder and Claire missed both questions. Both Tyler and Nicole and Rachel and Lare got their two questions right.

"All right couples, round three questions. Jennifer, if you please."

For the third time, Jennifer passed around the bowl. Talia and Jack took questions and again, Jack gripped his in his fist like it was about to bite him. Talia watched Jennifer set down the bowl and walk off set. Devin paused as the cameras panned across the other couples. Devin turned toward camera two.

"All right, Talia, read your third and final question please," said Devin.

Her hand shook as she read the third question. "What does Jack want most?"

"One more line of flake!" Lare shouted.

"That's it!" Jack snapped, storming toward Lare Dumont.

"Cut!" Herb shouted as Talia grabbed his right arm, trying to pull him back, but he jerked out of her grasp.

Armand was in front of him now, hands gripping his biceps, holding him back. "Let it go, Jack. He's a waste of your attention."

His light green eyes burned with fury, but Lare Dumont just laughed at him.

"Lare, I'm not going to put up with these outbursts. Not even from you. Can it or—"

"Or what, Herb?" Lare asked, still smiling at Jack and then at Herb.

Talia wanted to smite him right then and there. The little egomaniac was daring Herb to cross him and lose the estate as the show's setting. And two couples. If Herb fired him, the whole show would be delayed for months. And it would cost them a fortune."

"Or I call my lawyer and he sues you for breach of contract, Lare," said Herb, sounding tired. "You signed the rules of conduct, promising to behave in a respectful manner on set."

"Since when has stating facts been disrespectful?" Lare asked, his mahogany brown eyes bright. Enjoying every moment that he could hurt Jack.

"It's insulting," Herb shouted. "And I want it stopped. Are we clear?"

Lare didn't say anything. He just cast a hateful look at Jack and went quiet.

"Roll it back again," said Steve. "Devin, camera one in three. Three, two, one."

Devin exhaled and smiled at Talia. "Talia, what does Jack want most?"

She looked at him. He was seething inside, but that actor's mask was firmly in place. And he was so good at it, looking excited and engaged.

But she knew the answer to this question without thinking.

"Me," she answered.

He grinned at her.

"Exactly right, Talia. And looks like Jack's got that at last."

"Damned right I do," he said and slid his arms around her, dipping her into a slow, romantic kiss that made her weak in the knees.

She grinned at him as he set her on her feet again.

"Jack, please read your question."

He opened his fist and opened the crushed bit of paper. He read it and then looked at Devin.

"What is Talia's greatest fear?"

"Tell us, Jack. What is Talia's greatest fear?"

He looked at her, pausing, letting that question sink in as he laid a hand against her cheek, cupping it.

"It's never learning to soar, Devin," he replied, gazing into her eyes.

"Perfect response, Jack. And Jack and Talia are the first to grab all six points, congratulations!"

This time, she flashed a devious smile at him and then dipped him, kissing him hard on the lips. He laughed and kissed her back, dipping her again. That had been her worst fear on *The Cinderella Hour*. Now, it was losing Jack. She needed to tell him that.

Armand and Izzy got their two questions right. Mark and Morgan got theirs right too. Eric and Riya and Ryder and Claire missed both of their questions. Tyler and Nicole got both of their questions right. And then Lare missed his question, but Rachel got hers right. She glared at him and he looked pissed, arguing with her in a low whisper.

"And when we come back, our couples will each play Three Truths and a Lie with their partners. Stay tuned."

"Print it," said Herb. "Roll into Truth and Lies."

"You heard the man," Steve, smiling. "Everyone, stay at your podiums. Rolling in five minutes."

Talia watched Lare and Rachel step away from their podium to the window, Tyler Hughes and Nicole Reardon following.

Armand stepped over to Jack, looking concerned. He glanced over his shoulder and then back at Jack who looked sullen.

"Shake it off, Jack," he said in a quiet. "I don't know the history between you, two, but don't let him get to you."

Jack bowed his head. "Lare was my best friend when I was on SanFran Confidential. He was like the big brother I never had. I looked up to him. I wanted to be like him. But Rachel said it was all an act. That he really hated me."

Armand's brown eyes softened and Talia saw his compassion springing forth. "And he stole your girlfriend."

Jack shook his head. "Apparently, she'd been his girlfriend all along. Remember that article you showed me? She just played the part of my girlfriend for three years." He sighed, the sound so heavy and pained. "I don't even know why."

Armand looked horrified and she saw the mounting respect for Jack building in his gaze.

"That's just—monstrous, Jack. Why would anybody do such a thing?"

For the first time since she'd known him, the words didn't come. He just stared at Armand, looking a little lost, and shrugged and held out his hands.

"You were a threat to them, Jack," said Talia finally, unable to watch him suffer any longer.

"A threat?" he said, squinting at her.

That thought had never occurred to him. He'd spent four years trying to understand what had happened. And for over half of that, he'd spent it thinking he'd sacrificed himself for the good of the show. People he loved.

"Audiences loved this hot, heroic kid," she said, glancing from Jack to Armand and Izzy. "He had a heart of gold that bled through his bad boy persona. He was passionate and broke the rules to make the world right again. And the audience found a new hero in him and wanted more. Much, much more."

Armand was nodding as Jack shook his head.

"But Lare and I were buddies," he said and she could see that his heart refused to believe the truth. "Best friends on and off screen."

"Jack, Talia's right," said Armand, still nodding at him. "I watched your show. They tried to create a bad boy antagonist for Dumont, but you upended the whole role through your passionate, straight-shooting portrayal. Audiences loved you. They began to side with you. Saw you as the hero."

"And Laren Dumont wouldn't stand for an upstart dethroning him on his own show," she explained, trying to get Jack to see that none of this was his fault, that he'd been setup. "So, he concocted a plan to take you down, Jack. Completely. Permanently. With the coke."

Jack looked sick, the truth at last sinking into his heart.

"All this time, I thought I was saving them," he said in a tired voice. "I let them fire me and I didn't implicate the rest of the cast. Thought I was protecting my friends from suffering the same fate. We'd all been complicit, responsible. So, I took one for the team."

"You played the hero again, Jack," said Armand. "Doing what you thought was the right thing. And they were counting on that."

He nodded, a hand against his mouth. "The whole time, they were grooming me for that sacrifice. Getting me off the show had been their whole goal. And breaking me into little pieces." He rubbed his face. "And I was too stupid to realize it."

Talia shook her head. "No, Jack, you trusted them. You loved them. You couldn't see the horrible people they were."

"Are." Armand replied, correcting her.

"Places, people!" Steve announced. "Cueing up for the next scene. Devin, camera two and then camera one."

FOR THE NEXT part of the challenge, Devin reversed the order and explained the Three Truths and a Lie portion of the challenge. And started with Rachel and Lare, but Talia knew that nothing they said was truth.

It was all lies.

She could barely listen to them draw out their statements and fawn over each other for the camera. It made her want to retch and smite both of them. She knew they were playing it all up to rub in Jack's face. This whole show seemed geared toward hurting Jack and she knew it was all Lucifer's doing.

By the time they got to Eric and Riya, they were running late, already past the scheduled lunch break.

"All right, Riya," said Devin, shuffling the cards in his hand. "Tell us four statements and Eric, you identify the lie."

Eric nodded and gave Riya his full attention as she made four statements. "I have appeared in twenty-one episodes of American television."

Talia glanced at Jack and he was watching her intently, as if he recognized her.

"I was born in Bhopal." She paused.

"Jack Casey was the best series star I ever worked with." Paused again.

"I started working at fifteen as a model."

Eric studied Riya's face as he thought through the statements. Finally, he asked her to repeat them. She went through each one again, speaking slowly and clearly.

"All right, Eric, times up," said Devin. "Please tell us which statement is a lie."

Eric gave a shy smile, his dark brown eyes looking nervous. "You were born in Bhopal."

Devin looked at Riya now. "Riya, please identify the lie."

Her gaze hardened as she looked past him. At Jack. And Talia's stomach twisted.

"Jack Casey was the best costar I ever worked with," she said, staring at Jack.

He held onto his game face, but she felt him flinch.

The whole set went deathly quiet until she heard Lare's laughter cut through the silence.

"Cut!" Herb shouted. "What the hell is going on with you people? This is getting really mean-spirited and I'm getting a little tired of it."

"Maybe you should just cut Casey loose?" said Tyler Hughes. "For the good of the show."

"Obviously, he's the problem," said Nicole, staring at her hands, looking bored.

"See, it's not just me, Herb," Lare said with a shrug.

"Breaking for lunch," Steve announced, an irritated look on his face.

The crew looked tense, angry. Even Jennifer looked upset as she led the couples out of the game room and toward the dining table where lunch had been laid out. Cold sub sandwiches, chips, and little hot sliders. Hamburgers and chicken.

Jack was so deathly quiet and pale that it frightened her. She stopped in front of Armand and Izzy who stood beside the table stacked with white plates, thick white paper napkins, and cups of silverware, but Jack kept walking.

"Jack," she called, aching all over for him.

He didn't respond, but just kept walking into the hallway and out the front door.

Armand laid his hand on her shoulder. "Let him be for a little bit, Talia," he replied. "Let him sort through it first." Anger flared in Armand's eyes, his face tense, jaw set. "Jack didn't deserve any of that. And that garbage from Riya was totally uncalled for. It's like they're all targeting him."

Talia knew it was worse than that. Lucifer was targeting him. And right now, the chained ward shields and fourteen angels of death were all that stood between them and an unending horde of demons and hellhounds. If they left here now, she and Jack would both be dragged off to Hell. And without any of her death angel powers—not even her wings—she was powerless to stop it.

Where was Azrael? Why had he left them to Lucifer's mercy with no defenses?

16

The heat from the seraphim guttered around Archangel Azrael in a red-gold storm, swamping his halo and blackening his wings. His face hurt from the blast of heat that engulfed him and slammed into the opposite wall that burst into flame. Scorching the glistening white stone walls, turning them black.

"Archangel Samael. God's Scribe uncovered evidence in the forged Books. And there are more, but we don't know their identities yet. They have attempted to kill Pravuil. They must be stopped."

Which Books? Seraphina's question was a demand, her shadow burning across him.

"The Book of Life and Death created for Pravuil," he said and hesitated.

The last thing he wanted to do was to call down High House on Jack Casey. Especially after him rewinding time to keep Talia with him.

The rest of it, Azrael. Now!

He'd never seen the seraphim this agitated. He prayed that it was over his news and not his actions.

Azrael sighed. *Forgive me, Talia.* "And human mortal, Jack Casey who—"

It is identified. One of the seraphim spoke in his head, cutting him off.

Through him, they pinpointed Jack Casey from all the billions of lives with Books in the archive.

Leave now.

"Wait!" he shouted, knowing they could end him with a thought. "Please. I have more to say. Things you must hear beyond what's in my heart."

Enough. Go.

"Seraphina, I beg your indulgence. Please. You must hear me."

The room shook, the platform trembling, but he held his ground. He had more to say and he wouldn't leave here until they either heard him or disintegrated him.

"I must speak!"

The room stopped shaking. To his amazement, Seraphina landed on the platform beside him. Her form cooling in the winds buffeting the platform.

Speak. Quickly.

"Pravuil and I have a plan. To draw out our Heavenly traitors and trap Lucifer in his own scheme."

Why this risk?

"I want to stop Lucifer from causing a war in the Heavens. I want to stop Lucifer from claiming souls he has no right to claim. And I want to save one of my own, Seraphina. And her heart."

Selfish motives. Her statement made him pause.

"Completely selfish motives. You can see it in my heart and I won't try to hide it. But the Maker loves those stubborn, warring, emotional children made in His image. The Chosen we've been sworn to protect, to teach, to walk alongside. Chosen I've grown to love through my duties as an archangel of death. God only asked one thing of them and it's the one thing, as his Heavenly guardians and soldiers, we must give in order to teach them."

Name this thing.

"Love," Azrael replied. "In all its forms. With all its sacrifices! And they are many."

Love?

At last, it was a question, not a demand or a statement that things were just so and could never change.

Was the seraph truly listening to him?

"Lucifer tried to destroy that love, but my guard has fought long and hard to save it. Talia most of all. She found that love in her human charge, Jack Casey when she'd given up on all humans. And was quickly growing to hate them. Like Lucifer. Then she sacrificed everything to save this human. To stay with him and love him. As the Maker loved His Chosen. And us. Lucifer and Samael want God's Chosen destroyed because without them, He can only favor us. But they're wrong, Seraphina. We need these precocious humans."

Why?

Another question! Would she really hear him?

"The reason God made humans was because only they could love him back. In ways angels cannot even comprehend. And only these volatile, petulant humans can teach us, God's Heavenly guardians, to love."

Teach angels to love?

She was listening. She was hearing him!

"Once we've mastered that very human and Godly emotion, action, feeling, we can take our rightful place beside God's Chosen. And fulfill the reason for it all. Love. In the Maker's image. As He intended all along. That's why Talia must stay with Jack. To bring that understanding forward and educate the guard. Educate the Watchers and the guardians. And stubborn old archangels like me. She is our best hope, Seraphina."

Explain.

Azrael grinned. He hadn't been disintegrated and she was still listening to him.

"Talia's rare gifts are emerging. I burned away her angelic gifts in grand fashion in front of Lucifer and threw her from the Heavens. Because I knew her human soul would make her fall to the Earth and not Hell. And only an angel with rare gifts will experience a Phoenix shift."

There has been a Phoenix shift? In the death angel guard?

This comment chilled Azrael. Why had this information not been communicated to the seraphim yet? That troubled him.

"Yes, three human days ago. Lucifer doesn't know that my ruse was to test her powers. Her wings have already begun to grow back. When she regains her halo, her powers will magnify and the new ones will emerge. From the ash, she is reborn. Becoming an angel of Powers."

There has been no new Angel of Powers in centuries.

Azrael nodded. "One has emerged, Heavenly Hosts. It will take her rare gifts to drive Lucifer's attempts at starting a war in the Heavens all the way back to where they belong. In Hell."

In the blink of an eye, Seraphina was floating beside the other seraphim. Silent. Still. Contemplating.

Azrael stood in silence, wondering if they would dismiss him again. He sighed. Or disintegrate him. But they'd made no move to do either yet. He had to hope that he'd gotten through to them about Lucifer's threat and the traitors in their midst.

And shown them that Talia and Jack must stay together. But there was one more thing he had to explain to the seraphim. A complication from the Phoenix shift. He sighed. It was about Jack Casey.

He cleared his throat and glanced up at the seraphim clustered together. Unmoving.

"One last thing that must be said," Azrael began. "About the Phoenix shift. And Jack Casey. There's been a..." He sighed. "A complication."

17

JACK RAN DOWN THE PATH TO THE BEACH BELOW, ANGER MIXING WITH shame. He halted at the water's edge, but wanted to just keep walking. He couldn't face Talia. Or Gianni and Banks. What they must think of him. Was snorting flake the only thing he was good for now? Lare's taunts he could take, but Lare's, Rachel's, Tyler's, Nicole's, and now Riya's? On top of Lucifer and the rest of it?

It was too much, even for him.

"Giving up?" the voice behind him asked.

He whirled around. Only the ocean and the wind whispered around him. But something in the wind took on weight. Form. Movement. Almost wrapping around him. Touching his face. Running unseen fingers down his right arm.

It chilled him to the bone.

"Muriel? Anahera? This isn't funny."

"You're washed up, Jack," said the voice. "Let it go already and stop torturing yourself. You're just no good anymore. And no one wants to work with you. The others were just being polite by not agreeing, you know? Talia must have been so embarrassed. Nobody can love a coke addict. Sooner or later, they always go back."

"Shut up!" he shouted into the wind, but the ocean waves swallowed up the sound.

"Talia could never love someone like you," the voice continued, so soft and smooth. So calm and concise. "Angels hate human weakness, don't you know that? She says she'll never leave you, but she will. Everyone says that until they've had enough. Because sooner or later, they have to save themselves. Help Talia save herself, Jack. You'll destroy her if you don't let go. She already lost her wings and her halo because of you. Don't make her lose everything."

"Destroy her?" he replied, horrified.

Of course, it was his fault. She was supposed to take his soul as part of that wager and she didn't. That's why they cast her out of Heaven. Took her wings and her halo. She had to let him go to save herself.

He shook his head. No, he had to let her go. It was the only way to save her from Lucifer. From the wrath of her archangel boss.

"Yes, that's right, Jack," said the calm, cool voice in every rush of wind across the beach. "You need to let go to save her."

He nodded finally. To protect her, to save her, he had to walk away. He loved her more than his own life. Guess it was time he proved that. But he had nowhere to go that an angel of death couldn't find him.

"How do I do that?" he asked.

A hand caressed his shoulder. "You know how, Jack," the voice purred against his ear.

He stepped closer to the ocean waves. So cold against his feet now. It wouldn't take long in 59-degree water.

"Yes, that's right," said the voice, the wind so cold and hollow now. "You won't feel a thing. Just go to sleep and it'll all be over."

He felt so sick inside. He couldn't change what he was, a coke addict. Couldn't fix it. Couldn't walk away from the cravings. Couldn't escape the horrible person he'd become. Already ruined two television shows and one movie. Had he already tanked Gianni's career and ruined any chance of a comeback for poor Banks, the man who helped save his life?

He smashed his eyes closed. And poor Talia. Look what he'd done to poor Talia. Completely ruined her existence. She'd lost everything because of him. And the destruction just kept piling up, no matter how hard he tried to change it. Lare was right. He *was* the problem.

He stepped into the waves. The icy water rushed around his calves, soaking his jeans and Vans.

"See, it's for the best, Jack," said the voice, the hand stroking his face now. "Just another step or two and all the pain will end."

His chest ached with regret. Why couldn't he have been stronger? A better person? Why couldn't he be what Talia deserved?

All he wanted was to love her. He'd never meant to hurt her. Much less cause her to lose everything. He'd never meant to ruin *SanFran Confidential* either. Or the Hughes and Reardon film. Or *The Cinderella Hour*.

He'd ruined everything.

He took another step until the chilly water rose to his knees, rushing onto the beach in foamy swaths as the cold wind swirled around him.

"That's right, Jack. One more step. You were the problem with everything. This is the one good thing you can do for Talia and your friends."

Again, the waves surged past his legs and onto the beach, numbing his feet.

"Save her, Jack," the voice was a singsong in his ear. Soft, insistent. "Save Talia. Make the sacrifice for her. You owe her that."

The icy wind swirled around him again and as it hissed past his face, he thought he heard laughter. But it died away with the breeze.

"All of it's my fault," he said, his voice breaking. "She deserves better than me. I caused her to lose everything."

"Everything, Jack," the voice said in his other ear and it felt like a hand rested on his left shoulder.

He turned his gaze back to the waves, his heart heavy. "For her, I need to end this."

18

Talia couldn't concentrate on the food or Izzy and Morgan's conversation as she stood by the table, a hand on the back of the white leather chair, and glanced at the sunlight glistening on the ocean. Armand and Mark stood behind them, plates in hand, two or three sliders—as Jack called them—on their plates. Rachel and Lare stood at the window, smiling, and laughing as they gazed at the ocean and the beach below.

But this time, she could hear their whispers. Was her angelic hearing beginning to return?

"Keep it up, babe," Rachel whispered, hand stroking his neck. "It won't take much now. It's already getting to him."

"What about the flake?" Lare whispered. "Why don't we just OD him now? Or enough to black him out? Then a nice, evening ocean swim."

"And a nice big pay out on the insurance," Rachel whispered. "Turning over his soul will buy us another decade on top, Lare."

"Another stupid, trusting kid. Thought I was his best friend. He'll never know he had all of Hollywood at his feet and legions of fans."

"I made sure of that," said Rachel. "A shame we couldn't have turned him like Tyler and Nicole though. I miss that hot little property. In the beginning, it was so hard to get him on the flake. Even now, he's resisted it."

"Then we just have to try harder," Lare whispered. "Push harder. You know what to do this time. We left the job unfinished last time."

"I know," Rachel whispered. "I'll take care of it, babe. We've still got time."

Talia's heart smashed against her ribs, a mixture of horror and fear washing cold through her chest. She knew they were pathetic, selling their souls to Lucifer. And evil, delivering souls to him. That's how they stayed rich and on top. But what they'd done to poor Jack—and others like him—made her hurt all over. The pain and abuse they'd put him through. Grooming him, stoking him with drugs to string him out and then break him.

Jack was in terrible danger from these people. It made her sick. And she wished she had her angel of death powers to smite them all the way to Hell. Where they belonged.

She kept glancing over at the door, expecting Jack to walk back in the room, a surly, combative look in those sizzling, light green eyes. A fighting stance in his swagger as he walked up to her, full of fire and determination. Like every other time she'd seen him deal with adversity. She loved his never going to quit attitude. But she also loved those rare moments of vulnerability when he needed her to tell him to keep fighting.

But she saw neither of those in him when he had walked out of the room just now. Lunch was half over and he hadn't returned. That worried her. Especially in this house. With Lucifer trying to take their souls.

She noticed that Armand's gaze kept trailing back to the door, too. And he was just picking at his lunch.

Finally, she set down her plate with an untouched barbecue chicken slider on it and walked over to Armand.

"Armand, I'm worried," she said, staring at him. "It's been almost a half hour."

"Maybe he went to lie down for a while?" Armand offered, setting down his plate beside Izzy.

Mark glanced uneasily at the door. "Jack was never a nap taker," he said.

"Armand, there's something you don't know," said Talia in a quiet voice as she tried not to let her eyes get misty. "This house is where his costars held all their coke binge parties. This is where they got him hooked on the stuff to the point where he'd black out."

"That's a lot of flake," Mark said with a hiss.

Armand's eyes were wide as he shook his head. "Here?"

She nodded, her voice falling to a whisper. "He said they did things to him in this house." She nodded at Rachel by the window who was laughing and tossing her hair. "She did things to him."

"What kind of things?" Armand demanded.

Mark's eyes narrowed, his mouth pressing into an angry line as he moved closer to hear her.

"He said he'd start out downstairs and wake up in the bed beside her, his clothes gone. With no memory of what happened. With her touching him. Or he'd wake up in other places. Strangers leering at him. When he walked into our suite and over to the bed, he froze and his eyes were so haunted and frightened."

Armand laid his hand over his mouth. "My God, they assaulted him here."

"And got him addicted to cocaine," said Mark. "Man, and poor Jack let them fire him over the coke when this shit was going on?"

Armand sighed heavily. "Now, I'm really worried. He should have been back by now. He's under contract." He took her by the shoulders. "Just to be certain, go to your room, and see if he's there. If he's not, we go find him. Agreed?"

She nodded. "I'll be right back."

She rushed out of the room and into the hallway that curved south. She raced down it until she got to the end. To the Breckenridge suite. The door was closed. She fumbled her key out of her skirt pocket and opened the door.

"Jack?" she called. "Jack!"

The palpable silence made her skin crawl.

"Muriel. Muriel!"

As she peered at the couch, she heard the flap of wings. Muriel landed beside her.

"What's up?" she asked. "You and Jack schooling the other couples?"

She shook her head, her eyes welling with tears. "All through the first part of the challenge, they battered Jack with insults."

"What? Why?"

"Because Rachel and Lare are beasts! And so are their friends, Tyler and Nicole. And so is Riya Patel. They ganged up on him. When we broke for lunch, he just walked out of the room. He was devastated, Muriel. I was hoping he was here."

Muriel's eyes widened. "He's alone somewhere?"

She nodded. "I can't find him."

"If he's alone out there, he's easy prey for demons in this house. You know that, Talia. And through them, Lucifer can get to him. Lucifer doesn't have to even physically show up to do it either. I'll alert the guard. We'll start searching."

"Thank you," said Talia, feeling frantic. "Armand's going to help me look."

"Talia," Muriel said in an anxious voice. "I'm not sensing his presence in the house."

"He loves running on the beach. We'll look there."

Muriel grabbed her by the shoulders. "He's alone? On the beach?"

Talia shrugged. "I don't know. I'm going down there right now with Armand to look."

"Hurry," said Muriel. "I'll start scanning for him. The ward shield chains will protect him from outside demons, but the ones already in here can connect to Lucifer. Go!"

Talia ran out of the room and back down to the living area. She opened the door and Armand was there waiting.

"He's not in our suite. He likes to run on the beach."

"Let's head there," said Armand. "Don't worry. We'll find him."

"I hope so," she said in a quiet voice, the fear rising inside her.

"He looked devastated when he walked out of here," said Armand.

That's what frightened her the most. Lucifer might hone right in on that, especially after hearing from his minions, and attack Jack through them. And poor Jack would never see it coming. Like the attack that tried to force him to overdose.

"Let's hurry," she said and ran out of the living room, toward the front door with Armand in tow.

Between the guard and Armand, she hoped they'd find Jack fast. Before Lucifer harmed him.

19

Jack felt useless.

He was a liability. He was Talia's destruction. She should have let him overdose on *The Cinderella Hour* like he was meant to do. Like the world had originally planned for him. Everyone else would have been safer. And better off without him.

"That's right, Jack," the British-like voice hissed around his head, the wind rising again. "The whole room can't be wrong, can they?"

The ocean was stinging cold. He was shivering. Couldn't feel his legs. One more step. Where the beach sloped down another five feet. That's all it'd take.

He needed to do this last thing for Talia. She'd never been able to make this decision on her own. He'd do it for her. He was the biggest mistake of her life. Finally, he'd fix things for her. Maybe even save the show?

"I'm the biggest mistake of her life," he repeated into the wind.

"It's good that you've finally realized it," the voice replied.

It still felt like a hand gripped his left shoulder, even though he couldn't see it.

Jack sighed. "It's time I fixed that."

"Yes, it is, Jack," said the voice. "Hurry, now. Before the tide comes in."

His eyes stung. "I'm sorry, Talia," he said. "I never wanted to hurt you." He bowed his head, his heart aching. "I only wanted to love you."

"Jack!"

Talia's voice shrieked somewhere behind him. He smashed his eyes closed. For her, he needed to end this. Save her from herself. From him.

He took another step. Into the drop off. And sank under the chilly water. The burst of cold made him gasp. And suck in a mouthful of seawater.

But hands were grabbing hold of him, pulling him up toward the light.

He resisted. The cold sedated him, made him groggy and slow. Until he couldn't struggle anymore. The hand that been caressing his shoulder clamped down hard on it, twisting, gouging, tearing.

He screamed, the pain terrible. Another mouthful of water.

But he was rising, toward the sunlight and the roar of the surf.

Wind moaned across the rocks. And suddenly, wet sand was against his back, the sound of the surf so loud and wild.

He shook from the cold, teeth chattering. His shoulder throbbed and burned. Something sticky clung to the fabric of his soaked shirt and ran down his arm. The bandages were gone, pulled away in the current, his shirt twisted and up around his armpits.

He coughed and retched, sea water burning his throat and lungs as Armand Gianni's terrified gaze hung over him. And then Talia's big grey eyes stared back at him, pulling his shirt down, tears streaming down her face. Her hands were against his face, in his hair, against his chest.

"Just breathe, Jack," said Gianni in a soothing tone, rubbing his right shoulder. "C'mon, breathe."

"Oh, Jack," Talia cried and threw her arms around his neck. "What were you trying to do?"

"Save you," he said between coughs and wheezes.

"Take it slow," said Gianni, those Cary Grant eyes filled with fear and anger.

"Save me?" she shouted, sitting up.

"I'm the biggest mistake of your life," he mumbled. "Should have saved yourself and let me overdose."

Gianni frowned and his gaze snapped to Talia. "Talia, what's he going on about? Saving you? Overdosing?"

Tears streaked down her face. "When Jack thought I was using him to get to you that night at the pool, in the show's first season, he went back to his room and did a bunch of cocaine. Enough to stop his heart."

Gianni's eyes were wide. Jack felt nothing but shame. Shaking violently, he turned his head away, teeth chattering.

"Mark and I found him just before that. When his heart stopped, we did CPR and brought him back. Stayed with him until the next morning. Until he was out of danger."

"I never knew that," said Gianni in a hoarse whisper.

Jack couldn't look at him now. Or Talia. He closed his eyes.

Someone shook him until his eyes snapped open.

"Jack Casey, you listen to me and you listen real good." Talia grabbed his chin and forced him to look at her. "You get this through that thick skull of yours right now. You are the best thing that ever happened to me. And you did save me. Over and over. Every time I gave up on myself. Every time things got too tough and I wanted to quit. You were always there to tell me to keep fighting. And when I couldn't, you fought for me. Every. Single. Time."

His face contorted, the pain in his chest so tight.

"And even when you thought you were going to your death," she continued, pulling in a quick breath, "you kissed me and told me you were going fight to your last breath for me. And you got in that ring and faced a crazy man with a sword sharp enough to take your head off. With only a steel practice sword. And you know what, Jack Casey? You beat him. Like you've beaten every obstacle ever thrown at you. So, don't you dare quit on me now."

Gianni laid a hand on his right arm and squeezed. "She's right,

Jack. Those people were monsters to you. Way before their insults just now. Talia told me about this house."

He felt shame bloom through him as his teeth continued to chatter. He still couldn't look at Gianni.

"Jack, don't you understand?" said Gianni, shaking his head. "You were assaulted in this house. Multiple times. And practically force-fed drugs. And now these monsters are still gaslighting you."

Gianni helped him sit up and into Talia's arms.

"Gaslighting me?" Jack sputtered.

"You were never the problem with SanFran Confidential," said Gianni as he sat down on the rocks beside Jack. "It was their jealousy. You were the bright light that saved that show. All the critics said so. And now, Evan Bellows would kill to sign you back again. Same thing with You and Me. It was a mediocre screenplay with B-List actors at best—until they signed you. You gave a masterful performance and made that crap at least break even. All the reviews said so."

"Not the ones I saw," said Jack.

He remembered Devin Van Fossen's comments again about those reviews. The ones Rachel had read to him, emailed to him. They were horrific. And he'd believed her. Every line. Every word.

"I looked all of them up last night, Jack," Gianni replied. "Every critic praised you on SanFran Confidential. And every last review of that film singled you out as the only reason to watch it. They called Hughes a washed-up has-been and said that Reardon should stick to films that involved taking her clothes off. You were the one bright light in that whole production."

That's not how he remembered it, but back then, he was still hitting the flake hard enough to black out. Hughes always had a ready stash and Nicole threw lines at him during every break and every delay.

They were just as bad as Lare and Rachel.

"Guess I was too tanked up on flake to remember any reviews like that," he said, teeth still chattering. "And I don't even remember meeting Riya Patel, much less costarring with her on SanFran Confidential."

Gianni shook him. "That's what I'm trying to say, Jack. They've been gaslighting you. Today and four years ago. I don't know why, but they're still trying to harm you."

"He's right, Jack," said Talia, kissing his wet hair. "Their goal is to destroy you. Any way they can. That's what all of those taunts were." She pulled him tighter into her arms and held him closer. "And this. And if you try to kill yourself again to save me, Jack Casey, I swear I'll kill you myself."

He chuckled, but it faded quickly. He wasn't sure what had come over him. How'd he gotten from wanting to punch something— someone—to here? Ready to end his life. What had come over him?

"Let's get him off the beach and into some warm and dry clothes," said Gianni.

Jack yelped when Gianni took hold of his left shoulder. The daytime soap star's hand came away bloody and he gasped.

"Jack! You're bleeding."

He nodded, hunching over as the pain throbbed through his arm and chest. He began to pant, trying to alleviate the horrible pain that ached like a toothache through his shoulder now. The hellhound bite was bleeding a lot again. He needed to get it stopped and get into some dry clothes. Then try to figure out how he'd gone from furious to suicidal in the space of thirty minutes.

And that voice that had so convincingly urged him to end it. He had to figure out the source of it. He shuddered. A voice that so quickly and easily convinced him to walk into cold, turbulent sea water. And kill himself.

20

GIANNI CALLED BANKS, ASKING HIM TO GET A DELAY ON FILMING WHILE he helped Jack back to his suite. Talia seemed unusually subdued. She was probably pissed at him and he couldn't blame her. He'd been angry. Ashamed and humiliated when he left to go to the beach. To cool off. But something convinced him to take a permanent plunge into the ocean.

He couldn't even explain it. Couldn't voice it.

He was unsteady as he peeled off his clothes and draped them over the glistening white tub. He pulled on grey boxer briefs and another faded pair of Levi's then dried his hair with a white towel. But his shoulder kept on bleeding.

Grabbing some tissue from the silver box on the counter by the sink, he tried to soak up the blood running down his arm. He walked out of the bathroom, moving toward the dresser where he'd unpacked some of his clothes into three of the nine drawers.

"Jack, that looks horrible," Gianni cried, face contorting. "You need stitches!"

Talia was beside him now with a large, heavy gauze pad and pressed it hard against the wound.

He winced, the pain making him lightheaded as he struggled to hold still.

"Sorry," said Talia, holding the gauze in place as she lifted his arm above his head.

The movement sent sharp jolts of pain through his bicep and into his wrist. He gritted his teeth, eyes scrunching closed as he tried to breathe through it. It was excruciating.

"Armand, hand me that tube of antibiotic cream, please," Talia asked, holding out her left hand.

Wide-eyed, Gianni laid the tube in her hand, gaze frozen on the huge teeth marks crowning his shoulder and wrapping around to both sides. The whole wound was angry red and swollen, puncture wounds deep.

"Did you get attacked by a grizzly?" Gianni replied. "A tiger maybe? In South Los Angeles, that wouldn't exactly surprise me."

Jack sighed. *Just a hellhound, Gianni. With three heads. Just the guardian to the Gates of Hell. No worries. I'm sure I don't need a tetanus shot. Or chemotherapy.*

"Neighbor's dog. Part Newfie part Kodiak. Thought he was trying to rescue me from drowning in dogshit or my neighbor's Natural Ice cans."

Talia smiled at him, shaking her head.

"You should have a doctor look at that, Jack," said Gianni as Talia applied ointment and pressed another heavy gauze pad against it.

She grabbed another elastic bandage and wrapped it around his upper arm, then over the shoulder, around the back, across his chest and back around his bicep. Clipping it in place with three wrap clips.

When she was done, he pulled on a navy blue Henley and grabbed his tan loafers. He slid them on his feet.

"All right, let's get back to filming," he said.

"Just like that?" Gianni replied, standing there exchanging worried looks with Talia.

He nodded. "I'm fine." He sighed and ran his fingers through his damp blond hair. "I'm sorry you guys had to see that. But thank you. I lost every friend I had two years ago, so I appreciate your concern and support." He reached out and cupped Talia's chin. "Forgive me? I love you more than my own life."

Fear hovered in her eyes. "That's what I'm worried about, Jack," she said, taking his hand in hers. "I'll forgive you if you keep fighting."

He forced his most charming smile onto his face. "I'm back to fight. Show them they haven't beaten me yet."

"That's the Jack I know and love."

Gianni patted him on the back. "If you get tired, tell us. Banks and I have your back. So does Izzy. And Morgan. And Talia loves you with all her heart."

This choked him up. He'd almost gotten used to the jeers and bad treatment. Almost. He hadn't expected it from the whole room. But knowing that he wasn't alone in this horrible house where Rachel and Lare had done so much damage to him—it humbled him.

"Thanks," he said, his voice cracking as he bowed his head.

Talia hugged him. "I love you."

Gianni squeezed his shoulder. "It's going to be okay, Jack."

He sighed and turned toward the door. "Let's do this," he said and opened the suite door, his stomach in knots as he put on his best swagger and moved down the hallway toward the living area.

Pulling in a breath, he pasted on his game face, and opened the door. Smiling, he moved down the hallway and into the dining table and grabbed a plate. He plopped two cheeseburger sliders on the plate and a small bag of chips. And wolfed down the sliders. He reached for an iced cold can of Coke and saw Rachel and Lare glaring at him. They stood in front of the massive wall of windows that overlooked the ocean and the beach.

The anger tore through him. They'd watched that whole thing. Watched him walk into the ocean and try to drown himself. And they did nothing. They wanted him to end it. They were pissed because he was still kicking. That burned deep inside him, the rage building.

Banks gave Gianni a worried, questioning look. Gianni nodded at him and led Talia back to the table to get her lunch.

He felt bad that they'd left their food to go find him. The whole thing felt surreal now, but it made him feel so uncomfortable, knowing something had controlled him like that. It happened so fast, too. He didn't even realize it until he'd stepped off into deeper water.

"Jack," Banks said, laying a hand on his left shoulder, studying his face. Banks frowned at his damp hair. "Everything okay?"

The pain was sharp. He nearly dropped the plate. He smiled through it, rolling his shoulder out of Banks' grip as he turned toward him.

Probably smelled the ocean on him. He hoped Gianni kept quiet about what happened.

"Just needed to go clear my head for a bit," he said. "Sorry for the filming delay."

Banks smiled at him. "No worries. Herb wants to shoot the whole first challenge over anyway. He's delayed the Three Truths and a Lie until tomorrow. Gave you two more hours."

"Good to know," he said, keeping his gaze on his plate. He didn't want to face Rachel and Lare.

Banks glanced around and lowered his voice. "He read the riot act to those jokers after you walked out. Told Riya to rewrite her Truths and Lies so they were only about her. He said one more insult directed at anyone would result in immediate dismissal. Rachel and Lare just laughed."

Jack gritted his teeth, but held onto his game face. "Good to hear."

***

THE WHOLE FIRST round of the first challenge had to be filmed again. Jack got through it with Talia beside him, watching him intently through the whole ordeal. He put on his best camera smile and forced out an unaffected attitude, projecting a charming portrayal of himself on a good day. Jennifer smiled at him from behind the cameras and Steve kept him pumped up with thumbs ups and smiles from Roy and the camera crew.

The others looked quiet and a little subdued, except Lare who kept a sneering grin on his face the whole time. The dude kept staring at him, trying to intimidate him, but he held his head high and focused on Talia. She was the reason he was here. Okay, they were here so the death angel guard could protect them from Lucifer until their archangel boss decided to show his face. He and Talia needed to stay in this game as long as they could. He sighed. Or be dragged off to Hell.

No pressure there.

At last, filming ended. Jennifer called all the women out for interviews with Devin, leaving Jack to fidget beside the snack table in the living room. He didn't want to go back to the suite. Back to the hazy, half-formed memories of coke-fueled parties, blackouts, and bodies pressing against his, with him too numb and unresponsive to shove them away. Or even shout no. When he'd managed to say no, he had fuzzy memories of Rachel just laughing at him. Forcing another line of flake down him. Or putting her hands on him.

His stomach dropped into his feet as Lare and Rachel approached the table. And him.

"Jack," said Lare, slapping his left shoulder hard.

"Hello, Jack," said Rachel. She reached out and grabbed it with her long red fingernails. Twisting. Gouging.

Until he swallowed a yelp and slid back from them. Feeling blood seeping through the bandages.

"Get away from me," he snapped, glaring, trying to get his breath and control the terrible throbbing pain in his shoulder.

Lare clicked his tongue. "When are you going to finally learn that at Summer's Revenge, it's my house, my rules, Jack?"

Rachel chuckled as she slid her arms around Lare while taunting him with her gaze. "He should have already learned that, Lare," she said, a sultry look in her smoky eyes, those ultra-blue contacts making her eyes look so unnatural. "Every time he came to our parties." She winked at him.

He felt only revulsion.

She reached out and touched his face. He pulled away.

"I always had my way with you, Jack. No matter how many times you said no."

Then she laughed. Like he was an old coat she'd just donated to charity.

He had very little memory of those events, only tangled bodies and hands sliding across his skin, someone pushing a mirror and straw under his nose until the numbness returned. Until he couldn't say no or push someone away. He became a horrified observer, watching himself become their plaything. And for the first time, he was glad he couldn't remember it all.

"You were such a good little pet," said Rachel. "Sitting up and begging for more flake, rolling over on command. So obedient."

Then she laughed at him, a rusty, caustic sound that made him want to slap the hell out of her. She deserved it, but he just couldn't hit a woman.

And suddenly, Gianni was between them. Banks behind him, dressed in a tan sweater and jeans.

"There you are, Jack," said Gianni, an arm around his shoulders as he wedged past Rachel, Banks standing between him and Lare.

"Got an interview coming up," said Banks, keeping his body between them.

Lare glared at them. "You're way too late," said Lare, that sneering smile on his face. "Jack's home. And he still belongs to us."

Rachel laughed and the sound made him apprehensive. Filled him with dread.

Banks gave her a horrified look and shuffled him away, Gianni not turning his back on Lare or Rachel.

"Not now and not ever," Jack said with a growl, her response shaking him, creeping him out.

Rachel just tossed her hair off her shoulder and smiled at him as she slid one arm around Lare's shoulders. And watched him disappear out the door. Gianni hustled him down the hall to the Breckenridge suite.

"Key," Gianni demanded, holding out his hand.

Jack fumbled through his jeans pockets until he pulled out the brass key and handed it to the taller soap star, looking statuesque even in a pair of jeans and striped dress shirt.

He unlocked the door and Banks turned around and watched his flank until the door popped open. They hustled him inside and closed it.

Gianni whirled around and stared at Jack, looking unnerved.

"What in God's name was that about?" he asked, his gaze flicking from Jack to Banks.

"I don't know," said Jack, shaking his head, "but I don't think God's got anything to do with it."

Banks kept shaking his head and gazing at the door. "Not gonna lie. That whole interchange creeped me out."

"Jack, what do you remember about the parties here?" Gianni asked. "These people did some horrible things to you here."

Jack nodded, bowing his head. He only had flashes of visceral images that ran together in a continuous coke high. Uncomfortable memories of feeling violated. Of waking up without his clothes on many occasions. When moments before, he'd been at a normal party, talking and circulating, snacking on appetizers, and drinking wine. Until someone threw down that first line. And then it all just went haywire.

"I'd never done coke in my life before Lare and Rachel," he said, struggling to remember those parties, but only the snippets of bad memories remained. "It took them five months to get me to even try it. I didn't want it. Didn't need it."

He started to pace as more of the wildness of Lare's parties began to surface in his head. Like them twisting his wounded shoulder had shaken more memories loose.

"So, you didn't want the drugs," said Gianni, his expression sad now.

Jack shook his head. "I didn't need it, I told them. Coffee was more than enough for me. But they just kept pushing. Rachel especially. At home. On the set. At these parties. I hated Lare's parties. They made me uncomfortable."

He chuckled, hanging his head. He'd been a naïve Midwestern college kid with a bunch of commercials under his belt and a lot of regional theatre gigs. He'd only lived in Los Angeles a few months when he got cast on *SanFran Confidential*. He'd never dealt with the fast and loose Hollywood crowd before that. Much less stars that lived large and played hard. In ways that had horrified him the first time he came to Summer's Revenge.

"What made you uncomfortable, Jack?" Banks asked in a quiet voice. "I've been to some of these wild parties. Even thrown them. What made these so bad?"

Jack stepped between Banks and Gianni, running his hand through his hair, trying to recall the first time he came here. He was barely twenty with two episodes of *SanFran Confidential* in the can when Lare invited him up to Malibu to look at real estate. And Rachel had asked him out.

"It felt..." he struggled for a word. "Choreographed. Staged."

Gianni raised an eyebrow and glanced at Banks who shrugged.

"Explain," said Gianni, crossing his arms against his chest.

Restless, he began to pace again. "Like they were on their best behavior around me. Like they were trying too hard."

"Trying too hard at what?" Gianni asked.

"To get me to like them. To make sure I had a good time." He stopped pacing and stared at the bed.

Tangle of sheets. His clothes in a pile on the floor. His face covered in flake. Hands all over him. He was too numb to move. Too frozen to shout. Unable to shove away the drugs or the people. Strangers. Mouths against his, hands on his chest. He shuddered. On his thighs. Flash of horns. Leering red eyes.

"God, no!" he shouted, turning away from the bed.

He covered his face, trying to smother the images.

"Jack? What is it?"

At last, he pulled his hands away from his face. And he was shaking.

"They groomed me, Gianni," he said in a pained voice. "Lured me into their parties, practically forced the flake down me until they'd enslaved me with it. And then when I blacked out, they..."

He couldn't say the words. He just turned around and stared at the bed.

"Jack..." It was all Banks could say. "Oh, God."

Gianni laid his hand against Jack's shoulder. A supportive gesture.

"I can't even imagine the hell you went through in this house." He sighed. "What they did to you."

Jack swallowed a breath, trying to control his shaking. "The longer I'm here, the more memories come back." He pressed his face against his hands again. "I was nineteen. I'd walked away from college. Naïve and scared, but hungry to start my acting career. Moved out here, doing commercials and theater. A few months later—weeks after my twentieth birthday—I got cast on SanFran Confidential. After two episodes, I got invited to their cast parties."

He shook his head, staring out the window.

"I'd been to more than my share of frat parties, but they looked like church socials compared to this place. It would have made a Roman emperor blush."

Gianni turned him around. "You were a scared kid who just wanted to act. And you hit it big. They hated you for it. So, they decided to corrupt and ruin you." Anger flashed in his eyes. "It's nothing but sport to them. It's how they get their kicks."

Somehow, it felt darker than that. Something much more sinister. And somehow, he'd felt singled out. Special in some strange way. Maybe Gianni was right? Maybe Lare felt threatened, so they thought it'd be great fun to corrupt and ruin their new costar. Who was getting rave reviews, but never knew it because his girlfriend beat him down with lies and gaslighted reviews.

And together, his best friend and girlfriend were systematically shoving so much coke down him that he couldn't feel anything anymore. Until they got him fired. And then they cut him off, forgot they knew him. He sighed. Pushed him to the brink of killing himself or overdosing.

But he'd foiled their plan by grabbing for a lifeline. By signing onto *The Cinderella Hour*.

"I think it was more deliberate than that," said Jack, staring at Gianni who was nodding now. "I think you and Talia are right. They wanted me off the show because I was grabbing the spotlight away from Lare. And the quickest way to do that was coke me up and then just stop giving it to me. Let me self-destruct all by myself. My moods were shifting faster than the San Andreas fault and I didn't feel anything but irritation and anger."

Gianni put his hands on his hips, eyes burning with anger. "Of course not, Jack. They deliberately strung you out, withholding drugs so you'd explode at anyone and everyone."

"And get myself a hundred Gs in debt with drug dealers that wanted to end me."

Banks shook his head, looking horrified.

"That was after I'd paid it down some."

He was too ashamed to tell them that he'd been over three hundred thousand in debt when he got fired from *SanFran Confidential*. The film got him under a hundred thousand, but by then, no one would hire him. And Lenny Overton began hunting him.

"I propose a pact," said Gianni, looking from Banks to him. "Banks and I make sure that you're never alone with Rachel and Lare. And you make sure you stay alive, Jack. I like having you around to compete against. I don't have to work as hard."

Jack chuckled. He loved these dudes.

Gianni fixed Banks with his intense, silver screen brown eyes. "Deal?"

Banks smirked at Jack. "Yeah, I'm in. I like kicking Jack's butt and stealing his girls. Like Morgan."

"That include Hughes and Nicole Reardon?" Gianni asked him.

"They're good friends of Lare's and Rachel's. Found that out after I'd done that film, You and Me."

The flutter of wings behind Gianni startled Jack. He glanced at Banks and then Gianni, his gaze snapping to Muriel who landed about six feet behind Gianni, looking terrified. It sent a chill through him.

Neither of them seemed to notice her as she frantically glanced around the room. Or Anahera fluttering past them as she landed beside Muriel.

"Then we keep an eye on all four of them. Agreed, Banks?" Gianni asked.

Banks nodded. "Agreed. I'd like to add that we just don't leave Jack alone."

"Agreed."

An angel of death landed beside Anahera, grey eyes wide, staring behind him like he was being pursued.

Jack fidgeted. Okay, three angels of death in the room. Terrified angels of death, he told himself, a chill rushing down his spine. He tried to look nonchalant, his gaze flicking around the room.

"What do you two get out of this deal?" he asked, trying not to stare as another angel of death shot into the room, her gaze flicking over her shoulder.

That can't be good. He glanced over at Gianni and Banks. They didn't react.

Gianni bowed. "That I get to stand up to their bullying. And the satisfaction that Talia will live happily ever after."

"If her prince charming doesn't get murdered on the set of The Ever After Hour," Banks added.

Death angel number five stumbled past the rest and turned, wings extended, arms raised. Gold shield flickering in his hand.

Aw, dammit. Something got past their wards. And it was coming this way.

"Seriously, Jack, we're just paying it forward," said Gianni. "You were just a kid with his first big break. And you got horribly abused— and assaulted—by two psychopaths. And the system. Sooner or later, the truth will come out in Hollywood and you'll be vindicated."

Or dead after Lucifer got through with him.

"Guard, roundel formation! Wings out. Shields to the sun!" Muriel shouted. She turned to Anahera. "Anahera, wards up! Hold them as long as you can." She turned her gaze toward Jack. "Jack, an attack's coming. You need to stand in the circle. Now. So we can protect you."

He smiled as he walked slowly, calmly toward the couch. Where the circle of death angels crouched behind it. He ambled, but took big strides until he stepped through an opening between two death angels and stood in the center of their raised shields. The angels of death immediately closed ranks.

Muriel nodded at him and then tapped her wrist like it was a watch. Then pointed at both Banks and Gianni. On cue, both men glanced down at their watches.

"I need to meet Izzy back at the suite," said Gianni, moving toward the door. "For a walk on the beach. You text me if you even think about going alone, Jack. I mean it."

Jack nodded. "I will, Gianni," he said. "I promise."

"And if you can't get him, text me, Jack," said Banks. "Morgan's done with her interview, so I'm going to meet her for some wine and smooching."

"Don't do anything I wouldn't, dudes!" Jack called to them as something thumped against the suite door.

Damn. Showtime.

"That's a short list," said Gianni, moving toward the door.

"List implies more than one item, Gianni," he said as Gianni laughed and grabbed hold of the doorknob.

Again, something thumped against the door.

"This is going to be bad, isn't it?" Jack said in a half-whisper.

"Worse than that, I think," said Muriel, shield raised.

Gianni opened the door and he and Banks hurried into the hall.

Just as a large shadow stretched long and lean into the room.

Jack stared, dread a dead weight around his neck as a bone-chilling screech echoed through the suite, trembling through him. A sound he'd never heard before.

"What the hell was that?" Jack asked, staring at the door as something large and thumping approached.

"Accurate," Muriel replied. "It's definitely from Hell."

"Sounds too big to be a hellhound," he said, his mouth going dry.

"It's a greater demon," said Anahera, her gaze wide and glued to the approaching, screeching thing that cast a growing shadow.

"An Eater of Hearts," said Muriel.

"Probably don't mean artichokes or palm, do you?"

Muriel chuckled. "More of a carnivore really. Never seen one outside of Hell. Not sure how she got here."

"Let's hope she's become a vegan. To do commercials and a little modeling."

"You always make fighting Hell creatures a lot more fun, Jack," said Muriel, laughing as she glanced around the circle. "Ready shields!"

Golden shields of light turned toward the ceiling, charcoal-colored wings stiff and forming a closed circle around him as the angels of death closed ranks.

"Let me guess, she wants to get cozy with me," said Jack as something dark and shadowy ducked under the door's threshold. With red eyes, gaping jaws, and several tentacled limbs.

Muriel thumped her shield and raised her right hand into the air. "Yep, Lucifer's brought out the big guns since he couldn't get you to drown yourself in the ocean."

"You saw that?" he said, cringing.

She nodded. "Lucifer's powers of persuasion are incredible. Don't beat yourself up over it. He's a master at it, deceiving even seraphim and archangels. He plays on your weaknesses. Exploits and magnifies them."

The hideous, hissing creature belched fire and rushed toward them. The guard stood its ground.

"Hold. Don't break the circle." Muriel commanded in a calm voice. "Holy fire on my mark."

This thing was massive. Eight feet tall, its head almost touching the ceiling as it hit the front of the circle. Its gaping maw was filled with hundreds of sharp, pointy teeth that made Cerberus' three jaws look like a broken comb.

"Mark!"

All five angels of death lifted their hands and summoned balls of writhing white fire.

"Engage!"

Five balls of Holy fire hit this squirming mass of tentacles and shadow, setting it alight. It screeched like the dead, flailing and twisting, but turned and ran at them again.

Jack swallowed a breath. It was trying to get at him.

"Dude! Order some takeout!" Jack shouted. "You're not getting my heart. I'm still using it, thanks."

Muriel snickered. "Holy fire. Again! On my mark. Three...two...one—mark!"

Again, five baseball-sized balls of white fire sailed through the room. Striking this coughing, shrieking, gaping-mouthed Hell beast. That staggered. And came at them again.

Knocking two angels of death out of its way. Breaking the circle.

"Jack," Muriel said, her gaze fixed on the rampaging creature. "Get behind me and Anahera. Now." She looked up at the ceiling. "Two more from the guard. NOW!"

Jack moved behind them as one angel of death got up. The other lay crumpled and unmoving on the floor.

"Aren't you dudes angels of death?" Jack shouted.

"Yes, of course," said Anahera, closing ranks with Muriel, wings locking together, golden shields raised, balls of Holy fire clutched in their fingers.

"Death is your business, so kill it already," he replied as Muriel and Anahera flung more Holy fire at it.

"Killing demons is a lot harder than crossing over humans," said Muriel, raising her shield higher as tentacles swept across the floor.

Knocking all of them to the ground.

"What about supersized demons?" Jack asked, scrambling to his feet. "One trying to do cardio with my heart."

"An archangel would be good here!" Muriel shouted at the ceiling. "Where in High House is Azrael? Guard! Need some support—now!"

Muriel and Anahera rose to their feet and backed up, wings encircling him.

This was bad. This thing was still coming. Had Rachel and Lare summoned it somehow?

No, that was crazy talk. She was just a bitch, not a demon. Or was she?

The flashback of horns and red eyes hit him again, almost leveling him. Where had that come from? Had he hallucinated that or was his memory that jumbled.

The Eater of Hearts shrieked again, the sound like death and another angel of death fell to the ground, holding his head.

Again, Muriel backed up, Anahera locking arms with her.

Jack stepped back. And felt a wall against his heels.

Damn. Ran out of floor.

The shadowy, red-eyed demon screeched again, knocking the three death angels out of her way as she towered over Muriel and Anahera.

Jack groaned. And him.

"Wish Talia was here," said Anahera, raising her shield higher.

"I don't," said Jack.

"Why, Anahera?" Muriel asked, shield turning, blocking another swipe of tentacles.

"Could use her oblivion spheres about now."

"Oblivion spheres?" Jack replied, pressing his back harder against the wall. Wishing he could push it out six more feet. One of those spheres sounded handy about now.

"What spheres?" Muriel replied, swinging her shield at the shadowy monster.

She thwacked it in its gaping maw, staggering it.

"Oblivion spheres," said Anahera. She held out her left hand. "She just held her hand out like this and summoned one."

Jack held up his right arm, blocking a swing of tentacles that ripped through his sleeve. He held out his right hand, trying to grab hold of a tentacle, rip it off. Injure this bitch.

The greater demon lunged. Knocking both Muriel and Anahera sideways.

Anahera slammed against the wall and dropped. Muriel hit the floor and rolled, but tentacles wrapped around her. Holding her down.

"Jack!" she shouted. "Run!"

But the demon was on him in a flash, tentacles flailing, blocking him from either side. He was pinned.

Damn. Oblivion sphere would have been good here.

"Muriel, tell Talia I love her," he said with grim determination and held out his right hand again. Reaching out to try and snap off a tentacle. Wishing he had an oblivion sphere.

Something small and gold—the size of a large marble—materialized in his palm. Glowing white-gold and pulsing. A slow whine echoing through the room. The pitch rising.

He stared down at his hand. What the hell was this?

Muriel and Anahera stared at him, wide-eyed.

"Jack…"

The greater demon slid toward him, maw gaping, teeth snapping toward his chest. His heart.

He flung the glowing gold sphere in its face.

A thunderous blast shook the room, throwing him backward against the wall. Knocking the air from his lungs. Stunned, he slid down the wall as tentacles rained down on him in shadowy curls.

"Jack!" Muriel shouted, wings in motion as she traversed the room in a blink, Anahera a moment behind her.

They knelt in front of him as he lifted his head from the floor, the room swaying.

"You finally got reinforcements," he said, shaking his head.

Muriel's brow furrowed, eyebrows flattening over her grey eyes. She glanced at Anahera and then back at him.

"What are you talking about?"

"Oh, sorry, there's just two of you both," he said with a smirk. "Thought there were six of you. My bad."

"What in High House did you just summon and throw at that thing?" Muriel asked, shaking her head. "And next question is *how* in High House did you just summon and throw anything?"

He shrugged. "Where's the demon?" he asked. "She decide to order a pizza instead?"

Anahera giggled, making Muriel laugh, too. "No, because a crazy, stupid-brave human just used an extremely rare death angel power to summon an oblivion sphere and splattered it all over the room. How, Jack? How'd you do that?"

He shrugged again. "No clue. I was just trying to rip out a few tentacles. Slow her down from eating my heart too fast. Just wished I had one of those oblivion spheres and there it was. So, I shoved an antacid right down her maw."

Muriel laughed and helped him to his feet, Anahera on his right, guiding him over to the couch.

"Talia's never going to believe this," said Muriel, shaking her head. "I don't believe it."

"What am I not going to believe?"

Jack looked over at the suite door. Talia stood beside it, looking confused and concerned when she saw the five death angels slowly rising from the floor and the pile of tentacles on the hardwood.

"Greater demon stopped by while you were being interviewed," said Jack. "Restaurant up the street was closed, so she just wanted to borrow my heart. To eat. You know how those late-afternoon cravings get."

She moved toward him and saw his shoulder was bleeding through his shirt and down his arm. Shirt sleeve shredded.

"Jack!"

"It was an Eater of Hearts, Talia," said Muriel, moving over to the stunned death angels struggling up from the floor.

The color drained from her face and she slid her hand into Jack's right hand, holding him tight. He smiled, squeezing her hand.

"Went through all of us like toothpicks," said Muriel, helping up the angels of death.

Her gaze shot over to the pile of tentacles by the wall and then back to Muriel.

"But you took it down," she said.

She pointed at Jack. "Your crazy, stupid-brave boyfriend there's the one that took it down. It had Anahera and I pinned to the floor."

Her grey eyes were wide and filled with fear as she fixed him with her luminous gaze.

"You took it down?" She glanced around the room and then her gaze returned to him. "There are seven angels of death in this room and you're the one that took it down?"

"Still not sure how," he said with a shrug, "but yeah, I took it down."

Her gaze shot back to Muriel. "How, Muriel? That thing should have killed him."

"You sound disappointed," he replied.

She jerked her head around and glared at him. "I will shove you down on this couch and tickle you 'til you beg for mercy."

He couldn't hold back his grin. "Oh, God, please make that happen. But it won't be mercy I'll beg for."

Her mouth gaped, cheeks turning bright red. "Jack Casey!"

He busted out laughing. Muriel tried not to laugh, but she couldn't help herself. Anahera was giggling behind her wings.

"I just embarrassed the shit out of an angel of death," he said with a snort. "This day just gets better and better."

Talia smacked him in the face with a pillow and he laughed harder. She took hold of his face and kissed him hard on the lips and he kissed her back with an anxious kiss, pulling her against his chest.

"Okay, is someone going to tell me how Jack managed to take down an Eater of Hearts by himself?"

"Don't think you're gonna be ready for this one," said Muriel, sitting down in one of the turquoise chairs.

She looked at him and he just shrugged. It was a mystery to him. He was hoping Muriel could explain it.

"Spill it," she said, those haunting grey eyes narrowing.

"The human in the room summoned an oblivion sphere and disintegrated the greater demon," Muriel replied.

"What?" Her head swiveled around until she was staring at him again.

He held up his hands. "I have no clue how it happened, okay? I had my hand out, trying to rip out some tentacles and stop her from eating my heart. I just wished I had an oblivion sphere like Anahera mentioned. And boom! There it was in my hand. It sounded like a time bomb, so I threw it at the demon. And everything exploded."

Talia pointed at him, staring at Muriel. "Muriel! How's that possible?"

"Don't ask me," Muriel replied. "I've dealt with a lot of humans and I've never seen that trick in my entire existence. I've got so many questions to ask Azrael. If he ever escapes High House." She glared up at the ceiling. "Like where's our backup? And why isn't he helping us deal with Lucifer?"

Talia looked confused and angry. "And how about you ask him how a greater demon, an Eater of Hearts, got through a chained ward shield being maintained by fourteen seasoned angels of death. That shouldn't have happened."

Jack shrugged. "Unless it was already in the house. Or someone inside summoned it."

The silence in the room was palpable.

"Summoned it?" Talia said finally.

He sighed, turning to her. She wasn't going to like this either. "This afternoon, while you were being interviewed, Rachel and Lare started trash-talking me again."

Her eyes narrowed, her mouth an angry line as she glared toward the door.

"Gianni and Banks got in their faces, got between us. Got me out of there and back to the suite. They both told me they had my back and they'd work together to keep those two away from me. Or me from being alone with them."

That news made her relax a little and settle back against the sofa.

"Glad to hear that."

"While we were talking, I had more flashbacks from inside this room." He winced, not even wanting to give these images a voice. "Talia, I saw horns and red eyes when I came to on this bed once." He bowed his head. "Without my clothes. Before that, I'd been in Lare's kitchen, drinking white wine."

"That's horrifying, Jack," she said and slid her arms around him, holding him close as he shuddered.

Muriel groaned and held her head, halo tilting. "I really wish I understood what was going on here."

"Allow me to explain."

A dude with sun-washed blond hair and robin egg blue eyes

appeared, leaning against the wall beside the tentacles. He wore torn and faded jeans, black Chuck Taylors, and a faded black T-shirt with *SanFran Confidential* on it. He looked like the same dude that had appeared in the tux in his apartment.

This couldn't be good.

Talia's eyes turned fiery and Jack expected them to burst into white hot flames at any moment. She sat up, moving in front of him. Trying to protect him, he realized.

"Lucifer," Talia said with a growl, rising to her feet.

Jack grabbed hold of her arm. "Talia, don't."

She pulled away, crossing her arms, glaring at the tall, stately man. He had a deadly, hard glint in those blue eyes, his jaw GQ chiseled and his nose had a gentle curve to it. Perfect features like the highest paid male models.

"How'd you get in here?" Talia demanded. "It's warded like High House during festival season. How?"

Lucifer laughed and walked toward her, with all the poise and grace of a dancer.

"Like I'm some common burglar? I think not, my dear, Talia." He held out his arms, turning as he took in the suite, grinning. "I hardly need to break into my own house."

Jack nearly choked on his inhale. That feeling of dread rushed along his spine and turned as cold as the ocean below. He felt sick, those flashes of memory turning his stomach.

Lucifer laughed. "Yes, Jack, those awakening memories are real. And boy will your face be red when the rest of it returns. See, Rachel and Lare work for me, but you already know that, don't you?"

"No!" he shouted, grabbing hold of his hair. "No! I don't want to know this."

"Where do you think all the money came from, Jack? All the drugs? Your girlfriend. All of it belongs to me. Like you will soon, Jack."

He covered his face, wanting to scream and rage, the whole thing at last making sense. Rachel Daniels and Lare Dumont sold their souls to Lucifer. For money? Success? Beauty? They were like Satan's multilevel marketing associates, turning souls and delivering them.

And if there was one thing he hated more than liars, it was multilevel marketers.

And Lucifer's pyramid scheme was the worst in town.

He'd been their mark this whole time. They got him hooked on the drugs so he'd burn out and overdose. Off himself. Or sell his own soul to get it all back. Every part of it had been orchestrated, down to the debauched parties, Lare pretending to be his best friend, and Rachel gaslighting his reviews. Even her dumping him. It had all been according to some schedule. Including feeding him so much coke that he'd black out in this house. Holy shit.

In Lucifer's freakin' beach house.

"I love it when a plan comes together," said Lucifer, watching him with a dangerous glint in those pale blue eyes. "You've put all the pieces together at last, Jack. Figured it all out." He smiled. "As Rachel so eloquently put it…you were played, darling. By the entire band."

Talia laughed at Lucifer and he flicked his gaze to her, looking puzzled.

"It all comes together except for one tiny, little detail, Lucifer," she said, hands on her hips.

"What would that possibly be?" he replied.

"Choice," said Talia in a smug tone. "You're always forgetting that little point about humans having choice. They have to invite you in, remember? And unlike Rachel and Lare or Tyler and Nicole, Jack didn't invite you in, did he? He never signed a contract, he never wished for selfish things, and he never tried to buy the things he couldn't accomplish with hard work."

Lucifer glared at her.

"See, Jack," she said, turning back to him. "No matter what happened in this house, no matter what they did to you, you didn't sell your soul. And you didn't kill yourself, leaving your soul on disputed ground. That he could fight for and steal. No, you fought for everything in spite of what they did to you. Like you're still fighting. He's trying to make you think you've already lost, but Jack, you've won. He can't touch you." She laughed. "No matter how much coke they forced down you in this house."

Jack bit the inside of his cheek. "Even if I can't remember what happened at these depraved parties?"

"Even more so, Jack," said Muriel, nodding at the room. "You had no moral agency available to agree or disagree to anything. And Lucifer there knows that. He's trying to trip you up. Make you think otherwise." Muriel chuckled. "He pulls those tricks all the time in his contracts." She cast a sideways glare at Lucifer. "And his wagers."

Talia walked up to Lucifer and crossed her arms. "You did more than that, didn't you? You somehow waded into the time stream. It was no coincidence that all these things happened to Jack, was it? You've been setting the stage for those wagers with Azrael for years. It was no accident that I had to save Jack's soul."

Lucifer's smile widened into a broad, over-bright grin.

"But dear Talia, Azrael chose Jack as the first soul, not me."

Smug bastard. Jack didn't understand most of this angel and demon business, but this dude obviously knew a lot more than he was telling. And he was enjoying Talia trying to piece it together.

"Why, Lucifer?" she demanded. "Why Jack? Why me?"

He laughed. "Just call it a rebirth, Talia," he said. "By fire. I can't wait for you to see what I've done with the lower circles in Hell. And Jack, I've got a nice comfy rack all ready for you. Just waiting to flay the skin from your body. Talia will have so much fun counting the strokes, won't you?"

In a puff of smoke, he was gone.

"Okay," said Jack, standing up from the couch. "Is somebody going to explain to me how we ended up on season three of a reality TV show being filmed at Lucifer's beach house?"

Muriel rubbed her face, halo spinning faster as Anahera sank down in the other chair.

"If our boss was listening anymore!" she shouted. "Then maybe somebody in Heaven would be directing the guard and warning us before we just warded ourselves into Lucifer's place."

Anahera sighed and flattened her wings against her back. "I feel like we're working alone out here. I'm sorry I broke the strike to come here."

"Strike?" Jack replied. "Didn't know angels of death had unionized."

"Two archangels of death are warring with each other after one of them made wagers with Lucifer over Talia's fate," Anahera explained. "That's what started all of this."

"And now, the demons outnumber us," said Jack. "And we're trapped here. Not that we could run anywhere anyway. They'd just find us."

Muriel rose from the chair and began to pace. "We've got to hold out until we hear from Azrael, but I think it's time someone go look for him. Find out what's happening and how he plans to get us out of this mess. After all, he started all of it."

She turned to Anahera.

"Me?" said the taller angel, her grey eyes darker than Muriel's eyes. "You want me to return to Heaven?"

"Someone's got to contact Azrael. Tell him what's happening down here. Get help before Lucifer wipes out the guard and just takes Talia and Jack." She looked at Jack. "And find out how and why Jack Casey can summon an oblivion sphere—and see us in the first place. It's all connected. And Azrael has to know why."

Anahera nodded. "All right. I'll get the guard to let me through the wards. And I'll hurry back as fast as I can. Hopefully, with answers and help."

Anahera flexed her wings and they unfurled as she leaped toward the ceiling. And vanished.

"So, anybody know what all that bravado meant?" Jack asked. "That Lucifer tossed out at the end before leaving."

"That circles of Hell garbage?" Muriel asked.

He shook his head. "No, before that. He said something about a rebirth in fire."

Muriel shrugged. "Who knows?"

"Wait," said Talia, moving back to Jack. "He meant something by it. He loves to drop hints because he thinks he's much cleverer than anyone else. That we're too lame to figure it out."

"Maybe it has something to do with that Phoenix thing you mentioned at my place, Muriel?"

"What?" she said, staring at him. "The Phoenix shift."

He nodded. "That's it. That's what you said was happening to Talia."

"Right," said Muriel, staring at the floor. "Talia's powers are returning. And…" She glanced at Talia. "You gonna tell him?"

Talia's eyes widened and she shook her head. Muriel rolled her eyes. "Jack, you know Talia's powers are returning, right?"

He looked at her, feeling a little sad. Would she look at him one day with fire burning in her eyes instead of these expressive, bright grey eyes? Finally, he nodded at Muriel.

"Well, her wings are also growing back."

"Wait, what?" he said. "Talia? That true?"

She nodded, staring down at her hands. "I was going to tell you, Jack, but there hasn't been time."

"Right," he snapped. "You were going to let me figure it out when you just flew off back to Heaven again."

"What? No!" She moved toward him, but he stepped back from her.

"When were you planning to tell me goodbye?" he asked, the anger beginning a slow burn. "By postcard? On my deathbed?"

"Jack, it's not like that."

He couldn't deal with this. He'd fought so hard to be with her and now, that her powers—and her wings—were returning, she didn't need him anymore. Damn. That hurt.

"No, of course not," he said and stormed toward the door, blood still running down his arm.

21

Talia turned toward Muriel. "Couldn't you let me handle my relationship with Jack myself?"

Muriel propped her arm on her hip. "By not telling him that your wings were growing back? He'd have noticed in another day or two."

"I was going to tell him."

With everything happening, she hadn't had a moment alone with him. And then all the attacks on him by the cast and Lucifer almost convincing him to drown himself. She needed to tell him, to make him understand that getting her wings back didn't mean she was leaving him. Now, he felt betrayed and abandoned. Again. She had to make him understand. He'd never seen her with wings before. She didn't want to just spring them on him.

And now, he thought she was hiding things. *Azrael, this is all your fault!*

"When?" Muriel asked, giving her that look.

Muriel saw right through her. Knew that she'd been stalling, terrified Jack wouldn't want her once he saw her with wings and a halo.

"As soon as he and I were alone. Which I was hoping would be tonight."

Muriel gasped. "Jack's alone. Talia, you can't let him go off alone. Especially now that we know this is Lucifer's home turf. He could surprise Jack with any number of demons. Carry him off to Hell before anyone could stop him."

"Why hasn't he just done that, Muriel?" she asked. "Because either he can't or he orchestrated all of us together for a reason."

"Maybe you're right?" Muriel said, slouching into the chair again, her wings curving around her shoulders. "Why didn't he send a bunch of those Eater of Hearts after us? Could have easily overpowered us, but he didn't. Why?"

"It was a test," said Talia, moving toward the wall of windows that faced the ocean. "Or he's waiting for something."

"Maybe Jack was onto something about that rebirth and fire business?" Muriel replied, spinning her halo faster around her head until its hum spiraled up an octave.

Rebirth in fire. Like a Phoenix. Almost like Lucifer knew about the Phoenix shift. Or...by the Heavens! He'd orchestrated it. She whirled around, staring at Muriel in terror.

"Muriel, it was Lucifer," she said, dread chilling her fingers and toes.

"What was Lucifer?" she asked, a frown on her face.

"The Phoenix shift. He's been working toward causing one. Turning the right angels of death to his cause. Finding an in-road into the archive. Forging tiny snippets of Books of Life and Death. Testing. Trying to control God's Scribe. To find the right circumstances in time and on Earth that would cause a Phoenix shift. He needed just the right subjects and a live test bed, by hiding it in the guise of a wager with Azrael."

"That's way too complex for Lucifer to accomplish."

"No, listen!" Talia dropped down in front of the chair and gripped Muriel's shoulders. "He needed to test all of these variables on a live subject. One before the fall and after the fall. That's the reason for the two wagers. Once I'd fallen and he had all the other variables in place, he just needed to sit back and see if this legendary Phoenix shift would happen. And Muriel, it has!"

"But what's the point?"

It was terrifyingly clear. Didn't she see it?

"If all the conditions were met, he was able to orchestrate a Phoenix shift. On an angel that had lost her wings. If it worked on me, then there's nothing stopping him from forcing a Phoenix shift on himself. Regain his wings. And reclaim his full power."

At last, Muriel understood and she recoiled in terror. "By Heaven itself! If Lucifer regains his power and his wings, there's nothing stopping him from launching a full-scale war against the Heavens. And this time, he has an army at his back." She shook her head. "But Talia, what's he waiting for?"

Then she knew. One thing was missing. And the other was an enigma. Something Lucifer hadn't realized was possible.

"To see if my halo returns. With his halo back, he's got an infinite battery pack for his power. And the other thing is Jack."

Muriel sat up, studying her eyes, her face, trying to read her expression. Her heart, she realized.

"What's Jack's role in all of this?"

"Jack is beginning to exhibit mirrored powers to mine. Something Lucifer didn't expect. So, he's waiting to see what happens with Jack," said Talia.

"You mean he's watching rats in a maze?"

"Exactly. If Lucifer can cause a Phoenix shift and then mirror powers to his human minions, then he's got an infinite army with angel powers. He's studying Jack to see how much and what powers he receives from my transformation. To see what he can transfer to his human minions when he causes his own Phoenix shift. An army of turned humans in addition to his fallen angels and demons. With all of that, he could crush everything in his path. And maybe even God's throne."

Muriel looked terrified now. And very concerned. "Lucifer defeating God? That's too horrific to even consider. So, you think Lucifer's observing you and studying Jack."

Talia nodded. "Testing him."

It didn't make sense for Lucifer to wait otherwise. That had to be his plan.

Muriel winced. "So, if Jack gains anymore powers, Lucifer will just dissect him for answers. He won't keep a human alive that could overthrow him before he's regained his wings and powers. Besides, all he really needs is Jack's soul, right?"

Wait. Jack's soul. That's what he was really after. A human soul with rare angel powers? The energy in that one soul alone could devastate. He wanted Jack's soul in Hell to power his assault on the Heavens. And if he could transfer Jack's powers into the damned souls in his realm, he'd have another army. He wasn't waiting to see what powers Jack developed. He was waiting to pluck it at its most powerful moment. Waiting for it to ripen. To be the tree. And an endless harvest, transferring his powers to other souls. The moment her halo returned and mirrored that energy back to Jack, Lucifer would take him. Unless Rachel and Lare got to him first.

The mirror effect was the result of their connection to each other! That unbroken bond that had transcended human and angel, soul energy and death. It had survived everything.

"We can't let Lucifer—or Rachel and Lare—get his hands on Jack. They plan to sacrifice him for a huge insurance pay out and then sell his soul to Lucifer for more time on Earth."

"What? When did you find that out?" She looked stricken by this news.

"Today. In the living area during lunch. My powers are coming back, so I heard their whispering."

Muriel wrung her hands. "This is going to be a long reality TV show. And there are a million ways for you to lose Jack this time. Keep him close."

"I will. If he ever forgives me."

"One thing I know for certain," said Muriel, leaning her head against the wall, wings fluttering. "We need Azrael's help. Because someone up in Heaven has to be helping Lucifer. We have to find out who. And to keep Jack safe, I'm going to need an army."

Talia had never felt so afraid for Jack. And he wouldn't even talk to her. How would they stay on this show if they were barely a couple? She had to get through to him. Make him see how important to her he was—and that she intended to stay right at his side. With or without wings. But first, she needed to find him.

"Muriel, can you please scan for Jack? Put the guard on him until I can get to him. And get him to understand why I didn't tell him about my wings yet."

"You got it," said Muriel, rising from the chair. "Go find him before those horrible people do."

She had to, otherwise, she might have to watch Muriel cross him over. And never see him again.

22

The seraphim were losing patience with him. Azrael felt their irritation and anxiousness. But they had to know everything.

"Heavenly Hosts," he said, holding out his arms. "This Phoenix shift complicated everything. Lucifer has been attempting to orchestrate one for centuries and all of the forgeries, attacks on the Scribe, and the archive were part of his plan. I allowed him to create the conditions for it because it was necessary for Talia's transcendence. But to Lucifer, she is his test. To regain his wings and halo. And his powers. He is watching her now as her powers unfold, waiting to see if the shift will grant her a total recovery of her original powers. He doesn't know that she has rare powers that give her the ability to defeat him."

And the complication?

Azrael cleared his throat and leaned against the podium. He didn't expect the seraphim to forget that part of the story.

"The complication is the deep, unbroken connection between Talia and her human charge, Jack Casey. Because of her human soul, there has been a mirrored effect in her transformation."

Explain.

"The human charge, Jack Casey has begun to develop similar powers."

Angel powers? In a human? What angel powers!

That question chewed through his head, angry and aghast. This was completely unheard of in any of the original stories and had never been recorded in a single Book before. Not one case in the entire archive. No, this was a new and strange development that Azrael had no idea how to handle. But the seraphim had to know. He feared they would order Jack Casey destroyed.

But it was far too late for that now.

"From the moment that Talia landed in his arms on Earth, he began to see angels. All angels. Even the fallen. And demons."

The silence was painful. Dangerous.

He had no choice but to press on and hope they didn't destroy him where he stood. After a quick conference with Anahera, he dreaded telling them about this second ability. They might just smite him on the spot when they knew.

"And just a few minutes ago, Lucifer sent a greater demon after my guard and Jack Casey. An Eater of Hearts."

Silence. No smiting yet. He pulled in a quick breath and pressed onward with his story.

"The greater demon overpowered seven of the guard, leaving Jack Casey unguarded and at the demon's mercy."

Another breath. Exhale. Breathe. Here came the smiting part.

"Jack Casey had heard Anahera mention Talia summoning an oblivion sphere to destroy an assassin demon. So, Jack Casey..." He cleared his throat. "Jack Casey uh...well, he—"

What power! Now!

He pulled in a breath, his hands shaking. "Jack Casey wished he had an oblivion sphere. That statement allowed him to bring one into existence in his hand. He threw it at the greater demon and destroyed it."

The heaviest silence he'd ever felt filled the Cloud Chamber.

Azrael blinked and all three seraphim burned along the edge of the pyre. Burning across his halo and his wings. His robes began to smoke. Hair and eyebrows sizzled.

"I do not know the extent of this mirroring effect, but as Talia's powers and abilities return, they may also be mirrored in Jack Casey."

Jack Casey is now a weapon that Lucifer can wield.

Azrael had been expecting that response. And he feared they'd order the young human destroyed. Because he fell in love with a human woman disguising her true angel form. It was unfair and it was his fault. Somehow, he had to protect this human that Talia loved so fervently.

"That is why Heaven must wield him first. Under the protection of the guard and with some training, Jack Casey can be a Heavenly asset. He has already resisted every single temptation that Lucifer has thrown at him. And he fought valiantly for Talia. And that includes Lucifer when he possessed another man that was bigger, stronger, taller, and with a deadly sword. Armed with only a dull practice sword, Jack Casey defeated Lucifer. That kind of bravery, commitment to the light, and determination should be rewarded not snuffed out. And so should the one thing our Maker prizes above all else."

Seraphina appeared at the platform. Waiting for him to continue.

"Love. Talia and Jack Casey have both made tremendous sacrifices for each other in order to stay together. It is that love that will save us like it saves our human charges. And it raises us up in the Maker's eyes. This bond must not be severed, Seraphina! It must be strengthened. It must be saved!"

Love.

Her delicate statement made him tear up. Just one word, but the depth and intensity of a seraphim speaking it ached through him. In a way that he hadn't felt in millennia. By the way she let the statement float across the platform, along the cloud tops, and through the air currents surging across the crisp blue sky, she acknowledged its importance. Its need. Its existence. Something he'd never heard in a seraph about a human emotion.

It was a statement that it was universal. And it belonged in Heaven as much as it did on Earth. And in that one word, she acknowledged that such bonds should never be broken, even if dictated by protocols.

Let this bond stand.

His eyes burned with emotion, his hands shaking at her pronouncement. Talia and Jack Casey would be allowed to stay together if they wished. It was the best news he'd heard in millennia.

"Thank you, seraphim," he said, his heart full.

Deal with Lucifer. And Samael.

And in that moment, the seraphim vanished.

It was over. He had won.

He had protected Talia and the man she loved. And unmasked a traitor. Dealing with Lucifer and Samael was a new matter that he and his guard would handle. But first, he had to protect Talia and his death angel guard. And Jack Casey. Prevent them from becoming weapons wielded against the Heavens. Prevent Lucifer from destroying them. And stop Lucifer from regaining his wings. Failure in any one of those areas meant a war in the Heavens. And they just might lose everything.

What would the world look like with only evil in it? And only darkness? An existence he could not even contemplate.

23

IN A RAGE, JACK STORMED OUT OF THE SUITE, LOOKING FOR THE WEIGHT room at the opposite end of the house. Why hadn't she told him she was becoming an angel of death again?

Had she just outgrown him?

He found the brightly lit space with a heavy, grey rubber mat covering the floor. A green stripe ran along the white walls that had a rack of free weights, an elliptical machine, a rowing machine, a treadmill, and a weight bench with support rack. A grey metal shelf on the wall had stacks of white towels.

Hopping onto the treadmill, he turned it on and set it on a brisk walk. He was dressed in jeans and loafers, not for a run, but a walk on the beach might be deadly. He didn't want to have another run-in with Lucifer.

His shoes thunked against the treadmill's steady grind, the fear finally hitting him. At how easily Lucifer had twisted his despair into a fatal swim. Gianni wanted him to text him or Banks if he was alone. But he was as tired of having babysitters as he was of this whole nightmare. He wanted out of this house and as far away from Lare Dumont and Rachel Daniels as he could get.

And he didn't even care about this couple's competition. Now that

Talia had gotten back what she'd lost, she didn't need him anymore. He loved her more than his own life, but he couldn't compete with wings and a halo. He couldn't offer her the Heavens and the clouds.

He could barely offer her a place to sleep.

The treadmill trundled a little faster and he lengthened his strides.

Besides, she was an angel of death. She had no use for his human emotions or the love he offered. Even if she did, it was a blip. He couldn't offer her eternity. He could barely offer her tomorrow. Why would anybody—especially an angel of death—give that up? For him? He wasn't worth a second glance to her. To anyone.

But everything was happening so fast. The redo of Three Truths and a Lie started tomorrow and then the future part of the challenge, whatever that was. How could he match Talia's vision of the future when she no longer saw him in it?

The treadmill's pace picked up again and he moved faster, loafers scuffing across the surface.

And five more challenges after that. In Lucifer's beach house. How many more of those heart eater things waited for him out there?

It still chilled his bones to see that thing leap past Gianni and Banks and they never even saw it. Never felt it. Never sensed it. How many of those things had been around him in the first two seasons of the show? Leering in his face. Hungering for him in his sleep.

Or even the angels of death. Clustered around him with wings spread. Watching his every move. It made him shiver with dread. Had Talia stood over him like that? Watching him? Judging him. Deciding whether to cross him over or not?

Whatever that meant.

He shuddered, fighting the movement in his bloodied left shoulder that still seeped into his Henley as the treadmill whined, speed increasing. He was jogging now, keeping up with the droning pace, the motor so loud in his ears.

Did she know every memory in his head—including the terrible ones from this house that he couldn't remember? Could she see them all? Did she know everything they did to him? While he was blacked out? While he was too numb to move?

Couldn't make them stop touching him. Using him. Making him react to things he never wanted. Hadn't consented to.

Shadows straddling him. Hands running down his chest. Up his legs. Long red fingernails pressing white powder under his nose. Tamping it into his nostrils so he'd inhale it like air in order to breathe.

Treadmill whined, moving faster. He was running now. Hard. His breath coming in heavy huffs.

Memories of the muffled sounds of his mouth struggling to form the word, no. It had hung there, the n stuttering on his tongue, lips so numb he couldn't purse them into an o. And when he'd finally forced it out, it was just an ignored sound beneath their laughter.

He smashed his eyes closed, face contorting at the twisted, dark images awakening in his head. He didn't want to know this! Didn't want to remember it!

His feet beat hard against the treadmill as its pace became frenetic, legs pumping, arms churning, blood dripping down his arm and soaking into the navy blue Henley. Sweat dripped down the sides of his face, collecting like a mask against his cheeks and chin.

The treadmill was out of control, jerking and racing and he struggled to keep up with it. Soles of his feet burning. Breathing like a steam engine. Legs tangling.

He fell backward, rolling off the back of the treadmill. Onto the rubber mat. He laid on his back, the room spinning as he tried to stabilize his breathing.

The red-soled spiked heels startled him. Pale pink. Standing beside his head. Long, milky pale legs. Short, tight pink skirt. Tight white blouse.

He looked up. Wild auburn curls. Too blue eyes and freckled nose.

Rachel.

"Jack," she said, smiling, as she dropped down beside him. "I should have warned you about the treadmill." A hand against his hair. Stroking.

He shirked away from her touch. Glaring. His stomach in knots.

"Sorry about Lare's cruelty," she said, fingers brushing his cheek. "He's just jealous of what we used to have."

He stared at her, wary. Tense. Angry. She hadn't said a kind word to him in years. Long before she walked out.

"We had a good thing once, Jack," she said, long pink fingernails working their way through his hair. "I've missed you."

The cloying scent of her perfume hit him with too many roses, too much cinnamon, way too much patchouli and jasmine. Coiling through his brain with an ache that touched his heart. It had been so good in the beginning. Like everything in his life. Until she took him apart, piece by piece, moment by moment. Then tore out his beating heart right in front of him and slammed it on the floor.

"We used to have such good times here," she said, glancing up at the walls. "In this house. Champagne on the beach. Walking along the ocean. Spending days at a time in bed, watching the sun set. You still remember that, don't you?"

Like the meningitis he had in college that almost killed him.

He just stared. He felt only malice for this woman who'd gaslighted him for years about his career. His reviews. His love. The woman who fed him cocaine like three square meals until he reached blackout stage and even forced it into him when he'd blacked out. He was her spring house cleaning project. Remove him from *SanFran Confidential* and put the spotlight back on her real lover. The one she'd been with the entire time she was with him.

"Here, let's help you remember," she said.

There was white powder cupped in one of her long fingernails. She pressed the nail hard under his nose, smashing it against his nostrils.

"Just breathe, Jack, and it will all get better. I promise."

He fought, but she pinned his left shoulder with her knee. Straddling him with her right leg, spiked heel trapping his right arm against his side. The pain was excruciating.

"No!" he shouted. "Don't!"

She slapped her left hand over his mouth, forcing the powder up his nose. "Breathe, damn you!"

But he couldn't hold his breath. He sucked a breath through her fingers. But the powder was already numbing him, the taunting hint of gasoline and nail polish telling his brain this was high quality flake. Awakening the burn and the ache and the hunger all over again.

She was holding something in her hand now. Something glinting in the lights. Something sharp.

His eyes widened at the syringe she squeezed.

"That's right, Jack," she purred. "If you won't be a good boy, I'll have to tap a vein."

The pinch against his left arm startled him. The first wave of euphoria slammed through his body like a Formula One race car on its first lap. And he was floating. And it was all numb and white. And he couldn't remember why he'd ever stopped.

"There," said Rachel, leaning down.

She thrust her mouth against his, tongue pressing deep, hand sliding under his shirt. Into his jeans.

But he couldn't move. Couldn't speak. Couldn't stop himself from reacting to her touch.

24

TALIA RUSHED TOWARD THE WEIGHT ROOM, GIANNI BEHIND HER. Muriel at her side.

Until she threw her hands out, pushing Talia away from the doorway.

"You don't want to go in there," she said, face contorting. "Send Armand Gianni instead."

She glared at Muriel, trying to push past, but she held her a moment.

"She got to him, Talia," said Muriel, anger in her eyes. "Send Armand. Now."

Her eyes burned with fury, feeling the tiny brush of feathers across her shoulder blades. She scowled at Muriel, pushing past her. She grabbed hold of the doorway. Pulling herself inside the room as Armand hurried behind her.

Jack was on the floor, Rachel straddling him, mouth over his, her fingers at his jeans zipper.

Cold, icy rage cut through her. She lunged at Rachel, knocking her into the floor. Spiked heels stuck to the rubber mat as she rose up on her haunches, lip bleeding. Over-bright blue eyes filled with hate.

Gianni was beside Jack, calling his name in a quiet voice, but Jack stared at the ceiling, her pink lipstick clinging to his mouth and chin. Traces of white powder clinging to his upper lip and nose.

She wanted to rage. To pound this woman into a red stain against the rubber mat. She'd finally gotten to him.

"Jack? Do you hear me? It's Armand. Jack!" He patted Jack's face with his hand. "Jack, do you hear me?"

His faded jeans and light blue dress shirt had splotches of Jack's blood on it as he stared into Jack's light green eyes.

Jack didn't even seem cognizant of Armand's presence, the corners of his mouth pursed, lips moving. But not a sound emerged.

"What's he saying, Armand?" Talia asked.

Armand leaned close to his face, ear turned toward him. Finally, he looked up at her with sad eyes.

"He's saying no. Over and over."

"Oh, Jack," she said with a moan and laid her hand against his cheek.

Rachel had probably surprised him. And with that shoulder, it wouldn't have taken much to overpower him. He didn't understand this new power he'd exhibited with the oblivion sphere yet. Probably didn't even remember he had it.

Then Armand's gaze snapped toward something on the floor beside Jack's head. He grabbed Jack's left arm, touching the top of his hand as he picked up something from the rubber mat. He held it out to her and she squinted.

It reminded her of the woman doing crack in that alley so long ago. Where this whole journey began for Talia. Image of syringes and needles lying along the alley floor came back to her and her heart raced. Exactly what Armand held out to her.

Rachel was grinning now. "Shot him up with enough flake to turn a titan." She nodded toward Jack. "Blame Jack," she said. "Refused to snort it on his own, so I improvised."

"You bitch!" Talia hauled off and slammed her fist into Rachel's face.

Laying her out on the rubber mat.

"Nice one, Talia," Armand said with a smile, but his worried gaze traveled back to Jack.

Talia dropped down beside him, holding his hand as Armand checked his pulse and pressed his ear to his chest, listening to his heart.

"We have no idea how much coke she shot him up with," he said. "His pulse is racing. Heart's pounding. Skin's hot. Could have been enough to kill him." He scowled at Rachel. "Although, I doubt she'd tell us."

Talia felt sick. "This is all my fault. I let him go off alone."

Armand's eyes darkened. "He was supposed to text me or Banks if he went out alone. Dammit, Jack!" Armand pulled out his phone and his fingers flew across it. "Banks. It's Gianni. Get down to the weight room. Now."

She couldn't hear Mark's response.

"Don't care. Now. It's Jack."

He pressed a button and stuck the phone in his pocket. "Banks will help me carry Jack back to your suite. We'll have to keep watch on him in case he needs medical support."

She shook her head and gripped Jack's hand tighter, watching him stare past Armand who jumped up and grabbed some white towels from the shelf on the wall. Folding one, he lifted Jack's head and slid the towel underneath. He took a second towel and put it beneath Jack's shoulder, laying a third towel on top to absorb the blood.

"That shoulder needs stitches," Armand said with a groan. "Jack should have gotten it looked at when his neighbor's dog bit him."

"I'll see if I can convince him to see a doctor."

Armand scowled at Jack's face as he took the fourth towel and gently wiped the lipstick off Jack's mouth and chin. And the white powder away from his nose.

"What do we look for in an overdose, Armand?" Talia asked, laying her hand on his hot forehead.

She remembered Jack struggling to breathe on the set of *The Cinderella Hour* and how fast his heart had pounded against his chest. With Mark Banks trying to cool him down with cold compresses.

"Breathing difficulties, blue skin, fever among other things," said Armand. "I play a doctor on daytime television. Had several scenes where I treated a patient that overdosed. So, I had to research the symptoms and how they were treated. Best I can do until we can get the set doctor to look at him."

Footsteps pounded down the hallway and Mark Banks tumbled into the room, wearing a white sweatshirt and jeans, his spiky, light brown hair windblown.

"Jack!" Mark sprinted across the mat and dropped down beside Talia, his eyes wide, staring from Jack to Armand. "What happened?"

Then he glanced over at Rachel unconscious on the mat and smiled back at Talia.

"Your handiwork?" he asked.

"If she gets up, I'll deck her again," Talia said with a growl.

He chuckled, but the smile disappeared, his focus returning to Jack. "So, what'd she do to him?"

At last, Talia heard the whirr of the treadmill. Jack must have been on it when Rachel ambushed him. Talia pointed behind them at the machine.

"He must have been using that treadmill," she replied.

Banks squinted, jumping up to investigate the machine. He touched some buttons and the rushing sound slowed, the high-pitched whirr deepening. "Damn, this thing was set on Autobahn or something. It was flying. Maybe Jack got knocked off or something?"

Gianni stared at the treadmill and then back at Jack, nodding. "Makes sense," he said. "Especially from his position on the floor and the blood on the mat."

"I know how we can find out!" Mark cried. "There are cameras all over the house, remember? Bet this whole event is sitting on a hard drive somewhere."

"Mark, that's brilliant!" Talia cried.

She needed to know what Rachel did to him. To help him heal.

"Yes, quite ingenious, Banks," said Armand. "I intend to report this to Herb after we get Jack stabilized. I want these monsters kicked off the show. I don't care if it's their house or not. Coking up a recovering cocaine addict is brutal and I want them gone."

"I couldn't agree more, Armand," said Talia, cradling Jack's hand against her cheek. "Jack would probably pitch a fit, but this is unforgivable."

"Agreed," Mark said with a nod. "Let's get him out of here. Someplace where he can sleep it off safely while I get the footage."

"Help me, Banks," said Armand, rising from the rubber mat.

Mark bent down and took hold of Jack's legs. He nodded at Rachel as Armand lifted Jack gently under the arms.

"What about her?"

Talia shrugged. "Leave her."

"Couldn't agree more, Talia," Armand replied.

With Talia leading the way, Armand and Mark carried Jack out of the weight room and down to the end of the house. She unlocked the suite door and held it open while they carried him to the bed.

Armand nodded toward the door. "Get the footage and get Herb to meet us down here."

"I'll take care of it," said Mark. "I'll put it on my tablet, so we can show him what happened."

"Thanks, Mark," Talia replied, sitting down on the king-sized bed beside Jack.

Armand laid the back of his hand against Jack's forehead. "I'll get a wet towel, he's feverish." He sighed, shaking his head. "Wish we knew how much coke she gave him."

"Me, too," said Talia, watching the death angel guard gather around the head of the bed. Wings unfurled, grey eyes a mixture of pain and fury.

Her heart began hammering against her ribs again. Were they here in an official capacity? Or were they guarding Jack?

Armand disappeared into the bathroom. Talia turned to her right at the touch of a hand against her shoulder. She looked up. Muriel, halo burning, wings extended.

"Lucifer threw a bunch of assassin demons in our path," Muriel replied, looking forlorn. "Couldn't get to Jack in time. I'm so sorry."

The rest of the guard bowed their heads, looking ashamed. She relaxed a little. They were here to apologize to her. She winced. Not to cross Jack over.

"Thank you all for trying." She fixed Muriel with her gaze. "Can you open his Book? See what happens?"

Muriel shook her head. "The archive rejected our queries. Not sure what's happening up there. That's never happened before." Then she smiled. "So, in the absence of any data, I'm prepared to preempt any premature changes. And use my healing powers until told otherwise."

"You're my hero, Muriel," Talia cried, throwing her arms around Muriel, hugging her tightly.

"And you're mine, Talia. You and Jack. Ignoring protocols until he's okay." Muriel pointed at the guard. "We made the decision together."

Talia turned back toward Jack as Armand returned with a clear plastic spray bottle and a wet hand towel. Muriel winked at her and flicked on the wall switch. A ceiling fan whispered on, blowing cool air on Jack.

"Yes, that's the right idea, Talia," said Armand as he placed a wet towel against Jack's forehead. "By some crazy luck, I found this spray bottle in the bathroom. I filled it with water to spray him down and let the air cool him. But this fan will really help."

Muriel and the guard shrugged as they held a silent vigil for Jack.

Almost an hour later, Mark returned with Herb Rutherford, the show's director, and a tablet computer.

"Talia," he cried, rushing over to her. She rose from the bed and gripped his hands. "I'm so sorry. Mark said Jack's been injured." He leaned over Jack, his face turning dark with anger. "What happened?"

Mark held out the tablet computer. "I got Roy and Steve to download the camera footage from the weight room and grant me access. That's where it happened."

Armand touched Herb on the shoulder. "Herb, we think we know what happened and we found evidence on scene, but we won't know until we see the recording. We wanted you here as the official show representative when it was viewed."

Herb's face turned pale. "This sounds serious."

"It's worse than that," said Armand, trading anxious looks with Talia.

"All right, cue it up, Mark," said Herb, moving toward the couch.

Talia followed Armand and Mark over to the sitting area as Mark connected the tablet to the large screen television on the wall. The room was empty, a time stamp in the corner as Mark flicked on the fast forward. Until Jack entered the room. He hit play.

Jack walked over to the treadmill and climbed on. He pressed a button and the treadmill whirred to life. A slow walk. Jack looked upset, a faraway look in his eyes as he walked along the treadmill.

That kept speeding up without Jack touching it.

His gait quickened, strides lengthening.

He began to huff, feet pounding against the machine as it moved faster and faster.

"What the hell?" Armand replied softly.

"That treadmill looks like it's possessed or something," Mark replied and Talia felt the cold chill down her spine.

Because it was. By Lucifer or tampered with by Rachel and Lare. Lucifer probably alerted them to Jack's presence in the weight room while he kept Jack occupied. This was what Lare had whispered to Rachel. For her to handle it.

In a few minutes, Jack was barely keeping up with the treadmill's frantic motion until it flung him off. Into the floor.

"It did throw him off," Armand muttered, glancing at Talia.

She bit her lip and nodded, her stomach tightening as Rachel entered the room. But Jack hadn't seen her yet. He was struggling against the pain in his shoulder, disoriented.

And then Rachel was leaning over him.

"Jack," she purred, a dangerous smile on her face as she dropped down beside him. "I should have warned you about the treadmill."

She began stroking his hair and he pulled away, a look of revulsion on his face.

"Sorry about Lare's cruelty," she said, stroking his cheek. "He's just jealous of what we used to have."

He stared at her as if she wielded a knife in his face. His muscles were taut, anger pressing his mouth into a thin line.

"We had a good thing once, Jack," she said, smiling at him with a hungry look as she ran her fingers through his hair again. "I've missed you."

He looked confused. Disgusted.

"We used to have such good times here," said Rachel, glancing around. "In this house. Champagne on the beach. Walking along the ocean. Spending days at a time in bed, watching the sun set. You still remember that, don't you?"

He stared at her. Anger burning in his eyes.

"Here, let's help you remember," she said.

She had white powder in her hand, scooping it into a long fingernail. Pressing it under Jack's nose.

Talia's eyes welled with tears.

"Just breathe, Jack, and it will all get better. I promise."

He fought.

She pinned him to the floor, slamming her knee on top of his left shoulder. The pain subdued him as she straddled him with her right leg, pinning his other arm with her spiked heel. His face contorted with pain.

"No!" he shouted. "Don't!"

She slapped her left hand over his mouth, forcing the powder up his nose. "Breathe, damn you!"

It broke Talia's heart to watch him fight against the drugs. Watching him try to breathe through his mouth.

"My God," Herb said with a hiss, his hand over his mouth, eyes wide.

Armand winced, shaking his head as he glanced over at the bed. "That's horrible."

And then Rachel had a syringe in her hand.

Jack's eyes widened.

"That's right, Jack. If you won't be a good boy, I'll have to tap a vein."

His gaze jerked to his left arm after she leaned over it.

"There," she said and smashed her mouth against his, almost smothering him with a frantic kiss, her hand slipping under his shirt. Moving down to his jeans. Groping him.

Talia was seething with rage. "That monster!" she shouted, shaking with fury.

Armand took her hand in his and squeezed.

And then she and Armand appeared in the doorway. Talia watched herself hit Rachel, knocking her out the second time as Armand leaned over Jack.

Over and over, Jack's lips moved, mouth pursing. Soundlessly shouting no.

It broke her heart.

Mark paused the footage, turning to Herb. "The rest is just Armand finding the syringe and me investigating the treadmill. And then all three of us carrying Jack out of there."

Herb looked stunned. "I'm...I'm—horrified. Speechless."

Talia just wanted to go to Jack.

"Herb," Armand replied, staring at the director. "I demand that Rachel Daniels and Laren Dumont be fired immediately for what they did to Jack. It was insidious and brutal. The man's recovering from a terrible addiction and she may have jeopardized his entire recovery. And we don't even know how much coke she injected him with. She could have killed him."

Mark stepped toward Herb, tablet in hand. "And it's obvious that Jack fought her every attempt to feed him blow. Until she injected him with it."

The director was silent for several long moments, a hand over his face.

"I don't have a choice. If they try to fight me or renege on using the location, I'll show them this footage and agree not to sue them into bankruptcy if they graciously bow out of the show. And have them arrested."

"Thank you," said Talia. "This is unforgivable."

"Agreed," said Herb, getting to his feet. He went over to the bed and studied Jack's face. "Get better quick, Jack," he said in a sad voice. "This show will tank without you. But it won't even notice Rachel Daniels and Laren Dumont's departure. We'll edit the footage together that we have, redo the Truth and Lies and future portion, and film Jack's part last. Then we'll announce Rachel and Lare's dismissal. It'll shorten the show by one challenge, but we'll make up for it with camera footage and interviews. Audience won't care."

He nodded at Talia.

"If he needs a doctor, I'll have the set doctor here in minutes. Or an ambulance. We take care of our own." He smiled and touched Jack on the arm. "Especially Jack Casey, who made our success possible."

"Thanks, Herb," said Talia.

The director gripped her shoulders and then headed out the door, anger burning in his face.

Talia moved back to Jack, holding his hand as Armand sat down on the other side of the bed. Jack's face was a mask of sweat. Armand took his pulse while Mark stood beside the bed. Talia took the damp towel and mopped the sweat from Jack's face.

"Jack," Armand called, tapping him on the face. "Jack, can you hear me?"

"Man, he's in deep," said Mark, shaking his head. "Much too still and quiet."

"What do you mean?" Talia asked.

She had no experience with this drug. Her charges were usually blue and gasping for breath when she arrived to cross them over. Or just comatose.

"Coke's a stimulant," said Mark. "People like the energy blast it gives. They're excited. Restless. Frenetic. Not zoned out like this. Should we get the set doctor over here?"

Armand sighed. "Wish we knew what was in that syringe. I hope we don't have to involve the set doctor and explain about the drugs. She'd legally have to report that."

Mark shook his head. "And if paparazzi got wind of it, Jack's reputation would tank again—even though he didn't ask for these drugs." Mark nodded toward the door. "But just in case, I gave the syringe to Steve and he locked it up so it doesn't disappear. But Jack's not gasping for air or having convulsions, so I don't think he needs a doctor. Besides, the high from shooting up coke doesn't last as long as snorting it."

Armand stared at him, brow furrowing.

"What? Told you I used to be a coke slave. Not going to lie. I shot it up quite a few times."

"Talia, I'll stay with you until he shows signs of awareness and the fever breaks," said Armand. "I'm going to text Izzy and let her know where I am."

"I'm going to head out and find Morgan," said Mark with a shrug. "Left her on the beach with almost no explanation. Text me if you need me. Otherwise, I'll check in with you in an hour. See how he's doing."

Talia thanked Mark who hurried out of the room. Leaving Muriel and the guard at the head of Jack's bed, looking angry and concerned. Muriel was shaking with fury. She had a crush on Jack even though she'd never admit it. And he'd earned the guard's respect by fighting alongside them. He'd become an unofficial member of the guard since he took down that Eater of Hearts by himself.

She, Armand, Muriel, and the guard stood vigil beside Jack as he struggled through a fever and this terrible unnerving silence that had puzzled Mark and Armand. And waited.

25

J ACK BLACKED OUT SEVERAL TIMES, COMING TO ON A WAVE OF EUPHORIA. The world felt so hot, his face and hair drenched. His heart raced. And he was so tired. The wall of windows had gone dark, the ocean a smudge against the darkness as he became aware of the room around him.

He froze. Terrified. Expecting to see Rachel in the bed beside him and his clothes scattered across the bed. It made him sick.

"No," he said, the sound so weak and hollow as the high burned away.

Along with his willpower.

Already, he felt the low descending. His body so sluggish. His head aching, hands shaking. And that sharp hunger in his belly. Wanting another hit so badly that he could taste the ethery chemical on his tongue. Feel it numbing the inside of his nose. Whiff of that gasoline-like scent lingering.

He craved another hit. Burned for it.

And he hated Rachel for forcing it down him. Breaking down his defenses. His resolve.

"Jack?" Talia cried, climbing onto the bed as he lifted up his head.

"Where am I?" he demanded.

"Jack!" Gianni sat down on the side of the bed as Jack struggled to sit up.

But his left shoulder dropped him back against the pillows.

"Take it easy," said Talia. "Just rest."

"You didn't text me, Jack," Gianni said with an angry look. "Like you promised."

He sighed and bowed his head. "Sorry. Was pretty angry when I headed to the weight room. And then—it was too late. Treadmill malfunctioned and then that bitch was shoving flake up my nose." He felt the shame bubbling up. "She pinned my bad shoulder. Couldn't make her stop. I didn't seek out the blow."

"We saw the camera footage."

Oh, my God. They had his failure online? "Oh, no."

He felt a hand against his neck, kneading. Talia. He tried to hold onto his anger, his resolve, but it melted the longer he stared into her eyes.

"They're being kicked off the show, Jack," said Gianni.

"Tell that to Lucifer," he snapped.

Gianni gave him a funny look. "Lucifer?"

"He's gotta be their agent. You know, the devil?"

Gianni laughed. "Then he probably wants more than fifteen percent."

"Of their souls? Probably already owns a hundred percent and all their residuals."

Talia was smiling at him. She reached out and took his hand in hers, cradling it against her chest. He didn't pull away.

Gianni patted his arm. "Looks like Jack's going to be fine, Talia. Herb rescheduled your shoot until tomorrow afternoon. Competition will drop one challenge because they're announcing Rachel and Lare's departure on the live show on Friday. There will still be a dismissal."

"Thanks, dude. Again. For everything."

Gianni shook a finger at him. "Dammit, Jack, text me. I mean it. Rachel and Lare may be off the show, but this is still their house. You scared Talia half to death."

He glanced over at her. Her eyes were misty and his heart

clenched. God, he felt so conflicted. He loved her, but she was leaving. And he had no way to reconcile his heart with that.

"Sorry," he said to her. "I let my anger get the best of me."

"As long as you're all right, I'll forgive you," she said and pressed against him, giving him a gentle kiss.

He tried to enjoy it, but all that came back was the sensation of Rachel with her tongue down his throat, her hands grabbing his crotch. He broke off the kiss, but Talia had this understanding look in her eyes. She rubbed his hand and sat back against the headboard.

"Get some rest and I'll see you tomorrow. To kick your ass at Truth and Lies."

"You mean you'll try."

Gianni grinned and left them alone.

He glanced around the room. No angels peered at him from the foot of the bed or behind the headboard.

He cast a quick look at Talia. He needed to apologize for being an idiot.

They both spoke at once. He stopped in mid-sentence, motioning for her to continue.

"Go ahead," he said, staring at his hands.

"No, you first," she said.

"Just wanted to apologize for being a hot-headed idiot. I just lost my mind when Muriel said your wings were growing back and you didn't tell me." He fixed her with a hard stare. "But whether you told me or not, you'll be going home—or wherever—when you can fly again. That's what I was so pissed about."

"Jack," she said, giving him that look. The one that told him he was still being an idiot. "My place is with you. With or without my wings."

"But you're immortal. I'll be lucky to make forty at this rate. And you can blink yourself around the world. Why would you choose to stay in one place—in a shitty studio apartment—with someone like me, knowing it was going to feel like a weekend." He sighed. "Besides, won't your boss make you go back to your old job of smiting people and stopping their hearts?"

She shook her head, smiling at him as she drew closer. "No, no, no, and no. See, there are some epic things happening right now. And because of our bond, it's spilled over onto you. I think the archangel is going to want to talk to you."

He laughed. "Me?"

She nodded, brushing her lips across his. "Yes, you. We don't know what it all means, but you're changing, Jack Casey. And we're connected. My boss, as you call him, will want to see these changes personally. And decide what to do."

"You mean like me being able to see angels and demons?" That wasn't a power. That was just unfortunate. An actor feeling self-conscious with a constant audience just felt wrong.

"And summoning an oblivion sphere."

She looked at him like he should understand the magnitude of it, but he didn't really know what an oblivion sphere was or how it appeared in his hand. He didn't see that as a power. At best, it was a lucky break.

"Jack, I'm the only angel of death in centuries that can conjure an oblivion sphere. They must be losing their minds in High House when they found out a human can summon one. You might be transcending a normal human life. I don't know what that means yet, but things are changing."

That was ominous. "They could decide to smite me out of existence and solve the problem."

"And lose a rare ability like that?" Her eyes were wide and animated. "Another weapon to use against Lucifer?" She smiled at him. "Not very likely. No, I'm afraid you're just stuck with me, Jack."

He smiled. "So, this means you aren't going to just fly away and leave me for the Heavens?"

"Not if I had three pairs of wings."

He frowned. "You—don't, right? Do you? I'm still trying to get used to one pair."

She broke into a fit of laughter. "Only seraphim have six wings. I'm just a lowly angel of death. Seraphim are the most powerful angels in Heaven." She leaned up to him, gently kissing him. "Sorry, just some angel humor there."

He just rubbed his forehead and sighed, making her laugh again.

"At least it wasn't angel of death humor," he replied. "Not sure my head could handle that tonight."

Talia reached up and laid the back of her hand against his head.

"You've still got a fever, Jack. I don't know if it's from the hellhound bite or…Rachel injecting you with cocaine."

He winced, his memory spiraling back to her holding a syringe and him feeling a pinch on his left arm. His hand? That bitch mainlined him with flake. He wanted to tear her head off.

"I'm really struggling with the cravings, Talia," he said, feeling the ache down deep.

"I'll call Muriel," she said, glancing over the top of the bed. "She'll use her healing—"

He pulled her against his chest, kissing her. "This is just about the first time we've been alone since you fell out of the sky," he said and kissed her again.

"You're right," she said, sliding her arms around his neck. "And there are so many things I've wanted to tell you since I landed. So many things I need to say."

"Me, too," he said, struggling to move his left arm around her waist. He held her close and nodded toward the headboard. "Starting with a conversation we started over there. On that couch." He kissed her. "The one that got interrupted."

"Oh," she said, returning his kiss. "That one." She kissed him again. "Is that the one where I threatened to push you down on the couch and tickle you?"

He nodded. "It was something about me needing attention, but close enough. Let's start there."

He laid her back on the pillow, kissing her as he struggled out of his Henley. She pushed it over his head and onto the bed as his hands slid under her half sweater, rolling it up and over her head. It fell into the floor as he ran his hands under that pink tank top, stroking her breasts as he sipped her mouth. He pushed up her tank top, over her head onto the bed, pressing urgent kisses against her jaw and down her neck. Along her collarbone, down to her breasts.

Her hands slid across his chest, her body trembling as he kissed her breasts, right hand sliding down her hip. Up her thigh. Under that short skirt.

"I like this conversation," she said with a gasp as his hand slid between her legs.

Her breath was ragged, hands frantic against his body as he struggled out of his jeans and boxer briefs. She slid off her skirt and panties. Her arms enfolded him as he rolled her under the sheets and against his hard, lean body.

"Sure you want this?" he asked.

"You to make love to me?"

He nodded.

"I've waited for this moment for three seasons, Jack Casey," she said, kissing him, her hands sliding down his chest.

"So have I," he replied, kissing her mouth again. "Wasn't sure if angels—"

"Have sex?"

She tangled her fingers in his hair, pulling his mouth to hers. She smiled at him then smashed her mouth against his again, urgent, anxious.

He grinned, pressing his body against hers, her winter-pale skin silky soft. She moved against him, her hips lifting, thighs pressing against his as she slid them around his legs.

"Let's find out."

She wrapped her arms around his back, pulling him closer. Against her as he pressed his body against hers, moving until he gently entered her. With a gasp, she held him tighter, her hips moving with his rhythmic thrusts until they were moving in tandem.

Her hands slid up and down his back, fingers tangling in his hair, holding him closer. He pressed his face against her sweat-slicked skin. Her lean, smooth body felt so good against him, his breath huffing. Her hips thrust against him. His movements quickened, pumping deeper, faster.

Frantic, he moved faster inside her until he felt her body tremble against him. She gasped, pressing her hips against him, her arms tightening around him. Her breath burned across his neck as his body slid against hers in an aching rhythm of need, his heart pounding. He whispered her name in her ear, lips brushing across her earlobe.

"I love you," he said in a raspy whisper.

He nuzzled her neck, thrusting, the heat of her body pulsing through his until the first shudders of release rippled through him. Deeper, faster, urgent until at last, he collapsed against her, panting, losing himself in her touch, her heat.

She just held him, laying her face against his, a hand against his chest. Naked and entwined, they watched the moon rise above the ocean.

THE NEXT DAY, TALIA AND JACK ARRIVED ON SET IN THE GAME ROOM and stood at their podiums as the other contestants took their places. She wore her short red skirt and red blouse that Muriel had changed to match the reds together. Jack wore jeans and a dark green and gold-striped dress shirt, his left shoulder packed with two gauze pads and a bandage wrapping it. The dark shirt hid the bandages tucked beneath it.

He carried his left arm gingerly against his side, not telling her it was hurting a lot more than he'd let on this morning. Where Rachel had pinned it with her knee. His light green eyes narrowed as he pressed his lips together, wincing against the pain.

She held Jack close, her arms around him, loving the feel of his body against hers. The memory of him finally making love to her would stay with her for the rest of her existence. A tiny treasure within the bleakness of her role as an angel of death. But she knew that their bond was special, causing her emerging and returning powers to be mirrored within him. She felt that bond deepening. She would protect it from Rachel Daniels and the rest of Lucifer's minions. Including Lucifer.

She hoped that when Heaven recognized their bond and the

powers it brought, she would have every chance to stay with him. Jack had some role in defeating Lucifer which meant that somehow, he would transcend his human existence. She needed Azrael's guidance and the assurance of knowing where Jack stood in all of the chaos soon to come.

But for now, she was in his arms, at his side. And she'd fight all of them to stay there. And today, that meant not losing this challenge.

She glanced over at Rachel and Lare's podium. Empty. Good. If she saw that bitch again, she was liable to smite her with her bare fists.

The day was long, reshooting all the questions and the Three Truths and a Lie. She listened to Riya's rewrites, ready to react accordingly if she insulted Jack again. Armand and Mark both look nervous as Riya read off her statements. The one about Jack had been rewritten to her favorite food. And Eric still missed the lie.

Nicole and Tyler went next. They cast a dozen glares at Jack, but they kept their statements out of personal areas. Nicole got Tyler's lie wrong, but Tyler came up with the correct answer.

"Mark, please read your statements for Morgan," said Devin, dressed in khaki pants, black dress shoes, and a blue dress shirt.

Mark wore a brown blazer over dark jeans and a dark blue T-shirt. "I did my first commercial at five. I hate craft beer. I've acted in television shows for fifteen years. My favorite food is lasagna."

Devin turned to camera two. "Morgan, please tell us the lie."

She smiled. "My favorite food is lasagna."

"Sorry, the correct answer is I hate craft beer."

Mark winced and hugged her.

"Morgan, read your statements please."

Morgan looked disappointed as she read her statements from a notecard. "I'm from Iowa. My first job was handing out samples at a grocery. I earned my first acting credit for television. And my favorite food is Filet Mignon."

Devin turned to Mark. "Mark, what is the lie."

Mark grinned at her. "I'm from Iowa. You're from Illinois."

"Yes, that's correct, Mark."

Morgan threw her arms around Mark and kissed him.

"All right, Armand and Isabella. Isabella, your statements please." Devin turned to Izzy, waiting for her responses.

Izzy wore a burnt orange shirt dress with a black belt, her copper-colored locks in a springy bob, warm brown eyes bright as she turned toward Armand, smiling. "All right. I graduated with degrees in journalism and telecommunications. I went to Stanford. I drive a Volvo. I work in San Francisco."

"Armand," Devin said, "Tell us the lie."

Armand looked at Izzy, his brown eyes filled with infatuation. "I work in San Francisco. She now works in Los Angeles."

"Correct!" Devin responded. "Armand, your statements please."

He flashed a bright, charming smile through the room. "I was born in Italy. I love football, not the American kind. I own two dogs. I play a doctor on daytime television."

"Izzy, what is the lie?"

Izzy looked smug as she leaned close to Armand. "You own one dog, not two."

"Correct! Great job!"

Izzy kissed him hard and he enfolded her in his arms as Devin turned to Jack.

"All right, Jack and Talia," he said, watching them carefully. "Talia, please read your statements."

Jack stiffened beside her, chewing his bottom lip as he waited for her statements.

"I have only been in California for six months. My favorite hobby is flying."

He smirked at her.

"I love hot weather. I have never tasted shrimp."

She looked up from the card again and he was grinning.

"Jack, what is the lie?"

"You love hot weather," he said, gazing into her eyes.

"Correct, Jack!" Devin turned to camera one. "All right, Jack, please read your statements."

"I was born in Indiana. I have four sisters. My dad lives in New Jersey. I majored in marketing."

"Talia, tell us which one of Jack's statements is a lie."

She gazed at him for a moment, remembering all his stories about his dad being a carpenter and making furniture. His dad was dead.

"Devin, it's my dad lives in New Jersey. Jack's dad passed away when he was eighteen."

Jack bowed his head.

"That's correct, Talia! Great job, you two! And it looks like Armand and Izzy and Jack and Talia are tied for first place going into the future match questions. Let's see how our couples match on their visions of the future. After the break."

"Cut!" Herb called. "Print that. Move on to the future match please."

"All right, everyone, hold places while we cue up," Steve announced, his hair loose around his shoulders today, beard close-cropped. He wore a blue *Prince Charming Hour* T-shirt and jeans. "Two minutes."

Talia leaned over and kissed Jack. He smiled, brushing a lock of black hair out of her eyes.

"Last night was amazing," he whispered, his lips brushing against her ear, tingling down her neck.

"Yes, it was," she replied in a quiet voice.

"Thanks for getting me through last night," he said, suddenly serious. "I hope I can get through whatever comes next."

She whispered against his ear. "Are the cravings bad?"

He nodded. "First forty-eight hours are gonna be rough."

She ran her fingers through his hair. "I'll keep a close watch on you," she said.

"In case I need attention?" he asked, smirking at her.

She slid her hand inside his shirt, stroking his chest. "I take my job very seriously, Jack Casey."

"We'll discuss this when we break for lunch," he said with a wink and kissed her.

"Ready to roll. Places. Devin, camera one."

Devin stepped back to his place behind his podium and Jack stood up straighter, waiting for the next part of this challenge to unfold.

"And we're back, my royal subjects," Devin said into camera one. "And now, we move onto the final piece of our first challenge. The future match." He turned to camera two. "Will our couples share a similar view of the future together? Let's find out."

Devin shuffled some white notecards in his hand and turned to Tyler and Nicole.

"All right, Tyler and Nicole, let's start with you. Nicole, I'm going to read four possible futures to you. Nicole, you tell me which one is Tyler's and Tyler, identify Nicole's future."

Devin shuffled another card. "Together, our future will be traveling the globe, fast cars, and a beach house in Bali." He cleared his throat. "We will have a house in Portugal, a house in France, and a villa in Italy, tasting wine and the world together." Again, Devin shuffled a card. "Family and friends in abundance. Success in all ventures. And a beach house in Malibu," he read from the card. "And the final future is, successful long careers that we love, funds to cover our wildest dreams, and all the clout that comes with both."

Talia looked at Jack, seeing him struggle not to make a face.

"All right, Nicole, tell me which one is Tyler's vision of the future."

Nicole tossed her light brown hair off her shoulder, hazel eyes looking confused. "Could you read them again please?"

Devin reshuffled his cards and read them again. Waiting while she seemed to be lost in thought.

"Nicole, I need your answer."

Finally, she sighed, glanced at Tyler, and turned back to Devin. "The beach house in Bali."

Devin turned to Tyler. "Tyler, which one is Nicole's future?"

"I'm going with the beach house in Malibu," said Tyler, looking nervous.

Devin shuffled another card and looked up at them. "I'm sorry, but both answers are incorrect."

Devin moved on to Ryder and Claire, and neither one got the other's future statement right. He read off future statements for Eric and Riya and they just looked at each other and guessed.

"I'm sorry, Eric and Riya. Both answers are incorrect," said Devin.

He pulled another stack of cards from behind the podium and shuffled through them. "All right, Mark and Morgan, let's see if you can identify each other's statements."

"We're ready, Devin," said Mark, smiling at Morgan who looked nervous.

"I see a little cottage in the hills with dogs and cats and lots of fruit trees," said Devin, shuffling the first card. "I see nights together, snuggling and binge watching our favorite shows and weekends building a new life together," he read and moved to the next card. "Traveling, hiking, and skiing, and finding each other's strengths." He shuffled another card and looked up. "And finally, working together to build a life of fun and support in a place we can call home."

Morgan seemed to be running all those statements through her mind and Mark was smiling.

"Mark, you're smiling. Tell us Morgan's statement."

He glanced at Morgan. "Well, Devin, Morgan's from Illinois and her parents have an orchard there. So, I'm going to say the cottage with fruit trees."

Morgan's eyes lit up, making Talia smile. She looked so happy.

"Morgan, your response?" Devin asked.

"Mark likes to hike and ski, so I'm going to say that."

Devin paused, looking at his cards again. "And two points for Mark and Morgan. Nice work."

Morgan squealed and threw her arms around Mark, kissing him.

Smiling, Devin moved to Armand and Izzy. They both looked nervous. Talia felt those same nerves, hoping she'd know what Jack saw for the future. She glanced at him. He looked calm and cool, those Casey nerves of ice engaged. She had no idea if he was even nervous. He hid those things well under his *everything's just fine* mask. That always troubled her. She never knew when he was troubled until the trouble was huge. Unless she used her angel of death senses to find out.

She reached over and laid her hand on his. Shaking him out of his thoughts. He glanced down at her hand and then up at her, through that thick fringe of lashes and sizzle of those sexy green eyes. One corner of his mouth lifted into a crooked smile and he squeezed her hand with his other hand.

"Isabella and Armand," Devin replied, holding out a card. "Here are your responses. I see a future of discovering little coffee houses and festivals, enjoying outdoor concerts, and being together when things get difficult." He shuffled a card. "I see weekend trips to romantic little bed and breakfasts, Sunday mornings tangled together drinking coffee and catching up with the world in our own good time."

Devin paused and pulled out more cards from his pocket. "So many cards," he said with a chuckle. Another shuffle. "Late nights and dancing, exploring the world around us together, for better or worse. And the last one, "Days and nights of forgiving the little things and negotiating the big things as we fall in love a little more every week."

"Armand, please identify Izzy's statement."

Armand reached out and laid his hand against Izzy's cheek. "Izzy is a journalist and her job is to make sense of the world. That's important to her. I will say drinking coffee and catching up with the world."

Devin turned to Izzy. "Isabella? Armand's statement."

Izzy laid her hand against Armand's. "Armand is a realist, but he's also a romantic at heart. I will say falling in love a little more each week."

Devin grinned. "Nailed it. Both of you. Congratulations."

Armand pulled Izzy into his arms for a long, steamy kiss that left her a little shaken.

Talia's stomach dropped as she glanced at Jack. He gripped the podium with his right hand. She smiled. A chink in his armor. His knuckles were turning white as he smiled at Devin. He was more nervous than she was.

"Jack, Talia, identify the other's statement from these four choices."

"We're ready," said Talia, watching him pull out two cards and set them on the podium.

"First statement. I want to move forward together, with both feet firmly on the ground."

Talia dismissed that statement immediately. Jack would never say that. He liked to keep moving.

"Next statement. I want to find a quiet little place where we can both just be who we are and love each other without the world getting in the way."

Devin shuffled a card. "Third statement. I want to learn to fly with you in my arms, never letting my feet touch the ground or my heart ever knowing a moment without you at my side."

That was Jack. Such a romantic. And when he loved, it was with his whole heart and soul. She wanted to wade through every single word and let it roll over her.

"Last statement. "I want to soar above the cloud tops and ride the air currents, never leaving your side. Loving you without end."

Devin smiled and looked up at her and Jack. He seemed moved by those last two statements. And she understood why. They were two sides of the same future. Matching.

"Talia? Identify Jack's statement."

She turned toward Jack and took both his hands in hers, gazing into his eyes, the fire of attraction and need burning deep. "Jack's statement is never letting my feet touch the ground."

"Jack?" Devin replied.

He didn't even hesitate as he lifted his hands from hers, taking her face in his hands. "Talia's is soaring above the cloud tops."

He didn't even wait for Devin's response as he leaned forward with the gentlest kiss that left her weak in the knees.

"Nailed it, Jack and Talia!" Devin was grinning at them both. Then he turned toward camera two. "That was the closest match for this competition. Awarding one additional point to Talia and Jack. We'll have the final scores on Friday's live show, so stay tuned as we interview the princesses in our royal couples. We asked each of them how they planned to work with their prince charmings in this royal courtship. First up is Riya Patel and Morgan Boyer. Stay with us."

"Cut!" Herb announced. "Print it."

"All right, everyone," Steve called to the crew as they swarmed into the game room. He shifted his lanky frame back and forth behind the cameras, directing crew. "Let's get these podiums broken down. And I want that prop inventory for tomorrow in my hands by two o'clock. Let's get it done."

Jennifer stepped into the group of couples, clipboard in hand. "All right, princesses, lunch and then we need to continue with the interviews. Prince charmings, you have some paperwork to fill out. After lunch. And prince charmings, you'll have your schedules in your email for tomorrow and Thursday. And then Friday for the live show. Dress formal. Work with the stylists to approve your outfits."

Tyler glared at Jack and then turned to Jennifer. "So, where's Rachel and Lare?"

Jennifer looked uncomfortable now. "We'll discuss that on Friday."

Tyler turned back to Jack, animosity burning in his eyes. He moved past Jack and bumped into him on purpose, throwing his shoulder into Jack's left shoulder. Jack's face turned white and he slumped against the podium in silent agony until he could move again.

"Whoops, my bad," Tyler replied, glaring at Jack. "Better watch out there, Jack." Then his voice dropped to a whisper. "Accidents happen."

Jack sucked in a breath, lids hooded over his eyes as he waited out the pain. Talia moved in front of the podium, blocking Tyler and Nicole from getting close as they followed Jennifer. He'd chosen a moment when no one was watching. She wanted to smite him back to Hell, but those powers hadn't returned to her yet."

"Are you okay?" she asked Jack.

He nodded, catching his breath as he slid his arm around her and they filed out of the game room. Back toward the big dining table with the white leather chairs. He was leaning to the left a bit as the first spots of blood appeared on his shirt.

"I'm gonna run out of shirts soon," he said with a groan.

She ached to have her powers back, wanting to heal him or at least lessen the pain. He'd been struggling with that injured shoulder for nearly a week. But hellhound bites were tricky. They didn't heal well.

The table was spread with things Talia hadn't seen before. A stack of small, round, flat things beside a bunch of bowls. Shredded lettuce, rice, shredded cheese, diced tomatoes. There were two different kinds of beans and shredded meats. Bowls of white stuff, green stuff, and red stuff sat beside it. Sauces? And a steamy bowl of something that was pale yellow and goopy. It had a label on it. Queso.

"What is all this?" Talia asked Jack as he picked up a plate, placing it in his left hand. He picked up the tongs with his right hand, tossing two of the small flat things on his plate.

"Tacos," he said, whispering in her ear. "Watch me."

He smeared white stuff across both flat things. "Sour cream," he said, smiling, as he plopped some rice and shredded meat on top of the sour cream. "Rice and chicken." He spooned on shredded cheese, lots of tomatoes, and that hot, goopy queso. "Queso Blanco. It's a Mexican white cheese dip. Delicious!" He spooned a little bit of green stuff and lots of the red stuff. "A little guacamole—avocado dip. And lots of Pico de Gallo—fresh salsa."

"It looks wonderful," she said, wanting to try it.

"Want to make your own or eat the one I made for you?"

She loved that he'd made one for her. "I'll try the one you made."

He slid one onto another plate and set it down. He handed the other plate to her.

"Here you go."

She reached toward it, but he held up his hand. "A little maintenance first," he said. "Watch."

He took hold of the sides of the flat thing and folded them into the center and sort of rolled the flat thing closed. He held it above his plate. "See, comes in its own container. Makes it easier to eat." He grinned. "Your turn. But be careful or it'll all be in your lap."

He held over his plate and took a bite. Then wiped his chin with a napkin. He set a few napkins in front of her plate. "You'll need these."

She struggled to fold over the flat thing so it didn't leak out. He smiled, watching her until she got it settled enough to take a bite. The mix of flavors was enchanting. The warm cheese and the cold sour cream mixing with the tomatoes and the rice. It was incredible. She took another bite.

"Jack, how'd you put all that together like this? It's amazing."

He laughed. "Gotta give the credit to Mexico, not me. Not really authentic, but it was their idea."

Jack went back for two more tacos and brought her another one. They ate in silence until Jack, glancing around the room, leaned over to her and spoke in a quiet voice.

"Why does everybody in this house have to slam my bad shoulder every chance they get?"

She wasn't sure if they were doing their best to hit Jack from every direction or if there was a reason that they kept reinjuring that shoulder. They kept hitting it until it bled. Hellhound and demon bites didn't heal quickly and usually festered. Jack's wound was almost a week old and it would probably take months to heal. Without divine intervention. Muriel promised to heal it after she'd spoken to Azrael.

Why hadn't Anahera returned yet? Maybe Azrael was making preparations for something? But she was growing concerned about how much that wound had already bled Jack. It had weakened him. And so had the cocaine cravings.

She felt like they were setting Jack up for something, but she couldn't put a name to it. Couldn't figure out what.

"Promise me you'll stick close to Armand or Mark when I'm at my interviews," she said, laying a hand on his leg.

"Talia, I don't—"

She glared at him. "Jack Casey, you promise me."

"I can take care of myself," he said, getting that stubborn, angry look on his face.

He wanted to fight this and the others involved. And that included hellhounds and Lucifer. He needed to understand that he couldn't fight this alone.

"Not this time," she said, hands on her hips now. "Promise me."

At last, he sighed and slumped back in his chair. "All right! I promise."

"So, you will text Armand or Mark?"

He was silent and that worried her.

"Jack, they could kill you. What if all four of them ambushed you? Remember Lucifer on the beach?"

She watched the fear flicker in those light green eyes, the realization sinking in finally.

"You're right," he said, nodding. "I'll make sure Gianni or Banks is with me."

Talia finished her second taco and washed her hands in the sink. She moved back to Jack still working on his last taco and slid her arm around his neck. Kissing the side of his face. She ran her fingers through his blond hair.

"Dinner on the beach tonight?" she asked.

"I like that idea," he said. "I'll go scout out a spot while you're doing interviews."

She gave him an angry look, hands on her hips.

"What?" he said, holding out his arms.

She crossed hers, still staring at him.

"Gianni and I will scout out a spot," he said, his lip curling. "Happy now?"

She nodded and kissed him on top of the head. "Be careful."

"You, too," he said as she walked out of the room.

She turned left down the curving hallway toward an enclosed den where they were holding interviews. Jennifer stood outside the white, six-paneled door, clipboard in hand.

"Right on time, Talia," she said and checked something off on it. "Have a seat."

Two white leather dining chairs set in the hallway outside the room. She sat down, her thoughts going back to Jack and she worried what he'd do while she was apart from him. She was terrified that Lare and Rachel would get him alone and kill him. But something felt wrong. Like they were setting something up.

Had she miscalculated Lucifer's plan? And why hadn't Azrael addressed any of these breaches of protocols. No, it was worse than that. It was an act of war. And by High House, she couldn't figure out what Lucifer was waiting for. Were they safe here among the chained shield wards? Or was Lucifer letting them believe they were safe until he set his plan into motion?

She had to figure out what Lucifer was waiting for—before Jack paid the ultimate price for it.

27

FRIDAY CAME FAST. FIRST DISMISSAL. JACK DRESSED IN A SILVER SUIT AND white shirt, no tie, Talia in a red dress that made his blood boil. He worried that his shoulder would bleed all over the white shirt, but Talia wrapped it with extra gauze and extra layers of elastic bandage over the wound. And he worried what Tyler and Nicole would do when Rachel and Lare's departure was announced. He hadn't seen them at the house since Rachel attacked him. Were they even still here?

"How do I look?" Talia asked, twirling in a circle as he stepped away from the dresser.

"Hotter than the Las Vegas strip in July," he replied, taking in the curve of her hips, soft taper of her waist, small firm breasts. Full lips begging to be kissed.

Those incredible big grey eyes gleamed with an inner glow. Admiring him in his suit. She looked relaxed, settled, as if all the bad things were behind them.

He knew they were just a heartbeat away. And he couldn't tell her.

He'd struggled with the flake cravings all week, not telling her how bad they'd gotten. She'd slept through his nightmares. Him walking the floor, restless, agitated. He felt that familiar hollow ache, the hunger burning so hot in him that he'd nearly called Lenny three times that night. That life was still just a text away and he'd been fighting it all week.

He took her into his arms and pressed kisses against her mouth, his lips sliding to her neck. She nuzzled her face against his hair, hands sliding underneath his jacket.

"We'll be late," she whispered in his ear.

"Can't you freeze time or something?" he said, nibbling her ear lobe.

"Not until I get my powers back," she said in a husky voice, leaning into him now.

"Wow, that was a joke," he said, "but now that I know—"

"Jack…"

He let her go and she pulled on silver flats. "Ready?" he asked with a disappointed sigh.

She nodded and wrapped her arm in his as they hurried out of the suite and out to the back terrace. The sun had set, the ocean still illuminated with its glow along glassy, churning waves as dusk settled against the cool air. The set crew had placed about a hundred flickering ivory candles (beneath set lights) alongside clear vases of lavender roses and spiky white jasmine blooms across the stone terrace that overlooked the beach. The air was fragrant with jasmine, sea spray, and a touch of roses.

There were six colored tape marks spread in a half-circle around a single mark reserved for Devin Van Fossen. The ocean, the candles (and set lights), and the curved stone terrace were the perfect stage for the dismissal, reminding him of all those times he'd stood on the one outside Beverly Hills. At Cinderella's palace. Aching for Talia and this time, she was beside him.

He pulled her close, wanting to feel her beside him, against his body. This place haunted him in ways that he couldn't even articulate. It made him miss the palace, but not the times away from Talia.

He glanced around as the other couples found their marks, Gianni and Izzy beside him and Talia. Lost in their own little worlds and he felt a pang of envy. No hellhounds or demons or angels of death, just each other and that burning flame of attraction. His kept getting tamped by demons and angels barging into the bedroom. But as long as Talia was still with him, he'd put up with all of it.

This first dismissal wouldn't be difficult and he knew that next week, everything could change. But this week, he and Talia were safe. Still, it felt good having her at his side instead of facing off with each other, fearful that the other would be sent home. At least, if they went home this time, they went home together.

Unless Talia's boss had something to say about his angel of death loving a human. He worried about that. And about Lucifer FedExing him down to Hell via hellhound courier. But for tonight, they were safe.

Devin stood in front of the white and frosted glass French doors, wearing a black tailcoat, black pants, white shirt, and black bowtie. His customary attire for dismissals.

"We go live in five minutes, couples...so places," Herb announced, leaning forward in his director's chair behind the cameras.

"You heard the man," Steve announced from the cameras off to the right of the stone terrace. "Find your marks, stick close, and don't fidget. We're live in five."

Devin was studying the small stack of notecards in his hand as he did a sound check on his mic.

Jack watched Armand, wearing a charcoal grey suit and pale pink shirt, whisper in Izzy's ear. She laughed, tossing that coppery, bobbed hair, her burnt orange dress looking like a sunset, the sleeves a see-through, shimmery fabric. Morgan leaned against Mark who wore a brown tweed jacket, coral shirt, and blue slacks, Morgan wearing a short black dress. Eric wore a black pin-striped suit, white shirt, and yellow tie, Riya in a yellow dress. Ryder wore a tan suit and blue shirt, Claire in a pale mint dress. Nicole's dress glittered with silver and blue crystals, short and tight, Tyler in a royal blue suit, white shirt, and white tie.

He hoped that they'd be the first to leave, but he knew better. No, it would be one of the arranged couples that left. They had the lowest scores.

"Two-minute warning," Steve said. "Devin, camera one and hold."

Devin nodded, running through his cards again as crew stepped out of the scene, clustering behind cameras and moving into the background.

Jack wrapped his arms tighter around Talia's waist, resting his chin on her shoulder as they waited. She reached up, fingers cool against his cheek.

"You feel hot," she whispered.

"That an observation or a compliment?" he asked with a smirk.

"Both," she replied. "You feel fever hot."

He shrugged. He was a little feverish. Wasn't sure if it was the bite wound or the coke, but he was okay.

"Hot for you," he said, kissing her cheek.

She smiled and leaned into him again as he nuzzled her neck.

"Thirty seconds." Steve announced.

Jack glanced up, feeling someone staring at him. He glanced past Gianni and Banks. At Nicole Reardon. She was fixing him with a deep stare, her hazel eyes flickering red as the night darkened.

And then the world froze. Even Talia unmoving, stopped in mid-look toward him. Nicole began walking toward him. A slow, sultry walk. Past Banks. Past Gianni. Past Talia. She stood barely a foot in front of him, her eyes so red. He stood his ground.

"You think Rachel and Lare were the ones to worry about, Jack?" She tossed her lion's main of hair back and laughed. "Think again."

She waved her hand and red trails appeared across the terrace. Blood. He began to shake when she smiled at him.

It was his blood.

"Why?" he demanded.

"All in good time."

She grabbed his left shoulder with both hands, squeezing hard until he almost blacked out from the pain. He snapped his hand around her right wrist and bent her arm back, but the nails of her left hand sank into the tender, puffy bite. The air sparkled, Jack's shout echoing across the terrace as he dropped to his knees and then threw himself backward, dislodging her hand from his shoulder.

Already, wet, sticky blood soaked into his white dress shirt. Trickling onto the stone floor, lengthening the trail of his blood. It made no sense.

"Why are you doing this?" he shouted through gritted teeth.

She stepped over to him, bending down. She laid her hand against his face and he flinched away. She grabbed his chin and held it.

"Hellhounds need a trail to follow, Jack," she said with a chuckle. "And human blood to whet their appetites. So, they stay hungry." She glanced up at the dark sky. "The moment these wards lift, they will pounce. And drag you off to Hell. So, we're making sure the trail stays…" She laughed, a deep, throaty sound that made his skin crawl. "Warm. See, dead or alive, you're the prototype. Rachel and Lare got greedy. But Tyler and I are here to make sure Lucifer gets his weapon."

Jack jerked free of her hold and shoved her backward. She fell against the stone floor, still laughing at him.

"You may escape me and Tyler, but that wound leaves a trail for every demon and hellhound in Hell, Jack. If you manage to leave here, there won't be a place you can hide." She nodded at Talia frozen in place. "And your fallen angel of death girlfriend will be torn apart. With you, Lucifer can build an army of souls and turned humans. Talia was only the test."

"Test? What do you mean, test?" he demanded, moving in front of Talia.

"So gallant," she said, getting up from the ground. "He knows her wings are growing back. And her powers are returning. Confirmation of the path to his own return. But he'll still take her. To torture the archangel. And he'll enjoy making her watch you being tortured as your soul is used to churn out an endless army." She gave him another smug look. "For eternity."

He lifted his hand. And something small, round, and gold rolled under her feet.

She glanced down, eyes narrowing, and then back at him, a puzzled look on her face.

"Welcome to oblivion, bitch," he said with a grin.

The oblivion sphere exploded under her feet. Obliterating her into demonic fragments that turned to ash and floated away on the breeze.

"You son of a bitch, Jack!" Hughes shouted at him from across the terrace, red eyes flashing.

"I get that a lot," he said as Hughes turned to shadow.

"This isn't over." Hughes cast a withering scowl at him and rushed at him.

Jack ducked as the shadow leaped off the balcony and disappeared over the cliff.

He glanced around. Well, this dismissal was going to be awkward. He'd just dismissed another couple.

Herb was going to pull the rest of his hair out when he saw that Nicole and Tyler had vanished twenty seconds before going live.

And the world unfroze, the trails of blood disappearing.

Talia's eyes filled with fear, widening when she saw the blood soaking into his shirt.

"Jack? What—"

"This dismissal's about to get really awkward," he whispered.

"Twenty seconds," Steve called out. "Hey, where's Nicole and Tyler? Tyler! Nicole! Places! We're live in seventeen seconds."

Herb was out of his chair, eyes huge, frantically whispering to Jennifer and Steve. The crew members were shaking their heads, glancing around the terrace.

"Find them," Herb hissed as Jennifer and Steve rushed inside the house.

"Your shoulder," Talia said with a gasp. "What's going on?"

"Tell you later," he said with a smile, his gaze returning to Devin as he stared at the empty mark where Nicole and Tyler had been only moments ago.

"Muriel!" Talia whispered frantically. "What's going on?"

"Ten seconds!" Herb shouted. "What are we going to do?"

"Dismiss them," Jack called out. "For low scores."

Herb gave Devin a desperate look, hands splayed as Steve sprinted back behind the cameras.

"Five seconds, Devin. Camera one. In four, three, two, one. Go."

Devin's head snapped toward camera one and he pasted on a smile, game face on. Jack didn't know whether to curl up in a ball or rampage through this place, taking down everything with even a blush of red in its eyes. Talia would lose her mind when he told her what just happened.

He sighed. If he told her.

"Good evening, my royal subjects," Devin said to camera one. Welcome to The Ever After Hour as we must say goodbye to two of our couples." Devin suddenly looked inspired. "None of our couples knew that tonight was a double elimination. One of our couples that thought they were safe is also going home tonight. Scores were based on their answers to our past, present, future challenge. Earlier this week, our contestants answered questions about each other. We take you now to those questions. See how your favorite couples responded about their pasts, presents, and futures."

"And...tape is rolling. We're clear. Fifteen minutes and four seconds." Steve.

"All right," Devin shouted, looking visibly upset as he stomped across the terrace and stared at Herb. "What the hell just happened? They were standing right there in front of me on their marks. I blinked and now, they're gone."

He glanced around at the crew, but Roy and Steve were shrugging and shaking their heads.

"Jack, what happened?" Talia asked.

"Long story," he said in a clipped tone, the ache in his shoulder intensifying.

Devin turned back to Jack. "Brilliant suggestion, Jack. I'm going to sell it as a surprise double elimination. But I really don't understand what happened here."

Jack shrugged, the sharp pain in his shoulder making him wince.

"I'm as surprised as you are, Devin. They were right there. I think this house is possessed or something."

Devin shook his head and returned to his tape mark on the terrace. "I'm beginning to wonder."

Talia was glaring at him now. "The moment we're off this live broadcast, you better spill everything or you'll regret it."

He gave her his best smirk. "Like push me down on the couch and tickle me regret it?"

"You wish," she said. "More like you're sleeping on the couch for the next week regret it."

Gianni and Banks were looking at him, wondering what was going on, but he shrugged at them and shook his head.

"Jack, I just saw Nicole watching you," said Gianni, glancing around the terrace and then at him. "Where'd she go?"

Like he could explain any of this without their heads exploding.

They were demons, Gianni. Nicole stopped time and tried to put her entire hand through my shoulder. Until I tossed an oblivion sphere at her. Yeah, I just created it out of thin air and exploded Nicole's demon ass all over the terrace. Because, apparently Talia's powers are brushing off on me like dye on a cheap suit. Her being an angel of death and all. Of course, you understand.

"I don't know, Gianni," he said with a shrug. "She was right there."

"Jack, what gives?" Banks called to him. "Where's Tyler?"

Well, see, Banks, Tyler turned into a shadow and jumped off the terrace and down a hundred-foot drop, disappearing. And don't step in any of the blood trails running across the terrace and through the entire beach house. Yeah, it's mine. It's bait for the hellhounds and demons, so they can overnight me to Hell in a handbasket for Lucifer to torture. You know, the Prince of Darkness.

Again, Jack shrugged, his shoulder burning from the movement. "Don't know. He was right there glaring at me."

Talia was still staring at him. "I wish I could freeze time right now and make you tell me what happened."

"I'll tell you later," he whispered. "There were demons involved. It got ugly."

Her eyes were full of fear now. *Great, now she was worried sick.* He hadn't even planned to tell her, but the guard—and Muriel—probably saw everything anyway.

Pissing off an angel of death was not on his To Do List today, especially the one he was in love with. Being caught in the middle of warring angels and demons sucked for a human. Especially now that he discovered that he was now the fox in Lucifer's Royal Hellhound Hunt. He didn't have the heart to tell Talia that.

He laid his hand against his forehead, feeling lightheaded. The air sparkled.

Oh, God, he couldn't pass out. Between Rachel and Nicole's attacks, he'd lost a lot of blood. And now, Tyler was out there somewhere. Probably gunning for him now. Like Rachel and Lare.

How'd everything get into such a mess?

Nicole said that Lucifer no longer needed Talia. Maybe if he was enough of a prize, he could distract them. Lead them away from her until her powers returned? She couldn't even fight back yet. He didn't understand how he was doing things like calling up oblivion spheres and seeing demons, but however long he had these abilities, he'd use them to draw Lucifer away from her.

"Five-minute warning," Steve announced. "Cutting to commercial break for four minutes and fifty-three seconds…now!"

Talia reached up to his suit jacket and opened it, her face contorting when she saw the upper quadrant of his white shirt soaked and dark red.

"Jack, this is bad," she whispered.

He nodded. "Think maybe Muriel could pause time?"

"Of course, she can, why?" Talia asked.

He felt so hot all of a sudden.

"Because I think I'm gonna pass out."

She gasped and pressed her hands against his chest. "We're back on the air in three minutes!" she said with a hiss.

"I tried to pause it, but…can't."

He felt his weight shift and she was holding him up. But not for long.

"Two minutes forty-nine seconds. Hold your places." Steve.

"Not gonna—be able to—do that," he said as the stone terrace began to tilt.

"Jack, no—hang on…"

"Can't…" he said, his voice trailing off as the world began to rise.

And he was sinking.

28

TALIA WANTED TO SHOUT TO HIGH HOUSE, BEGGING MURIEL TO intercede, but no response. Not even a whisper of wings aloft or in the wind. Jack's wounded shoulder was bleeding profusely now, soaking his shirt, and running down his arm, staining his suit jacket lining.

He began to sink, his eyes rolling back. She put her hands up, holding him on his feet.

"Two minutes thirty seconds," Steve called out, looking a little frazzled. "Stay on your marks. Devin, camera two."

He was about to have a whole new world of problems. In about three seconds. Jack's knees buckled and he began to slide away from her hands.

"Jack!" she shouted.

And he was on the floor.

"Shit! Jack! This is a disaster!" Herb was now wringing his hands as Steve bolted onto the terrace, Armand rushing to Jack's right. Talia clung to his left side, hand against his neck.

"My God," Steve cried when he saw the blood soaking Jack's shirt. "He's bleeding badly! Call an ambulance!"

Jennifer was behind Herb now, looking frantic. "Live in one minute and fifty-seven seconds."

At last, Talia heard the rustle of wings.

"Pause." Muriel said as the world froze around Talia.

"I'm so relieved to see you," said Talia.

Muriel looked shaken.

"What's wrong?"

Muriel glowered around the terrace. "The guard and I just fought off a horde of demons and three hellhounds. That's why we couldn't get here until now. Anahera's still not back. What happened here?"

Talia shook her head. "I wish I knew. All I know is Nicole and Tyler are gone, vanished, and Jack's bleeding like an alley knife fight. He said there were demons. They must have frozen the moment. I didn't see it. And then he passed out."

"Wow, I need to heal that. Get him on his feet."

"Can you rewind the moment back to just before he collapsed?"

"Isn't that why Azrael's in trouble?"

Talia shook her head. "Because he rewound time and significantly changed it. This is only preempting."

Muriel nodded slowly. "You're right. It won't affect the outcome, preempting will keep out unwarranted attention."

She held up her index and forefingers, turning them counterclockwise, slowly, as the moment moved backward. Steve ran backward behind the camera. Armand ran backward to his mark, standing back beside Izzy. Herb froze. Jennifer stayed back behind the director's chair. And Jack rose from the floor, his eyes rolling forward, some of the color returning to his face as Talia's hands moved back against his chest.

She felt his weight against her palms and then it shifted backward.

Muriel touched him and he unfroze from the rest. He looked at Muriel, confusion in his eyes.

"Come to join the demon party?" he asked. "Worst party ever. They didn't even bring a bottle of wine."

She laughed and slid her hand into his dress shirt, moving her fingers toward the wound.

"At least buy me a drink first," he said, sounding woozy.

Muriel grinned at him. "It won't hurt, I promise."

"That's what she said," Jack replied.

Muriel laughed again, but she squinted at him. "That wasn't entirely a joke, was it?"

He shook his head, beginning to sink. Talia grabbed hold of him and eased him to the floor.

"Nicole," he said, his eyes glazing over. "She tried to put her hand through my shoulder. Her eyes were red. And not because she was baked either."

"She's a demon?" Talia asked in surprise.

"So is Hughes."

Muriel glanced around the terrace, dread in her eyes. "They're probably still here then. I'll call in the guard."

Jack gripped Talia's arm. "Hughes is. Turned into a shadow and jumped off the terrace. Nicole is well..." He pointed toward Banks. "Over there." He pointed at Devin. "And over there and some by Herb and by the ledge over there."

Muriel shook her head and gave Talia a confused look.

"Jack, you're not making sense," she said as she summoned gold healing light and bathed Jack's shoulder in it.

He shrugged, one corner of his mouth rising into a smirk. "Oblivion sphere. Sorry. Couldn't help myself. She was pissing me off."

Muriel busted out laughing. "He's starting to sound like you, Talia."

"Very funny," Talia snapped, crossing her arms.

"Like I'm kidding here." At last, Muriel pulled her hand back from Jack's shoulder. "That should hold for a few days. I'm an angel of death, not a healer, so I can't do much about the blood loss. But there was enough healing there to keep him on his feet for the evening." She wagged her finger at him. "But no theatrics and no heroics, got it?"

He struggled up from the terrace floor and Talia anchored him on his right side, getting him on his feet.

"How do you feel?" Talia asked him, pressing her hands against his chest.

"Lightheaded," he said, "but I think I can get through tonight's show."

"Thanks, Muriel," said Talia, feeling relieved.

"My pleasure," she said. "Can't wait to tell the guard that Jack took out another demon with an oblivion sphere. They'll flip. Now, we're going to search for the other demon, Tyler Hughes. He was so good in that Hellsgate series. Now, I know why."

"I read for that role," Jack replied. "Before SanFran Confidential. They told me I was too blond. More kid than demon."

Talia grinned. He looked so incredibly hot in that silver suit, his blond hair disheveled, light green eyes fever-bright, and that cute little smirk that quirked his mouth into a crooked smile. She laid her hand against his over-warm face.

"I couldn't agree more."

He smiled.

"All right, I'm out," said Muriel. "Three-second warning."

Talia nodded and slid her arms around Jack's waist. She'd make sure he stayed on his feet as she counted to three.

"Two minutes and forty-nine seconds. Hold your places." Steve announced.

Talia looked into Jack's eyes. They looked weak, but he was alert and smiling at her.

"Doing okay?" she asked, reaching up to his hair to brush a flyaway lock back into place.

He nodded. "Holding my own." His gaze fell to her hands pressed against his chest and then he looked back at her. "More or less."

"Two minutes thirty seconds," Steve called out, looking a little frazzled. "Stay on your marks. Devin, camera two."

Devin nodded, turning his body as he reviewed his notecards.

"Think the guard will locate Hughes?" Jack asked.

"I hope so."

"Me, too. He wasn't real happy when I splattered his girlfriend across the terrace."

Her stomach did a somersault. "Did he threaten you?"

Jack twisted his mouth, staring at her. And her stomach dropped.

Tyler Hughes threatened him before disappearing. She fixed him with her penetrating stare, trying to see past that actor's mask he'd put up. What else wasn't he telling her? She'd never felt this afraid before. Rachel and Lare scared her, but Tyler Hughes and Nicole Reardon terrified her.

She'd been around them for a week, but without her powers, she couldn't detect that they were demons. Muriel and the guard had their hands full scanning the whole house, but these two were more dangerous. Not like the Eater of Hearts. Those were greater demons and quite powerful, but they were an old race of demons. Not complicated and devious like Lucifer and his fallen ones. Or Tyler and Nicole.

Eaters of Hearts and other greater demons had raw and terrible powers, but assassin demons like Nicole and maybe Tyler were sophisticated and deadly. Able to hide themselves until it was too late.

"Thirty seconds, Devin," Steve announced.

Devin nodded, looking at camera two. Jack leaned against her and she braced herself in case he passed out.

"Fifteen seconds. Places."

Talia's heart beat faster as she held onto Jack, wanting this to be over. She felt so vulnerable out here right now. Even with the shield wards in place.

"Live in five. Four. Three. Two. One."

"Welcome back, my royal subjects," Devin said into camera two, his famous over-the-top dramatic delivery making her tense tonight. "It's time to announce the first couple moving on to the second round." Devin stared down at his cards, drawing out the announcement in theatrical fashion. He looked up at camera one. "In no particular order, the first couple moving on is…" He turned back to camera two. "Mark Banks and Morgan Boyer."

Cameras moved in on Mark and Morgan as he kissed her and held her in his arms.

Devin turned to camera two again. "And the next couple moving on in this competition…"

Another dramatic pause. Talia wanted to scream. She just wanted this broadcast to end.

"Eric and Riya, you're moving on to the next competition."

Riya put her arms around Eric and he kissed her. She looked surprised, but happy.

Devin turned to camera one. "One more couple is moving on. And that couple is…"

Talia did her best not to roll her eyes, waiting for the false tension to pass.

"Talia and Jack! You're still in the game."

Jack wrapped her in his arms and planted the most heart-stopping, bone-rattling kiss she'd ever felt. It exploded through her like a firestorm, his hot mouth covering hers in a deep, urgent kiss, his arms setting her alight. When he finally let her go, she was lightheaded and a little disoriented.

Devin pointed at camera one. "The next couple moving on in the game is next, following this commercial announcement. Stay tuned."

"And we're clear," Steve said, motioning at Devin. "Three minutes fifty-three seconds. Everyone, stay put. And for God's sake, nobody else disappear."

Jack's hands were so hot against hers. His eyes so bright, but looking weak now. He was hurting a lot more than he let on, that actor's mask firmly in place again. But the fever in his eyes showed through it.

"Hang in there, Jack," she said, holding his hand. "It's almost over."

"Good," he said, sounding tired now. It softened his voice, hooded his eyelids.

That demon attack had taken a lot out him. Probably Lucifer's plan all along. He'd keep Jack off kilter and step up the attacks. Weakened prey were easier to subdue.

Her wing tips had emerged, the feathers at last blooming. They were no longer the tiny buds that Jack had barely noticed when he'd made love to her. He would notice this. But she worried about when her halo would emerge, fearing that would be the point of no return.

When Lucifer and a legion of demons descended on them and dragged her and Jack off to Hell.

Without more of the guard and Azrael, she and Jack had no chance against a legion of demons. Not even if she had her full powers and Jack could wield them, too. She prayed that Anahera returned with the cavalry soon.

"Thirty seconds. Camera one, Devin."

"I need to get you to bed," she said to Jack.

That devious smirk rose on his lips as he laid his hand against her face. "You gonna have your way with me?" he asked. "In my weakened condition."

She gasped, shaking her head. How could he think such a thing about her? "Jack, I'd never do something like that!"

"Oh, God, please say yes," he replied.

"Jack Casey—"

"Ten seconds. Places."

Devin stood up straighter, cards in hand.

"You're impossible," she said to Jack, still frowning.

"And easy," he said, those sexy green eyes and that charming smile melting right through her frown. "Very easy."

She couldn't help but laugh. By High House, he was the sexiest thing she'd ever seen. Lean body, tight abs, and gently muscled like a runner's body. And that devastatingly handsome face.

"Live in three, two, one."

"Welcome back, my royal subjects. The next couple that will move on in the competition is…"

Talia groaned. *Just say it, Devin!* She was tired of the theatrics.

"Ryder and Claire."

Claire smiled as Ryder hugged her.

Devin shuffled his cards. "And the final couple moving on to the next challenge is…Armand and Izzy, congratulations!"

Devin stared into camera one, a look of sadness on his face. "Unfortunately, that means that Tyler Hughes and Nicole Reardon will be leaving us tonight. As well as Rachel Daniels and Laren Dumont."

The monitor behind the camera played the cut scene of Rachel and Lare leaving the house in a black limousine that Steve had run with Devin's voiceover bidding them good luck. With a sleight of hand, implying that all four were in the limousine.

Devin turned to camera two. "Join us next week as our royal courtships take our couples into the royal kitchens. They must work together to complete a unique cooking challenge and other surprises. Until next time."

"And we're clear." Steve's voice sounded exasperated as he sank down onto a stone bench, looking frazzled.

"All right, nobody better disappear next week," Herb shouted, jumping up from his chair. "Steve, get the kitchen setup and ready to go for Monday morning. Jennifer, I want prince charming interviews scheduled all day tomorrow. And then schedule reaction interviews for Sunday. And I want a clam bake or some kind of romantic group supper on the beach in the can by Wednesday. And winners of the kitchen challenge will get a candlelit supper on the beach or the terrace. Make it happen."

Jennifer walked toward the remaining five couples, gathering them around her.

"I'll email schedules tonight for Saturday and Sunday and slide a paper copy under your doors. Next week's schedule will be out Sunday. Dress casual for the interviews. Dress up for the beach dinner. The stylist will contact you with suggestions and any other wardrobe assistance. All right, the rest of the night is yours." She gave Jack a look up and down. "Get some sleep, Jack. We don't want you disappearing on us either."

"I'm planning on an early night."

She smiled. "Good. The rest of you get some sleep, too. There will be a lot more interviews to cover the sudden departure of Tyler Hughes and Nicole Reardon. Wherever they went."

Jack leaned down to Talia's ear. "Gonna need a vacuum, too," he said and made an explosion motion with his hands.

Sending her into a fit of laughter.

Everyone turned around, staring at her. Jack looked at them

innocently and shrugged, pointing at her and shaking his head. She smacked him on his right shoulder. Making him laugh out loud.

"Okay, you're free to enjoy your evening," said Jennifer. She smiled at Talia and Jack. "And each other."

"We will," said Jack, sliding his arm around her and he felt so warm. "Talia promised to take advantage of me in my weakened condition."

Talia gasped, her mouth falling open. "Jack Casey!"

"I volunteered," he said. "Taking one for the team."

Armand rolled his eyes as Izzy burst out laughing. "Thanks, Jack. You're a real hero."

Talia glared at him.

"Probably why I'm sleeping on the couch for the rest of my life. After that look."

"Good night, everyone," said Talia, taking hold of Jack's hand.

His hands were really hot. She needed to get some cool compresses on his forehead and maybe get him to take some ibuprofen or something to bring down that fever. Maybe then she could tease out the rest of what happened on the terrace? He wasn't telling her everything. She felt it even in her burgeoning wings.

WHEN SHE GOT Jack back to the suite, he had gotten quiet. No more jokes or even a crooked smile. His eyes looked weak. He wasn't feeling well. He draped his suit jacket over a chair and sat down heavily on the bed, kicking off his shoes. With his left arm hanging at his side, he unbuttoned his bloody white shirt and struggled out of it.

"Let me put this in the sink to soak," Talia said and carried the shirt into the bathroom.

She filled the sink with cold water and wet a hand towel. After wringing it out, she put the shirt in to soak and carried the towel out to the bed. Jack lay on the bed in only grey boxer briefs and slid under the sheet. He was shivering.

Talia sat down beside him and pressed the cold towel to his forehead. Making his teeth chatter.

"God, that's cold!"

"No wonder," she said. "You've got fever. Just lie still."

"No worries, I'm frozen solid now."

She left him with the compress on his forehead as she hurried into the bathroom to change out of her red dress. She hung it back on its hanger and took off her bra. She slipped into a short, light blue silk nightshirt and hung the dress in the armoire. When she slid into the bed, snuggling up to him, his eyes were closed. He was out, breaths deep and even.

She smiled at him, running her fingers through his short blond hair, and kissed his steamy hot mouth. He was burning up. She reached over to the light beside the bed and switched it off. She watched the ocean waves through the glow of moonlight and listened to Jack's heavy, even breaths beside her, thankful that he was still with her. That those demons hadn't killed him or dragged him away from her. She laid her head against his chest and closed her eyes.

29

Jack felt relieved when he finished his last reaction interview. He was still running a fever and his shoulder ached, but he was on a roll, helping Devin cover the sudden departures of two couples with his reactions to their relationships and why they may not live happily ever after. Without mentioning the fact that Hughes and Reardon were demons or that he'd splattered Nicole all over the terrace. Or that Hughes had turned into a shadow and fled, threatening him.

Yeah, he kind of knew when he exploded Nicole into little demon bits that Hughes would probably want to take some revenge out of his hide. He hoped that he'd at least see Hughes coming before the dude tried to kill him.

Or before Talia found out.

But he helped Devin explain Rachel and Lare's departure. Then he was out the door and at the dining room table, eating bacon and eggs with Gianni and Banks. If Talia had found him anywhere alone, she'd have brained him.

He felt guilty for passing out on her last night, but he was burning up and freezing all at once by the time they got back to the suite. Still, he felt her beside him all night, head on his chest, arm stretched across him, that swath of gorgeous black hair across his stomach.

Having her beside him got him through a couple of nightmares. Including one where Hughes slid out of a dark wall, a shadow behind him, and stabbed him in the chest with a huge sword. And then Hughes became Jordan Bellamy, laughing as he cut off Jack's hands.

As Jack began to bleed out, he'd crawled to the bed, calling for Talia. Her beautiful form became Rachel lying on the bed, laughing at him as she forced more cocaine at him and dragged him into the bed, her eyes turning red and her skin turning red and leathery. Horns appeared on her forehead, Lucifer's grin leering back at him.

Waking with a shout, he was out of the bed and rocking on the edge.

Until Talia slid her arms around him and coaxed him back into bed. She'd covered him up as his teeth chattered and put her arms around him until he fell back asleep again.

He made it through the group scenes shot around the house, including footage of the five prince charmings working out in the weight room. And a group dinner at the dining table, also filmed. He'd pushed himself, game face on, jokes turned up to maximum, keeping everyone laughing and off guard, so they wouldn't notice how badly he felt.

Or see the shadow against the window. That he'd seen twice during dinner. Smoky. Red eyes gleaming. Horns clear and glassy in the growing darkness.

Staring at him. Waiting.

Even if he turned his back, it shifted. A blur. A blink. And it was in the corner of the room, just out of reach. But within range. Making his skin crawl and his heart race. He wanted to blame the fever, but couldn't. It was too prescient. And so very patient. Like it had been there when the basalt cliffs had first formed. It felt so very old and evil. It filled him with a deep, poignant dread.

Like his whole life had been leading up to some moment, some confrontation that he didn't even understand. Like a part of his life had been destined for this moment and no amount of fighting could change it. A choice he'd never made. A destiny he couldn't stop. A fate he couldn't avoid.

And it ached through him. Because he knew then that he and Talia could never truly be together. Not long term. All they had were moments now and it made him so sad. But he would own those moments, fight for them with everything he had left to give.

Before those things got to him and tore him apart.

He didn't understand any of it. How he was suddenly able to see these creatures or do things that just flat-out defied reality. Or why Lucifer hunted him. Why him? It made no sense.

Had his fall from Hollywood grace been a much more damning fall than he realized?

By evening, he was exhausted, the fever rising again. This time, Muriel was beside the bed with Talia, laying hands on his shoulder and forehead as he collapsed against the pillow.

"Jack, I wish I could heal this for you," said Muriel, shaking her head. "But it's demonic in origin and I don't have the healing power to remove or reverse it. I can ease the symptoms a bit and slow the bleeding. But it's going to take an archangel to fix this. Where in Heaven is Azrael? Doesn't he know that the guard needs him?"

Talia looked fearful, anxious, and he hated that he couldn't ease her mind. And he couldn't tell her about the demons getting closer. Or what Nicole said about his wound. He couldn't tell her about the trails of his blood running all through the house and along the terrace. Bait for hellhounds and demons. A trail for them to follow. So, he couldn't escape.

And he really couldn't tell her about Lucifer's plans for him.

He didn't know if anything Nicole said was true. He'd been in Hollywood a while. He knew liars when he heard them, but there'd been kernels of truth lurking in Nicole's words. It made him a little crazy thinking about it. Especially now that he saw demons lurking close to him. And trails of his own blood throughout the entire house.

But he couldn't tell her.

She'd lose her mind worrying about him. Besides, she was in danger. He'd play the decoy if it kept her safe. She might kill him for it, but he'd cross that bridge when he came to it. He sighed. Even if it led to Hell.

"Thanks for trying, Muriel," he said, already sleepy but fighting that fall toward sleep.

Where the shadows and demons had free rein. And he couldn't stop them.

HE WOKE UP TO STILLNESS. The first fragile light of a December dawn warming the world and brushing pale yellow fingers across the deep blue ocean as he watched it flutter across the waves. Talia was already up and dressed. Off to another interview. And they had an early set call. Seven-thirty.

It was Monday. The start of the second challenge.

He staggered into the shower, shivering, and let the hot water try and rinse away the persistent fatigue and fever. He did his best to keep his bandaged left shoulder out of the spray. Muriel's healing had staunched the bleeding and eased some of the ache, but it still wept blood. He shaved and dried his hair, dressing in jeans, a charcoal grey V-neck sweater, and his blue Vans slip-ons, then hurried out of the condo for the kitchen.

And the next challenge.

When he got there, the rest of the cast was waiting in the kitchen, talking quietly. Especially Eric and Riya. She looked up and glared at him, her eyes filled with animosity. He didn't even remember her. Maybe that was the problem? Maybe he'd been too coked up and ego-fueled to have even been polite to her? Regardless, he felt like he owed her an apology.

Ryder and Claire were huddled together, doing a lot of flirting. He smiled. Might have created a little magic by arranging that match. Mark and Morgan were laughing and having fun. Gianni and Izzy were lost in each other's eyes. And Talia, dressed in jeans and...he smiled, his Van Halen T-shirt. It never looked that good on him. Talia was tense, worry shining in those haunting grey eyes as she fidgeted. Until she saw him enter the space.

He smiled at her as he walked toward Riya and Eric who stood in front of the long L-shaped kitchen with its glossy turquoise Italian cabinets and stainless-steel appliances. The white quartz countertops sparkled with flecks of silver and glass.

He passed the island with a bar counter overhang and a sink that set between the dining room and the kitchen cabinets. Four white, padded bar stools nestled under the bar counter and four mercury glass pendant lights hung over the white quartz bar top, making the silver and glass accents sparkle. The scent of fresh lemons and rosemary was strong as he paused beside Eric and Riya.

Eric smiled and extended his hand. Riya crossed her arms and scowled at him.

"Jack, how are you this morning?" Eric asked as Jack shook his hand with a quick, firm shake.

"Good," he answered. "How are you? Ready for a kitchen challenge?"

Eric laughed and shook his head. "Not so much. I'm a disaster in a kitchen."

"Same," he replied with a shrug. "Unless you need leftover pizza warmed up."

Eric nodded. "Y'know, you're not what I expected from such a big star. Thought you'd be arrogant and above talking to people like me."

"Me? What do I have to be arrogant about?"

"You're famous. You were nominated for a couple of Emmys. And you were fantastic on SanFran Confidential."

"It was only one nomination, but thanks. And I appreciate the comments about SanFran Confidential."

Riya looked like a tea kettle boiling over.

He bowed his head a moment and then looked at her. "Look, Riya, I wanted to apologize to you for whatever happened on the set of SanFran Confidential. I was a real dick back then and I'm sorry if I said or did anything that hurt or insulted you. Whatever I did, you didn't deserve it and I'm sorry."

"Save your apologies, Casey," she snapped. "I have nothing to say to you." A slight smile lifted the corners of her mouth. "Looking forward to giving you hell for the rest of this show." Her eyes flashed red for an instant, startling him.

"Fair enough," he said, stepping back. "I'm sure I deserve it, but I'm still sorry."

Eric looked uncomfortable, but didn't say anything asJack walked away toward Talia. Her grey eyes were narrowed, sparks there as she laid her hands on Jack's elbows, moving close.

"Wow, what was that about, Jack?" she asked.

He shrugged. "I have no memory of working with her, Talia," he said as Riya went back to a deep conversation with Eric, her eyes warming and laughter echoing. "But whatever I did made a lasting impression."

"I'll ask Muriel to consult your Book and see if she can find out what happened."

And then Jennifer stood behind the bar, dressed in a pink *Ever After Hour* sweatshirt and black leggings, her hair back in a clip at her nape. She held her clipboard high, a pair of pink reading glasses balanced low on her nose.

"Good morning, couples," she said, smiling. "Welcome to the set of your next challenge." She handed a stack of white papers to Talia. "Take one and pass it around."

Talia took one sheet and handed it to Jack. He grabbed the schedule and passed the stack. He and Talia were scheduled for Thursday. With a bunch of interviews scheduled before then, separately and as a couple. And there was a group dinner scheduled every night.

"This is the revised filming schedule for the challenge, so recycle the one under your door this morning. Each couple will be scheduled for two-hour sessions with an extra hour blocked for makeup and styling and post-session cleanup. Pre-interviews and follow-up interviews will be scheduled throughout the week according to your challenge schedule. We'll be filming all week. Devin and the crew will critique your results and assign a score. You won't know how you performed until dismissal night, so good luck."

She looked over at Eric and Riya. "Eric and Riya are up first, so we need to get you both to interviews with Devin and then makeup. The rest of you, use your free time while you have it, but clear out of this area. Good luck to all of you."

Jack took Talia's hand. "Walk on the beach with me?"

She grinned and nodded at him.

"Let's get you a hoodie first," he said, a hand against her cheek. "Don't want you getting cold."

She slid her hand into his and they headed back to the suite for a hoodie. He grinned. Eventually.

EVERY NIGHT THAT WEEK, there was a filmed group dinner and Jack dialed up his public persona, keeping everybody entertained as they drank cocktails and ate a multi-course meal fit for royalty on the terrace. Or sipped wine and ate grilled seafood at a romantic beach dinner. Each night was either a magical, intimate affair or a boisterous party.

Either way, Jack kept up the game, the appearance that everything was light and fun, but at every meal, he saw demons at a distance. Standing motionless in the cold sea water, watching him in silence. Or glaring at him from the shadows with flashes of terrifying red eyes. Revealing red trails of his blood in the sand, along the rocks, and across the stone terrace.

Like the tangle of coke-fueled hallucinations that surfaced in his head whenever he stepped into certain rooms, the memories still haunting him.

He had to act his way through all of it, but he wondered why Talia hadn't said something. Surely, she'd seen the demons, too.

He sighed. Or was it the coke—or whatever it'd been—that Rachel shot him up with?

The cravings still gnawed at him in weak moments. Like when that horrible hellhound fever flooded his veins. Muriel's healings never kept it down for long. Like some sort of demonic malaria.

But he made it through the next round of interviews, joking with

Devin about his lack of cooking skills. Truth was he knew his way around a kitchen. As the youngest with four sisters, he'd learned that roles were for actors and dinner tables. In the Casey household, people learned to take care of themselves. He learned woodworking and other skills from his dad on weekends (before the divorce), but through the week, his sisters taught him how to read and write, cook, hem his own pants, and use a computer. He taught them how to joke their way out of trouble, drive a stick shift, throw a curveball, and use firecrackers in new and inventive ways.

He and Talia showed up in the kitchen, both dressed in jeans. She wore a loose chambray blouse, her raven black hair clipped into a messy bun. He'd rarely seen her with her hair up and it gave her a sexy, inquisitive look. He had on a red Henley with the sleeves pushed up to his elbows and his shoulder wrapped tight with fresh gauze.

The shimmery white L-shaped counter top had a chef's knife and cutting board laid out to the left of the stove along with measuring cups and spoons, some bottles, and a handful of spice jars. Hints of fresh garlic and onions warmed the kitchen. To the right of the stove was the refrigerator. And on the bar countertop was a photo stand with five numbered, red envelopes clipped to it. Talia looked terrified and he wanted to laugh.

An angel of death doing a cooking challenge. Muriel had to be watching and laughing her ass off. He glanced around the room until he caught the twitch of wings. By the window, Muriel and two of the guard's death angels stood. Muriel was grinning.

"Jack," Talia whispered, staring wide-eyed at everything around them. "I barely know what some of the human food looks like. I can't cook."

He smiled. "No worries, we got this."

"How? You said you could barely heat up pizza."

"I had four sisters. They made me learn to cook. And actually, I enjoyed it. I'm not a chef or anything, but we'll be okay." He kissed her. "Relax."

She nodded, but her gaze shot daggers across the room. He snickered. Toward the window.

"Muriel, I will smite you," she said with a growl.

"Not today, chef," said Muriel with a chuckle. "Gotta wait until you get your halo back. I can't wait to see this. Azrael's gonna laugh his halo off when he hears this."

Jack laughed until Talia glared at him. He pretended to clear his throat.

Jennifer walked over to the counter and Jack turned toward her.

"Welcome to the couples' cooking challenge, you, two," she said with a smile. "Because the couple that cooks together stays together, right?"

"Or gets their head thunked with a skillet," he said, casting a sideways glance at Talia who gave him that *I will smite you* look of hers.

He smiled. Angels of death got mean when they were out of their element.

"Either way, it'll make for good TV, Jack," said Talia.

Jennifer laughed. "All right, Devin will explain how this works as soon as he arrives from styling."

She motioned toward the cameras and Steve hurried over, dark hair tied back, black glasses over his jovial brown eyes, short beard cropped close.

"Okay," said Steve, grinning as he clapped his hands together. "While we're waiting, everything you need for your challenge is laid out on the counters. Spices, utensils, measuring cups. Pans are on the gas stove, ready to use. And the refrigerator is stocked and labeled, so you can grab what you need quickly."

"Wow, can you come to my house and set it up like this?" Jack asked. "So, I don't have to order so many pepperoni pizzas?"

Steve laughed. "I know, right? The crew's starving, so make us something yummy."

"We'll do our best," said Jack as Talia began to fidget again.

Then Devin was hurrying over to the kitchen, dressed in a black polo shirt and khakis, highlighted blond hair pomaded into submission, and those snow-bright teeth stretched into a toothy grin.

"Okay, I'll leave you in Devin's hands," said Jennifer, stepping away. "Have a good challenge."

"Thanks, Jennifer," he replied as Steve hurried behind the cameras and Herb took his place in the director's chair.

"All right, Devin," said Herb, leaning back. "Take them through the rules of the challenge and then step out of frame. Talia and Jack, just be yourselves and cook up something incredible for the viewers."

"All right, people. Find your marks on the floor. Places. Cueing up first take, cameras one, two, and three rolling in fifteen seconds."

Jack motioned Talia toward the purple tape on the floor between the cabinets and the sink as Devin found his black tape to Jack's right, at the bar top edge. He turned toward Talia and waited. Jack pulled in a breath.

"Slate it and roll, Roy," said Herb.

"In three, two, one," Steve called out.

The slater held the slate in front of the camera, LED time stamp displayed for the camera.

"Cooking challenge, Talia and Jack, first take," said the slater and stepped out of camera range.

Devin smiled at Talia and then Jack as the cameras captured several angles. "Welcome to the couple's cooking challenge, my royal subjects. We're here with Talia and Jack, ready to see how well they cook together. And let's begin."

He moved toward the photo stand with its five numbered envelopes. Then he reached behind the stand and picked up five yellow envelopes. He fanned them out in his hand.

"Jack and Talia, I have here five yellow envelopes and five red envelopes. In each one of these yellow envelopes is a recipe with five ingredients. You will choose one of these envelopes and cook the recipe inside it." He motioned to the bar top.

Talia's eyes got huge and she stared at Jack, looking fearful and nervous again.

"And together," Devin continued, "you will answer five questions about each other. These are answers you both gave before the show started. For every correct answer, you will earn an ingredient for your recipe. Then you will complete the recipe with the ingredients you earned. To be judged by myself and the crew. Do you have any questions?"

"Is the show insured for injuries or illnesses resulting from eating our cooking?" Jack asked.

Devin laughed. "We'll find out, Jack."

"You ready to kick some butt and make some food, Talia?" Jack asked, turning toward her.

She nodded. "With you, I'm game for anything."

He leaned over and kissed her.

"Let's do this, Devin," said Jack.

Devin held out the five yellow envelopes to them. "Select your recipe."

Jack motioned to Talia who studied all five envelopes carefully and then reached out and plucked the middle one from Devin's hand. She handed it to Jack who tore through the royal gold seal on the back. And slid out a large yellow recipe card.

"Read the name of your dish please," said Devin.

Chicken Marsala. One of his favorites. He hadn't made it for years, but he knew the dish.

"Chicken Marsala."

"Mar what?" Talia asked.

"Marsala," he repeated. "It's a type of wine."

At last, she smiled. "I like wine."

"You'll like this, too," he said, squeezing her hand. "Especially our take on it."

"All right, Jack, Talia, while we get you both washed up and outfitted in aprons, we'll start with question one to get your first ingredient."

Jack moved to the sink and washed his hands with soap and dried them with paper towels. Talia followed his example. Jennifer and Steve both moved into the kitchen, slipping coral-colored aprons over their heads, and tying them in back. Both aprons had the show's logo in blue on them. They slipped out of frame right before Devin turned around with the first red envelope.

"All right, Jack," said Devin, sliding a card out of the envelope. "The first question is for you. What is Talia's favorite hobby?"

Smiting people? Probably not the answer they were looking for. He smiled and looked at Devin. "Besides me? It's gotta be flying, Devin."

Devin and Talia were both smiling.

"Correct, Jack. Pick your first ingredient."

Jack moved toward the big stainless-steel refrigerator, recipe card in hand, and motioned Talia toward it. He opened the door. Inside, everything was organized. Meats on one shelf. Vegetables on the next shelf. Condiments in the door. Butter and eggs beside liquids on the next shelf. Couldn't make chicken marsala without chicken.

"Let's go with chicken," he said.

"Agreed," said Talia. "It's in the recipe title."

Jack grabbed the container with four chicken breasts and carried it over to the counter. He held it up to the cameras.

"We're going with chicken," he replied.

Devin nodded. "All right, prepare your first ingredient."

Jack set down the container and looked around until he found a roll of oven bags and a rolling pin. He unrolled a bag and opened it, placing the chicken breasts inside.

"What are you doing?" Talia asked, squinting at the bag and then Jack.

"We're going to flatten these out a bit," he answered. "Make them a little more tender." He smiled at her when he saw her getting anxious again. "You read the instructions to tell me what to do, okay?"

She picked up the recipe card, the instructions calming her. "Oh, I see," she replied, her expression brightening. "It's all explained."

"See, no worries," he said.

"Okay, it says to..." she looked at him, a smile lighting her eyes. "To do what you're doing."

He nodded, picking up the rolling pin, and ran it across until the chicken breasts weren't so thick.

"Next," he asked.

"It says to use salt and pepper to season the chicken. I'll get them."

Talia reached across him to grab the two wooden grinders marked salt and pepper.

He leaned over and kissed her.

"I'm going to like this seasoning part," she said with a grin.

"Me, too," he said as she returned his kiss.

"I think we'll have to answer another question before we get to use those," Jack replied when he saw Devin reach for another envelope.

She nodded, those grey eyes so luminous and intense. He loved her eyes. "That means I get to kiss you again."

He grinned.

"All right, Talia," said Devin. "Your turn to answer a question."

Jack and Talia turned around to face Devin as Talia nodded.

Devin opened the second envelope and pulled out another card. "What was the best and most favorite gift that Jack's ever received?"

She grinned, remembering his long-ago story about the best birthday gift he'd been given. By his dad.

"Devin, it was a flight in a glider. It was just Jack gliding through the clouds, sun at his back, wind in his hair, and the silence of the world around him."

Devin was already grinning. "That was a beautiful description, Talia. And a perfect portrayal of Jack's favorite gift. Well done. Please select your next ingredient—and you can now use the salt and pepper."

Talia grabbed the recipe card and they headed back to the fridge. Jack opened the door as Talia read from the card.

"Jack, it says after we season the chicken, we have to brown it on both sides. So, we should get butter next."

"See, you got this, Talia! I agree."

There were four glass cups, each containing unwrapped half-sticks of butter.

"How much butter?" he asked.

"Half a stick," she said.

"Perfect," Jack muttered and grabbed one of the containers.

He carried it over to the counter, returning to the chicken. "Salt and pepper," he said, winking at her.

She leaned against him, picking up the salt grinder, watching him as she gave it two turns on each chicken breast. He leaned down and kissed her. She picked up the pepper grinder, kissing him as she gave it one turn over each chicken breast.

"Turning them," he said in a husky breath and used tongs to turn them over.

She gave each piece of chicken one turn of the pepper grinder, kissing him again. She set it down and picked up the salt grinder. He kissed her again. Then she gave it two turns for each piece.

"Cut the butter in half and put it in the skillet. On medium heat." Her voice was soft, breathy as she read the card to him.

Jack fanned himself with the envelope. "Is it hot in here or just you?" he asked with a smile and cut the stick of butter in half. He stepped behind her and slid the butter into the skillet.

"Medium heat," she repeated.

"Oh, no," he said. "You're smokin' hot, never medium. I'll turn it on after the next question."

"You've already turned it on," she said, kissing him again. "Oh, you mean the stove."

She was grinning as they turned around. And so was Devin as he plucked the third envelope off the stand.

"Jack, your next question."

"Hit me, Devin."

"What was the worst moment of Talia's life?"

Jack paused, staring at her a moment. Her eyes turned glassy as she watched him, as if trying to convey the answer to him. But he already knew that look and it was a punch to his gut. And a reminder of how stupid he'd been. Thinking she'd betrayed him, using him to get to Gianni.

"The night that I almost made the stupidest mistake of my life and hurt her badly when I dismissed her from The Cinderella Hour. I can still see the pain in her eyes when I said her name. Thank God Banks saved me from being an idiot. Otherwise, I might have lost her forever."

He leaned over and kissed her as a tear ran down her cheek. "I hope you'll forgive me for that someday, Talia." He pressed his hand to his heart and held out his open hand to her.

She closed her hand and pressed it to her heart. "Ancient history," she said and kissed him.

"Perfect answer, Jack," Devin said in a quiet, solemn voice. "Pick your third ingredient please."

Talia grabbed the recipe card, following him to the fridge again. "The next step after browning the chicken calls for mushrooms."

"Mushrooms it is," he said, grabbing a container of sliced mushrooms.

He carried it over to the counter and set it to the left of the stove.

"Okay, let's brown the chicken," Talia said as he turned on the stove. "Three minutes on each side."

He grabbed a wooden spoon off the cutting board and swirled the butter around the large black skillet until it melted. He set down the spoon, grabbing tongs. He laid each chicken breast in the butter and it sizzled.

"I'll tell you when three minutes is up," Talia said, watching the clock on the stove.

He adjusted the temp down a little. "You're too hot, Talia," he said with a quick nuzzle to her neck. "Don't want to burn the chicken."

She laughed, keeping her eye on the clock. In three minutes, she motioned to the skillet.

"Time to turn them."

"Done," he said and use the tongs to turn each one over, making sure they were in the melted butter.

Time moved fast and so did the next three minutes.

"Done," she said, holding out a white plate. "Set them aside."

He took the chicken out of the skillet and set it off the flame, turning around to face Devin again.

"Good instincts, you two," said Devin, holding envelope number four in his hand. He looked at Talia as he slid the card out of the envelope. "Talia, what was the worst moment in Jack's life."

Her eyes turned misty, choking him up. "I hate that there's been so many," she said, fixing him with her intense grey gaze. "But the worst one has to be the finale of The Cinderella Hour. When Erica Thomlin walked onstage with a gun." She bowed her head. "And I stepped in front of him as she fired."

His eyes stung, welling with moisture and he couldn't blink it all back. He thought he'd lost her forever at that moment and he hated that she'd taken a bullet meant for him. He wanted to rage at the world, but all he could do was hold her as his heart broke into a bazillion little pieces. Not even stepping under those ropes to face Bellamy with that sharp-ass sword hurt as much as seeing her take that bullet. It broke him.

He huffed out a breath, trying to rein in the painful memory that still haunted him. And her hand was against his face, cupping his cheek as he swallowed another breath, eyes still stinging. Finally, he looked up and Devin was watching him patiently.

"And by Jack's reaction, we can all see that you've got the right answer, Talia." Devin gave him another moment and then motioned toward the refrigerator. "Take a moment, Jack, and then the two of you select your next ingredient."

He nodded and moved toward the refrigerator, Talia beside him with the recipe card.

"Are you okay?" she asked with wide eyes.

He ran his sleeve across his eyes and nodded. "What's the next step?" he asked.

"It's that I love you," she said and kissed him.

He returned her kiss with an urgency that surprised even him. He needed to feel her against him for a moment, reminding him that she was here and that things were okay right now.

"I love you, too," he said. "What's next?"

"Marsala wine," she replied.

He found the bottle on the refrigerator shelf with the other liquids and carried it over to the counter. He set the skillet back on the burner and turned it up to medium heat.

"Melt the rest of the butter," she said and dumped the rest of the butter out of the container, into the skillet.

He used the skillet handle to swirl the butter around the skillet.

"Next?"

"Brown the mushrooms."

He nodded toward the container. She picked it up and emptied the mushrooms into the skillet.

"Three minutes."

He grabbed the wooden spoon and stirred the mushrooms until they were brown.

"Add the marsala wine," said Talia, handing him the liquid measuring cup. "Half a cup. Simmer for two minutes."

She held the cup while he poured in a half cup. Then Talia poured it into the skillet. He gave it quick stir and then turned back to Devin.

"Final question to Jack," said Devin, the fifth red envelope in his hand. He slid out the card. "Jack, what does Talia want most in the world?"

He grinned, turning toward her. "To stay at my side." He kissed her softly and she kissed him back. Hard.

"Didn't even hesitate," said Devin, smiling. "Exactly right, Jack. Get your final ingredient and finish your dish."

He rushed to fridge, Talia beside him. "It's the heavy cream, Jack," she said. "Two minutes are almost up."

He reached inside the fridge and snatched the little carton of heavy cream and hurried over to the skillet. He poured half a cup of cream into the liquid measuring cup he'd used for the wine.

"Time," Talia called and he poured in the cream. She grabbed the salt grinder and did three turns of the grinder into the pan as he stirred the cream and put the four chicken breasts back in the pan.

"Hand me the lid, please," he said pointing to the glass top.

She passed it to him and he covered the skillet, turning down the heat a tad.

"Three minutes," said Talia.

He watched the cream rise, mushrooms floating around the chicken breasts until the sauce began to thicken.

"Time," Talia called.

He removed the lid and stuck the spoon into the sauce. Creamy, not watery. He turned off the burner and returned the lid.

"All right, Talia and Jack," said Devin. "It's time to hand off your dish to my wonderful assistant, Jennifer. She and I will evaluate and score your dish. And you'll find out the results of the challenge." He turned around and faced the cameras. "Tomorrow night during Friday's live dismissal show."

Jennifer stepped into the frame and picked up the skillet, carrying it to the table where she placed it on a turquoise hot pad. A pile of little white scorecards, a basket of silverware, and a stack of plates were already on the table.

"Cut and print that!" Herb called. "Great job, Talia and Jack. Couldn't have asked for a more romantic challenge. Jennifer, get Talia and Jack off to their post challenge interviews and then we'll score their dish."

Talia slid her hand into Jack's as he stepped out of the kitchen. Walking hand in hand, they followed Jennifer down the hallway to the left. Toward the den. And more interviews. At least during the first one, they'd be together. He looked forward to hearing an angel of death talk about cooking for the first time. After that, separate interviews and a group dinner on the beach. He looked forward to sharing some wine and moonlight with her tonight. Before they faced tomorrow's dismissal show.

30

TALIA WANTED TO FLOAT AFTER THE COOKING CHALLENGE AND THE interviews. Cooking with Jack had been a lot more fun and so much more romantic than she'd ever dreamed. He'd been so sweet and patient, finding ways to include her and help her contribute. And so romantic.

And seeing the pain in his face when she described his worst moment burned through her. He hadn't been wearing his game face this time and she felt so much closer to him.

She wore a pale pink dress that sparkled with crystals, cut low and short, her black hair in ringlets, eyes with a soft pink and smoky shadow contrast, and a smudge of sugary pink lip gloss. Thanks to the show stylist. When Jack stepped out onto the balcony, moving toward her, he wore a slim cut black suit, the material a little shiny, and a white silk T-shirt, making his light green eyes and blond hair look so bright.

He was so steamy hot in the flicker of candles and set lights along the terrace, night settling like watercolors against the ocean swells. She couldn't believe he was with her.

"You are the most beautiful thing I've ever seen, Jack Casey," she said, sliding her arms around his neck.

Kissing him hard on the lips.

He grinned, his mouth so hot against hers.

She laid her hands against his face. Hot to her touch. She pressed the back of her hand against his forehead and he tried to pull away. His temperature was up again. From the hellhound bite. She wanted to choke the breath out of Lucifer.

"It's spiking again," she said.

He shrugged. "I'll live with it," he said.

"Well, you shouldn't have to," she said. "Where in blazes is Azrael?"

He glanced around. "That your archangel boss?"

She nodded. "Anahera still hasn't returned. But your time on Earth is different than ours. A week of your time is a day in ours."

"So, to her, she's been gone a day or so?" he asked, his gaze flicking around the terrace again.

"Exactly. Well, that's not that long then."

He was right. She was too anxious. She wanted Azrael to come and fix everything.

Armand walked onto the terrace with Izzy, cameras filming their arrival. Izzy looked stunning in a long emerald gown with spaghetti straps and Armand wore a black tuxedo jacket and black pants. Mark and Morgan stepped out behind them. Morgan wore a short ivory dress and Mark wore a blue pin-striped suit. Ryder and Claire were already on the terrace, Claire in a red dress and Ryder wearing a charcoal grey suit. They were talking and laughing and looked really intense.

Next, Eric and Riya stepped onto the terrace. Riya wore a short black dress with crystal straps and Eric wore a black suit with white dress shirt and black tie.

Talia glanced back at Jack as his gaze darted across the terrace, around railings, behind planters, like he was searching for something. His eyes looked intense and a little haunted.

He was probably thinking about last week's dismissal. Expecting an attack. It frightened her. Because she didn't have her abilities back yet, she wasn't immune to those time freezes. She had horrors of being frozen in place while demons tortured or took Jack.

His gaze dropped over the balcony, following something with his eyes. A troubled look touched his face, jaw set, cheeks taut, lips flattening. What was he looking at now?

"Jack?" she said, a hand on his arm.

"Yeah?" he asked, not looking at her.

"What are you staring at?" she asked finally.

His gaze jerked up from the ground and he stared at her wide-eyed for a moment. "Uh, looking for more—evidence of demons." He glanced over at Eric and Riya and his voice fell to a sharp whisper. "I saw her eyes flash red this week."

What? And she was just now hearing this from him?

"When did that happen?" she demanded, gripping his forearms, staring into his eyes, wishing she could sense emotions and truth with her angel abilities, but they hadn't come back yet.

"When?" he asked.

"You heard me," she said.

"Uh...Monday."

Monday! She'd sensed that he wasn't telling her everything, but through her own intuition. Hearing this only confirmed her fears.

"Jack Casey, you're just now telling me about this? It's Friday. That was days ago."

He shrugged. "Didn't want you to worry."

"Way too late for that." She pulled in a breath and held it, trying to calm down. She didn't want a repeat of last week's dismissal. "I'll make sure Muriel is aware. That Riya is also a demon apparently. Guess there's no need to check your Book now."

"Why?" he asked.

"Because she's a demon, Jack. She was never on your show. She wanted everyone on this show to think she was though. So, she could bash you. Undermine you in front of the cast and crew. Like they've been doing to you since you arrived in Hollywood apparently."

"But why focus so much attention on me?" he asked in a quiet voice. "I was a dumb kid with a lucky break. Why would demons be interested in that? Beyond wanting to take another human soul?"

Talia sighed. The answer she needed from Azrael.

This didn't make sense. Except for her theory that Lucifer had waded into the time stream and discovered that Jack would soon connect with her. So, he started sowing the seeds early in Jack's life, setting her up to fall. Had Lucifer done all of that to test his forced Phoenix shift experiment? Ruined Jack's life to run an experiment. That was horrible.

"I wish I knew, Jack," she said. "That's why I need Azrael here. To answer these questions. And protect us while he confronts Lucifer."

Devin stepped onto the terrace, finding his mark. He worked with the crew, testing his microphone as they adjusted candles and some of the camera lights.

She called to Muriel in her head until the flutter of wings whispered above the soft rush of ocean waves.

Jack looked up as Muriel and one of the guard settled on top of the roof, halos bright in the growing dark. Seeing Muriel and another angel made her relax, hoping they'd keep Jack safe when she couldn't.

She was nervous tonight. No one knew how they'd scored this time. It was a little like the uncertainty of *The Cinderella Hour* when she'd feared that Jack, Armand, or Mark would call her name and send her home. But having Jack beside her made it bearable. If she was dismissed, they were a couple this time.

"Two minutes, Devin," Steve said, pointing at him. "Camera two then camera one. Places everyone. Stay on your marks." He cast a look around the terrace. "And I'll end anyone that decides to disappear this week."

Everyone laughed, including Jack. Steve always had a smile on his face, but this week, he looked a little grumpy. She couldn't blame him. If he only knew what had really happened on this terrace, he'd look terrified.

Jack leaned toward her ear. "If he only knew," he said.

Talia nodded. "He'd run screaming."

He snickered, but the sound disappeared quickly as his gaze darted around the terrace again. Looking for Tyler Hughes. That had to be it. She tugged on Jack's sleeve and nodded at the roof. Muriel waved at him. He smiled and some of the tension drained from his face.

"See, everything's fine," she said.

He still looked haunted and his gaze didn't track so much across the terrace, but he seemed relieved to see Muriel and one of the guard watching over them.

"Ten seconds." Steve announced.

"Places, people," Herb called. "And keep the energy up. I know this one's nerve-wracking, but that's part of the game."

"Live in five," said Steve. "In four, three, two, one."

"Good evening, my royal subjects," Devin said, staring into camera two. "Tonight, is a tense night for our contestants as we dismiss one couple. Our five couples have no idea how they did on the royal kitchens challenge, so tonight's results will be a complete surprise for them."

Devin turned toward camera one. "As I said, this week's challenge is called the royal kitchens challenge. Our five couples had to work together to cook a main dish and answer questions about each other in order to get the ingredients to make their dish. Final scores include questions correctly answered and dish completion. As well as taste. Our couples have no idea what their scores were. Before we announce the first couple moving on to the next challenge, let's see how well Armand and Izzy cooked together."

The monitor behind the cameras displayed the footage of Armand and Izzy's cooking challenge. They worked well together and didn't seem to have any mishaps. Talia couldn't hear the audio. She could only see the video.

"Three seconds, camera one," Steve said in a quiet voice. "Three, two, one."

Devin looked at camera one. "Afterward, the couple had this to say."

Interview footage appeared on the monitor. She had no idea what was said, but Armand and Izzy were holding hands and looking at each other a lot. She glanced over at Izzy and she was still smiling.

"In three seconds, camera two," Steve announced. "Three, two, one."

"Let's have a look at Eric and Riya's experience."

Riya and Eric's challenge didn't go quite as smoothly as Armand and Izzy's. From the video, it looked like they missed two questions. Talia didn't know what recipe they had, but each dish only had five ingredients. Two missing ingredients were a big deal.

Devin introduced their interviews next and the couple's interview played.

Jack fidgeted beside her and she wondered if the fever was making him restless and uncomfortable, but he looked so incredibly handsome tonight. She wanted to walk along the beach with him and just touch him. Listen to him to talk about his life and what he wanted to do with it. She smiled. And how she fit into that life now.

"Next up, Mark and Morgan's royal cooking adventure. When we come back from a commercial break. Stay tuned."

"Clear. Four minutes two seconds," Steve announced, lifting his arms as he grinned. "Everyone, relax and take a deep breath. You're doing great."

Jack sighed and turned toward the ocean. He was nervous, she realized. She was surprised.

"Why so nervous?" she asked.

"Because I have no idea where we stand, I guess. And I'm really worried about what happens when we walk out of this place."

She understood that fear. And he didn't mean going back to Los Angeles or what happened to his acting career. He was still concerned about the demons. About Tyler Hughes still out there somewhere. About Riya's proximity. She wanted to curse.

Where was Azrael?

She glanced over at Riya. She was glaring at Jack, looking at him with hungry brown eyes, like she wanted to devour him.

Talia glanced up at Muriel, shouting in angel notes for her and the guard to keep a close eye on Jack. She glanced at Riya as Muriel nodded her understanding.

But Riya was staring at her now. With a smug, ugly expression. Then the demonic woman smiled. A taunt? A challenge?

Talia wasn't sure, but Riya was acting like she'd already won something. And it unsettled her a little more than it angered her. No wonder Jack seemed so preoccupied.

"One minute," said Steve.

Jack didn't seem aware that Riya was staring at him. He was still scanning the terrace, watching for Tyler Hughes. Talia now had her sights on Riya. And she'd gotten the guard's attention on her, too.

"Thirty seconds. On your marks. Devin, camera two and stay."

Devin nodded and pulled a card out of his jacket pocket, turning his body toward camera two as he scanned the card.

"Ten seconds. Places." Steve looked tense. "Live…in…five. Four. Three, two, one."

"And we're back to see how Mark and Morgan cooked together," Devin announced. "See for yourselves."

And then their cooking challenge ran. Mark and Morgan seemed to get through all the questions and the actual cooking without any problems. Next, Devin introduced their interviews and after those ran, he introduced the next couple.

"Our next couple, Claire Olsen and Ryder Kurland, was one of our arranged marriages. None of us expected sparks to fly. As you'll see next in their cooking challenge."

The footage ran and it was clear that Claire and Ryder were quite taken with each other while they cooked. Standing close, arms around each other, lots of smiles, and sultry looks. But from their expressions, it looked like they struggled with the questions. Which wasn't their fault since they had no history together yet.

Devin smiled into the camera and his reaction was so genuine that it made Talia smile.

"And the last royal kitchens challenge is full of fire and sparks as Talia and Jack heat up the kitchen, cooking up a romantic dish that you won't want to miss. After the break. Stay tuned."

"We're clear," Steve announced. "Three minutes and forty-eight seconds."

Jack turned to Talia, taking her hands in his. "It was pretty steamy there a few times," he said and kissed her. "I think I'm gonna like spending time in the kitchen with you."

"Are you now?" she asked, brushing her lips across his. "No more pepperoni pizza?"

"Let's see, cooking with Talia or pizza delivery," he said, that delicious, sexy smirk lifting one corner of his mouth. "Hmmm, let me think now." Both corners of his mouth curved into that crooked smile and she wanted to melt. "Add a little wine and I'm a fixture there."

"Done," Talia said and brushed her fingers through his bangs and down the side of his face. "Do I need to draw up a contract?"

He took her left hand in his and laid his fingers on the thin silver band he'd placed there during *The Prince Charming Hour's* finale.

"Contract delivered," he said, kissing her.

"Two minutes," said Steve. "Find your marks."

"What are the terms?" she asked, returning Jack's kiss.

"The rest of my life," he said and winked as he pressed his forehead against hers, still smiling. She felt the heat against her skin. He was so warm. "With an option to renew."

"Where do I sign?" she asked.

He pointed to his heart. "Right here."

She laid her hand against his heart. "Here?"

He nodded.

"One minute, places," Steve announced.

"Is there a signing bonus?" she asked with a chuckle.

He nodded and laid his hand over hers, the one against his chest. "My heart. All of it. Free of charge."

"Sign me up," she said, kissing him.

He gave her his most devious smirk. "I'll tell you about the fringe benefits later. After the show."

"You'll have my undivided attention," she purred in his ear.

"I will definitely need your attention," he said and kissed her.

"Ten seconds. Devin, camera two. In…five, four, three, two, one."

"Welcome back. As I present a royal treat. Talia Smith and Jack Casey cooking up some serious romance in our royal kitchens. And in their couple's interview."

She settled into Jack's arms, watching the footage on the monitor, but she didn't need sound. She felt every moment and every look in her heart, her skin tingling every time he leaned down and kissed her or spoke softly and sweetly to her about cooking and working together. He'd been a joy in the kitchen, but it broke her heart when she saw that pained look aching through his eyes, his mouth tightening as she described the moment that she'd taken a bullet for him.

She felt his arms tightening around her and held him closer until the footage ended.

Devin still looked a little affected when the camera focus returned to him.

"And now, in no particular order, we announce the first couple moving on in the competition. That couple is…Mark and Morgan."

Morgan screamed and leaped into Mark's arms. He kissed her and turned toward Devin, grinning.

"And the next couple moving on to the next challenge is…Armand and Izzy."

Armand put his arms around Izzy and kissed her. She was excited, kissing him back, a big grin on her face.

Devin turned to camera one. "And the first couple in danger of going home is…Eric and Riya. Eric, Riya, please come stand beside me."

Eric looked disappointed. Riya looked pissed. Talia hoped they went home. Without her and Jack having to fight another demon.

Devin looked back into camera one. "The next couple moving on. Will be announced after these announcements. Stay tuned."

"Four minutes, thirty-two seconds. Everyone, hold positions." Steve frowned. "And don't even think about disappearing or I swear I'll hunt you down."

Jack laughed. He looked calmer, but she wondered if it was his game face. Was he as nervous as she felt?

"Good luck, Jack," Gianni called to him.

"Thanks, Gianni," Jack replied. "Congratulations, you two."

Izzy leaned around Gianni, her brown eyes filled with laughter. "Thanks, Jack, but you and Talia don't need any luck. After that steamy cooking lesson, I'm thinking about signing Armand and I up for cooking classes." She fanned herself with her hand. "You let us know if you decide to teach a course."

Jack laughed, a deep belly laugh that was infectious. "Got a new career gig if I don't get any more callbacks, Talia."

She shook her head and put her arms around him, holding him close. "Oh, no you don't. You're only cooking with me."

"You got that right," he said and kissed her.

"Two minutes. Devin, camera one 'til the end."

Devin nodded and took out a notecard from his jacket pocket, running through his lines.

"Izzy's right," said Gianni. "After that performance, you won't need any luck."

"What can I say, she makes my blood boil," he said, resting his chin against Talia's hair as he stood behind her, arms around her waist.

"Believe me, Jack," said Izzy, sliding her arm around Armand's waist. "It showed."

Talia grinned and looked up at him. He nuzzled his face against her cheek.

"Ten seconds. Places. Don't you dare move. Or disappear. In three, two, one."

"And we're back," said Devin into camera one. "Before the announcement, we were about to tell America the next couple moving on to the next competition. One couple is in danger of leaving us tonight and the other couple is safe."

He looked around the terrace, cameras giving a view of all the couples now.

Talia wanted to scream. *Say it already, Devin!*

"And the next couple moving on is…"

Another dramatic pause. Her body tensed, but Jack whispered in her ear.

"We're fine," he said. "You'll see."

"Jack and Talia," Devin said, grinning.

She couldn't contain her grin. Jack took her hand and spun her around. He leaned her back in his arms and kissed her with an anxious kiss. She kissed him hard, dipping him backward. He couldn't contain his belly laugh as she let him stand up. He pulled her back into his arms and held her.

Devin looked into camera one again. "Unfortunately, that means that Ryder and Claire are in danger of leaving us tonight. Ryder, Claire, please come stand on my other side."

They looked sad as they entwined fingers and moved over to Devin's left. Ryder put his arm around her waist.

Introducing a filmed montage of Eric and Riya, Devin kept his focus on camera one as the footage played on the monitor behind the cameras. When Steve pointed back to Devin, he introduced another montage of Claire and Ryder, the highlights of their time on the show playing on the monitor off stage. Again, Steve pointed at Devin whose expression turned serious, his voice sharp with a dramatic edge.

"America, one of our royal couple's won't continue with their royal courtship on The Ever After Hour. But we hope that their courtship will continue. And now, the couple going home tonight is…next. After this announcement."

"Three minutes fifty seconds, people. Stay on your marks." Steve again. Sounding nervous. Like he expected something to happen.

Three minutes rushed by in Jack's arms.

"Live in thirty seconds. Stay on your marks."

Jack began to tense, staring past Devin. At Eric and Riya? His gaze was too low to be on Muriel. She glanced up. Muriel had her head turned. In the same direction as Jack.

That's when she saw the shadow. Just behind Eric and Riya. A dark, foreboding shape crouched there. Watching. She glanced back at Jack. He looked pale, eyes wide.

Taunting or hunting Jack? Was it Tyler Hughes? She couldn't tell from this distance. And in the dark.

Muriel and another angel of death were alert and ready, shields out. Wings completely unfurled and ready to swoop.

Then the shadow vanished.

"You're safe," she whispered to Jack.

He exhaled and finally looked back at her, nodding, but he was clearly disturbed by the shadow.

"Welcome back, my royal subjects," Devin announced to camera one.

Talia's gaze shot back to Ryder and Claire and then Eric and Riya. Riya was leering at Jack, a malevolent look in her eyes.

"And now, we must say goodbye to one royal couple. Based solely on their scores from this week's challenge. The couple going home tonight is...Ryder and Claire. Eric and Riya will join us again next week as our four remaining royal couples face many obstacles in their royal courtship. Until next week, my royal subjects. Good night."

"And we're clear." Steve collapsed into a chair, looking relieved that everything went smoothly.

Armand and Izzy moved over and congratulated her and Jack again, Mark and Morgan joining them.

"Damn, that was smooth, Jack," said Mark, grinning at him with Morgan at his shoulder.

"What?" Jack asked, still distracted.

Another slip in his game face. That shadow had really rattled him. Talia wondered if there was more to it than one shadow. She needed a report from Muriel on what she and the guard found around the house and grounds.

"The cooking challenge, man," said Mark. "You and Talia really shined in that."

"It was so romantic," said Morgan, her smile bright. "You, two are so good together."

At last, Jack grinned and folded his arms around Talia. "I couldn't agree more."

"Why don't we celebrate with some champagne on the beach again?" said Armand. "Izzy and I are treating this time."

"Next time, Jack's buying," said Mark.

Jack nodded. "You bet, Banks. Talia and I will host the next one."

"All right, everyone, get changed," Izzy announced, taking Armand's hand. "And meet us on the beach."

Talia grabbed Jack's hand and tugged him toward the door. He lingered a moment, glancing over his shoulder, and then followed her inside to their suite.

He was unusually quiet as they hurried out of their dress clothes and pulled on jeans. Jack left on his white T-shirt and grabbed a black hoodie, zipping it up halfway. He pulled out a navy hoodie from the armoire and held it out to her as she pulled on Jack's Van Halen T-shirt.

He motioned for her to slide her arms in, holding it for her until she had it over her shoulders. He took hold of the zipper and slowly threaded it, gently zipping it up to her stomach.

"Don't want you getting cold," he said.

She slid her arms around his neck and kissed him. "So, what was going on tonight? On the terrace? I saw the shadow behind Eric and Riya, but you saw something else, didn't you?"

He shook his head and stepped out of her embrace to grab his slip-on sneakers. She bent down and pulled on a white pair of sneakers.

"Hughes' demon shadow was unnerving enough, don't you think?"

"I do, but you saw something else. Jack, talk to me."

"I saw another shadow," he said. "Behind us. Creeped me out. Maybe it was a bird or something from the set? I don't know. Just made me uneasy." He smiled at her. "Ready?"

She nodded and they headed out of the suite. Toward the beach. And champagne with friends.

31

THE WEEKEND BROUGHT ANOTHER HECTIC SCHEDULE AND REHEARSALS. More interviews. By Monday, all the remaining couples were scheduled for a walkthrough of the next challenge. Courtship obstacles as Devin called it.

Jack wondered if it was an actual obstacle course as he and Talia got ready for the seven A.M. set call outside. He dressed in a black pair of sweatpants and grabbed a black T-shirt from the drawer. He looked around the suite. No sign of Muriel or the guard.

He unfolded the black T-shirt. Judas Priest. *Sad Wings of Destiny*. With a big fallen angel on it.

"Dammit, Muriel!" he shouted as he pulled it over his head.

He heard her laughing as she came out of the bathroom with Talia who looked amazing in grey leggings and a long-sleeved pink T-shirt.

"Ready?" he asked, pulling on a black hoodie.

He zipped it up halfway and headed toward the door in black and white checked Vans slip-ons.

When Talia nodded, they hurried down the hall and out the front door, heading to the right, away from the huge white garage. Beside the house, the crew had built an obstacle course with several parts. It stood on the bluff with basalt rocks and sea grass, the air crisp and smelling like sea spray.

Jennifer and Steve brought everyone to the entrance of the course. The walls surrounding it looked like castle walls. Jack couldn't see past the wooden white gate installed at the front of the course.

"All right, everyone, welcome to the courtship obstacles challenge," said Jennifer, clipboard against her chest, voice rising as a gust of wind raked across the bluff. "You and your partner will have to run this course together." She smiled. "With one catch." She unclipped something from her clipboard and held it up. "A blindfold."

The group fell silent, including Jack. This one looked tough.

"I know what you're thinking," she said and lowered the blindfold. "How can you do an obstacle course blindfolded? Because your partner is going to guide you through the obstacles. You'll have to trust your partner to get you through it. You'll have one chance to run the course, but you must complete all the obstacles for your time to count. The slowest time will send you home."

She pointed at Steve who smiled, his hair blowing in the wind. "I'll take you through the course and give you the nickel tour. You'll get a chance to walk through it a couple of times with your partner. And then your run will be scheduled this week. When you arrive for your scheduled run, you'll have to identify who's wearing the blindfold and who's directing. Any questions?"

"You have a place picked out to bury the bodies yet?" Jack asked.

Everyone laughed.

"We'll pile them on the beach and let the tide carry them out," Steve replied with a grin.

"That's a good plan," Jack replied.

"Glad you approve," said Steve. "All right, let's walk through it."

Steve opened the gate and led them inside. A big green arch with Start in white capital letters stood to the right. Jack took hold of Talia's hand as they entered the first part of the course. They passed a purple sign with big white letters that read, Maypole in Old English lettering.

"There are six poles lined up in a single column." Steve veered left around the first pole, then to to the right around the next pole, weaving between them until he got to the end. "You must weave around them until you clear the last pole. Miss one and you start that obstacle over again. Questions? Simple enough."

They walked past the six tall poles, each with a purple banner flag fluttering from the top. The next section had five elevated planks in succession, about a foot off the ground. Another purple sign with the same Old English lettering read, Royal Steps.

"You have to jump over each plank in the order they're laid out." He jumped over each one as he came to it, moving left or right to jump over the next plank, until he'd jumped over all five. "Questions?" He paused. "None? Good. On to the next obstacle."

A large, green canvas tube stretched ahead with three big turns in it. About forty feet or so long and four feet wide. The purple sign read, Secret Tunnel.

"Simple. Duck through the tube and get out the other end."

Steve ducked into the opening, following its turns until he came out the other end. He tumbled out and stood up.

"Questions on that one?"

Everyone shook their heads.

"Moving on," said Steve as they moved about ten feet to a sandbox across from the tube.

It was a ten-foot square filled with sand. A red and blue beach ball leaned against the corner of the sandbox frame. The purple sign on this obstacle read, Royal Retrieval.

"For Royal Retrieval, your partner has to direct you to the beach ball. Pick it up and hand it to your partner to get credit for that obstacle. Any questions?"

Silence.

"Excellent," said Steve, walking around the sandbox. "Let's move to the fifth obstacle."

A long plank about eighteen inches wide stood between two green ramps. The sign on this obstacle read, Drawbridge.

"For Drawbridge, your partner has to talk you across the plank. You've got to walk up the ramp, across the board, and down the opposite ramp to complete this obstacle. Clear?"

Everyone nodded.

"And the final obstacle is ahead," said Steve walking past the plank.

Talia looked overwhelmed by this point. Jack squeezed her hand and offered her his best reassuring smile as they reached a fifteen-foot square of artificial grass. Scattered through the artificial grass were about a dozen or so red rocks about the size of softballs. The sign read, Trebuchet.

Steve grinned and motioned at the artificial grass. "We call this one the Trebuchet. And the red rocks are all the rocks flung by a trebuchet. You have to talk your partner around the rocks to the archway ahead. Getting through the archway without touching a rock completes the challenge. From there, the finish line which stops your clock. The whole course is a big square."

"Do the rocks explode if you touch them?" Jack asked.

"No, Jack," Steve said with a chuckle. "This isn't a horror movie."

"You sure?" he replied.

Apparently, Steve couldn't see the demons rampaging around the beach house.

"Yes," said Steve, a hand against his short-cropped beard, "but a good question because if you touch a rock, you have to start that obstacle over. Any questions?"

No one had a question.

"Wow, you guys are either scared to death, tired, or quick studies," said Steve, sliding his glasses back up his nose.

"Two out of three ain't bad," Jack replied.

Steve smiled and brushed his hands against his jeans. "Okay, have at it. Walk through a few times, so you understand all the challenges. Then decide who gets blindfolded. You get one run at it, so give it your best shot. Good luck, gang."

Then Steve stepped out of the gate as Jack turned toward Talia.

"What do you think?" he asked, glancing around at the different areas.

He was fast. With Talia directing, he could get through this course and make a decent showing.

"This is a lot, Jack," she said, her gaze flitting from each of the obstacles, looking unsure and shaken.

"I think I should do the obstacles and you should direct."

She studied him a moment. "Are you sure? With that injured shoulder and the fever, you may not be able to do this, Jack."

"I don't have to climb anything or pull myself up," he countered. "I'll need to be careful through the tunnel."

She sighed and ran a hand through her black hair. "I don't know. With that fever, you might not be up to a run like this. There's a lot to do here, Jack."

"I don't want you getting hurt," he said and moved close. "What if your wings grow out by then? You'd never get through the poles or the tunnel. It could happen any time."

She nodded. "You're right. Okay, I'll direct and you'll do the obstacles, but only if you promise you'll be careful."

"Careful's my middle name," he said with a smirk.

"No, it's not," she said. "It's reckless. So, be careful."

"Guess you've seen my driver's license," he replied and she smiled at him finally.

"And your Book, Jack Casey. I know better."

He shrugged and motioned her over to the poles. "Okay, let's walk through it. I'll close my eyes and you try your hand at directions."

He closed his eyes and faced the first pole.

"Make a half-turn left and take four paces forward. Veer right around the first pole," said Talia.

He followed her directions and didn't hit anything. So far, so good.

"Good, you cleared it," said Talia. "Now, make a half-turn right. Take three paces forward. And turn left around the next pole."

He turned, took three paces, and walked slowly left until Talia told him to stop.

"Take a half-step left. Turn a half-turn to the right and walk around the pole until I say stop again."

He took the half-step left and then angled right, hoping he was moving around the pole as he veered right and then circled left.

Talia got him around all six posts without running into one.

"Good job, Jack," she said and led him by the hand to the next obstacle. Royal Steps.

———

THEY WERE able to walk through each obstacle two or three times until Steve kicked them all out and handed them schedules. Jack looked at it. Thursday. Like the last challenge. And then more interviews. This challenge would be a big one. He hoped he was up for it.

Talia's wings had started to become small feathered appendages and required Muriel's powers to hide them. It had been a little disturbing when he'd rolled over in the night and gotten a face full of feathers. He'd have to get used to the wings. And the halo when that appeared.

He hoped Muriel was only messing with him about the scythe. That thing wasn't coming near the bed.

He was still struggling with the whole angel of death concept. *So, Jack, what's your girlfriend do? Oh, she smites people and stops their hearts. Then crosses their souls over to the other side. Wherever that is. With a scythe. Yeah, she's an angel of death. Oh, your girlfriend works for the IRS? That's cool.*

He sighed. Guess he needed more time.

He got through his Thursday interview schedule and hurried back to the suite. They had a couple's interview after their obstacle course run. Talia looked hot in her black leggings, purple tunic, and black sneakers. And terrified about something.

"Hey, you okay?" he asked, moving over to the couch where she sat, and knelt down beside her.

He brushed the hair out of her eyes.

"What if we lose this one?" she asked. "What if we—"

He laid his fingers against her mouth. "Win or lose, it's going to be okay. We'll get through it."

Her eyes misted. "Azrael still hasn't contacted us. No one's heard from Anahera. There are demons still here, trying to harm us. And I don't have my powers back yet. If we leave the chained wards, they'll swarm us before we even spread our wings to fly off—without the entire guard. We can't hold them all back without someplace defensible. Your apartment is a death trap."

"You're telling me," he said, smirking at her. "That Murphy bed is an accident waiting to happen. Or a makeshift trebuchet!"

She slapped her hand against the cushion. "I'm serious, Jack. We can't fight them outside an isolated, warded location without Azrael and the rest of the guard to even have a fighting chance."

"Can't you just fly off once your wings grow back?" he asked, frowning. He'd seen the other death angels fly through the ceiling. "Through the walls like your colleagues?"

"I can," she said, a sad look on her face. "But you can't pass through those obstacles in human form."

Then he understood. She was protecting him again. Alone, he'd be a quick mark for these things. And she knew it. He ran his hand through her hair.

"Then we'll have to come in third place or better. We'll make it happen, okay?"

She touched his face, her fingers tracing across his lips. "How do you do that?"

"Do what?"

"Stay so positive like that?" she asked. "You always find the up side and give me hope that things will work out."

"If I don't, I go for the joke," he said with a shrug. "Either blind optimism or laugh in doom's face. It's how I roll."

She laughed. "Okay, let's go laugh in its face then."

He helped her up from the couch. "Let's do this."

WHEN THEY GOT out to the course, they found the show's crew finishing camera installs throughout the course. About a dozen cameras in all. He walked up to Jennifer who stood beside the gate, talking to Steve and Roy, the cameraman.

"Jack! Talia!" she called to them, waving her clipboard. "Ready for your run?"

"No, but we're here anyway," Jack replied as Talia stood beside him, looking scared.

"Talia, are you all right?" Jennifer asked, moving closer, her gaze scrutinizing.

"I'm worried that Jack's going to get hurt," she said. "If I mess up the directions."

Jennifer laid her hands on Talia's shoulders, clipboard under her arm. "Don't worry," she said. "Jack will be fine. There's nothing out there that can cause him injury. Maybe a turned ankle, but that could happen on the beach. So, don't worry, he'll be fine."

He slid his arm around Talia's shoulders and hugged her.

"So, obviously, I'm the maze rat and she's giving directions," said Jack, motioning toward the first obstacle.

Jennifer held up a long black piece of cloth. "And here's your blindfold. If you're ready, I'll tie it around your eyes at the start line."

He looked over at Talia. "Ready, babe?" he asked, giving her his best *everything's okay* smile.

She sighed and finally nodded.

"Okay, let's do this," he said as Steve opened the gate.

"Roll it, Roy," Steve called over his shoulder.

Jennifer led them to the right as Roy began filming. Where the green starting arch stood. Steve gave directions to Roy who got cameras focused on the starting gate. Steve had a stopwatch in his hand.

Draping the blindfold across Jack's eyes, Jennifer tied it tight against his head. He couldn't see a damned thing. Not even slivers of sunlight from the afternoon sun that slid slowly westward toward the ocean.

"Okay," said Steve. "Ten-second warning, Talia. Get ready to direct Jack through. And good luck to you guys."

"Thanks," Jack called, Talia's voice joining his.

"Five seconds. Get ready to move, Jack," said Jennifer, turning him toward the poles.

"Three, two, one. Go!"

"Okay, Jack, walk five paces forward and stop."

He quickly took five steps and stopped.

"Half step right. Veer left around the first pole and stop."

He veered left and stopped.

"Half step left and veer right. Then stop."

He took another half step and stopped.

"Third pole. Half step left and veer left."

He followed her directions to the letter until he heard her cheer.

"We're through the maypoles! Ten steps straight ahead and stop."

He counted off the steps and stopped. Waiting.

"Okay, the plank is six inches wide and a foot tall," she said. "Jump over it and stop."

He held his breath, taking a leap of faith. And landed on level ground.

"Great job! Move four steps to your left and stop."

He moved left in the darkness, counting off, and stopped.

"Half step forward."

He took a baby step.

"Perfect. Jump over."

It felt so uncomfortable jumping into the dark, but he trusted Talia with his life. He shifted his arms back and jumped.

"Six steps to the right and stop."

He moved swiftly. Waiting for the next instruction.

"One more step right."

He took another step.

"Jump over."

Again, he leaped into the darkness. Landing on flat ground.

She got him past the next two jumps and directed him left then right until she made him stop.

"Okay, the tunnel entrance is right in front of you. Grab hold with both hands and slide inside. The first left curve is ten feet inside. I'll stand beside it."

"Go," he said and grabbed hold of the circular entrance.

With a quick breath, he heaved himself inside, ducking as he felt along the side with his left hand. He moved toward Talia's voice.

"Okay, Jack, follow the curve to your right. Ten feet around."

He reached out with his right hand, following the second curve toward her voice.

"Third curve left, about ten feet or so. Follow my voice."

He held out his left hand and hurried around the curve, Talia calling his name. When he heard her clearly, he fumbled for the opening until she clapped.

"Perfect, Jack! You're out!"

He grinned.

"Straight ahead now. Twelve steps and stop."

He counted out the steps and stopped.

"Two more and then step over a board that's six inches wide. Into the sand."

His foot hit the top of the board as he stepped over and he face-planted into the sand.

"Found the sand," he said.

She laughed.

He struggled to his feet as she directed him, left, right, forward until he felt like a computer cursor. Finally, she told him to bend down and carefully pick up the ball. The first time, he knocked it forward and couldn't get a grip on it. She guided him to it again and he carefully and gently reached down until he gathered it in his arms.

"Four steps forward and stop."

He still felt the sinking sand under his feet as he stopped.

"Carefully step over," she said, a smile in her voice. "A big step and don't fall."

He held his breath and waded over in a big, long stretch. Finding solid ground. He pulled his other leg over, straightening up, and then held out the beach ball. Talia clapped then took it from him.

"Great job, Jack."

He grinned.

"Okay, ten steps forward. And stop."

He took the ten steps quickly and stopped.

"There's a ramp in front of you. Four steps to the top. Then stop."

He felt the incline as he took each step.

"One step left. Half step forward."

He took one normal step left and then a tiny step forward.

"One more half step forward."

He took another careful, half step forward and waited for her next command.

"Keep your feet close together. Right next to each other. And step forward one step with the right. And one step with your left."

He felt off balance as he took the right step, and then left, but he hadn't fallen.

"Good," Talia replied. "One more of those."

He took another right step and then the left.

"Two more."

Pulling in a breath, Jack took a deliberate right step and then left. He felt off balance and uncomfortable, but he kept moving.

"Halfway across, Jack! Two more of those."

He exhaled, right then left. Right then left. "What next?"

"One more of those."

He hesitated. Then another right and left.

"One more, Jack and you'll be at the ramp."

Nodding, he let out a heavy breath and took another deliberate right then left and paused.

"Okay, scoot forward a half step, left and right forward."

Scoot? Okay. He'd try that.

With a sharp inhale, he slid his right foot and then his left forward.

"Perfect, Jack. Now take a deep step forward with your right foot. And then your left. Then you'll be on the ramp."

He hesitated, feeling disoriented, the blindfold claustrophobic.

"You can do it, Jack," Talia replied. "One long step onto the ramp."

He worked up to it and then stretched his right foot forward.

Slamming it down on the ramp. He pulled his other foot after it. Solid ground.

"All right, Jack, walk four steps forward down the ramp. Then twelve steps toward the last obstacle. Almost there!"

Feeling shaky, he hurried down the ramp with four steps. Then he counted twelve steps, stopping when he felt the artificial grass under his feet.

"Okay, Jack," said Talia, sounding anxious. "Three steps forward."

He took three steps and waited.

"One more forward. Turn half a step right and then take three steps."

He was about to take step three when Talia's voice rang out.

"Stop! Don't step down!"

He halted in mid-step, turning his body, and stepping down.

"That was close. Sorry."

He smiled. "We got this."

"Two steps forward and then a half step left."

He took them cautiously, but not so much that it slowed him down. He moved left and right, a heartbeat behind her directions, moving across and through the Trebuchet obstacle. Until he stepped onto a rocky surface.

"Run straight ahead, Jack!" she shouted. "And don't stop until you feel my arms around you."

Grinning, he broke into a run, sneakers slapping the flat, rocky ground until Talia enfolded him in her arms.

"Time!" Steve called off to his right.

He reached up and ripped the blindfold off his face. He was standing under the red finish banner, Talia in his arms. Three cameras around him and a handful of crew. She was beaming at him, those grey eyes filled with excitement as he kissed her.

"You were brilliant, Talia! Got me through all of it."

"Thanks for trusting me," she said, hugging him.

He brushed the hair out of her eyes. "Are you kidding? I trust you with my heart, my soul. All of it."

Steve walked up and patted them both on the backs. "Good run, you, two. Hope tomorrow's dismissal goes well for you."

"Thanks, Steve," Jack replied and walked off with Talia.

He slid his arm around her back. And felt the folds of her wings. They'd gotten longer even since yesterday. They were growing back fast.

"Something wrong?" she asked.

He shook his head. "Surprised at how much your wings have grown."

"Me, too," she said in a quiet voice. "Are you bothered by it?"

"Not bothered," he replied.

He didn't want to make her feel bad, but he'd never seen her with wings and a halo. It would require some adjustment on his part.

"Getting used to it. Never saw you as a full-fledged angel before."

"That's true." She looked sad now. "I wish I'd told you from the beginning, but when I met you on Cinderella Hour, I didn't know if I'd ever be an angel again. On Prince Charming Hour, I didn't know how to tell you."

He stopped walking, turning her around by the shoulders. "Talia, it's all right," he said, flashing his most charming smile. "When I offered you my heart, it didn't have a million riders attached. The only condition was that you love me back. Whatever happens, we'll deal with it together. Even if my girlfriend can fly without a plane and can smite anything that moves."

She threw her arms around him. "I love you, Jack."

"I love you too, Tal. No matter what. Even if demons carry me off, I'll always love you."

She pulled away, her eyes shining with fear. "Jack, don't say that."

"I just meant that good or bad, I'll always love you."

She let him take her in his arms again, but her eyes still gleamed with apprehension.

"I feel like you're not telling me something," she said.

He swallowed hard, holding her close as he stared at the empty space between the bluff and the house. A dozen demons in black

Wayfarers stood there, wearing black suits, black shirts, and black ties, arms behind their backs. Waiting. Watching him with hungry smiles.

And winding between him and the demons was a trail of his blood.

"Only that I love you—always," he said, arms tightening around her.

Why couldn't she see them?

A female demon grinned at him. "Because we're only here for you, Jack," she said with a hiss. "The interruption of her powers is only temporary. Until then, we can exploit this loophole—as long as we stay away from the angels of death." She bared sharp pointed teeth. "And we get to torture you until you're plucked from the Earth."

The demon laughed, the sound rough and caustic as he hurried Talia across the expanse toward the house.

On Friday night, he and Talia arrived on the darkening terrace for another live dismissal show. The ocean whispered below, soothing sound of the waves washing across the rocks and sand, calming him as he stepped under the set lights and candles flickering across the stone terrace. To his purple tape mark.

He wore a crisp navy blue suit and grey silk T-shirt. Talia wore a mint green dress with little spaghetti straps and a short skirt. Her silver flats clicked against the stone, wind tousling a headful of black waves that tumbled down her back. She made his breath catch as she walked toward him.

He laid a hand against his chest. "Don't think my heart can take you in that dress," he said, smiling at her.

"Why not?" she asked, looking surprised.

"Because it might explode on impact," he said and pulled her into an embrace.

At last, she smiled, understanding what he meant.

"That means you like it," she said.

"Like it?" he said. "You look amazing!" He brushed his lips against her ear. "And I'm imagining slowly taking it off you," he whispered.

He held her close as Gianni and Izzy walked onto the terrace. Gianni wore a dark blue pin-striped suit, Izzy in a short red dress and grey heels. Banks walked in next with Morgan, dressed in a strapless raspberry-colored dress and black heels. Banks wore a charcoal grey suit and no tie.

Then Eric walked in wearing a tan suit and white t-shirt. Riya had on a tight-fitting black dress. She glared at Jack as they walked past. He nodded at Eric as they moved beside Morgan and Banks, standing on their marks.

Waiting for Devin and the show to begin.

Five minutes before the broadcast began, Devin showed up with notecards in his hand, that familiar black tux on, and his hair pomaded into stone. Steve stood beside him, doing mic and lighting checks. Until Herb called places and Steve returned to his position behind the camera crew, calling the two-minute warning.

"Nervous?" Talia asked him.

Nervous that he'd be swarmed by demons that could stop time and carry him off into thin air? That was a silly thought. He wasn't nervous. He was terrified.

Finally, he nodded. What could he say? Even his game face couldn't blot out all these demons surrounding the house. Counting down the minutes until they could attack him.

"Ten seconds, Devin. Camera one then two until first commercial break."

Devin nodded, turning to camera one as Steve counted off the seconds. That's when Jack saw the demonic shadow against the wall of the house. Behind Devin as he began the broadcast.

"Welcome, my royal subjects to the next Ever After Hour live dismissal. Where our four royal couples ran the royal obstacles challenge together." He pointed toward the monitor on the wall. "Let's take a look."

"Tape montage rolling," Steve said, showing highlights from all five runs.

He watched Gianni's long legs sprint across the planks, Eric's poise at crossing the drawbridge without a single bobble. And Banks' dexterity as he weaved through the posts. Then he saw himself fumble into the tunnel and slide his way through it.

Back to Devin. Devin turned to camera two. "And the moment has come to announce our first couple moving on to the next challenge."

Devin paused, glancing around at all four couples.

"Armand and Izzy, you're in the next round."

Gianni kissed her as she put her arms around him.

Jack glanced at Talia. She looked so nervous. He felt the soft feathers of her lengthening wings against his fingertips. How long before she could fly again? Judging from their growing width, she'd have her wings back in days.

He slid his hand in hers.

Devin announced another montage from the obstacle course and Jack squirmed, hating to see himself stumbling around in that blindfold. But he hadn't fallen on his face—much, so it wasn't as painful as he'd expected.

Everything paused for a commercial break and he couldn't help but look around the terrace. Counting the demons standing around like they were part of the show. Of the crew. All of them turned toward him. Watching him with red eyes. Until his skin began to crawl.

When the broadcast returned, Devin introduced interviews and ran more footage. And then he turned to camera two.

"My royal subjects, our next couple moving on to the next challenge is…Jack and Talia."

Jack grinned as Talia threw her arms around him. He held her tight, kissing her as he felt all the tension release, wings lying flat at her back.

"And unfortunately, both Mark and Morgan and Eric and Riya are in danger of leaving us tonight. But before we get to the last safe couple, let's see what our royal courtiers had to say about their challenges."

More canned footage. Jack looked up.

More demons had joined the others. Dressed in tuxedos, red bowties, and black shirts. Watching him. One of them bowed and motioned toward the stone floor. Twisting between Gianni and Banks was a glistening red trail of blood. The demon lifted a hand toward Jack and snapped it closed.

Like a hot poker, something pierced his left shoulder. He gasped, staggered as the horrible pain ripped through him. And the wound began to bleed again, soaking through the bandage and seeping into his grey T-shirt until it dripped from his jacket sleeve onto the stone floor. Every drop sizzled, skittering across the stones like it had hit a hot griddle. Making another trail.

The demon grinned at him and slid on a pair of sunglasses.

He blinked and it all disappeared again.

He barely heard Devin return from break or the next montage of interviews and obstacle play. Even when Devin began the wind up for the dismissal, his brain struggled against the raw pain in his shoulder and all the demons surrounding him.

Had he truly been damned? Doomed to spend eternity as Lucifer's chew toy? He didn't even know why. And it made him shake all over.

"And the last couple moving on to the next challenge is…Mark and Morgan. That means Eric and Riya are leaving us. Thank you for watching, America. And we'll see you next week for the next challenge on…The Ever After Hour."

"And we're clear," Herb called out. "Thanks everybody. Look for next week's schedule under your doors tomorrow morning. Now, get some sleep."

"Sleep, hell!" Banks shouted. "Jack and Talia's buying champagne tonight on the beach."

Banks pumped the air with his fist, Morgan hugging him.

Jennifer led Eric and Riya off the terrace. Jack glanced around him. Down to three couples. Two challenges left. He'd given Jennifer money to get some bottles of champagne delivered, including a few for the crew. They were chilling in the fridge. But all he could think about were demons and the pain in his shoulder as he led Gianni and Banks to the kitchen to retrieve the champagne, ice, and a cooler while Talia, Izzy, and Morgan gathered champagne flutes from Morgan and Banks' suite.

Thirty minutes later, they were on the beach, the fire pit crackling above the ocean swells, smell of sea spray mixing with wood smoke, the soft feel of Talia's hair against his face as she huddled beside him.

"A toast to good friends," said Gianni, raising his glass.

"And to being alive and still in this contest," Banks added.

Jack stared at the demons gathering on the dark beach and standing motionless in the cold surf, red eyes gleaming in the darkness, and he felt hollow. Dread numbed his fingertips as he drank a hard mouthful of champagne that bubbled down his throat.

With the terrible feeling that he was about to lose everything.

32

On Monday morning, Jennifer Collins met Talia and Jack, Armand and Izzy, and Mark and Morgan at the beach. The next challenge was beginning. Jennifer wore a yellow windbreaker over a long-sleeved green blouse, black pants, and boots as she stood beside the blackened fire pit.

Talia smelled the stale scent of burned charcoal that hung above the cool breeze and salty sea smell. She watched Jack stare off into the distance. Like he was a million miles away. He was dressed in faded jeans, a grey Henley, and navy blue windbreaker. She ran her hand across his back and he turned around, those light green eyes lighting up, corners of his mouth lifting.

"All right, couples," said Jennifer, greeting them all warmly, "the next challenge is a scavenger hunt. Work together to solve the clues and find your five objects. They're hidden along the beach. You lose points for every object you miss. Clues are based on answers to questions we asked each of you when you arrived. Fastest time gets the most points."

She handed them each a paper schedule. "Like the obstacle course, you'll run this event at a scheduled time. You'll get the list of objects and clues then. And there are interviews scheduled throughout the week. Any questions?"

No one spoke.

Talia looked at Jack, expecting him to make a joke. Everyone paused, glancing at him. But he didn't say a word. That wasn't like Jack. He always made jokes to cover his fear or apprehension. Right now, though she couldn't tell if he was afraid or distracted. Or maybe both?

She needed to tell him that she'd felt the first hum of her halo returning this morning, wings getting longer and stronger. When she regained her halo, she'd have her powers back. Maybe then she could protect him from demon attacks, but her stomach twisted into knots, knowing that only Azrael and the entire guard could help them now.

"All right, good luck, couples!"

In silence, she and Jack returned to the suite. Empty. No sign of the guard or Muriel. There hadn't been for days and it made Talia uneasy. Muriel hadn't appeared even when she'd called her. Was the guard still protecting them or had they been suddenly recalled to the Heavens.

She shuddered. Or High House.

Jack stood in front of the window, staring out at the ocean, hands in his jeans' pockets, navy blue hoodie bunched around his shoulders.

"Jack? Is everything all right?"

"Yeah," he said with a sigh.

"Oh, that was convincing," she said and moved toward him.

He turned around, all smiles, that game face on now. But she wouldn't have it this time.

"You were a million miles away from the beach this weekend and all morning." She laid her hand against his warm face and caressed his cheek. "What's the matter?"

"Worried about Hughes getting me with my back turned," he said, his light green eyes sparking. "His shadow is never far away from me."

That made her want to rage. That this demon was stalking Jack. And that Jack hadn't told her that he was a constant presence. Only an occasional sighting.

"So, when were you going to tell me that this demon has been stalking you, Jack?"

"Didn't want you to worry since you don't seem to be able to see him every time."

She hadn't realized that until right now, but Jack was right. She had most of her angel of death senses except her ability to detect lies. But she was an angel, a creature of light. She was born with that innate sense to see creatures of light and dark. Why couldn't she see this demon shadow stalking Jack?

"You're right," she said, the fear returning. "Why can't I see them? As an angel, I was created with that sense. This is very troubling. Why isn't Azrael here to help us?"

Jack sighed again, turning back toward the window.

"Looks like your boss isn't coming, Talia. We're going to have figure out a way to fight these things without him. Or…"

He shook his head and stared out at the ocean. He didn't even finish that thought, like he'd almost given up. Like he'd accepted that the demons would win.

"Jack," she said, laying her hand against his right arm. "We can't give up now."

"We're not giving up," he said. "Looking for another way out because we can't fight them and win."

She knew he was right. She hated to leave him in this state, but she had an interview and he was meeting Armand and Mark for lunch. Or face her wrath if he stayed here alone.

INTERVIEWS KEPT her and Jack busy until Thursday, the day of the beach scavenger hunt. The day was cool, requiring layers. Jack dressed in jeans, an olive Henley, grey hoodie, and a blue windbreaker and she wore grey leggings, purple tunic, and one of Jack's windbreakers in a charcoal grey.

This morning, her wings had grown out to their full length and for the first time, she was able to control them. Stretching them out behind her, shifting them up to the sky. She didn't want to test her flight skills yet though, not until she got her rudder back. Her halo.

Already, she'd seen sparkles of light above her head. It was returning. When she had it at full light and motion, she'd test out her flying. And her powers. Until then, any sort of flight might harm her.

How would Jack react when she was back in full angel of death form? She feared that his feelings for her would cool and he'd slowly fall out of love with her. But she had to hold onto that trust they'd forged together during *The Prince Charming Hour*. When he'd given up everything for her.

Camera crew was filming along the beach with several cameras as Jennifer met them at a row of fluttering green flags. The starting point of the scavenger hunt. Jennifer wore a long tan windbreaker over a blue blouse and tan pants. She had on blue glasses and hugged her clipboard against her chest.

"Good morning, Talia! Hi, Jack! Ready for your royal scavenger hunt?"

Jack nodded.

"We are, Jennifer," Talia answered quickly as Jack slid his hands into his jacket pockets.

Jennifer glanced at him and then back to her as she handed Talia a big manilla envelope, a map of the beach, and a purple tote bag with *The Ever After Hour* logo on it.

"Here's a bag to carry your items, a map of the beach, and the list with questions is inside the envelope. You can open it now. When Steve calls time, start your hunt and then head to the big red flag when you've finished. Good luck."

Jack mumbled thanks and took the bag from Talia's hands as she opened the envelope.

The first page had five numbered items listed at the top. "A gold starfish, a glass heart, a wooden cloud, a toy detective's badge, and a toy airplane."

She smiled. These items had been handpicked for them.

"Sounds tough," said Jack, squinting at the map.

"Not if we work together," she said, taking his hand.

"And together, we're dynamite," he said, that sexy smirk brightening his face.

Then Steve walked up with a stopwatch as a blonde, curly-haired woman planted herself beside the start line with a camera on her shoulder. She wore an army jacket, cargo pants, and a yellow blouse.

"Start rolling, Rhonda," said Steve as the camera woman turned the lens toward Talia and Jack.

"Okay, get to the start line and head out when I say go," said Steve.

Talia and Jack moved to the starting line, green flags fluttering above them in the wind. She held the papers tight against her chest and waited.

"Going in five," said Steve. "Five, four, three, two, one. Go!"

Jack trotted away from the start line that began at the edge of the terrace and stretched about three hundred feet to a cliff that marked the end.

"Okay, first clue for the starfish," Talia said, reading. "How Jack feels when he looks at Talia."

He grinned and nodded her forward. "That's an easy one," he said.

He ran ahead, purple bag in his fist, rushing past the terrace to the right. Toward the path that led up to the house. He stopped in front of the blackened fire pit and pulled out an envelope.

"The answer's on fire," he said, kissing her as he tore open the envelope.

Talia was already smiling.

"Okay, an REO Speedwagon song and the sea. Or what Jack's going to do to Talia."

He was grinning now, that smirk deep. "Gonna have to think more about this one later in our suite," he said as he grabbed her hand and pulled her toward the water. "An REO song," Jack muttered. Then he stepped on something stringy and green. And laughed. "Over here!"

He led her to a pile of cold, wet tubes with balls at the end. Thick and green. That had washed up from the ocean and dried in the sun. He bent down and dug around, coming up with another envelope.

"What was the answer?" Talia asked.

He chuckled. "Gonna Kelp on Loving You. Bad pun, but it works. Thanks, Steve!" he called out. "I know that was you."

He ripped open the envelope and read the card inside. "What Talia wants from Jack."

He gazed at her with a devious smile.

"Jack Casey, don't make me tickle you," she said, shaking her index finger at him.

Then she glanced at the ring on her finger. Wait! The ring of chairs around the fire pit!

"This way!" she shouted, running across the beach.

And he was right behind her. Running toward the ring of chairs.

"Not what I was thinking," he replied, shaking his head.

She leaned up and kissed him. "I know what you were thinking."

He shrugged as she grabbed the envelope out of one of the chairs. She tore it open, throwing the envelopes into the bag that Jack held.

Inside was a three-inch gold star fish!

"First object!" she cried, handing it to Jack.

"Sweet! Next clue."

"A glass heart. First clue, what Jack held when he offered Talia his heart."

Jack's face lit up and he rushed over to the path leading up to the house. Where a trash can stood. Beside it was an empty cardboard box that held champagne bottles.

"An empty box," he said, motioning at it.

He reached inside and snatched out the envelope. Tearing it open, he pulled out the next clue.

"What did Talia give Jack at the finale when he matched with her?"

"A crown!" Talia shouted.

Jack started looking around as she looked back at the terrace, the cliffs, and the sand rolling toward the rocks ahead.

"Wait," said Jack, grabbing the map from her hand. "There are all kinds of little points and nooks and bluffs with names along this beach." He ran his index finger across all the landmarks, eyes narrowing. "Crown Spur. Over this way!"

He ran down the beach and she rushed after him. He stopped at a heel of basalt rock that stuck out into the ocean. It almost looked like the points of a crown. He walked around it and plucked an envelope out of the top of the rocks. It had been hidden in a deep crevice. He tore open the envelope and slid out the card.

"What did Jack do to match with Talia on The Prince Charming Hour?"

Jack laughed and motioned her back down the beach toward two small basalt cliffs that faced each other. Between them was a tiny crevice just big enough for a bird or two. It was shaped almost like a sword.

"Looks like a sword, doesn't it?" he said, nodding toward the map she carried. "It's called Claymore Crevice on that map."

He reached inside, fumbling a bit, and pulled out a glass heart.

"I give you my heart again, Talia Smith," he said, but there was something hollow in his eyes. Something a little sad and a little jaded that hadn't been there until now. "But be careful...it's a little fragile and it can shatter."

Gently, she took the glass heart from his hand and kissed him, holding him tight in her arms.

"Your heart is the most priceless gift I've ever received, Jack Casey," she said, running her hand through his windblown hair. "And I will guard it with my life. To my last breath."

She echoed his own words back to him, wanting him to know how much he meant to her.

He grinned and kissed her, an urgent kiss that burned deep, making her want more.

"Next object," she said and placed the heart in the bag. "Wooden cloud. Where is Talia most at home when away from Jack?"

Jack immediately looked up at the fluffy white clouds scuttling across the crisp December sky.

"Okay, the sky, the clouds—what else?"

Sea gulls winged overhead, chattering in their laughing singsong. And Jack's eyes got wide.

"Seagull Point! This way."

They ran back down the beach, past Crown Spur, and toward

beach grass growing along the cliffs to the right. Where a dozen or more seagulls clustered. They scattered as Jack ran through the grass beside a small outcropping. He bent down and held up an envelope.

Tearing it open, he slid out the next clue. "Jack's best gift?"

He frowned, a pensive look sliding past his game face.

"We answered this question during the cooking challenge," Talia replied as Jack's face scrunched, the thoughts whizzing past his eyes. "Remember? The glider."

He was nodding, beginning to pace now. He looked down at the map, down the beach.

"Kite Landing!" he cried, motioning her back down the beach.

To a flattened mound of sand and grass in front of a horizontal slab of rock. He stood on the mound, glancing around in a circle. But Talia saw the envelope peeking out of the sand. She bent down and grabbed it.

"Great job, Jack!" she cried, tearing open the envelope. She pulled out the next clue. "What Talia sees when she looks at Jack?"

He flashed her a smug smile. "It's the fire pit again, isn't it?"

She laughed.

He held out his hands, walking toward her. "So, Talia Smith," he said, laying his hands on her shoulders as he mocked her always calling him by first and last name. "What do you see?"

He turned around in front of her and held out his hands again.

"I see…the most incredible man I've ever met," she said to him, taking his hand. "With a heart of gold. That he offered to me once. And finally gave me. And every time I look at him, I get lightheaded and my heart pounds."

His smile turned into a grin as he stared down at the map again. He laughed and pointed at something on the map. "Heart Rock, Talia." He grabbed her hand and pulled her along beside him. "Down here."

They ran back toward the terrace and the rocky cliffs that framed the side of the house. He moved around the edge, stopping beside a small outcrop. Shaped roughly like a heart. Lying on top of it was a six-inch cut-out of a cloud. Jack picked it up and held it in the sunlight. It was about three inches thick and painted white with pale blue highlights.

He slid it into the bag as Talia read off the next clue.

"Fourth object, a gold badge," she said. "First clue. Jack's character at sea."

Jack laughed. "Easy one," he said. "This way."

He pulled her along the water, toward a tall clump of rocks in the middle of the beach. Toward a flat area. He bent over some large indentations filled with sea water, plants, and tiny creatures. She grinned. And a couple of bright orange starfish.

"Jack! It's beautiful!" she cried, watching the little fish and the fleshy starfish slowly ooze across the rocks.

"Tidepools," he said. "They call this one Davy Jones' Locker because it's so large and deep."

Leaning against the rock was another envelope. Talia grabbed it, tearing it open. "Number of seasons Jack was on his first television series."

Her gaze snapped to Jack.

"Three," he said. Then his brow furrowed. "Wait." He glanced down at the map in his hand again. "The three pillars," he said. "It's down at the other end of the beach," he said, tugging her hand.

They ran toward the cliffs at the southern edge of the beach, stopping at a tall basalt rock, worn away in two spots to create three pillar-like shapes in the rock. Tucked in one of those openings was another envelope.

Jack climbed up and grabbed it. He jumped down and tore it open, sliding out a card.

"What did Jack's character want?" His eyes narrowed. "A paycheck and top billing?"

Talia moved closer to him. "Think, Jack. You said Davy was a rule breaker. What was he fighting for?"

"It was complicated," said Jack, rubbing his neck. "He was fighting for people outside the system. To solve his brother's murder. To change the system. Any way he could."

"Fighting injustice? Wanting vengeance?"

He got pensive again, studying the map. His finger poked the map and he looked up. "Wait—Justice Point. A rock that looks like a gavel. Over here!"

He dragged her across the beach toward the grass and seagulls again. Past them to the northeastern corner of the beach. To a rock with an odd shape. Sort of like a hammer. Or a gavel as Jack called it. The gold badge glinted in the sun as he swept it off the rock and tossed it in the bag.

Grinning, Talia grabbed the list again. "Okay, last object. A toy airplane." She scanned down to the clues. "First clue. What do you need to soar?"

"Wings!" Jack cried. "This way!"

She ran down the beach with him as he headed toward the base of the terrace. Where two tall beach flags fluttered in the wind.

"Wings," he said, grinning, holding out a hand.

Talia saw an envelope wrapped around the base of one flag pole. She pulled it free and opened it, pulling out the next clue.

"What makes you rise?"

Jack frowned, glancing at the map and then around the beach.

"Don't see any jet fuel," he remarked, looking around him. Then he looked over at her. "You're the flying expert," he said. "What makes you rise?"

She thought about flying through the clouds, sliding along the airstream, and diving through the cool air pockets. Floating along the air currents as they ran across her wing tips. Rising on updrafts.

"Updrafts," she muttered.

He turned around. "What?"

"Updrafts," she repeated. "Like the birds. They hit a pocket of warm air and it lets them float upward on it. Let's them rise."

"Warm air," he said. "Like the fire pit or the grill."

He hurried around the edge of the terrace and Talia followed as he checked out the grill and the fire pit again.

"What else, what else," Jack chanted to himself as he gazed around.

Then he glanced at the path leading up to the house. It snaked around the front of the house and then wound around the garage. He squinted at the house's white walls, arranged in white cubes. Grinning, he rushed up the path, toward the wall. And reached into something. Pulling out an envelope!

What was it?

Jack ran back, opening the envelope.

"What was that thing, Jack?" Talia asked, shaking her head.

He grinned. "The dryer vent," he said. "It puts out the hot air from the dryer."

He pulled the clue out of the envelope. "What makes planes fly?"

Talia shrugged. She knew nothing about planes.

"Wings, fuel, pilots," Jack replied, brainstorming as he paced. "Propulsion, engines, force."

Then he gazed at the circle of chairs, his brain cycling a mile a minute as he gazed around the beach, toward the house, and back at the rocks. He walked past the fire pit, repeating everything he thought of about planes. But he stopped at the grill again, staring at it.

"Fuel," he said finally. "Fuel." Then he grinned. "Propane." He reached under the grill, toward a small silver tank, and pulled something free from it.

A toy airplane that fit in his hand.

"Finish line!" he shouted, grabbing her hand.

They ran as hard as they could toward the waving red flags.

Steve was there when they crossed the finish line.

"Good job, guys!" he shouted as Jack handed him the bag.

Steven opened the purple tote bag and pulled out the objects until he had all five displayed in the sand for the cameras.

"You got all five and your time's recorded. Have a good night and we'll see you tomorrow at the live show."

Talia wrapped her arm in Jack's and together, they moved toward the house. Cold and tired. But happy.

Back in their suite, Talia shucked off the windbreaker as Jack draped his across a chair. And then he was beside her, picking her up in his arms and carrying her to the couch.

He laid her down on the couch, kicking off his shoes. Leaning down, he kissed her gently. With a grin, Talia grabbed him around the waist. And pulled him onto the couch.

33

JACK ENDURED ANOTHER ELIMINATION ON *THE EVER AFTER HOUR* WITH Talia beside him. Another candlelit ceremony under the set lights. On the terrace, live. Devin presided in his black tailcoat, white tuxedo shirt, and white bowtie, giving another overdramatic presentation with just Gianni and Izzy, Banks and Morgan, and him and Talia this time.

The taped footage played much longer for this elimination, showing lengthy highlights of each couple's hunt along the beach, interspersed with interviews. Kisses in the sand. And more commercials. Still, the whole time, he felt on edge.

And then demons began to climb onto the terrace.

The hair stood up on the back of Jack's neck at the first three that planted themselves along the railing. Leaning. Watching. Dressed in black tuxedos, black shirts, and red bowties, looking bored. Mocking him with those red eyes.

And then more climbed up from the beach, over the railing to stand on the other side of him. Hands stuffed in their tuxedo jacket pockets. Watching him. Standing so close that he smelled the sulfury burn of brimstone in his nose and the electric burnt smell of ozone in the air.

Thunder crackled. Wind rose. Leaves clattered across the terrace.

He glanced around. No one else seemed to notice the stormy weather. Or the eight demons clustered around him on the terrace. Crowding him.

Two more clambered out of the house and slouched against the wall beside Devin. Two more brushed past to stand behind him at the terrace overlook.

Until he was surrounded.

They began to laugh as red trails of his blood crisscrossed the terrace, looking dark and shiny in the flicker of candles as Devin introduced another segment after the commercial break.

"See, Jack," one whispered in his ear. "We're everywhere."

"You thought getting rid of your pals, Rachel and Lare made a difference? Think again."

"Nicole was only a warmup," Jack said with a growl.

"What was that, Jack?" Talia asked, leaning against him.

"And so is this, Jack ol' boy," one of the demons to his right whispered. "If you give up now, we promise not to hurt her."

"Devin didn't even need a warmup," he repeated in a whisper to her.

One of the demons to his left was in front of him now.

"Come on, Jack," he said, those red eyes laser-bright on the dark terrace. "Do you really want to watch us tear her apart? Either way, it won't change your fate. Give up now and save her."

"No," he said through gritted teeth.

Not until he was backed against the wall with no way out. And right now, he didn't feel backed into the corner. Close, but he still had room to maneuver.

But he knew that moment wasn't far off. The moment her halo returned, she'd be whole again. Would it be enough to defeat these bastards? His heart told him the answer right away and it made him ache all over.

He was losing her. And not even winning this competition would keep him with her. Her only salvation was to fly off to Heaven.

Someplace he couldn't follow her. But maybe, he'd be just enough decoy to get her out of here? Safe. Where they couldn't touch her.

"And the first couple moving to the final challenge...Armand and Izzy."

Gianni threw his arms around Izzy and kissed her. She held him tight.

"That means that both Jack and Talia and Mark and Morgan are in jeopardy. The couple leaving us tonight when we return. Stay tuned."

"Three minutes forty-eight seconds," Steve called from behind the camera. "Stay on your marks and hold position."

"Are we going to make it, Jack?" she asked, those grey eyes burning holes through his heart.

God, he wanted to curl up in a ball and rage. There was no way to escape these demons.

And she had no idea how many had already gotten inside. Gotten past those angel shields. Not until her powers returned. He hadn't seen Muriel or another angel of death in a week or more. They were alone. At Lucifer's mercy.

And the only way he saw out of this was to get Talia aloft. On those wings. Maybe she'd be able to fly them both out? It was his last hope.

Otherwise, those demons would tear him apart.

He turned to her, the biggest game face of his career on tight, and grinned.

"We got this," he said, kissing her, feeling his heart beginning to crack. "Don't you worry."

She smiled, stroking his face. "You always see the upside. That's what I love about you, Jack."

He fought to keep his voice steady. "I love everything about you, Talia Smith," he said and kissed her again.

"Thirty seconds. Places. Devin, camera one 'til the end," Steve called out.

Jack stood up straighter and kissed Talia again as he glanced over at Gianni and Banks.

"Whatever happens, dudes," he said, feeling overwhelmed. "Thanks for everything. Gianni, Banks, you're the best."

Gianni smiled at him and Banks gave him a thumbs up.

"You, too, Jack," said Gianni, "It's been a pleasure and you've become one of my true friends. No matter what happens here, I plan to annoy the hell out of you and make sure we stay friends."

He couldn't hold back a grin.

"Same, Jack," said Banks. "The first barbecue's at my place. No matter what. And if I have to come after you, you are going to be there. You and Talia."

He wanted nothing more than to accept that invitation.

"You got it. Don't think I deserve friends as good as you, two. But regardless, thanks for the ride. It's been the best one of my life."

Gianni had a funny look on his face as he glanced at Banks and then Talia.

"Jack, this isn't a eulogy," said Gianni. "It's only a game."

A game of lost souls. And this time, he'd lose his heart and his soul.

"Welcome back, my royal subjects!" Devin's voice echoed across the terrace and Jack turned back to the host, Talia's grip on his hand like hellhound jaws. "Tonight, we have to say goodbye to one of our most popular couples on the show. Jack and Talia and Mark and Morgan both began their royal journeys on season one, The Cinderella Hour."

Devin paused and opened the flap on the envelope that Jennifer had handed him. Devin held up the envelope to camera one.

"In this envelope, is the name of the couple moving on to the final challenge."

Again, he paused and Talia sighed, a heavy, flustered sound.

Jack wrapped his arms around her and held her. Alone, without the angels to help them, they would be torn apart by demons. And he couldn't do much to stop it. He had to hope that their scavenger hunt performance had been enough to keep them behind the wards. Safe for another week.

Hoping for a miracle.

Devin tore open the envelope and slid out a card. He looked it over a moment and then stared into camera one.

"And the couple moving on to the final challenge is…"

It was the longest pause of his life.

"Talia and Jack! And we're out of time. Goodnight, my royal subjects. Until next week."

Stunned, he staggered a moment. And then he felt Talia's arms around his neck, kissing him in the mouth.

"And we're clear," Steve announced.

Jack kissed Talia back hard, relief flooding out as he laughed.

Laughed at the demons surrounding them. Laughed at the shitty cards they'd pulled this turn. Laughed at all the people that had tried to take him down this season. He threw his arms around Talia, holding her tight enough to stop his shaking.

Then he looked up at Mark Banks and Morgan. Tears ran down Morgan's face and Banks looked dejected.

He let go of Talia and moved over to Banks.

"Thanks for everything, dude. You're the best," he said and hugged Banks.

Surprised, he stared at Jack a moment and then hugged him back as Talia hugged Morgan.

"Thanks, Jack," he said, looking serious now. "You're a really good friend that I'd like to keep. I mean that."

"Done, dude. As soon as Talia and I get a new place, I'm having you and Morgan over for dinner. Gianni and Izzy, too. Seriously. Don't know how I'm going to get through without you, two watching my back. And it's time I returned the favor."

Banks grinned at him. "I'll text you my contact information. And I will harass the shit out of you if you ghost me."

"Never!" Jack said with a laugh.

Banks hugged Talia and then he and Morgan hugged Gianni and Izzy and departed the terrace.

Gianni and Izzy moved toward them. "Looks like it's only you and me left, Jack. Feels like old times."

Jack nodded. "Can't think of anyone I'd rather compete with. Or hang out with. Besides Talia."

Talia wrapped him in her arms.

Then Herb was standing beside them on the terrace, Jennifer, and Steve behind him.

"All right, gang, the final showdown is next week," said Herb. "Two of America's favorites. Couldn't have ended better than this. Next week's challenge is called Royal Escape. Jennifer and Steve will give you the orientation and then we start shooting Monday. You'll have the weekend to rest up." He glanced at Jennifer.

She smiled, red glasses on, coral *Ever After Hour* sweatshirt over jeans. No clipboard in sight. That made Jack uneasy.

"The final challenge is elegantly simple, but deceivingly difficult," she said. "We have an escape room setup in the den. The couple that escapes the fastest wins."

"That's it?" Gianni replied.

Jennifer nodded, her brown eyes bright. "That's it. You'll get the scenario when you walk into the room. There are cameras all over it. Any questions?"

"I hope that escape's possible," Jack replied, his gaze centered past Jennifer.

At twelve demons clustered into a group. Hughes was at the front, part shadow part horns. Behind the demons stood Lucifer, wearing a black tailcoat, black shirt, and a red bowtie.

And the world froze.

"We're going to have so much fun when you arrive," Lucifer replied in his precise British accent. "It's a shame your dear little Talia won't survive the trip. But in time—that's eternity, Jack—you'll get over it. Slowly, day by day, century by century, until you won't feel anything at all. Nothing except pain."

He glared at Lucifer. "You won't get even a shot at her," he said through gritted teeth. "I'll make sure of that."

"I'm always willing to negotiate, Jack," he said with a dangerous glint in those pale blue eyes. "You for Talia. Think about it. You're going to suffer either way. So, wouldn't it be best to suffer alone? Without having to watch her torn apart without her angel powers?"

He couldn't take watching that. If her angel powers didn't return by the show's end, he'd have no choice but to end this. His way. Protecting her.

"Think about it, Jack," said Lucifer and waved his arm in the air. "When the time comes, you'll know what to do."

In a puff of smoke, Lucifer disappeared, the demons along with him.

And the world was moving again.

But he'd never felt so cold and heartsick as he felt right now. Watching the woman he loved slowly slip through his fingers.

34

On Monday morning, Talia awoke to an empty bed. She sat up, wings flexed, feathers rustling, and felt more like herself than she'd felt in the weeks since she'd fallen from Heaven. She couldn't help but feel a sense of dread though. The final competition was this week with the finale on Friday. Shot here at the house instead of back in a theatre in L.A. like the first two seasons of the show.

Jack still wasn't himself, even though moments of his easygoing, uplifting persona bled through when he let his game face slide. When he wasn't preoccupied. She knew he was in turmoil about the demons and the disappearance of Muriel and the guard. She felt that way, too.

But she also knew that as she changed back into her angel of death form, his distance grew.

A dull whine hung in the air above the tick of the clock as she rose from the bed in a red nightshirt and headed into the bathroom. She glanced at the mirror and her heart leaped in her chest.

A thin gold band of light glimmered above her head. Her halo!

Her powers were returning. She felt the hum of them at her fingertips. The well of Holy flame beginning to fill. It was only a drop or two, but it was back and it was filling.

She had no idea how this Phoenix shift had changed her powers, but she couldn't wait to find out. When her halo was at a full gold-white glow, she'd be able to test her wings and summon her powers again. Maybe it would be in time to carry her and Jack out of here before demons descended on them?

And maybe Azrael would get here in time to stop Lucifer from dragging her and Jack off? Anahera and Muriel had to come through.

She took a shower, the water sloughing off her wings like water off a duck's back, and dressed in jeans and a light blue sweater. Waiting for Jack to return from his interviews. They had their Royal Escape session this afternoon. Then more interviews, a candlelit dinner alone, and another one on the beach with Armand and Izzy.

And then the finale. And maybe then, if she and Jack escaped the demons—and Lucifer—she and Jack could find that new place he talked about. And be together at last. She wanted that ever after with him. It was the only thing she wanted. And she'd fight to the last breath to keep it.

To keep him beside her.

NERVOUS ABOUT THE LAST CHALLENGE, Talia met Jack down the hall from the den. Where the escape room had been set up. He showed up looking pale, wearing a navy hoodie over a grey Henley, blue slip-on sneakers he called Vans, and faded jeans. She kissed him, his face so warm, light green eyes a little misty.

"Any word from Muriel or Anahera?" he asked in a half-whisper, looking around, apprehension shining in his eyes.

She shook her head. That's when his gaze snapped to hers, looking above her head.

"Your halo," he said with a gasp.

"It appeared this morning. It's only a thin ray of light now, but—"

He was shaking his head. "It's expanded," he said, looking terrified.

"Does it frighten you?" she asked, feeling sad at seeing fear in those beautiful green eyes.

"No, but Lucifer returning does," he said as she leaned over toward a hallway mirror.

The almost full-blown gleam of her halo glowed back at her from the mirror. She was a breath away from having one hundred percent of her powers back. She was nearly restored as an angel of death. Just a little more Holy flame and her well of power would be fully charged. She could summon her abilities now. They weren't full strength, but she had enough power to use them. She turned toward Jack, lifting her index and middle finger, and turning them counterclockwise.

Everything froze.

She grinned. She had her powers back!

She turned her two fingers clockwise and time resumed.

"Jack!" she cried, throwing her arms around him. "I've got my powers back!"

He bit his lip, looking so sad, moisture collecting in her eyes. "It isn't enough, Talia. They'll tear us apart."

"Don't you understand?" she cried, gripping his hands. "I can fly us out of here now. Most of these demons can't fly."

His whole demeanor changed, the hope returning. "What? Are you sure?"

She nodded at him. "We don't need Azrael to save us, Jack. I can fly us out of here."

He was grinning now. He threw his arms around her and held her so tight that she felt his heart pounding against her chest.

"That's the best news I've ever heard," he said, his voice breaking. "Come on," he said, taking her hand, nodding at the den. "Let's go win this thing."

"The escape room?" she asked.

He nodded.

Together, they walked hand in hand to the end of the hall. Where Jennifer stood, clipboard in hand. She wore an orange, long-sleeved tunic, grey flats, and charcoal leggings. Those red glasses perched on her nose and she clutched her clipboard.

"Jack! Talia! Welcome to your final challenge. The escape room. Fastest time wins a million dollars. Are you ready?"

Talia nodded as Jack gripped her hand tighter.

"Okay, here is the scenario," Jennifer began, glancing at her clipboard. "You and your princess slip into this private room for a kiss and overhear courtiers plotting to kill the king. They lock you in the room to keep you from saving him. Together, you must find the key to the door and escape to save the king. And find the evidence in the room to expose the courtiers plotting to kill the king."

"In that room?" Talia asked, pointing toward the den.

Jennifer nodded at the door. "You'll be locked in this room for an hour to solve the mystery and escape. You can request one hint without penalty. There are cameras throughout the room. Any questions?"

"And we can have one hint?" Jack repeated.

"One hint. Don't waste it. Ready to start?"

Jack nodded at her. Talia glanced around, feeling suddenly uneasy. Sensing demons. And the wards beginning to crumble.

Why hadn't she known this until now? If her powers were getting mirrored somehow to Jack, maybe he'd been sensing the same thing? Without knowing the cause. Maybe that's what had been bothering him? Sensing demons would do that.

She was startled by the number. It was a lot and they were finding ways past the wards.

This wasn't good.

"Jack," she said, her gaze darting to shadows in the hallway. "Shadows."

He nodded, his gaze flicking toward two shadows at the end of the hallway.

"Why didn't you say something?"

"Didn't want to alarm you," he said. "Since you weren't—able to do anything."

He'd been carrying this around for a week or two and she felt awful. It was her job to protect him and the rest of her human charges from demons. And all this time, he'd been protecting her. Again.

"The escape room might be a good defense," she whispered,

sending up a desperate shout to the Heavens, one that only an angel could hear.

Come on, Muriel! Anahera! The wards are crumbling. We need you!

She needed Azrael now. To defend them. Long enough for her to get airborne and fly her and Jack out of here. Without Azrael, their best defense was to barricade themselves in a defensible space and ward it. With her powers. Until they could make a break for it. She needed a little more time for the full charge. She'd need it to get them both to Heaven. To protect Jack and sort this out.

Before Lucifer got back his halo and wings. And summoned an army.

35

JACK COULDN'T STOP STARING AT THE MASSING SHADOWS AT THE END OF the hallway. Talia stepped back from the mirror as it began to vibrate. A shadowy hand reached out from it, almost grabbing her.

He pulled her backward, away from the mirror.

Jennifer stared at him, looking surprised and confused.

"She's checked her hair a dozen times," Jack said with a chuckle. "She looks fantastic, doesn't she?"

Behind Jennifer, demon claws tore down the wall. Slicing open the wall.

"She looks fabulous," said Jennifer.

Jack pasted on the best game face of his life, pulling Talia against him.

"They're breaking through," he said in a sharp whisper.

All Talia could do was nod as he backed the two of them toward the den door.

"We're ready, Jennifer," he said as the demons poured out of the hole in the wall. "Open the door."

Red eyes flashed like laser points, more and more sliding through the slit in the wall.

She bent down to unlock it as the horde massed on both sides of the hallway. Blurring.

The door opened and he dragged Talia inside and slammed the door shut.

"Ward it!" Jack shouted. "Hurry!"

Talia closed her eyes, hands pressed together as her dove grey wings unfurled. A heavy gold light illuminated the door as he backed into the room. The room smelled like stale wood smoke and hot with ozone and smoky brimstone.

Dark wood paneling covered one wall, the rest had bookshelves that wound around the entire room. Crammed full of leather hardcover books.

Dammit! Nothing sharp or blunt for defense there.

One wall was deep green with a roll top desk and a green, leather and wood chair against it. In the center of the room were two leather burgundy couches and a walnut coffee table between them. Flameless torches hung on all the walls, creating a warm flicker of Medieval light through the dimly lit room. Behind the far couch stood a library table and two wooden chairs.

Nothing he could use as a weapon!

Scratching began at the door. Pounding. Screeching. Like someone had awoken the dead.

Talia looked stunned as she backed against Jack.

"How long will that ward hold?" he asked.

"With that horde? Ten minutes or so," she said in a shaky voice, those beautiful grey eyes wide. "But by then, we can go through the wall and fly—" Her voice cracked, eyes welling with tears. "Oh no— the walls! Only angels can go through walls."

"What about—"

Clawed hands shot through the walls and grabbed him.

He slammed against the bookshelves as Talia screamed and flung a handful of Holy flame at the wall.

Demons shrieked, shrinking back from the gold fire as they released him.

He stumbled away from the wall, panting.

"Answers that question."

Shadows began to flutter along all four walls.

"Talia," he said as deathly calm as he could. "Ward the walls. Quick. Or we're demon chow."

She held out her arms, eyes burning with gold light as the glow began to adhere to the walls, floor, and ceiling like plastic wrap.

And the shadows vanished.

"So, what—ten more minutes?" he asked as something slammed against the door.

She nodded and opened her mouth, but no sound came out. "I sent another call to Azrael and Muriel."

"Let's hope their commute's less than ten minutes," said Jack as the pounding against the door turned to thumping and slamming.

He glanced around the room again, trying to find a weapon, an exit, something to stop this horde of demons from tearing them apart.

They were surrounded.

And then Lucifer's voice echoed through the room.

"Do you really think there's a way out of this?" he asked from the other side of the wall.

"We're just getting started," Jack replied, hurrying over to the roll top desk. He rifled through the drawers, on top of the desk, around it.

"If you give up now," Lucifer called out, "I promise to end your miserable existences quickly."

"And take the express elevator to Hell? Forget it!" Jack shouted.

Talia smiled. "Jack, I sense Azrael approaching."

Game changer. Now, this was going to be a real fight and not a slaughter.

"Hear that, Lucifer? An archangel of death and his winged cavalry are on their way. Ready to express mail your ass all the way back to Hell. And your demons. If you give up now, I promise not to laugh too hard as you leave."

Talia gave him a hard look. "Don't, Jack."

He couldn't help himself. He'd had a lifetime of this dude.

And his demons.

"Ever wonder how my horde found you so quickly, Talia?" Lucifer continued. "Jack knows. He's kept it a secret from you this whole time. Did you know that? He's been lying to you."

What was he blathering on about now? He shrugged.

Until she gasped and pointed at the floor. "Jack!"

Spiraling across the floor was the trail of blood—his blood—that had wound through the entire house.

Lucifer was laughing now.

"Jack, why didn't you tell me about this?" she demanded.

"Didn't want to worry you. We already knew this bite had marked me, so it's not like this was a surprise. But I didn't lie to you, Talia. He's trying to drive a wedge between us."

She shook her head, eyes filling with tears. "Jack, it's not a trail. It's—"

A flash of white light exploded underneath the door. As the clawing stopped.

"Azrael! Muriel! Hurry, we're in here!"

Lucifer was still laughing as the tears kept spilling down her face.

"Talia, what is it?" Jack rushed to her, taking her in his arms.

"Jack, that isn't a trail that's leading demons to you. It's a cable. A tether."

"A tether?" he cried.

What the hell did that mean?

Something jerked him hard backward, his whole body lurching. Talia held onto him.

The doorframe cracked open, gold light spilling into the room. Soot-colored wings unfurled, red-gold halo glaring in the dim-lit room as Azrael, Archangel of Death, swung his sword of Holy fire, cutting through demons and shadows. Forcing his way into the room. Muriel, Anahera, and the guard of death angels behind him.

Talia grinned. "Azrael!"

The cavalry was here! Jack kissed Talia with a desperate, urgent kiss.

Lucifer was done here.

"Lucifer!" Azrael thundered, his eyes gold with fire, sword raised, gold armor glistening as Muriel and Anahera rushed into the room, the entire guard of death angels pouring in behind them.

The wards in the room fell.

Jack turned as Lucifer, grinning, stepped through the walls, an army of shadows and demons at his back.

"Azrael. Back so soon from High House?" Lucifer asked, arms crossed against his burnished gold breastplate.

It was the same armor that the archangel wore. But Lucifer didn't have wings or a halo. Horns began to lengthen beneath his curly blond hairline, blue eyes turning red as he glared at Jack and Talia.

"Much sooner than you'd anticipated, Lucifer," Azrael replied, his voice dark and heavy like thunder. "You expected me to be there a little longer though, didn't you? Giving you time to snatch my angel of death and her human charge. Sorry to disappoint you."

Lucifer nodded at him. "I'm never disappointed, Azrael. Not when I have the upper hand."

Azrael's eyes still burned with flame. "How do you figure that?"

In a blink, Lucifer was across the room. He grabbed Talia and dragged her backward.

"Simple math, my dear Azrael," he said, Talia fighting to break his hold. "I have two minutes until her halo is at full power. Enough time to overpower her."

Lucifer reached down and plucked the red trail of blood off the floor. The tether. Jack felt the resonance against his chest.

"And a line to her charge. Rare powers, Phoenix shift, and the mirror. All mine. And you have nothing."

Azrael moved toward Lucifer, Muriel and the guard shifting forward, gold shields up and humming to life.

"Last chance, Lucifer," Azrael commanded. "Then I smite you into oblivion."

Suddenly, Jack understood what Talia had been trying to say about the trail. The tether. It wasn't leading the demons to him. It was connecting him to the demons.

It was a leash. Terror welled cold inside him. To Lucifer.

That had been the whole point.

Lucifer had led them here to the Malibu beach house to spring a trap. And Jack was already caught. Hook, line, and sinker. All this bastard had to do was reel him in now that he had Talia.

Time to fight back with everything he had.

Jack reached down to the ground and picked up the red tether made from his own blood.

"And destroy precious, rare Talia in the process, Azrael?" Lucifer replied as Talia struggled. "I think not."

Jack opened his hand and summoned an oblivion sphere. He only had one shot at this. For Talia, he had to get it right.

"Let her go," Azrael said with a feral growl. "Now!"

"You have nothing to bargain with," Lucifer shouted. "Unless you wish to trade places with her. I'm always willing to negotiate, dear Azrael."

Jack pulled in a deep breath, held it, and turned toward Lucifer.

"Negotiate this, bitch!" he shouted and tossed the oblivion sphere at Lucifer.

His red eyes widened as Jack yanked on the tether with everything he had. Jerking Lucifer toward him.

As he collided with Lucifer, Jack pushed Talia out of his grasp and shoved her toward Azrael.

"Jack! No!" Talia shouted.

Lucifer exploded with rage, slamming Jack against the floor. He grabbed the tether in his fists and yanked it backward. Jack careened forward, against the far wall. As demons poured through it, swarming all over him.

"What have you done?" Talia's frantic scream tore through him. "JACK!"

He couldn't save them both. He had to pick one of them.

And he chose Talia.

The ache of an eternity without her pounded through his chest.

"I still walk away with my prize. The mirror." Lucifer said with a laugh. "Until next time, Azrael."

Lucifer yanked the tether and Jack tumbled forward, swarmed and overpowered by demons.

He turned his head for one last look at Talia, his heart in pieces.

Laying his hand against his heart, he held it out to her as Lucifer blew a hole in the side of the wall.

"Come along, Jack," Lucifer snapped, like he was the bastard's cocker spaniel. "Time to regret the day you were born."

Talia's desperate screams echoed in his ears as he fell through the wall. And kept falling.

The End of THE EVER AFTER HOUR: A Game of Lost Souls, Book Three

The story continues in…

A GAME OF LOST SOULS

THE FALLEN HEARTS SEASON: A Game of Lost Souls, Book Four

Read Chapter 1 Now!

AWARD-WINNING BESTSELLING AUTHOR
LISA SILVERTHORNE
THE FALLEN HEARTS SEASON
A GAME OF 4 LOST SOULS

Novels by Lisa Silverthorne

Standalones:
ISABEL'S TEARS
LANDFALL
PACIFIC BLUE TATTOO

A Game of Lost Souls series:
THE CINDERELLA HOUR
THE PRINCE CHARMING HOUR
THE EVER AFTER HOUR
THE FALLEN HEARTS SEASON
THE RISING SPIRITS SEASON
THE ETERNAL SOULS SEASON
THE ROYAL WEDDING HOUR
THE HEAVENLY HONEYMOON HOUR
THE DIVINE NEWLYWEDS SHOW
THE CELESTIAL COUPLES SHOW
THE ENOCHIAN APOCALYPSE SHOW

Curse and Crown series:
THORN & BLADE

The Spiral series:

BETWEEN

REPRISE

AVENGE

The Resurrectionist Papers

GRAVE RECKONING

Short Story Collections

THE SOUND OF ANGELS

THE MAGIC OF ORDINARY THINGS

TIMELESS

Science Fiction Writing as L.S. Silverthorne

Standalones:

REDISCOVERY

Experiencing True Purple series:

RECOMBINANT, Book 1

HELIX, Book 2

SPLICE, Book 3

FORTHCOMING!

A Game of Lost Souls series:

The Angelic Anniversary Hour, Book Twelve

The Perdition Picture Show, Book Thirteen

Curse and Crown series:

Storm & Steel, Book Two

Dagger & Flame, Book Three

The Spiral series:

Ruin, Book 4

Descent, Book 5

The Resurrectionist Papers:

Corpses Delicti

Stiffed Again

Cease and Deceased

SCIENCE FICTION WRITING AS **L.S. SILVERTHORNE**

Experiencing True Purple series:

Cipher, Book 4

Renascence, Book 5

SNEAK PEEK: THE FALLEN HEARTS SEASON

CHAPTER 1

1

He was gone. And she would never see him again.

The grand hall of Eolowen's glistening white walls felt hollow and empty against Parrish blue skies and billowing Constable clouds, the soft wind cold against Talia's face.

Her heart ached as she lay in the mossy green grass beside the winding stream. A willow tree swayed in the breeze that carried the soft scent of roses and honeysuckles as her tears gleamed like pearls against the thick silvery-green blades of grass. Glowing in the white-gold light of her spinning halo.

Her wings flattened against the grass and she didn't have the will or the desire to lift them into the wind. She didn't want to fly. Or soar across the sky. She would never soar again.

Not without Jack.

She watched several members of the death angel's guard flit across the sky, casting rivulets of white-gold light across the willow tree's shade as they passed overhead, Azrael leading the way.

It had been three angel days since Lucifer took Jack from her arms.

From the Malibu beach house as she and Jack were about to do their royal escape couple's challenge for *The Ever After Hour* reality TV show. It had been the final challenge and they were against good friends, Armand Gianni and Isabella Castilla.

Win or lose, Jack planned to find a new place. For her and him.

And she planned to spend a lifetime with him. When she lost Lucifer's wager and had her wings and halo taken by Azrael, she never expected her wings and halo to return. She thought her fall from Heaven was permanent. But she had Jack and he was everything she'd ever wanted.

But then her wings began growing back. And her angel powers began to return, strangely mirrored in Jack. Apparently, it had all been part of Lucifer's plan from the very first wager. A test. To regain his halo and wings. So he could march against the Heavens and take them over—finish what he started millennia ago.

And now, she'd lost Jack forever.

He'd sacrificed himself to free her from Lucifer's hold. Then Lucifer and his demons dragged Jack away to Hell.

Her halo hummed, churning with white light, and sparkled with blue, lavender, and green bursts. Green. A watercolor green, soft and pale. Like Jack's eyes. Her eyes welled with fresh tears.

She ached all over, her heart in shreds, the pain so deep and pervasive she couldn't move as it thrummed alongside the oscillation of her halo.

More crystalline and pearl tears fell into the grass. She didn't want to move. Didn't want to think or feel ever again, but she did feel and she hurt so much from her head to her feet. Aching with the memory of his touch, the feel of his mouth against her lips, the feel of his body against hers.

She ached to see that hot little smirk of his, feel his soft blond hair against her fingertips, and touch his smile that burned her down to her wing tips. She stared at the silver ring he'd placed on her finger during the finale of *The Prince Charming Hour*.

She'd finally earned his heart in that moment and had only wanted to love him.

Tears burned new pearly trails down her face, knowing that

Lucifer was torturing him right now. Breaking him piece by piece, memory by memory, heartache by heartache.

She balled her hands into fists, striking the ground. It should have been her in Lucifer's clutches! Not Jack. Who'd done nothing to deserve that torment. She hadn't earned an eternity in Hell either, but Jack's Book of Life and Death was clear. He hadn't earned eternal damnation either.

Why hadn't someone intervened? Why hadn't Azrael stopped it?

"Talia! Are you listening to me?"

Muriel's voice echoed behind her. She didn't even lift up her head.

"Go away," she said.

"Talia, the archangel is standing beside me," Muriel said in an anxious voice. "You know, your boss. Commander of the guard. Oversees death and soul crossings. And all angels of death—like you."

"Go away, Azrael," she replied.

He hadn't done anything to save Jack. No one had.

They just let him get taken by demons. By Lucifer. She had no use for Azrael or the guard right now. And she didn't care if they took her wings and halo again. For good. She'd lost everything anyway.

As soon as she'd gathered her wits and her abilities, she planned to storm through Hell's gates and fight her way through with everything she had. And find him. It had a trillion to one chance to succeed, but she wouldn't give up. As soon as she had all her strength.

And not the guard, not Azrael, or High House would stop her.

Azrael knelt beside her, charcoal robes and soot-colored wings fluttering in the breeze, silver-black hair windblown from flight, red-gold halo surging in its orbit.

"Talia, I—"

"I have nothing else to say," she said, her facing scrunching as her voice broke. "To anyone. Ever again. And I don't care what you do to me either. I don't care anymore."

She was going into Hell after Jack.

Azrael sat down in the grass beside her. "I think you care very much, Talia. Especially for that young man who sacrificed himself to free you."

Her face screwed up, grey eyes smashed closed, mouth contorting as she shouted a harmonic note of grief and collapsed into the grass, the sobs quavering through her, wings trembling.

She felt Azrael's hand against her hair and she remembered how Jack used to stroke her hair, looking at her with such adoration. The memory of that soft cedary cologne he sometimes wore, the clean soapy scent of his hair, buttery smell of his skin. His voice like hot caramel, like sun-warmed velvet. And how his constant jokes always made her laugh, even when she was furious at him. The light in those hypnotic green eyes had only been meant for her.

The last image of him burned through her brain. Flooding her eyes and face with more tears. His heart gesture to her. Laying his hand to his heart and holding out his open hand. Giving her his heart.

She'd hold it safe in the palm of her hand for the rest of her existence. Which she hoped was short.

"There's nothing you could have done, Talia," said Azrael as Muriel knelt on her other side. "You couldn't fight all of those demons. There were too many."

She snapped her head up from the grass. "But you could have! You had the guard at your back! You're an archangel! Why didn't you fight for him?" She struck the ground with her fists. "Why didn't I fight for him?"

He took her by the shoulders. "Talia, think. Lucifer wanted us to fight him. Even Jack knew that. If we'd fought him, he'd have taken both of you. And he had Jack tethered. Jack had no way to escape that. And in that moment, we had no way to free him from that tether. Remember your training, Talia. Remember who you are!"

"I'm…lost, Azrael." She shook her head. "Lost without him," she said and collapsed into his arms.

He clasped her to his chest as she wept. Behind her, the guard bowed their heads, wings lowered, halos dimming.

"We all feel your pain, Talia," said Muriel. "And we share it."

"Especially me," said Azrael in a pained voice. "This is my fault. I only wanted to help you love your human charges as the Maker intended of his soldiers and teachers. We were meant to walk beside them. But I never expected you to fall so hard and so completely for one of them."

"You gave me a human soul," Talia fired back, pulling away from him. "What did you expect?"

Azrael nodded. "You're right. I should have expected human responses from even an angel of death with a human soul." He sighed. "I thought that when you regained your angel of death abilities, your angelic nature would overcome it. That tells me your love transcends its presence."

"Meaning what?" she snapped.

"Meaning that even without that human soul, your deep love of Jack Casey would remain. You have such rare powers, Talia, abilities that the Heavens need to fight Lucifer and his demonic army. And your rare love for Jack Casey created a unique bond, so unusual that it mirrored your powers in him. The mirroring is why Lucifer tethered and took him."

Every time he said Jack's name it was a sword thrust to her heart. Every memory was a painful stab to her chest.

He smiled at her through his fiery stone exterior, those granite grey eyes softening. "And that's why we've got to get him back."

She stared at him through blurry streaks of tears filling her eyes. What had he just said? Had he really just said that they had to get Jack back?

"What are you saying, Azrael?"

He took her hands in his and squeezed them.

"I'm saying that Jack can't be left in Lucifer's hands. Lucifer intends to siphon off Jack's mirrored abilities and infuse them into the humans he's turned. And into the damned souls in Hell. Creating an unstoppable army to march on Heaven. As soon as he forces another Phoenix shift. On himself. While his allies here in Heaven kill God's Scribe and take over the archive. All of that is already in motion, but it will take time to accomplish. Time we need to use against him. By thwarting his traitorous accomplices." He grinned. "And marching straight into Hell to rescue Jack."

Rescue Jack! The words flooded over her like warm rain and made her grin through her tears. The archangel intended to march into Hell beside her!

"You're really going to help me rescue him?"

He exchanged a wary look with Muriel and then smiled back at her. "If I don't, you're going to go down there alone and try. So, we do this right. With enough force to succeed. Much better odds, wouldn't you say, Talia?"

She threw her arms around him and hugged him tightly, her tears beginning to dry. Azrael already knew what had been in her heart since she'd returned to Heaven, but he wanted to help her save Jack. Even though Heaven needed his mirrored powers, they needed them out of Lucifer's hands. And they wanted to right this injustice.

And bring him back to her.

Finally, she let Azrael go. She sank back on her knees and wiped the tears from her face.

"How do we proceed?" she asked, wide-eyed as Muriel reached out and hugged her.

"First, the guard needs to learn some new skills, Talia. Like breaking a demonic soul tether. It's a complex, multi-step process. And then we need to improve our demon-fighting skills. A Holy armor upgrade would help, too."

She nodded at him and rose to her feet. "I'll do whatever it takes, Azrael!"

He reached out and patted her shoulder. "So will I. And my guard. We have official sanction by the seraphim."

By the seraphim? "The seraphim approve?"

He nodded. "I told them everything," he said. "Including my break with protocol and everything about the wagers. They understand what's at stake and they approve."

Muriel motioned toward the ground. "Also, we need to handle the mess Lucifer left back on Earth."

Talia frowned. "What mess?"

"The one he created in California," said Muriel, shaking her head. "We thought he'd just frozen time in that room." She sighed. "Don't know if it was accidental or on purpose, but he stopped time.

Completely. Everywhere. Burbank to Budapest. Toronto to Taipei. London to Lima. All human time has been stopped."

Time had been completely stopped? Every human being frozen in place, every movement, every thought, every action stopped? Could it even be fixed?

"How do we fix that?"

She'd never seen time stopped before on the whole of Earth. Never even heard it mentioned.

"Pravuil has gone into an emergency conference with the Time Keepers," said Azrael as he got to his feet, wings flexing. "They are devising an emergency plan to identify all necessary events and actions and keep them on schedule. And figure out how to restore it all. It's not a simple fix. It will require a lot of angels to get time to resume."

Lots of angels? Maybe that was Lucifer's goal all along? Get as many angels on Earth as possible. Leaving the Heavens vulnerable.

"Azrael, won't that leave Heaven—and High House—open for attack?"

Azrael was nodding. "Exactly right, Talia," he said and walked out from under the willow tree. "That's why we need to rescue Jack. We're going to need his mirrored powers—and yours—to defend Heaven. From Lucifer and the traitor. Who has a formidable army of his own."

Talia frowned. Who in Heaven had their own army?

"What army?" she asked.

"A guard of death angels. Archangel Samael. He's turned, Talia. And we have to hold the line while our angels try to restart human time. And protect God's Scribe. Otherwise, there will be no Heaven and no humans. And Lucifer will rule the ensuing wasteland."

If they didn't stop Lucifer and Samael, there would be nothing left. And stopping them began with rescuing Jack. Only with Jack beside her, she had a fighting chance to stop all of this destruction.

ABOUT THE AUTHOR

LISA SILVERTHORNE, an award-winning bestselling author, has published 25 novels and 150 short stories and novelettes in many genres. She is the author of *A Game of Lost Souls* series, *Experiencing True Purple* series, *The Spiral, The Resurrectionist Papers,* and a new series, *Curse and Crown.* She lives in Las Vegas, Nevada.

Before you go, you are invited to please leave a **review of this book**!

Reviews are a wonderful way to help an author. They are also an exciting opportunity to share your honest thoughts with other readers, so **please post yours,** in as many places as possible!

9 781955 197328